Fireside Chats

by

Fran Steinmark

Fireside Chats
By Fran Steinmark

Published by Fran Steinmark Boca Raton, FL

ISBN: 978-0-9977582-5-2

Interior and cover design by Fran Steinmark
www.fransteinmark.com

Printed in the United States of America

Author's Note

All of the characters, organizations, and events portrayed in this novel are either products of the author's imagination or are used fictitiously. Any resemblance to actual persons, living or dead, is purely coincidental.

Dedicated to

Ann Bloom

Chapter One

Seated at Carl Hoppl's, a nightclub in Baldwin, Long Island, Jan's father, Norman, a stout, burly, and impatient man, hailed a waiter to his side and asked for HP steak sauce, insisting that the fellow run quickly to fulfill his request. "Don't bother serving anyone else, just go get it, as fast as a bullet out of a gun, and come right back pronto! You hear me?"

It was 8:45 p.m. on a Saturday night, and the atmosphere in the club was a jovial one. Subdued conversations and the clickety-clack of china and wine glasses, added to the intermittent clanging of silverware, fueled a cacophonous undercurrent in the air. The lights over the audience were turned down low, allowing for a romantic glow to emanate from the lit candles on each of the tables, but the stage, bared by its parted gold theater drapes, was fully illuminated. Many of the patrons, outfitted in their fanciest attire, were finishing their entrees, about to dip into their peach melba desserts or take a twirl around the dance floor.

Wearing a grey Prince of Wales plaid suit, starched white shirt, gold cufflinks, and a textured silk tie, purchased from Harrods of Knightsbridge, and accustomed to speaking at full volume, Norman hardly had to raise his voice to be heard over the band's rendition of *Roses are Red My Love,* a hit song with a lilting melody, made popular by newcomer Bobby Vinton, that was prompting legs, heads, and shoulders to sway.

Norman had expressed concerns that his well-cooked, to-a-crisp sirloin steak was getting cold before being properly seasoned, his mashed potatoes appeared to be lumpy, and his green beans seemed too stringy and unevenly cut. Not liking when things did not go his way, he took these imperfections as a personal affront and intimated that the entire contents of his dish would be dumped on the floor if the waiter didn't bring him what he wanted soon enough.

"And let me tell you something else you may not know," he barked at the waiter, who, in his matching vest and bow tie, was projecting the guise of someone not wishing to be anywhere but standing stiffly next to Norman. "If I can't enjoy eating my meal the way I like it, then neither will any of the others at my table! Somehow, all of their plates will end up on the floor as well, and if that is the case, then I will expect to be given a full refund for the show's tickets and cover charges to compensate for the gross inconvenience. Do you get my drift?" His beastly scowl told the waiter that this was no empty threat.

Walking briskly past rows of partygoers and special occasion celebrants, the young, eager-to-accommodate waiter sped away amply alarmed, hoping to reach the kitchen before succumbing to his buckling, jelly legs. Unfortunately, what he grabbed and was about to deliver to Norman was a bottle of A-1 steak sauce—not the desired HP brand. In the server's defense, the shapes of these two, dark brown, bottles were almost identical. The steak sauce bottles had been sitting next to each other in the kitchen on a crowded shelf with lots of spices and other condiments, amidst the frantic chaos of waiters and chefs scurrying in all different directions.

Norman plucked a wooden toothpick out of his mouth, as expeditiously as a pair of pliers pulling a loose wisdom tooth, and let loose a thunderous roar. "*I asked for*

HP Steak Sauce you moron!" He yelled so loudly; he could have been heard all the way to Manhattan. The musicians stopped playing their instruments. Dancing couples halted mid-step on the dance floor. The bartenders and waiters stood dead in their tracks. The house lights were turned on. Among the hundreds of people in the audience who had come to enjoy seeing scantily clad, feather-topped showgirls, performing with precision eye-high kicks in the Las Vegas-type revue, there was now absolute silence, and everyone's eyes were turned on Jan's father and his family seated at a table two tiers away from the stage.

Red-faced, sweating profusely, and visibly shaking, the waiter apologized and hastily retraced his steps. "I'm so sorry, sir. I'll get it for you right away."

"Right," Norman bellowed, accentuating his pronouncement with a slap on the table. "You bet you will." Appearing to be nonplussed by the amount of attention he was receiving, Norman retrieved a handkerchief from his trousers' pocket and blew his nose with a man-sized, gushing sound. The image of a whale powerfully and explosively exhaling air through a blowhole entered Jan's mind.

Norman accepted the exchanged bottle, which was presented to him on a platter. He unscrewed the top with such venom he almost ground it into powder and generously poured the HP over his charred meat. He took two elephantine-sized bites of his steak, threw his scrunched-up napkin on his plate, shoved back his chair, and hollered to his family, "We're getting out of this shitty joint! Pick your arses up and get to the car *now!*'"

Twelve-year-old Jan, devastated and distraught, gathered her Duffle coat, obeying her father's instructions. As she did so, she recognized the tune, *I Can't Stop Loving*

You, that the band was now playing, having recommenced its stalled program. Sequestered many nights in her bedroom, hiding from the battles and pandemonium taking place outside her locked door, she had listened to Ray Charles sing that same song on her clock radio. His sorrowful version resonated with her own painful and unavoidable wounds, buried deep inside her.

Gobbling up two french fries she had just popped in her mouth, she hoped there would be no further incidents that evening. To wish as such, however, ran contrary to their family's history, ravaged by one tumultuous, mortifying event after another. She wondered if apologies were going to be made to the members of her mother's cousins club, who were seated all about them and from the look on their faces were at a loss as to how to properly respond to the disruptive scene. Jan conjectured that this first annual outing would be the very last one to which she and her family would be invited.

Without apparent provocation, Norman picked up his chair and slammed it against the table. The explosive whack startled Jan and stifled the drone of whispers that just a few moments ago had begun to spread in the spacious, well-appointed room. Jan sensed an intense heat rushing to her cheeks. She wished she were a sparrow that could take flight and never return.

Jan's father took his time putting on his navy, trench coat and planting his pinch front fedora on his wavy, black hair, while the rest of his family went scrambling to the exit. He swaggered to the lobby, a smirk glued beneath his painter's brush mustache, and marched with his head held high through the polished, decorative doorway to the parking lot.

Once seated in the back seat of their brand-new, turquoise, 1962 Oldsmobile and choking from Norman's chain-smoked cigarettes, neither Jan nor anyone else dared utter a single word. The air hung ominously, and despite the spacious legroom of the back cabin, Jan was feeling claustrophobic, a not uncommon sensation for her to experience. She tried erasing her brain of all thoughts, a practice proven beneficial throughout her young life. Maureen, Jan's older sister, and Henry, the girls' only brother, stared straight ahead. The children's mother, Alice, wearing a beaded black cocktail dress with matching bolero jacket under a mantle of resignation, leaned heavily against her door. She managed to lower her window an inch, but Jan's father threw his lit butt at her face and commanded her to shut it.

***

It was in a different automobile that Jan learned how to drive four years later. She had hoped to sign up for private lessons like the other girls in her school, but that required a sum of money she did not have. Whatever she had earned from her baby-sitting jobs had to be spent on such necessities as clothing and school supplies.

Minutes after she had slipped behind the steering wheel of the gargantuan, avocado Ford LTD, with its stretched-out hood, her very first time in the driver's seat, Norman directed Jan to enter Grand Central Parkway, demanding that she *'floor'* the pedal. The car was traveling at over sixty-five, perhaps seventy miles per hour. Judging from his posture, it looked like Norman was reclining in a movie theater waiting for the entertainment to begin, popping his unfiltered cigarettes into his mouth like kernels of buttered popcorn.

"You're going too slow, you idiot!" her father kept on shouting, in between taking drags on his Marlboros and temporarily disappearing behind screens of smoke. "Press your foot all the way down and keep it there."

Drivers honked and swerved all about them, but her father directed Jan to weave across the asphalt, saying it was important to know how to steer properly. Both the car and Jan's nerves were shaking at the same rate. She felt as if she were being held captive in the caboose of a runaway train.

"*Fangul*. Don't you hear me?" her father yelled. "Drive as I tell you! Turn here. Go over there. Make a left. Move further left. Now switch to the right!"

"I am. I'm doing everything you're telling me to do."

"No, you're not," he lambasted her. "You're driving like a baby; like a fraidy-cat."

"I'm trying, but I don't think…I don't think there's enough room to pass." Breaking out into a cold sweat, Jan was scared out of her wits. She tried to anticipate what a crash would feel like and how she would react to it. She hoped not too many of her bones would be broken. She clung to the 3-spoke steering wheel that seemed to have a mind of its own, making full rotations with just a slight touch of her hand. The red Chevrolet in the lane beside her was approaching too quickly. She could see its broad grill in her side mirror. The distance between their LTD and the rear taillights of the tan Buick just ahead was diminishing rapidly.

"It's not your job to think or to wait until the other car gets out of your way. Let *them* move if they don't want to get hit. You be the aggressive one! Faster. Faster."

Jan saw the speedometer reach up to seventy-five. To the young, inexperienced teenager, fifteen miles per hour had seemed fast enough. Jan was more than petrified, believing with all her heart that her father had intended to kill them both.

Chapter Two

In 1985, Alice was seventy years old. Her two girls had long been married and living in their own homes, and no one could say with any degree of certainty where Henry, Alice and Norman's one son, had run off to. Alice was sick as a dog and fighting exhaustion much of the time. She had a long history of showing up in emergency rooms and recuperating in ICU wards. Whenever Alice would suffer a new medical calamity, an obliging neighbor or considerate friend would notify her daughters and urge their confluence at the hospital as soon as possible. "The situation is critical". "We might lose her". "She's screaming in pain". On these occasions, more often than not, Norman would remain glued to his television set watching his favorite shows in his living room.

That year, Alice had already spent three weeks in the hospital for treatment of angina. The prior year, she had undergone spinal surgery. The year before that, she had a severe bout of colitis. At an earlier age, she had undergone a complete hysterectomy, with half of her stomach and a partial intestine being removed. Despite the intensity of the pain and uncertainty of her multiple conditions, the emergency room and intensive care units unwittingly provided Alice with her only safe haven.

Norman, despite lacking a propensity for making good business decisions, had invested heavily throughout the years in various ventures in the garment industry. Not one of his pursuits, however, had succeeded in turning the slightest profit. His knock-offs of famous brand designs were being knocked-off by other manufacturers at even more affordable prices, squeezing him out of the market and causing his sales to plummet. He remained, nevertheless, a stickler for high quality, well-made staples of clothing, refusing to utilize synthetic fabrics or adapt his production line to the popular, innovative styles of the times, both ignoring and detesting the revolution taking place in the world of fashion. Having to borrow money to pay for money owed, he could have more easily poured the money down the drain and saved himself the aggravation of outstaring union officials and fighting off threats from the mob.

In the month of April, Norman, whose hair had turned silvery gray and thinning and whose most recent commercial endeavor had been shut down for six months—courtesy of the federal bankruptcy laws, was facing insurmountable debt and possible eviction from his home. He was financially insolvent; a condition that did not appear to be going away on its own anytime soon and was a major source of friction between him and Alice, causing a persistent, irritating needling, real or imagined, to come streaming out of her mouth. Late one Monday morning, he took off his robe, which had been his cloak of armor for half the year, dressed himself in trousers, shirt and a floral silk cravat, and went to purchase several newspapers at the corner coffee shop. When he came home, he drank a steaming cup of tea, sweetened with three lumps of sugar, and with a red pencil, marked dark circles around the want-ads that most piqued his curiosity. One by one, he scratched off the ads for which he had made enquiries but had come up empty. There was one individual he spoke with, however, that didn't seem to mind how old Norman was, which Norman had shared over the phone, slashing his real age by five years.

Two days later, Norman went to meet with Burt at his liquor store in Queens, New York and was offered the job. It was a small store on a bustling street with considerable foot traffic, in a multi-ethnic, middle class neighborhood, called Rego Park, a ten-minute drive from the apartment building where Norman and Alice lived. In the early 1920s, the developer of Rego Park gave it its name by contracting the words "Real" and "Good," but Norman's tenure at the spirit shop proved to be not very good at all. The fact that he was filling a managerial position took away some of the crushing sting of his being a paid employee, but Norman did not like to kowtow to anyone.

Not thrilled to be out of the comfort zone of his living room, where he was used to idling his days away, he now spent hours studying the different brands of alcohol—developing expertise on the various whiskies, ryes, and vodkas, which products to push, and which favorites to stock for the store's most loyal customers. He had to familiarize himself with the State's regulations, review his profit margins, apply procedures to avoid under stocking or over stocking, learn how to purchase in bulk, and find ways to maintain a high turnover. To motivate his shoppers, he even explored special reward programs. In spite of his initial reluctance, Norman was becoming quite proficient at being a store manager. As an added bonus, he welcomed the free samples, especially the exotic liqueurs in their stylized decanters, that Burt, the owner, provided every once in a while, which Norman displayed on a shelf he personally had built on his dining room wall. Alice had said the shelf looked to be a bit unsteady, but Norman had told her that it was none of her goddamn business.

The crew that worked in the store was an amiable lot, who spoke little and steadfastly attended to their chores except when their manager interrupted the flow of work to share a joke or humorous anecdote. Norman enjoyed being the center of a captive audience. Sometimes, he would rant on for long, tedious periods, lecturing the crew about matters that were pertinent to him alone, demanding zero feedback and allowing for no additional commentary. Nevertheless, he was perceived to be a warm, intelligent, well-groomed, outgoing gentleman. Although the others poked fun of his formal, custom-made shirts and hand-tailored suits, Norman actually began to enjoy the camaraderie and experience he was gaining.

Every once in a while, when something truly quirky did occur, like Norman losing his temper over a spill or snapping at a supplier for an inaccurate shipment, the crew just put it down to Norman getting out of the wrong side of bed that day. They had no reason to suspect their immediate boss of being the Dr. Jekyll to Alice's husband, the evil Mr. Hyde.

One evening, Alice was suffering from severe heart palpitations. Norman tried to convince her that she'd be all right and that her probable indigestion would pass— "Don't you know what gas pains are, you idiot?"— but Alice insisted on calling her doctor, who arranged for an ambulance to take her to the local hospital. She was admitted as an inpatient and subjected to a battery of tests, but nothing conclusive regarding her condition could be deduced. Nevertheless, Alice savored the attention she received from the medical staff and the additional short respite away from her husband's iron fist.

Jan, who was well established in her New York law practice at that time, paid a visit to her mother during her lunch break, looked her straight in the eyes, and told her that she was a battered woman. Alice replied that she didn't know what that meant.

"I have a heart condition, Jan. That's why I'm so weak," Alice moaned. "I could drop dead from a heart attack at any given moment."

"You do not have a heart condition," Jan instructed, well aware that she was rattling the superficial foundation of her mother's existence. "You have emotional issues that have been suppressed over your entire lifetime."

Alice sat up, unfazed by her mint-green shawl sliding to the floor, baring a fair share of her cleavage. She eyed her daughter's appearance, looking up and down, taking in the cut of her navy suit, the shade of her pantyhose, the style of her shoes, the fullness of her bangs and haircut. "You do know, Jan, if you wore shoulder pads in your suit jacket you would make more of an impression with your clients. You can buy the ones with Velcro and have a dressmaker sew them in. Come on; get with it and stop looking so puny."

"I'm here to discuss your health, not my fashion," Jan responded, stooping to pick up the shawl. She wanted to scream, "Mother! This is about you and not me," but said instead, "As I was saying, you do not have a heart condition."

Reaching for the half donut remaining on her tray, Alice demanded, "Well, what am I supposed to do about that?" She nibbled on the strawberry icing and sprinkles, scraping off the ones sticking to her lip and chin. "And furthermore, you're a lawyer, not a doctor. What gives you the right to say I don't have a heart condition?"

Observing Alice as crumbs fell down into the neckline of her nightgown, Jan thought, *You're really in your element here, aren't you?*

"I had a long talk with your cardiologist, and that's what he told me," Jan stated with confidence.

Alice licked her fingers clean and then draped the shawl behind her back and across her chest. "All right then," she said, elevating her chin with a flare of bravado. "So, if you're so smart, why don't you tell me what I'm supposed to do about it?"

"I'm going to smuggle you out of your apartment and bring you to someone who can help you," Jan advised, capturing her mother's interest so her entire demeanor began to liven up.

Since Alice had been insistent that there could be no possibility of Norman finding out about their secret mission, Jan made an appointment with Family Services at a local Jewish Center for a day when her mother was supposed to be at work. When that day arrived, however, Alice had offered a million and one excuses as to why she couldn't attend. To Jan's proposal about rescheduling, she responded, "Let me think about it; I'll let you know," but she never mentioned it again.

Chapter Three

The first time there was a holdup in the liquor store, Norman had been more angry than scared. He and Jake, a salesclerk, had been forced onto the floor by two masked men, one of whom pointed a gun at Stewart, a stock clerk, directing him to open the cash register and dump all the cash into a pillowcase.

This was not the first time, however, that someone had ever pointed a gun at Norman. The most recent incident occurred one Saturday while he was still the owner of the dress factory. He was cutting through a stack of cotton, broadcloth fabrics, reproducing shapes of pattern pieces to be sewn into sundresses for an overdue store order, when a young, mob soldier had emerged from the freight elevator, brandishing a weapon in his shaking, outstretched hand. Hesitant and visibly nervous, seemingly on his very first mission, he had approached Norman and demanded payment for protection, vowing the dress company would otherwise be destroyed. The ultimatum was barely audible over the loud screeching noise of the industrial circular saw in use, which Norman then swung into the air without missing a beat.

"If you don't immediately get out of here, I'll slice your face in half before you can say, 'Jack Rabbit,'" Norman yelled. "What a sorry excuse for a wannabe hoodlum you are. Go on. Vamoose! Go, you stupid punk, before you shit yourself. No one is going to extort money from me! You can tell the big guys who sent you that I'm not interested!"

The trembling assailant took Norman's threat to heart, jumping backwards before speedily departing and knocking over a clothing rack full of samples on his way out. Other emissaries for both the union and the mob were far more competent and successful in inflicting significant damage to the factory's stock and equipment in the days that followed.

This go-around, Norman had hoped Stewart would at least be smart enough to push the panic button to alert the police, but Stewart had been too afraid to do anything but follow the men's demands. The two robbers ran out of the store, their pillowcase filled with bills and change. Norman took off to chase them down the street, but Jake caught up with him and pleaded with him to let them go.

"It's no use, man. Even if you catch up to them, they'll grind you to a pulp."

"No one does that to me and gets away with it," Norman roared. "I'll tear them into a million pieces before they have any idea what's going on."

The robbers disappeared, descending into the subway entrance at the corner of Queens Boulevard and 63rd Drive.

"C'mon Norman. Let's go back." Jake put his arm around Norman, which Norman furiously shoved away. "C'mon," Jake repeated, jerking his head in the direction of the liquor store.

That evening at home, Norman couldn't stop ranting. Nothing on his dinner plate tasted good. He complained that his London Broil was overcooked and the vegetables were too raw. His soda was too cold, but the kitchen was too hot. He found fault with everything Alice said as she tried to calm him down.

"Alice," he said, screaming his head off as usual, "what do you mean it was an isolated incident? Are you a moron? This is a liquor store; everyone knows there's going to be a lot of change in the till. I wish I could have pounced on them; I would have torn those bloody *schvartze*s to shreds."

"Norman, it's not your place to get involved. You're not such a young man anymore. These things are best left to the police." Alice drew her hands into her lap.

"The police are probably in on it. Everyone is corrupt in this city." He puckered his lips as if he were chewing on rancid meat.

"Well, it's better for you to keep on doing your job, and let them do theirs," she offered in hushed tones, her eyes fixed on her crisscrossed thumbs.

"With a wife like you," Norman yelled back, "I don't need enemies. I get no support even in my own home. If those shitheads come back again, they'll have me to deal with, and it won't be pretty."

There was a second holdup four months after the first one. It took place while Norman was trying on leather moccasins and corduroy scuffs at Thom McCann's, three bays to the south of the liquor store. He had told Jake that he would be right back after stepping out to the bank for change for the till. Stewart had originally volunteered for the errand, but Norman needed a pair of slippers, and Thom McCann's was just a stone's throw away from the bank. For the next pair, Norman had promised himself he would be perusing the samples in the men's department at Saks Fifth Avenue in Manhattan instead.

Again, the silent alarm had not been activated, adding to Norman's fury and further discontent. He wanted to sack the entire crew for acting so cowardly, but Burt refused to let them go.

"Let the police handle it," Burt advised.

"The police don't do shit," Norman ranted.

Burt was adamant. "I don't want anyone getting hurt. I know Stewart and Jake; they're good guys. They've been with me from the beginning, and I'm not letting them go."

When he returned home, Norman hauled Alice over the coals all night long. The dinner was deplorable; she looked like a dishrag; and the house was a filthy mess. He threw the pillows off the couch, complaining that there was no place to "park his arse," and smashed a glass ashtray to the floor. Alice was thankful that it was not the hand-blown Murano one her brother, Morris, had bought her on his trip to Italy.

Muttering and cursing to himself, he fell heavily into a side chair before turning on the television with the remote control. Diverting his attention away from the nightly news, he informed Alice, who had been doing her best to sit a safe distance away, "I'm going to quit. I've had enough of this shit."

"Norman," she said, keeping her voice as restrained as possible, "don't quit. You seemed to be enjoying this job—at least in the beginning—and the money has been good. We need that money to live on. You'd be making a terrible mistake. Just don't wear your good gold watch to work anymore."

"What a brilliant suggestion!" he sneered back at her. "Not wearing a gold watch is going to thwart the store from being held up? Do you have any brains in your head at all?" He looked around the room for something to grab and settled on the *TV Guide*, which he flung at Alice's face. She ducked and the magazine landed at her feet.

Norman didn't quit his job, but he did apply for a gun permit, specifically to defend against future break-ins and to "teach the bastard scumbags a lesson they will never forget." Jan and Maureen worried endlessly, fearing their father's access to a deadly weapon increased the likelihood of his shooting their mother during a frenzied episode.

With the Christmas and Chanukah season approaching, Norman had the store's windows decorated in accordance with the festive spirit permeating the neighborhood. Alexanders department store, within walking distance of the liquor store, had erected an enormous tree, decked to the nines in bright lights and colorful ornaments. The atmosphere along the Rego Park streets was merry and hopeful. There was even talk of a few snowflakes approaching the eastern seaboard in time for the holidays, which spurred people into spending generously. The healthy profits and constant activity in the liquor store buoyed Norman's mood, expanding his already inflated sense of self-importance. He bragged to his crew and Burt about how much the store had benefited under his leadership— "You'd all be in the toilet if it wasn't for me."—and shouted them down if they begged to differ, even somewhat humorously.

It was almost closing time and Norman had started to count the receipts for the day's sales. Slipping in through the back door which led in from the parking lot, two armed, masked men shouted to Norman to hand them the money. They screamed at the other employees to lie on the floor with their hands behind their heads. Norman eyed the panic button and one of the robbers instructed Norman not to do anything foolish.

"Just give me the money old man, and we'll be out of here real soon," he warned Norman. "No one will get hurt. And while you're at it, you can take off that nice shiny bling and put it in with the cash."

Jake called out to Norman, "Just give them what they want, please!" but Norman was not about letting anyone push him around. He stepped toward the cabinet below the cash register and reached for his gun.

"Fuck you," Norman shouted. "You're not getting away this time."

"Man, what do you want to do something like that for?" one of the robbers called out.

Three bullets were shot into Norman's chest before he could even raise his weapon. He fell to the ground and died instantly.

Chapter Four

As there was next to nothing in Alice and Norman's bank accounts and Norman had believed insurance policies to be scams, the funeral arrangements and all of its associated expenses were paid for by Maureen and her husband, Jack, who had assured Alice she no longer had any reason to be worried about unpaid bills, repossession notices, and debt collectors. Within two weeks after the funeral, Maureen and Jack had also purchased a two-story townhouse not too far from where they lived and had Alice moved to a suburb on Long Island. They provided Alice with a monthly stipend and had obtained health insurance for her as well. Alice's life had gone from abject misery to *Queen for a Day* marvelous.

She became a lady who lunched and dined with a gaggle of other women at fashion shows, charity events, and tea parties. With an expanded social life calling for a more extensive wardrobe, Alice had set about acquiring new outfits, accessories, manicures, pedicures, and hairdos, all with the use of her son-in-law Jack's credit cards. Jack would question Maureen, and Maureen would question Alice if this excessive spending had been necessary and perhaps a little too self-indulgent.

"He refused me everything, your father did," Alice would cry. "You've no idea what it feels like to be a battered spouse and have someone breathing down your neck, trying to control your every move. For the first time in my life, I don't have to be humiliated, regulated or hunted every time I take a step outdoors. Oh my God, I feel truly liberated!"

Over an eight-year period, Jack continued to foot the bills for Alice's extravagant lifestyle while Jan and Maureen made certain to keep tabs on their mother's safety and welfare, calling her daily.

"Margo keeps pressing me to go on a twelve-day cruise with her," Alice mentioned in passing during one such phone call. "It's a lot of money to spend, but given my poor health, who knows if I'll ever have an opportunity to go anywhere else again?"

She whined another day, "It's just a week in Atlantic City, for goodness sake! Meals and transportation are included. I'd be the only one in the Hadassah chapter not going if I had to stay home. Without the neighbors around, I could drop dead and no one would even know it. *Do you know how badly* a rotting body *smells* when it's left undiscovered?"

"The drapes are being installed Friday," she complained months later, in classic, grandiose style. "I want them up before the new living room furniture is delivered. My place looked like a shithole compared to the other homes in this community. Who even knows if I am allergic to the mold and mildew from what was here before? It would explain my declining state of health."

"Your mother is great at scheming and feigning heart attacks, but she pours it on a little too thick, don't you think?" Mike, Jan's husband, questioned, after learning of Alice's latest protestation.

Jan replied, "I feel sorry for her; I always will. She's had such a rough life."

"That's her claim to fame," Mike said. "For a woman who has never been officially diagnosed with a heart condition, you and your sister spend an inordinate amount of time worrying about her suffering some catastrophic cardiac event. Don't you realize she uses that to her full advantage?"

"Yes, we are all well aware of that," Jan conceded, none too pleased to be discussing her mother once more with Mike, "but at this point, what can anyone really do about it? Please, let's not discuss this yet again."

Not too long after Mike and Jan's conversation, Alice accidentally dropped the phone during a call with Maureen, and Maureen, fearing the worst, assumed her mother had suffered a major heart attack. Emergency crews raced to Alice's home after Maureen dialed 911. The medics and firefighters knocked down the front door and ran up the staircase to find a healthy, robust Alice, wearing nothing but a pink, nylon negligee, propped up in bed, eating bonbons and watching TV. Without skipping a beat, Alice said, "I can only take you on one at a time." That was when the decision was made in August 1993 to pack up the seventy-eight-year-old Alice and send her to Florida, where Jan and Mike had already moved. Maureen said she believed the environment in Florida to be more conducive for seniors, but Jan suspected that Maureen and Jack had had their fill of Alice's shenanigans.

The move worked well for Alice. She was surely in her element when she came to live in Century Village in Boca Raton. There wasn't a single show, movie, or enriched-living class she didn't attend. Painted vases and figurines—produced weekly in the ceramic workshop—were proudly displayed on shelves, counter tops, and cubbyholes everywhere in her apartment. Each Thursday, she played Kalooki; Monday and Wednesday afternoons were set aside for Rummikub.

During this busy schedule, Alice still managed to book a plethora of doctors' appointments, but she could not be trusted to attend them alone. She had a habit of reacting to the medical staff incoherently or with gibberish, leading them to believe there was a language barrier, despite English being Alice's native tongue. Jan presumed Alice's behavior was attributable to a well-founded fear of authority figures, and, therefore, took it upon herself to accompany her mother on most of these visits.

"She was just impossible," Jan would report back to Mike. "I felt like climbing the walls, listening for hours upon hours to her nonsensical small talk."

Mike would shrug and say, "Whatever" or "Sounds awful" and then would quickly add, "If you're looking for sympathy from me, which you'd be a fool if you were, you're definitely barking up the wrong tree."

Throughout the week, Alice would have no compunction about sending Jan on multiple errands to the supermarket, butcher, or drugstore. "I'm all out of milk", "I've lost my pills", "My freezer and refrigerator are empty and I'm starving". Typically, when Jan would arrive at Alice's apartment, she would find her mother at the head of the table, holding court in her dining room surrounded by friends, eating M&M's and pretzels, and shuffling decks of playing cards.

"Be a dear and put everything away," Alice would command. "Then you may leave." Jan would comply with her mother's orders and then run to her car, silently fuming with rage.

"I don't recall my mother ever being this bossy before," a harried Jan shared with Mike one evening. "How did she ever manage to function on her own?"

"What difference does it make?" Mike responded angrily. "She probably never did and now she doesn't have to. She treats you as her slave. She tells you to jump, and you ask 'how high?'"

Chapter Five

Labor Day of 1993 was celebrated in Mike and Jan's backyard with a lavish barbecue, to which Alice and her new Boca Raton friends had been invited. The very next day, Jan was startled to receive an early morning call from her mother, who sounded much more melancholy than usual.

"I haven't been sleeping well," she declared between yawns. "Besides getting up in the middle of the night to tinkle, I'm also now getting up at all different hours."

"Does anything hurt?" Jan inquired, stretching across her pillow to read the time on her clock radio.

"No."

Jan had shoved Mike over from his back to his side to stifle his snores and whispered to Alice, "Is your mind too active before you go to sleep?"

"I usually try to convene the United Nations Security Council session a good half hour before I get into bed. "

"What are you talking about?" Jan demanded, her voice raspy.

"What are *you* talking about?" Alice shot back, incensed. "How much of my mind do you think I use to watch *Wheel of Fortune* or *Jeopardy*? I'm not one of the contestants, you know! All I do is watch the bloomin' shows!"

"I'm trying to help you," Jan said before clearing her throat. "Why are you attacking me?"

Alongside Jan, Mike muttered, "What's going on?"

"Nothing," Jan answered. "It's only 5:45 a.m., and it's my mother on the phone. Go back to sleep."

"What does the old shrew need now?" Mike's words came out muffled as his head sunk into his pillow.

"I need tranquilizers," Alice stated. "Why is your husband referring to me as an old Jew?"

"He must be dreaming," Jan suggested. "How do you know you need tranquilizers?"

"My new friend, Muriel, takes them all the time. She gets headaches."

"And you get headaches?"

"No, but I've been having a load of nightmares and it's making me feel very depressed."

After taking a deep breath, Jan asked, "What do you have to feel depressed about?"

"I don't know; a lot of things: my life, my marriage, dying." Alice's voice trailed off into a hush, ever so desolate.

"Oh, I see," Jan replied, unsure of what else to add. "Perhaps you would like to talk to a therapist about this?"

"Will they be able to give me tranquilizers?"

"They *might* be able to prescribe them, but maybe you won't need them so much if you're able to get some things off your chest. Would you like me to make an appointment for you?" *She doesn't know the difference between a psychiatrist and a psychologist, but now's not the time to clarify the distinction.*

"I'd prefer talking more to a woman than a man," Alice insisted, "although men do tend to be smarter. Can women write the same prescriptions as men?"

"Yes," Jan uttered, biting her tongue. "All therapists, regardless of gender, have the same training. Okay, I'll get on it first thing this morning."

Four hours later, Jan supplied her mother with the date, time, and location of the appointment with Dr. Sarah Solowitz.

"You'll have to drive me to see the shrink," Alice responded with trepidation. "I get lost a lot, since I still don't know my way around."

"She's not a shrink; *she's a psychologist*," Jan corrected, adding, "yes, I will certainly take you there."

"Will you stay with me in the room? I've never done anything like this before. I won't know what to say or what's expected of me."

"I'll stay as long as it is appropriate to stay. I'm sure Dr. Solowitz will be very nice and will put you at ease right away."

"No. I want you with me every time I have to go." Alice was adamant in this request. "I hate it when I get lost. It's very confusing by Military Trail and the overpass."

The day of the appointment, Jan entered the parking lot of the Century Village complex just as a balmy blast of warm air blew over the robellinis and ferns, causing the water in the lake to undulate. Shrieks of delight arose from the bridge players occupying the sundeck by the pool. Despite the temperature being in the high 80s, Alice had chosen to wear a wool pleated skirt, silk blouse, and a navy jacket with a gold mask pinned to its lapel; she looked nervous and discombobulated despite her formal outfit.

"You look like you're dressed for the cold weather up north," Jan commented as her mother slipped into the front passenger seat. *Oh my, did you forget your royal felt hat?*

"This is what I'd wear for *shul* for Rosh Hashanah. I thought it was appropriate to dress up for this occasion as well."

"What occasion?" Jan asked, bewildered.

"Seeing a shrink."

Jan checked the temperature setting for the air conditioning in the car. She was suddenly starting to sweat. "But it's really not that big of a deal."

"To me it is," Alice explained. "I want her to have a good impression of me."

Alice tapped her fingers on the armrest for the entire fifteen-minute journey, chatting non-stop about the weather, ice cream, and the unbearable number of commercials on Florida television stations. It irked Jan to no end because Alice's tapping was totally erratic and undecipherable. *There's no distinguishable rhythm. What could she possibly have in her head other than nonsensical gobbledy-gook?*

Once the two women were shown into the therapist's office, Alice sat erect with a pensive look on her face, as if she were trying to be a really good student and not be called upon in class. "Jan will tell you," was the response she gave to every question asked of her.

Dr. Solowitz, in her mid-forties and on the chunky side of a size fourteen, asked Alice if she had a speech impediment, to which Alice replied, "I'm not good at talking. Jan knows everything. She'll tell you what you need to know."

The therapist then asked Jan what she perceived the issue to be.

"My father was an extremely abusive man who demeaned my mother throughout their marriage." She looked straight at Dr. Solowitz's face, expecting a sympathetic reaction, but Dr. Solowitz remained stoic. The

34

chrome-rimmed glasses on the bridge of her nose didn't budge even a millimeter.

Dr. Solowitz reached for a legal pad and pen from her desk to jot down her notes. "Alice, how would *you* describe the abuse?"

"Huh?"

"Well, would you say the abuse was physical, mental, or both?"

"I've no idea what you or Jan is talking about."

Dr. Solowitz set the pen and pad down on her desk while she uncrossed her legs and forced a smile in Alice's direction. "Well then, how about you tell me a little about your married life?"

Alice glanced at her lap. "Mmmm, it was all right I guess."

Dr. Solowitz tented her fingers. "Alice, are you sure you wish to engage in this process?"

"Not really," Alice uttered, rotating the charm bracelet on her wrist.

"Why are you here?" Dr. Solowitz asked, leaning forward on her chair. "Are you experiencing any sleeplessness and/or depression?"

"No. Not really," Alice answered softly. "I thought it would be a good way to see my daughter at least once a week."

Jan's eyes darted about the room. If she had found a hammer or loose heavy object nearby, she would have smashed it over her mother's head.

Dr. Solowitz pulled on her paisley shirt cuffs so they extended equally beyond the sleeves of her red cardigan and then stood. "Perhaps you need some time to reconsider. When you feel comfortable enough to talk with me, I will be more than happy to make another appointment."

Alice took this last comment as her cue to depart, but before rising from her chair, she asked Dr. Solowitz for a prescription for tranquilizers. "That's what I really need, and then I won't be back to bother you anymore. You can even refill the prescription over the phone if that works better for you."

"I'm sorry, Alice. That's just not at all possible."

Dr. Solowitz was about to say more, but Alice immediately swung around to face Jan. "Please don't be mad at me. I hate it when you're mad at me. It's very lonely for me in Florida and I would never have seen you if I didn't agree to see this shrink—I mean psychiatrist."

At her wit's end, Jan felt her blood pounding in her temples. "Mom, I've been at your apartment every day!"

"Not really, you haven't."

"Yes, really, I have! Your 'poor me' performance is going overboard. Either you acknowledge that I have been to see you practically every day or we're leaving this office immediately and going straight over to see a neurosurgeon to have your brain cut open and examined, and I'll make sure to tell the surgeon not to give you any anesthetic ahead of time."

"I wouldn't mind doing that if the neurosurgeon would prescribe the tranquilizers."

Jan glared at Dr. Solowitz and shouted, "*Can you now see what I'm dealing with here?*"

Alice sank her head into her chest, sighing heavily.

"It's not unusual for some people to experience memory loss as they get older," Dr. Solowitz said, sitting pensively in her chair. "Please Jan, there's no need to use scare tactics with your mother. We don't want to needlessly add to her apprehension. There are many options and resources available to deal with forgetfulness."

Jan's right foot started tapping. She dug her fingernails into the palms of her hands. "She's playing you. My mother is not *this* forgetful!"

"Well, in any case, you might want to consider making a private appointment for yourself. It appears to me you are harboring some heavy-duty anger issues."

"Tell her the truth," Jan demanded, focusing on Alice. "Without embellishing it with any funny business or it will be years before you'll ever see me again."

Slowly and willfully, Alice raised her face toward the therapist. "My daughter wants me to tell you she does come to visit me once in a while."

Jan shook her head in disbelief, her jaw wide open in total exasperation. "That's not what I meant," she yelled, "and you know it! I see the game you're playing. Don't try to act all coy and innocent because you're not either of those things!"

Dr. Solowitz arose, looking none too pleased. "The dynamics of your relationship definitely warrant further examination," she announced with solemnity and ushered Jan and Alice toward the door. "Perhaps, the two of you can engage in a worthwhile dialogue over a cup of coffee. If either of you should choose to make another appointment, please feel free to contact my secretary."

"We're tea drinkers," Alice blurted out. "We drink tea, not coffee! But only tea with milk; that's the proper way. I was born in England. Couldn't you tell by my accent? You shouldn't go by Jan because she lost her accent in Brooklyn when she was a little girl. It happened right away. The schoolchildren had asked her what language they speak in England. Can you imagine that; people being so ignorant? She should have answered them, 'The King's English!' As timid as she was, she just kept her mouth shut and let them ridicule her. Norman, that was her father, gave her a bloody-good what-for. Anyway, we came over on the ocean liner, the *Queen Elizabeth*…"

Jan rolled her eyes while Dr. Solowitz anxiously interrupted Alice. "I'm sorry, but I do have another patient in the waiting room. Why don't you enjoy a lovely conversation over a cup of tea then? It might be therapeutic."

Chapter Six

While Alice continued to live in her one bedroom, lake-view apartment in Century Village, Jan felt obliged to cater to her mother's growing needs with regard to her health, car maintenance, occasional floods, condo association regulations, and other daily essentials—all the while struggling to maintain her own law practice.

In 1995, making the decision to greatly cut down on her own work hours, she dissolved her full-time practice and signed a contract requiring her to pick up or drop off files twice a week at the Trusts & Estates Law Firm of Susan Walsh. Susan's office was located in the renovated Tuscan-style center on State Road 7 in Boca Raton, Florida, where Jan had once maintained her own office.

It didn't bother Jan too much to pack up all of her framed diplomas and certificates and store them on a shelf in her bedroom closet, but it peeved Mike to no end. These items used to be publicly displayed on the wall behind Jan's antique walnut desk—the one-of-a-kind, expensive desk she fretted over for weeks before purchasing. While Jan had deliberated back and forth in the furniture store, Mike had insisted the desk was worthy of the super-duper, intelligent, professional his wife had become, but now it was assigned to a legal associate Susan Walsh had hired after assuming Jan's commercial lease.

"It's a disgrace," he objected as the two were preparing dinner together. "You worked so hard to get to this point, but your mother has totally taken over your life, making you her puppet. It's almost like you can't walk or talk without her pulling your strings. As it is, she has you running silly, back and forth, up and down, and sideways on her behalf. What more could she possibly expect from you?"

Mike stopped what he was doing and set his hands on Jan's shoulders, gripping the fabric of her blouse, to make sure his point was getting across. "So many of your clients are referring more clients and you've developed an admirable reputation, even with the fewer hours you're devoting to your practice. Why not cut down on your volunteer work instead? You don't have to serve on every board or committee that recruits you."

"I'll start my practice over again when I'm ready," Jan claimed, ducking out from under Mike's arms. Being pegged in like that set off warning signals in her head, making her feel imperiled.

"You're shortchanging yourself," Mike continued. "There's no reason at all to be placing your own life on hold."

Walking over to a cabinet, she handed him two water goblets to fill and place on the kitchen table. "The clients will still be there when I want them to be. People die all the time, so there never can be a shortage of probate or estate planning work." After she placed a French baguette in the toaster oven, she added, "And as far as my charities, the world would be a far better place if more people decided to help."

"But you've taken being goody-two-shoes to the nth degree," he stated, pressing the cold-water tab on the refrigerator door and then placing the filled glasses on the counter next to him. Standing with his back to the refrigerator, he kneaded his palms together and watched Jan scoot from one end of the kitchen to the other as she set the table and warmed up soup on the range. When she spun around to announce that dinner was ready, Mike pressed his cupped hands against his chin. "I thought that was one of the reasons we originally moved here: leaving your nutsy family behind. I saw the damage it was doing to your relationship with Daniel. You and he were screaming at each other practically every single day."

"As you well know, it was our son who walked around with a constant chip on his shoulder. That was none of my doing."

"Don't you see; it's all connected. It's as plain as black and white. Why can't it be that visible to you? This nonsense has got to stop!"

A veil of panic rippled across Jan's face. "Why are you bullying me? You sounded like my father just then."

"I am nothing like your father, and you know it! I sincerely love you. I am hoping to free you from his craziness once and for all." Looking directly into her eyes, Mike delicately placed a hand on each of her elbows, barely touching the surface of her blouse. "The last thing in the world I would ever want to be is a man who abuses or manipulates people through fear."

The heat from Mike's palms stirred a momentary tingling in her skin which she tried to dismiss. "My mother's well-being has to be my priority," Jan responded, shoving Mike aside so she could retrieve bottles of salad dressing from the fridge.

"I hate when you get like this, Jan. Not even a bulldozer can budge you off track. I'm trying so hard to protect you, but you just won't let me." He looked up at the ceiling, inhaling deeply, stewing in disappointment.

Well aware of Mike's burgeoning frustration, Jan hoped his plentiful reserve of patience was not about to dry up. He had always been the pillar of strength upon which she leaned, her buttress against all the ills of her world.

Losing his support would be an insuperable crushing blow. Despite desperately wishing their conversation would end so they could just sit down and eat their dinner in peace, she reiterated why she chose to close her practice in hopes of finally winning Mike over to her side.

"My work is very labor intensive. I have too many filing deadlines to meet and I'm swamped with tax forms, bank reconciliations, and accounts to balance. All of this adds to the mounting pressures from my overhead expenses. I just can't think straight anymore, and what makes matters worse, worrying about my mother totally inhibits my ability to focus."

Mike's mouth fell open. He began to stomp out of the room but stopped abruptly and backtracked to where Jan was standing. "Obviously, I'm a thick-headed simpleton because this is something I really don't understand. Why do you worry so much about her, especially since Norman is no longer around? It's the ever-present, million-dollar question that never gets answered. I wish you'd divert more of what I consider your wasted time to me!"

"Oh my God, Mike," Jan groaned, bunching her hands into fists, as an intense fear wrapped itself around her body like a slithering boa constrictor. She was on the brink of finally telling Mike what compelled her to act the way she did, but a heavy-duty, invisible clamp fastened over her mouth, precluding her from doing so. She had experienced this fear many times before since she was a little girl, sucking the life out of her, asphyxiating her, deadening her. A threat thrashed at her brain, ricocheting between her ears and tightening her jaw. "Keep your mouth shut. Do you hear me? You are to tell no one about this. No one at all!"

Jan closed her eyes and took a deep breath, snatching a comeback from a stockpile of plausible excuses in her memory bank. "Because she's a little old lady, and I don't want her to suffer anymore."

Mike threw his hands in the air. "Your sole purpose in life is not to act as a servant or a whipping child," he shouted, losing the battle to keep his temper under control. "For some preposterous, unfathomable reason, you've got blinders on with this regard. Don't you think it's time to stop clinging to the past and end our life sentence? And I purposefully said '*our* life sentence' because I feel like I'm forever stuck in this muddle with you." Mike's arms fell to his sides, his muscles stiff and unyielding.

Jan stretched on her tippy toes to kiss him, but he pulled away.

"For God's sake," she shrieked, her fingers now tugging at the many knots in her curly hair until clumps of fuzz fell from her hands. "You're overreacting. We both are. Please, let's give this a rest."

"I'm going out," Mike shouted, slashing the air with his hand. "You can have fun eating your soup and salad alone!"

For seven more years, Alice continued to flourish in Boca Raton, making the most of the sub-tropical climate and a more relaxed life than she had ever experienced in New York, but she remained a divisive wedge in Jan and Mike's relationship. Barely reaching over the steering wheel, she resembled the Mr. Magoo cartoon character, beep-beeping herself about town in her cobalt blue Toyota Corolla, which at times erroneously signaled an upcoming left or right turn because Alice was oblivious to the ticking of a switched-on indicator. Mike constantly claimed that Alice was a menace on the road, especially the way she cut off other drivers to change lanes or pulled up diagonally into parking spots. Jan would respond that her mother drove in the same manner as all the other retirees: no better, no worse.

Alice's frequent excursions brought her to the movies, department stores, casinos, and downtown Mizner Park, allowing her to enjoy a fun-filled social life. Her days and nights were occupied with strolling with friends along the marble glitz of Town Center Mall, chatting with them over lunch at The Cheesecake Factory, or humming to the songs performed at the grand Century Village Recreational Facility Theater. At little to no cost to Alice, her life had become truly idyllic.

Chapter Seven

At Alice's urging, she and her friend, Muriel, had waited a few days past the actual date in order to celebrate the New Year at Ming's Chinese restaurant. It was an inconspicuous, local restaurant in the middle of a strip mall, frequented by many of the Century Village residents because of its large, economical early bird menu.

"I can't stand the ballyhoo and trumped-up prices of the holiday," Alice had shared. "Although those Chinese people love to take advantage of us elderly Jews, I don't want to have to spend money on atmosphere. I'd rather pay good money for a meal I enjoy than pay for la-di-da dishes you need a magnifying glass to see what they're serving you."

"Yes, I agree, but if my son's paying, then I don't mind going somewhere a little fancier than Ming's," Muriel had commented.

"Well, we're going to Ming's regardless," Alice had asserted. "Does it ever bother you, though, how much those Chinese people smile all the time? I could be talking in French or Italian, but they just keep on smiling at me— that's all they ever do. You never know what they're really thinking. They could be cursing us out in their brains, wishing us dead, but they just keep on smiling all the time."

"Isn't that what they call an unfair generalization?" Muriel had asked.

"Not if I'm stating a truth," Alice had defended. "You've even said the same when the lady in the laundry store charged you an arm and a leg to shorten a maxi skirt."

"I think she's Korean," Muriel had recalled.

"No difference," Alice had replied. "In any case, our food will taste the same as always, just as salty, even with the non-stop smiles. I'll pick you up at 4:45 sharp; I want to be sure to be home for my two handsome boyfriends, Pat Sajak and Alex Trebek."

"Here's to 2002," Muriel said cheerfully, raising her wine glass. "May it turn out to be a wonderful year for the both of us!" The two women, sitting opposite each other, had been ushered into a booth in the corner of the main dining room, under a wall display of gold fiery dragons. Alice, wearing a purple, silk blouse and black slacks, complimented Muriel on her black and white dotted dress. The outfits had been purchased on their last outing together at the Festival flea market, the costs discounted by dollar coupons. They clinked their glasses and went back to munching on their appetizers.

"Muriel, look around you," Alice instructed her dinner companion in a hushed tone. "Tell me if we're not the only ones here without a caretaker."

Muriel surveyed the restaurant. "I hadn't noticed before you pointed that out, but why are you whispering?"

"I don't want *them* to hear me," Alice responded, her voice as lowered as before. "Seems to me these colored people do all right when they come to America, eating in restaurants they wouldn't ordinarily be able to afford."

"You've got a point there," Muriel spluttered, choking on a chestnut while speaking and chewing at the same time.

Alice waited for Muriel to finish clearing her throat. "Would you want your girl to be black or white?"

"You mean if I needed someone to take care of me?"

"Yes. Not that either of us is at that stage right now." Alice picked up a spare rib and began chewing on the meaty part. "We're both only eighty-six years old, but you can never tell from one year to the next."

"I'm eighty-five," Muriel snapped. "Please don't make me any older than I already am. Anyway, I plan on leaving that detail to my son when the time comes."

Alice wiped the grease from both her hands and leaned in. "Well, I'd probably trust the white ones a lot more than the blacks, but the black women tend to be cheaper, more doting and attentive. From what I can tell, they understand who's the boss."

Muriel again raised her wine glass. "Alice, let's hope we sail through this new year without needing anyone but ourselves." She chugged the contents down to the very last drop.

Shortly after watching her beloved game shows on television that night, Alice slipped as she stepped out of the shower, hearing a loud clunking sound when she landed on the cold tile floor. Several hours transpired before she regained the strength to crawl into her bedroom; it was impossible, though, for her to hoist herself up onto the mattress. With an exerted stretch, she reached the telephone cord hanging by her side table and jerked the phone down to the carpet. Exhausted and in excruciating pain, she chose not to make the call and closed her eyes.

The next morning, the receptionist in the cardiologist's office was trying to reschedule Alice's appointment. The phone just rang and rang, and the receptionist, after several attempts, was growing concerned. It was common knowledge that Alice liked to lull away her mornings watching TV in bed. As a precaution and following standard procedure, the receptionist notified the paramedics and also alerted Jan, who threw on her clothes and dashed into her car. Driving along the well-traveled route to her mother's apartment, Jan bellyached, "Here I go again. Off to being suckered into yet another earth-shattering crisis in the life of Alice Block."

Spurred on by the siren of the emergency vehicle speeding past the guardhouse and heading towards Alice's building, a sizeable crowd of nosy bodies had already congregated in the lot when Jan parked her car and hurried to find her mother being lifted onto a gurney. There appeared to be much more of a blanket and much less of a person being tied down by a series of straps. Jan had to squeeze through the swimsuits and shorts-clad spectators who refused to budge even an inch, lest they surrender their decent viewing spots.

"It hurts, Jan. It really hurts," her mother whispered. Her face was badly bruised and her lip was crusted with dried blood. "Such a wonderful year Muriel had wished us," Alice complained. "She put the kiss of death on me! From now on, I hope she won't be so quick to wish me anything."

"I understand, Mom," Jan said, rearranging strands of her mother's hair to cover a large pinkish bald spot in the center of her head. "The doctors will take care of you now; you'll be okay. I'm here by your side." She would need two hands and a foot to count how many times she had said these exact words before.

The officer in charge of the medical unit approached Jan, informing her that Alice had probably broken her hip, her pelvis, or both; she had been lying on the ground all night long by herself. Jan tried to dismiss the thought *because she's a nincompoop and never does what's right* from her head, but it kept popping back up over and over again. Her reaction was a mixture of bafflement and annoyance and she hoped the officer would not judge her too harshly.

"Why didn't you call me when this happened?" she asked her mother.

"Your rule: no phone calls after 10 o'clock," came Alice's reply. "I was afraid you'd lose your temper." Considering the lunacy of Alice's explanation, Jan wanted to scream out of sheer frustration, but the officer had already shot her a menacing, disapproving look.

What kind of monster am I? Isn't there a part of me that cares she's suffering?

"Well, next time you'll call me no matter what," Jan insisted, being sure to keep her voice in soothing, hushed tones as she gently stroked her mother's hand. "Don't you dare worry about how late it is."

"Let's all hope that there won't be a next time," the officer warned as he directed Jan into the ambulance in which her mother was about to be taken to the nearest hospital.

Chapter Eight

After a month of rehab and physical therapy, following the surgery to repair Alice's broken hip, and two months of Alice wreaking havoc on three different full-time caregivers ("I don't need any colored people in my home", "All she does is read her bible", "If she's going to eat that much, then let her pay for the groceries!"), Jan's sister, Maureen, arranged for Alice to be brought to North Miami to live in Platinum Heritage, a brand new sleek building catering to the elderly. It was equipped with state-of- the-art computers, modern furniture, and a devoted staff.

Jan transported Alice and her possessions to her new address and lunched with her in their trendy haute cuisine restaurant before saying an appropriate, not too mushy goodbye.

Appearing both angry and perturbed, Alice took several minutes to review the menu. "How can they not have matzo ball soup? They make that everywhere."

"They are serving something different today," Jan answered, making every effort to contain the level of stress at the table. "There's vichyssoise instead."

"What's with a cold soup? Have you ever heard of a cold soup?"

"Borscht."

"Well, that's different. That's perfectly all right. I can't eat something I can't pronounce."

Jan's shut-off resentment valve took a quarter-turn. "How about *gribenes, miltz, and holishkes*? Do you have any trouble pronouncing any of those dishes?"

Alice stared defiantly at Jan. When the waiter approached, she asked for a tuna fish sandwich on rye. After being informed there was only white bread or a Kaiser roll, she muttered, "Nazi bastards," under her breath.

By the time Jan returned home, the phone was ringing off its hook; Jan picked up the receiver and heard Alice screaming, "Get me out of this place now!"

She tried to calm her mother down, but it was to no avail. "You're not listening to me," Alice shrieked. "I don't want to give this place a chance. I don't want to stay another minute longer. I'll be waiting for you downstairs inside the lobby by the water fountain that looks like a coffin. My goodness gracious, of all the designs to choose from, that's the one the brilliant architect came up with? Seriously, how much reminding do these old people need? Whatever happened to using common sense or a little *sechel*?" Jan couldn't get a word in edgewise.

"I'm putting this on your shoulders; if you don't come soon, I'm going to jump out the window—and don't forget, Jan, the room they stuck me in is on the sixth floor. You'll find my splattered body on the sidewalk; God forbid it strikes an innocent bystander on the way down. That will make it murder! Let it be on your conscience; you're the one who will have to live with the consequences and guilt, not me."

Jan was pretty sure the windows on each of the upper floors of Platinum Heritage were kept locked. She placed a call to the director's office and was informed that her mother was causing a ruckus. Several of the residents were becoming upset by the disturbance. "We can administer tranquilizers, if need be," the director had informed Jan, to which Jan replied, "Yes, I will give you permission to do so, but only if it can be on a permanent basis."

51

The second time Jan arrived at Platinum Heritage, she discovered her mother sitting in the lobby in the middle of a coffee klatch. Hoping not to be detected right away, Jan stood off to the side, catching fragments of the ongoing conversation.

"Last year's fashions were definitely more wearable than this year's. Have you seen the newest Armani's?"

"I'm having the larger diamond re-set, but the smaller ones will be made into earrings with the emeralds."

As Alice caught sight of Jan approaching the group, her cheeks broadened into an indisputable smile. Springing to a standing position, she broadcast with an air of pretension, "Ladies, I see my daughter has arrived. It was a pleasure meeting all of you. It really is too bad, but I simply do miss my life in Boca."

While traveling north along the I-95 highway, Jan tried to impress upon her mother that they were heading straight to Glenbrook, another assisted-living facility.

Alice, recoiled in her seat, refusing to accept this inevitable defeat. "I have no other choice but this?" She pronounced these words with the precision of a hunter's blade peeling off the skin of its prey.

"That was the deal," Jan stated, determinedly impassive. "If you don't want to stay in Platinum Heritage, then you'll have to live in Glenbrook."

"How do you know they have a place for me there?"

"I called them before I left to pick you up."

Alice sat brooding, sliding her tongue over her dentures and smacking her lips until a smear of chocolate on her elastic waist pants grabbed her attention. She spat on the corner of her button-down cardigan, using it to arduously rub the stain, her head bobbing up and down.

Jan studied her mother. "They're getting the apartment ready now." A darkened blob expanded across Alice's thigh. Jan raised her voice to overcome her mother's wheezing and puffing. "The one they showed us last time. Do you remember it?"

"Just my luck it's still available." Alice spoke into her chest and then looked up to glare in Jan's direction, her fingers gripping the moistened fabric she was using as a wash cloth. "What kind of place is this? How can you be sure they're not killing the residents so they can have a quick turnaround?"

Jan took her eyes off the road long enough to fully absorb Alice's disdainful expression, suspecting a truck load of evil thoughts brewing behind it. "I can't tell if you're being serious or not. Glenbrook is a high-class institution. It's completely safe; there's absolutely no killing going on there. Don't you go comparing it to Bates Motel!"

"Bates Motel-Schmates Motel; either way, it's still a death sentence."

They passed by Fort Lauderdale, heading toward Deerfield Beach.

"It's a wonderful place," Jan offered. "You've got to give yourself the chance to like it. Chicken soup is a staple on their lunch and dinner menus. You can have it with noodles, matzo balls, or both."

Exiting at the Glades Road ramp, Alice uttered a heartbroken "*Oy vey iz mir.*"

"You'll like it better here. You can go to shows, attend seminars, play Bingo. You'll even be around the corner from your friends in Century Village."

"I could do all those things from your house, too."

"No you couldn't," Jan yelled back as if she was castigating a naughty puppy after it had defecated on the floor. "You'd be by yourself most of the time. And what about seeing to all of your medications? They have an entire system in place at Glenbrook."

Alice glanced sideways at her daughter while clutching her chest. "Stop your hollering. You could give me a heart attack. I almost feel one coming on."

"Yeah, right. No matter what, I'm staying on course."

"System-schmystem," Alice griped, bringing her hand back to her lap. "You would do a better job giving me my medicine—that's when you're not hollering your head off."

"I wish that I could, but I can't. This is the best solution for both of us." Feeling a rumbling in her chest, Jan added, "Please hand me the TUMS from the glove compartment. You're making this entire process extremely difficult."

Having quickly located the tube of antacid tablets, Alice handed them to Jan. "See how nicely I listen to you? I wouldn't be in your way at all. In fact, I could even help you and Mike around the house."

"Doing what exactly? You can hardly walk or stand up straight. I'm not going to have you do any housework and you haven't cooked a decent meal in years."

"So, this is what it has come down to?" Alice moaned. "It wasn't supposed to be this way, Jan. You're letting me down."

Chapter Nine

"And what will you do if your husband doesn't want me in his house?" Alice would sporadically drill her youngest daughter as part of a game, play-acted during Jan's childhood.

Janice, as she was called then, would crane her neck to take in the wholeness of the person she worshipped, admiring the voluminous, golden curls cascading over her mother's shoulders, her perfectly pancaked and rouged cheeks, her lips freshly dabbed in the most popular, non-smear, seasonal shade, her hour-glass figure draped in up to the minute printed, silk dresses with cinched-in waists and sensuous folds . Silently, Janice wished time would speed up so she could be a grownup and look just as glamorous as her mother. *Perhaps, she will notice me more then*, she had hoped. *Maybe, she'll spend some time with me once my ugliness disappears.*

Accompanied by a broad, victorious grin, Janice's eager response would gush out of her mouth; no dam existed strong enough to stem back her excitement. "I'll hide you in the back yard and after my husband goes to sleep, I'll run and bring you to your own bedroom."

In a tone indistinguishable between teasing and serious, Alice would then ask, "And for how long will I be able to stay with you?"

Janice, standing on tippy toes and giddy with anticipation, would affirm, "You'll live with me forever and ever." At that moment, but never one second sooner, her mother would bestow her approving hug and kiss. Oh, how much that little girl desperately wanted those priceless hugs and kisses dispensed on other occasions as well.

"You promise?"

"I promise."

The day in April 2002, when Jan had deposited Alice at Glenbrook along with her selected furnishings and suitcases filled with clothes and linens, Alice reminded Jan of all the childhood promises she had made way back in the mid-fifties. Jan made believe she was too busy unpacking and hanging paintings to respond. "So, go sue me," she muttered under her breath.

Alice stepped into the bathroom to check out the support bars in the shower and the emergency pull switch. Pausing to wash her hands, she took a minute to inspect her reflection in the medicine cabinet mirror. "I never thought in a million years that I would end up with these many lines on my face," she sorrowfully remarked. "I also don't understand why I have to end up in a place like this."

Choosing to ignore these last comments, Jan asked, "Do you have a preference if I hang the framed watercolor over your bed or above your sofa?"

"I pretty much don't care where you hang it," Alice responded. "You can string it around your neck and plant yourself in the corner; it makes no difference to me. Or better yet, you can shove it up your backside." Alice then purposefully flushed the toilet. Her expression was so venomous that Jan could sense hundreds of invisible daggers flying straight to her heart.

At 2:15 p.m., Sondra, the daycare worker, strolled into Alice's apartment to welcome her new charge with a display of enthusiasm as huge as her oversized body. Sondra's offer to escort Alice to the lobby to introduce her to the other residents had been received coolly. A very reluctant Alice, appearing wounded and bleak, insisted such a trip was totally unnecessary and that her preference was to stay alone in her new residence without eating so much as a crumb. Sondra, however, insisted it was Glenbrook policy for new residents to be introduced to one and all immediately upon arrival.

"We'll all be taking the elevator down together," Sondra instructed. "And that way your daughter can go about doing her own business. I'm sure there be plenty of other things be waiting for her to do." The sinister look that abruptly appeared on Alice's face sent a chill down Jan's spine.

"Why does this giant, maroon troll have to speak to me like I'm a child?" Alice asked directly of Jan. "And who is *she* to send you away when I'm not ready to let go of you just yet? She should pay more attention to what she stuffs into her mouth. Do they hire only fatties around here?"

Jan was grateful not to hear her mother use the "N" word or its Yiddish counterpart.

"In case you hadn't noticed, I can hear yous loud and clear," Sondra addressed Alice. "I understand that yous be feeling a little put off being in a new place and such, so's I'll be making some allowances for them things yous be saying." Turning back to Jan, she said, "Your mama sure is spunky; doesn't hold back none on what she be thinking. That don't bother me. Lets me know right up front where I stand with her."

"There's just one of me, "Alice announced sanctimoniously. "I don't understand why you keep referring to me as 'yous.' Jan, is there even such a pronoun as 'yous'?"

Jan went about stacking packages of pantyhose and panties into neat columns to be stowed away and purposefully ignored her mother's question, but Sondra extended her arm to thwart Jan from proceeding any further. "Hon, I'll be happy to finish what yous be doing. Don't worry none; it will all be put away in due time. It's best if we get going now!"

Hurriedly, Jan approached the land phone she had acquired from the Deaf and Hard of Hearing Services program, with its enlarged buttons and amplification switch, to make sure the numbers of her home and cell phones had been entered correctly on buttons numbers 1 and 2 on the instant dial feature. A very audible "Ahem" coming out of Alice's mouth caused Jan to cease what she was doing and spin around in her mother's direction. The expression on Alice's face said *Leave now and I will kill you!*

As if on cue, Jan lowered her head, extracting two pink receipts from her wallet, and nervously announced, "Oh, I almost forgot to pick up Mike's shirts." She then took tentative baby steps toward the door. "I hope I can get to the cleaners before it closes. Mom, I've got to rush, so be nice and have a good time. Remember the deal we made. Be kind to Sondra and listen to what she says. I'll say goodbye for now."

Sondra gave Jan a nod of approval while Alice continued to sneer at her daughter.

"So this is what it has come down to," Alice moaned, rocking her head from side to side. She feigned falling into a chair. "I haven't lost all my marbles quite yet, so you can quit the cleaner's act. And by the way, you're not one to talk about any deals made."

With a heavy heart, Jan walked over to where her mother had collapsed. She saw her as a mass of withered autumn leaves all tied up in knots. Gone were her voluptuous, blond curls, her curvaceous proportions, her statuesque over-all loveliness of yesteryear. As she leaned over to kiss her mother's cheek, she was struck by how far down she had to lower her own face to hit her target, but Alice squirmed away, dodging her daughter's mouth completely, and Jan ended up kissing the air.

"Don't bother to kiss me," Alice snapped, sounding both furious and fearful. "You're washing your hands of me like I'm a dirty nuisance. I know you can't wait to get out of here."

"That's not true, Mom," Jan answered, trying to make her voice sound more confident than she was truly feeling. "There are things I have to do."

"Yes, go pick out my coffin. I'm ready for it." Alice braced herself into a steel wall, not even a hacksaw could cut. "Make sure it's made of solid mahogany. I refuse to be buried in a low-priced, pine box. It could open up and I'd fall right out, but what would *you* care?"

When Sondra approached Jan to silently tug on her sleeve, Jan whispered, "Yes, I know. It's time for me to go." She recollected all the times her mother had asked, "And for how long will I be able to stay with you?" *Were these words truly more reflective of a secret strategy and less a part of a silly game? How often had she planned to escape? When did she stop searching for ways to be free of Norman?*

Taking a moment to survey Alice's apartment once more before departing, Jan double-checked that the furniture had been placed just so and all of the accessories had been properly positioned. The carpet stains she previously reported to the maintenance crew had been spot cleaned to her satisfaction. The children's and grandchildren's photographs, exhibited in a variety of metal and plastic frames, had all been given equal billing with one family not having more exposure or table space than another. *When*

Maureen comes to visit, if she ever does, that will be one of the first things she'll notice.

She was pleased to see how well the newly purchased comforter and bed shams matched the fabric on the couch and chairs, all blending in hues of peach, teal, and beige. In actuality, the apartment was just one decently sized room, artfully divided into two equal sections for "living" and "sleeping." The "living" section contained a three-seater couch, a coffee table configured of three small white faux-stone hexagons, a side chair, a club chair, a television on its own stand—which she and Mike had spent over four and a half hours putting together even though the catalogue specifically had said "easy to assemble"—and a standing lamp. The "bedroom" section was furnished with a twin bed, two night tables, table lamps, and a dresser. Jan tried to convince herself that it was the best living accommodation for her mother given her age and physical limitations. *The larger unit came with a kitchen, and that would have been superfluous, but I hope this one doesn't turn out to be too small. She should get used to the space in no time. I just hope she doesn't trip over the nesting tables Maureen insisted on buying. Not only that; I hope she doesn't have a heart attack the minute I shut the door.* Jan then called out, "I'll speak to you later," while awkwardly and guiltily exiting her mother's apartment as fast as she could.

As Jan suspected, there was no one on the stairs to impede her descent. The generously wide staircase, girthed by an oak balustrade, was covered in a hunter's green, wool carpet, which complemented the ivy, flocked paper on the walls. It had given Jan an impression of "old world" charm and grandeur when she had first seen it, prompting her to nudge her mother's side with her elbow as she exclaimed, "Pretty fancy, huh?"

To which Alice had responded, "What good is that going to do me?"

Jan had added that she could picture debutantes making grand entrances down such a staircase, and Alice had argued that this was a place where people went down and out in gurneys.

"They're going to heaven or hell but not to some highfalutin ball! Besides, Jewish people don't know from such things."

She sprinted two steps at a time, and after passing by the silk palms positioned on either side of the administrator's office, she exited the lobby, bypassing the first level social room where many residents were gathered to be entertained by the men's choir from the Episcopalian Church. Jan ran directly to her car without so much as glancing back up at her mother's window, lest she catch sight of her trying to jump out of it. As she pulled her white SUV out of the parking lot and onto Seacrest Road, Jan prayed repetitively, "Please God, let my mother at least stay the night."

She's behaving as badly as a three–year-old! Jan complained while steering toward the shopping center where she had planned to pick up Mike's shirts and salad greens for that night's dinner. *Accusing me of faking having to go to the cleaners; how ridiculous! She's just as bad as Daniel was during his first week of nursery school. No, make that worse than him.*

Once she parked her car in the area designated "For drop offs only—8-minute maximum stay", Jan took a few moments to calm down and rebalance her own nettled emotional state. A woman driving a Ford sedan pulled up perpendicularly behind her spot and called out, "Are you leaving soon? You're not supposed to stay here that long!"

Before Jan could offer the woman an explanation, a balding man carrying a batch of shirts in each hand approached the Honda next to her, secured the hangers on a rear compartment hook, and drove off, accommodating the woman and her Ford without Jan having to move.

It's been twenty-nine years since Daniel started nursery school and those feelings of impotence and doubt continue to reemerge and haunt me, making me feel inadequate all over again. She thought about Daniel's uncontainable tantrums when he would first notice the yellow school bus turning onto their street, triggering tremendous grief and misgivings in Jan, who was just twenty-four years of age then, and prompting many of the curious neighbors to peek out of their windows with concern. What did such a young mother know about raising a child the proper way? The only thing Jan knew for sure was that she was *not* going to follow her parents' lead in the way they negligently and painfully raised her and her siblings.

Throughout those challenging mornings, Jan had nervously called the administrative office to check up on her son's wellbeing, but the reports were always the same: "He's perfectly adjusted, Mrs. Fisher; he's playing with the wooden blocks". "No need to worry at all; he's happy and enjoying his snack". "Daniel's sitting with the other kids listening to story time".

"Has he initiated any fights?" she would nervously ask his teacher. "Has he exhibited any bullying traits?" she wanted to know, but at the same time, she did not want to know.

"No, not Daniel. He's a sweet, well-behaved little boy. Not one of the problem children in the class at all."

Throughout her pregnancy with Daniel, Jan worried that Norman's antisocial, deviant behavior would be passed along to her future child. "What if I give birth to a monster?" she would cry to Mike. "Do you remember when I had to leave the cinema in a panic in the middle of watching *Rosemary's Baby*? What if that was some kind of premonition or psychic communication from the universe giving me a heads-up?"

Mike would pat her belly, massage her feet, rub her back, kiss her all over and say, "I want you to let go of all these harmful fears and just concentrate on how much I love you and how much we are going to love our healthy child."

Once Daniel was born, however, Jan had not been willing to risk having any more babies. "We dodged an awful bullet. I can't subject myself to that terrible fear ever again." It had taken some time and unrelenting coaxing on Jan's part, but several years into their marriage, Mike did finally relinquish his dream of raising two more children.

Now Jan was seated in her car, trying to reassure herself that things would work out well for Alice at Glenbrook as it had eventually worked out for her son. *Daniel's married now and has a child of his own. He turned out all right. Well, sort of. We've had our issues to deal with, and he's constantly mad at me, but that can't be just because I sent him to nursery school.*

She exited her car and walked towards the supermarket, crossing paths with the driver of the Ford, who was exiting the cleaners and holding a red printed dress under a clear plastic bag. As the woman unlocked her door, she gave Jan a dirty look and muttered, "You think you're above all the rules, lady?" But Jan stared at the awning in front of her as if the woman's message had been intended for someone else's ears. *Be as spiteful as you want. I'm used to playing this game.*

Chapter Ten

Alice was on the phone with Jan and up to her usual tricks, feeling pretty smug about it to boot. For the most part, she was accustomed to getting everything she wanted. So far that morning, her wheedling and wangling had hit a home run. *Battered a six,* as they might say in a more refined cricket match. Whatever she desired, needed, or just plain fancied was soon to be delivered —requisitioned and fulfilled —without her having to earn a single penny to pay for it. Each item on her current wish list could now be checked off with hardly any effort expended on her part and without her taking one meager step outside into the hot, humid Florida air.

Not one to go begging, Alice had developed her own refined method of acquisition This method —referred to in some circles as *method acting* —worked every time. She had perfected her role, cultivating it to an art, knowing exactly when to sob, when to raise her voice, and when to act as defenseless as a guinea pig in a testing lab. It was as if a conveyor belt, carrying a never-ending inventory of products, stopped at her front door.

Jan, as dependable as a sunrise, as predictable as a novel's obvious ending, and as obedient as a small pet wanting to please its master, was proving to be the same putty in her mother's hands as always. *Such a malleable dear*, Alice mused.

With nothing left for Alice to add, such as: "How are you feeling?", "Are you enjoying a nice day so far?" or "Have you taken on any interesting cases?", she threw a curt, dismissive goodbye to Jan and plunked down the receiver.

Smiling with satisfaction, Alice ran to sit by the windowsill, taking up only half of the seat cushion. She was wearing her navy knit pants with the elasticized waist and an ecru over blouse trimmed with blue embroidery. Alice was always put together well. Her closet was filled with outfits galore because she cared about the impression she made. No one would ever call Alice badly dressed or unfashionable. They might call her acerbic, rude, racist, and even cold-blooded, but that was something she didn't give a rat's arse about. People used to say she had a nice, eye-catching figure—had branded her a real-looker—but somehow during the last five years and to her immense displeasure, her body had shrunk, shedding its plumpness and size-sixteen, buxom curves. Alice would often wonder what ever happened to that youthful girl of the 1930s and '40s with the Hollywood starlet physique; her svelte stature; the "hey girl, you're hot" whistles when she passed by.

Stooped over and thin except for a bulbous belly, eighty-eight-year-old Alice now felt obliged to wear a girdle every day. If there were not so many *meddling Minnies* in the place where she currently had the misfortune to live, the ones who checked in on her during their 10 o'clock shifts, brought her medications to swallow, and saw that she was safely tucked in under her covers, unrestrained by girdles or bras, she would choose to wear one each night as well. For no other reason than because she liked to look more presentable than not. Corseted in spandex and peppered with anticipation, Alice continued to peer out the window as expectant as a child hearing the ding-a-ling of a neighborhood ice cream truck.

Despite Sondra's assurance that she still had plenty of time, Alice scrutinized the sparse parking lot below while tapping the windowpane with her pointed, cherry red nails. They made spasmodic clicking sounds that were neither harmonious nor tuneful. Looking up to the sky, she noted the weather seemed fine enough without any storm clouds lurking on the horizon and groaned, "She's got no excuse to be this late," which drew a rapid response from Sondra, who according to Alice spent both "way too much" and yet "never enough" time in her company.

"Jan isn't late at all. Yous just be overly anxious to have her here; that's all."

Gazing down the three flights of the building and between the queen palms and patches of grass, Alice zeroed in on the yellow outlined "Guest" spots and was dismayed to find them still empty. In the middle of the lot, she eyed several passengers—many with canes, walkers, and wheel chairs—being helped out of the transportation van. Muriel, wearing a gold and orange bomber jacket, stood out among the crowd, not escaping Alice's scrutiny.

"I guess Muriel went to the casino after all; so much for her bad luck and being short on money." A trickle of disdain coiled its way through her words. "Sondra, don't you think that with that hideous get-up, Muriel looks like a beefsteak tomato or someone who's still stuck in the 80s?"

Sondra clucked her tongue before answering in her thick Bahamian accent. "No. I do not think that at all Miss Alice, and I do prefer you not to be talking so spiteful, even though with your way of speaking it comes off a little less mean-like. I do love how you be saying the word 'tomahto' instead of 'tomayto,' like most Americans be saying, but that doesn't be making you sound any less catty."

Alice raised her chin. She pulled back her shoulders to align with her hips, mimicking a queen reviewing a procession of mounted guards. Not just any queen, though, —Queen Elizabeth of the British Empire—the monarch for whom she still maintained supreme loyalty and admiration. "How I say the word 'tomahto' is the correct way to speak. More people should choose to speak the way I do—and I'm not being catty. I'm merely stating the truth." She fanned out the fingers of her right hand across her clavicle for emphasis. The V shape of her neckline disappeared, but the middle nail where Alice had scraped off some of the polish drew Sondra's keen attention, causing her to swoop in like a red-tailed hawk about to grab its prey.

"Oh, why'd you go and ruin your manicure like that? Jan's going to think I'm not taking proper care of you. Let me fix that finger for you before she gets here; it'll give your mind something else to concentrate on."

Sondra, overloaded with excess pounds and laden with her own family burdens, waddled and huffed her way toward the medicine cabinet. She returned with acetone, cotton wool, and a bottle of Revlon's nail polish labeled "Divine Diablo." Alice stretched out the culprit nail onto Sondra's lap as soon as Sondra lowered herself onto the corner of the bed.

"You do know," Sondra said as she gently held Alice's finger in the palm of her hand, "people go speaking the way they was taught in the countries they come from."

Short gasps interrupted her smooth, rhythmic voice as she rubbed the cotton ball back and forth until it became saturated with the color drained from Alice's nail. She then tossed the dirtied cotton ball into the trashcan and picked up the small bottle of nail polish, twisting its elongated black cap to take hold of its brush.

Alice regarded Sondra's bowed head as she busily worked on repairing the damage Alice had created. Eyeing the tufts of hair jiggling around Sondra's multi-creased neck and the blonde pageboy sitting on top of her head, Alice asked. "How many of these wigs do you own?"

"I have a few," Sondra answered matter-of-factly.

"Are they all as old as this one?"

"I guess so. Why you be asking about that?" Sondra's focus remained fixed on her task.

"I was just wondering how often you wash them," Alice answered. "This one looks like it could use a really good de-greasing."

Sondra looked up and then back down, tensing and releasing the muscles of her cheeks. "I'll be sure to wash it when I gets me home," she stammered.

"Based upon your choice of words and speech patterns, I surmise that you're a mixture of West Indian and uneducated poor black from the south. It seems like both places have had equal impacts on you; I'm not so sure which one is worse. I obviously come from a far superior place, and in England we learned proper English." Alice's pomposity kept pricking at Sondra like a hungry mosquito targeting type-O blood.

"Uh huh. If you be saying so."

Sondra dabbed a stroke lengthwise across Alice's nail. She lifted the brush midair and halted her actions to study Alice's face. There wasn't any hint in Alice's expression to match the hatefulness of her speech.

"No matter what comes out of their mouths," the training administrator had coached Sondra on her first day at work in Glenbrook, "we do not take kindly to anyone mouthing off to the residents. I reiterate: no matter what is said and no matter how justified you may feel in doing so, be sure to keep it to yourself! Otherwise, plain and simple without any further ado, your employment here will be terminated."

After a heavy sigh, Sondra turned her face toward the window, leaving Alice in the dark as to the intensity of discomfort and chagrin her verbal jabs had inflicted.

"Yes'm, you just about got that right," Sondra murmured, half swallowing her words. She licked her lips and sighed deeply again before quickly dabbing two coats of polish on Alice's cleaned nail. "I'm done now. Don't you go messing it up. Just sit like a lady by the window and be waiting for Jan to arrive." Then Sondra clenched her mouth tight and forced a hum through her teeth.

Returning the items to the medicine cabinet, she caught her reflection in the mirror. Her eyes were stinging and enraged. She filled a cup of water from the bathroom sink and sipped it slowly. "I didn't say nothing about this twenty minutes ago 'cause I didn't want you to feel bad about it, but it sure is smelly in here. That Giorgio is giving me a headache bad enough to make me want to stick my head in a butcher's freezer. What did you do: douse yourself in it and then pour the rest of the bottle down the drain?" She scrunched up her nose and face and energetically shook both hands in front of her. "I should wash you down with a washcloth to get that stink out of you. Even people with no sense of smell could catch a whiff of it from miles away."

"You're not doing any such thing. It's a high-class cologne, and I like making my presence known," came Alice's indignant reply.

"Suit yourself, but you do smell nasty!" Sondra called back. "You be sure to let Jan know that it ain't none of my doing."

There was a stack of freshly laundered towels that needed to be placed in the vanity and a mess of clothing that lay on Alice's bed waiting to be sorted through. Sondra tossed the remaining water down the sink and proceeded to her tasks.

"I want you to leave those things just as they are," Alice ordered.

"Are you sure? I can do them in no time."

"I'm quite sure," Alice responded, pivoting around to look out onto the parking lot once more.

Down below, Alice spied curly haired and dimpled-faced Charlotte, Glenbrook's gregarious social director, leading the troupe of hunched backs and broken-down bones into the lobby where a late afternoon reception had been set up.

"Such a sorry lot of dried-up prunes," Alice remarked as she followed the line of returnees across the parking lot until it disappeared under the porte-cochere of the building's facade. "I know I'm up there in age, but I'm told all the time how much younger I look and act than everyone else around here."

"They're out there having fun and you're stuck in your room," Sondra said with one hand hooked into the cerise pocket at her hip. "Now who you be calling a dried-up prune? You should rinse your neck and hands, fix yourself up, and go join them for the social hour."

Alice had no intention of joining the others in their social get-together—even if the Dixie cups filled with wine were free; none of those people were her type. They were a consortium of hillbillies and barbarians. Very old ones. And who even knew if the wine, described crassly as either red or white, was a Chardonnay or a Merlot? Those people were chugging it away as if it were moonshine. Sitting squarely on a peach and white herringbone cushion, she crossed her legs to indicate she was hunkering down for the long haul. Involuntarily, the foot on her supporting leg began to tap. Her top leg bobbled up and down, exposing the rim of her knee-high.

"Alice, you uncross your legs right now," Sondra demanded, walking hastily toward her. "You knows better than to sit like that; ain't no good for the circulation. Why don't you let me help you get ready? Jan won't mind joining you downstairs instead of up here."

"These people are too decrepit for me; they're all invalids," Alice complained. "I knew from the minute Jan and I first stopped by to look this dump over that this wasn't the right place for me, and nothing's changed in the entire time that I've been here. She wouldn't let on then but from the look on Jan's face, I knew she had the same thoughts as I did when we first sat down with Charlotte and Mr. Dean, the administrator. All I could see were wheelchairs parked by the oak benches and doorways, and the sunken, stooped demeanors of the residents with their blank stares and drooling mouths. I might limp and hobble a little, but those people should have all been shot long ago to be put out of their misery, just like they do with failed racehorses. They do that at Ascot even. Pack them up and send them to a glue factory. They would be doing them all a favor."

Sondra grimaced. "Surely, Alice you be exaggerating."

"Glenbrook is the last outpost of God's waiting room," Alice announced sadly, "and I am not a happy camper being here."

"Listen, hon," Sondra said softly, retaking her seat on the edge of the bed. "God has a plan for everyone. It's not up to us to decide when a person be going. Those other people have plenty of life left in them, and you do too Alice, whether you want to be admitting it or not."

Turning away from Sondra, Alice refocused on the scene below her window and with disappointment commented, "Nope. She's not here yet."

Sondra patted Alice's back and advised, "Don't you worry none. Jan will be here real soon."

"Not soon enough," Alice muttered. "She's tardy; an undesirable trait that won't get you very far in this world."

"Won't you *please* reconsider joining the folks for the Meet and Greet?" Sondra pleaded. "The accordionist is back again. You like singing the old songs—I knows you do. I even heard you humming *Que Sera Sera* just a few moments ago; sounded just like Doris Day, you did."

"In that case, I'd say you need to get your hearing checked. My old man used to say that my singing was worse than chalk scraping on a chalkboard. As screechy as an owl marking its territory. No, I'd rather stay in my room and watch *Jerry Springer* with all the fighting and name-calling; his show is much more entertaining. I like the parts where those poor women still want their men back even though they've knocked up some other broads."

Alice motioned to Sondra to pass her the Limoges candy dish sitting on the dresser, now filled with toffee crunches and red licorice bits. She placed a few sweets in her lap and offered the dish back to Sondra, saying, "Help yourself, and put some in your pocket for later too." Sondra's "Thank you" and Alice's "You're welcome" were followed by the unwrapping of papers and loud chewing sounds.

"You do know that lots of them fights are false, don't you?" Sondra asked while munching with her mouth wide open. "Much of the yelling and carrying on is overblown for the camera. The television audience loves that stuff, gets them all sorts of stirred up and rowdy."

"Black people act that way all the time," Alice stated with the certitude of a PhD scholar in Sociology. "You of all people should know that, Sondra." She swished her jaw to dislodge a piece of the licorice stuck between her teeth and was just about to scrape her finger against her gum when Sondra, despite having become inured to many of Alice's tactless insults, wagged her own finger at Alice and warned, "I just painted that nail. Do not—and I repeat, *do not*—stick it in your mouth. And another thing: no Miss Alice, black people do not behave like that all the time—and they don't eat watermelon all the time neither!"

Alice, temporarily taken aback by Sondra's unanticipated umbrage, furrowed her brow. "Well, maybe not the colored people you know. I'm not talking about you specifically or the people where you come from, although I must say, with the black beads around your neck and the pink uniform you have on today, you do resemble a *zaftig* watermelon." Alice chuckled out loud. "I see what you eat, and it certainly isn't just watermelon."

Sondra spat her candy back into its wrapper causing Alice to hastily add, "Now, now, there's no need for you to become so ticked off."

"Miss Alice, why don't I just call you Miss 'All right and proper and everything be so ha-ha funny' today?" She sounded a tad less than outright impertinent. "You is such a fancy, knowledgeable lady, 'specially with that red blotch right smack in the front of your teeth. Why don't you tell me just how I'm supposed to react to what you just said?"

"Take it in a good way; I meant it as a compliment," Alice replied, grasping Sondra's hand and hoping to get back on her good side. She kissed each one of Sondra's knuckles, leaving an imprint of her lipstick, and then left smudges as she tried to erase the marks. "Sondra. I'm teasing you. I like to tease. You should know that already. You're such a big, easy target to kid, but I love you anyway."

Sondra's forced smile revealed two gold teeth in the upper row of her mouth. "Uh huh."

"I meant it in fun. Why not take it that way?"

"Uh huh."

Alice tilted her head to one side, raising her eyebrows. "Just lighthearted fun."

Sondra glared at Alice. "Well that being the case, I guess I'll *just* let this latest nonsense of yours *just* slip by." She handed Alice a toothpick from her pocket. "Here, *just* for fun, do something useful. Don't go poking out any fillings or your crowns, *just* the licorice."

After Alice finished clearing all the crevices between her flattened, decayed teeth, she proposed that Sondra feel free to go to the 'Meet and Greet' without her. The ligaments surrounding Sondra's jawbone immediately began to relax.

"Suit yourself then. I knows that Jan should be here any minute, so I'm going to treat myself to a nice full glass of wine; I believe I need it, and the Lord knows I've earned it. You could do with a little pepping up yourself."

"Make sure you don't get yourself too *shickered*," Alice advised.

Sondra placed her hands on each side of Alice's face and tenderly kissed her forehead. "My other lady was Jewish too, so I know what that means. *'Kerpunkle up,'* we'd be saying where I grew up, but don't you be worrying none; one glass will do me just fine. Be putting me in a joyful mood."

"I certainly hope so. I don't need you going all nuts from the alcohol."

Sondra sighed and took two deep breaths before replying in a back-down-to-business tone. "Do you have to go potty before I leave?"

"No, I do not. Jan will be here soon; she'll help me out if I do."

Chapter Eleven

Alice watched as Sondra navigated the short hallway of the studio apartment and exited through the extra wide entry door. Sondra's headband and dangling earrings were almost the same scarlet color as the shoes she wore. Her plump thighs brushed against each other and her backside wobbled from side to side. Alice suspected Sondra of stealing from the batch of chocolate chip cookies that Jan had recently baked for her, so Alice made a mental note of hiding the last remaining cookies behind the bedpost. *I can't let her get any fatter; she'll explode,* she thought. *As it is, she almost had to turn sideways to get out into the hallway.*

Alice was tired of having to protect all of her personal belongings. It was getting so burdensome that she was having trouble remembering every one of her hiding places. Her photographs could not be found in the dresser drawer beneath her bras. Her stash of Sweet'N Lows was not on any shelf in the medicine cabinet. Her bracelets were missing from her black pumps with the three-inch heels that she could no longer wear. *Everyone knew that the staff stole things in these places. What was one supposed to do?* She had pleaded with Jan on her last visit to take the prettiest and most expensive of Alice's nightgowns home for safekeeping, but Jan, in a surprising act of defiance, would not hear of it. "They're after them. I won't be left with any at all," she had cried to Jan.

"But if I take them home, you won't have them to wear anyway," Jan had said.

"At least they won't get them!" Alice had responded in a panic.

"Firstly, I don't know who you mean by 'them.' Secondly, if that happens then I'll buy you more nightgowns, so don't worry about it."

"Oh, they love the new things. They see them come right out of the boxes and shopping bags with the tags still on and *POOF*, they're taken away immediately! Audrey's Mother's Day present from her grandchildren was swiped right before her very own eyes."

"Audrey can't see a thing," Jan had been quick to argue. "She's legally blind in both eyes."

Alice had pointed and jabbed her finger at Jan while crying, "Just because I'm elderly, you dismiss everything I say as poppycock? Well, that's what happened! Are you calling me a liar now?"

Jan had stretched backwards to avoid being hit. "No, Mom. I do understand how you might be disconcerted about losing some things."

"Let God be my witness; thieves are taking them," Alice had continued. "You never had to live in a place like this. Did you? You and Mike are in a gated community with a guardhouse and roaming security cars. Do you go to sleep each night worrying about someone entering your house and having their way with you? Don't bother answering that because I know the answer is no."

Jan had shuddered, losing her footing. She reached out to pat her mother's shoulder. "Nothing like that will ever happen to you here."

"Well, what about them invading my privacy?" Alice had hounded. "I no longer have any privacy at all. You do. You have it all, but I have nothing. And while I'm at it, why don't you take that look off of your face?"

Jan had denied having any look on her face, but Alice repeated her accusation:

"Oh yes you do: the one that says you can't wait to get out of here. When my mother was a much older woman and suffering from rheumatoid arthritis, I would wait on her morning, noon, and night. Knelt on the floor to wash her feet and cut her toenails. I loved her so much. It was a privilege to do whatever I could to help her. Nothing would have been too much for me to do."

Now, Alice tried to recall the image of Jan approaching the dresser to gather her pocketbook and car keys and speculated about whether there were any other objects in her hand. As she chewed on the fleshy part of her finger, her eyeballs slowly shifted from left to right. She could remember Jan saying, "Well, one good thing about your being here is that you meet monthly with a chiropodist." Then, Jan had hastily headed toward the door. *Didn't she add something else just as she was leaving? Didn't she say: "I will bring your fanciest nightgowns to my house and keep them in a special place for you; just don't forget that you gave them to me, all right?"*

No matter how much she wracked her brain, Alice couldn't be a hundred percent certain that Jan had actually taken some of the nightgowns home. She remembered having the specific discussion but now believed she and Jan had resolved the issue by choosing a good hiding place together instead. *Where was that? Did we stuff them in the TV cabinet? How about in one of my pocketbooks?*

Chapter Twelve

As soon as she stepped into her garage that morning, Jan was enveloped by a suffocating blanket of stale air which did little to alleviate her already peeved state. Before moving any further, she opened the garage door and heard the clamor of chains creeping laboriously along their tracks. The noise, an uninvited intrusion on her eardrums, was nevertheless comforting in its rhythm and familiarity.

Little by little, chunks of sunlight trudged in from the outside. Toolboxes, paint cans, and accumulated clutter, haphazardly stacked and unlabeled, piled on the floor and rising along the walls, were caught in the light's encroachment; their tiredness and dust becoming illuminated, but not the objects themselves. It was as if everything had been painted drab. By the time the door had stopped moving, the atmosphere inside was just as stifling and clammy as it had been before.

As Jan neared her car, beads of sweat began to dot her forehead and upper lip, diluting the effect of her beige, age-defying makeup and forcing her to spin around and race into the laundry room to rip off a paper towel to dab her face. *Enough already with this unbearable heat and humidity. How much longer can it possibly last?*

For what seemed to be an eternity, the nightly weather reports for southeast Florida had consistently predicted oppressively high daytime temperatures and pelting afternoon rains with no letup in sight. Jan was enduring the discomfort as best she could but longed for the cooler days and balmier nights of winter, her patience drawing rather thin.

A harvest-gold wall clock—one of the first purchases she and Mike had made as newlyweds and which she had insisted on bringing from New York despite Mike's objections ("Everything is digital now. It's a clunky, obsolete eyesore!")— hung above a shelf of detergents and fabric softeners, catty corner to the electric dryer. After checking the time, Jan bemoaned how late she was running. *For sure there'll be hell to pay. No, I'm not going to rush over there. Screw her. I'll get there whenever I can.*

Jan reentered the garage teeming with resentment, but as she stepped off the Welcome mat, she landed on an oil spill that sent her reeling. Her arms and legs went flying in all different directions. As she struggled to regain her balance, she caught sight of a flailing, overturned palmetto bug close by on the concrete floor. *How come I didn't see that earlier?* It appeared to be on its very last legs. *Mike believes I got overdosed with compassion genes, but I don't feel sorry for that bug in the least!* Coming to a final standstill, Jan raised her right foot. Within seconds, the last breath of that struggling creature had been stamped out.

After sliding behind the driver's wheel of her car, Jan tossed her pocketbook onto the passenger seat but continued to shift and squirm. *Perhaps one or two of those pesky plastic tags from my new outfit are poking my skin?* She pulled and patted her straight skirt. *I wonder if she'll notice I'm wearing a brand-new blouse today—or will she have something nasty to say about it not being suitable for my complexion? 'It's a little too young for you, don't you think? They didn't have it in the next size up? Perhaps a fuller cut would have been more flattering?'* She tried varying the angle of her car seat and the tilt of her steering wheel, giving some consideration to the fact that she wore ballet flats instead of the two-inch heels she typically chose on workdays. She pressed down, up, down, up, a little more, a little less, but none of these adjustments ended up being compatible with each other.

Maybe it's the rearview mirror that's throwing me off. She tried moving the mirror ever so slightly, but images of the cabin light and rear passenger seats took turns rapidly reflecting back at her. *Great going; I'll never get rid of that blind spot again. Someone must have changed my settings. Oh, why does Mike have to mess with my things?*

Jan turned the ignition before buckling up, taking a few deep breaths to savor the cool air emanating from the dashboard. She undid the top button of her blouse and stuck her head even closer to the air conditioning vent as the symptoms of a hot flash made their presence known at the back of her neck.

A buzz arose from Jan's shoulder bag as her car reversed slowly out of the driveway. Trapped in her mental meandering, it took a while for her to acknowledge the ringing which stopped shortly and then she heard, "Are you there? Are you there?" Alice sounded just as discontented as ever. Jan picked up the call with a sullen "Hello."

"What's taking you so long?" Alice asked impatiently. "Exactly, where are you? You should have been here ages ago!"

There was a void of inflection in Jan's response, "I'm on my way." *Or suppose I first went to the beach for ten minutes?* She visualized with a longing in her gut, the three-mile drive to the wooden pavilion overlooking the shore, east of the Intracoastal.

"Well then, since you're heading this way—which you just said you are—you wouldn't mind picking me up some pocket tissues?"

"You have as many tissues as you'll ever need at Glenbrook," Jan stated, purposefully pacing her words so she didn't come off trying to jump down her mother's throat.

Alice shouted back angrily, "They don't have pocket-sized ones here!"

"What are you getting all hepped up about? You sound like someone just shot you in the foot!"

Alice emphasized, "My *preference* is for the *smaller* ones and *only* the *smaller* ones."

Jan pictured her mother digging in her heels, preparing to go to combat over an absolutely absurd requisition. Her grittiness was as annoying as ever. *For the umpteenth time this week, here I go into that miserable cloud of doom and gloom.* The ever-present yoke of responsibility made Jan's shoulders sag.

"But if it's too much trouble Jan, I don't want you should bother yourself on my account. I'll force myself to learn somehow how to live without them."

Oh Mother, I can so read you like a script. Here come the violins and another one of your tear-jerking soliloquys.

"I don't see why you can't…," Jan began, but then she happened to spot Gillian McVey wearing black yoga pants—the kind Jan had tried on in the department store and didn't buy because they had made her thighs look too fat— and a short cropped shirt—which Jan would never in a million years consider given her expanding waistline— sprinting out of her house and crossing the pavers in her front yard. *Any time of the day, she's one of those women who always looks good. Damn it!* Gillian's ponytail bobbed up and down as her trim, enviable body glided through the air. After reaching her mailbox, she stopped and waved, forcing Jan to likewise smile and return the gesture while Jan's mother continued to squawk over the phone, "Life is hard, I know, believe me. It's hard for everyone, but some have it worse than others. Suffering? You only know a fraction of the suffering I've had to endure. Your life is a breeze compared to what others have to go through—What *I* had to go through; well, it certainly has taken its toll. I'm weak. I'm alone. I'm totally dependent upon others—even for the bare necessities of life… the things most people consider insignificant but for me are essential. I don't want to put you out, but really now, what's the big deal about stopping along the way?"

"Hold on a minute," she told her mother, placing the phone in a square cutout in the center console. Lowering the driver's window, she called out to Gillian, "Mike mentioned he saw you in the gym the other night. He said talking with you helped him do twice the workout."

"It worked wonders for me, too," Gillian responded as she sorted through a stack of envelopes and magazines. "Your husband is sooo obliging. I'm going to borrow him to do some chores in my house—which he said he wouldn't mind doing at all."

"Hmm. Well, good luck with that," Jan replied, feeling an ever-so-slight unease.

"Do you know if it's supposed to rain later today?" Gillian asked, looking inquisitively up at the sky while flexing and pointing her sneakers one at a time.

Jan stared at Gillian, thinking *what an idiot,* but then decided to cut her a little slack given that Gillian had moved down from Philadelphia with her eight-year-old son just a few weeks ago. "Today's no different than any other day so far. You can pretty much expect a downfall every afternoon."

Gillian scrunched her face, scaling down the usual cheeriness it reflected. "I try not to listen to the weather reports. Most of them are pretty scary."

"Well yes, ever since Hurricane Andrew, the meteorologists don't want us to be caught off guard so they tend to turn every storm into a major event."

A shadow of concern passed over Gillian's face. "Were you here for that? It must have been simply awful."

"Yep, we were," Jan said ruefully. "Although we were lucky to get away with just broken trees and some badly banged-up outdoor furniture. That was 1992," she informed Gillian, "but over the last eleven years, there hasn't been anything nearly as horrible."

Gillian stretched from side to side, bouncing from her waist a few times. "Mike said he would help me get my windows covered if we ever got hit with a hurricane."

"Of course," Jan commented. "That's what neighbors are for. We all pull together in times of emergency."

"I seem to have an abundance of emergencies arising in every corner of my house right now. Mike said we should tackle them one by one."

There was that unease hitting Jan again. *What's with the "we" part?*

"Well, wherever you're going today, you be sure to have some fun," Gillian called out as she marched herself back home.

"You too, hon. I hope Mike gets to your chores a lot sooner than he gets to ours."

As Jan drove away, she was overcome with an unidentifiable angst, which triggered the memory of a run-in with her son to emerge. It tied in with the reference to

Hurricane Andrew and how contentious Daniel's behavior had been immediately thereafter.

Having saved much of his allowance and wages from his part-time job, the teenage Daniel had purchased a ticket for the Lollapalooza band fest in Orlando that week, but Jan had adamantly refused to allow him to go.

"You suck! All my friends went and they said it was unbelievably fantastic. I wish you weren't my mother! I wish you were dead!" he had yelled. "You're worse than Godzilla. You're a pain in my ass. All you ever do is make my life freakin' miserable!"

"Let's keep things in perspective," had been Jan's response. "Billions of dollars in losses, over a hundred thousand homes destroyed, and countless human fatalities—that's what I and the rest of the world consider true devastation. You have absolutely no right to complain about not going whatsoever!"

For the following months, Daniel had sought revenge by acting up at home and school, keeping Jan forever on edge.

"What's that?" Alice questioned. "Did you hang up on me? Is a hurricane coming? If so, you'd better come and get me. I'm not relying on the jerks here to know what to do."

Jan exhaled.

"Speak up, I can't hear you!" Alice yelled. "You need a better cell phone service, the kind where that nice young man roams all over the country and keeps asking if they can hear him."

Jan retrieved her phone. "My current phone service is plenty good enough."

"What about that hurricane then?" Alice grumbled. "I'm a sitting duck over here, waiting to be clobbered."

"No, there is no current forecast for a hurricane; not on any television station or in any newspaper."

Despite Jan's reassurance, Alice's concerns regarding the weather would not dissipate; neither would the kernel of unsettledness growing in Jan's stomach regarding Mike's promises to Gillian.

"Did they mention a hurricane on *ABC*?" Alice continued. "They didn't mention anything about one on *CBS* or *NBC*. I don't know where in this friggin' *fercockta* place they store the water bottles. If you don't come and get me Jan, I'll be stranded high and dry!"

"As I've already told you," Jan said, trying her utmost to remain composed, "there isn't going to be a hurricane any time soon."

"Your voice is coming in and out," Alice complained. "You need to have Mike look into this. Men know about electronics better than women."

"There's no need for that," Jan managed to squeeze in before her mother returned to her "woe is me" recitation.

"If only I could still drive," Alice began, "I would never think to ask you this, but you've already taken away my car together with my independence and…"

Placing her phone back into the center console, Jan half-listened as Alice continued to rant dejectedly.

"…It's my unhappy lot in life that I now have to rely upon others for everything, even for such a silly little thing like pocket tissues. I hope you should never know from such *tsoris*. Forget about it; I'll use my sleeve if I have to wipe my nose. So what if it gets a little red and full of pus? They say that's how disease spreads, but don't worry about that. Please don't make the extra stop. You should have been here already as it is. I've survived this long without them.

I'll learn to make do. I'm hanging up. Goodbye for now; I'll see you soon."

Her mother had not sounded any angrier or more disappointed than usual. *One more masterful performance by the supreme, whining martyr. She's as cunning as ever. Mike and I should move back up north, leaving her alone to her own devices. Who am I kidding? That's never going to happen!*

She edged her car onto the other side of the street, maintaining a steady thirty-five miles per hour even after entering the public thoroughfares. If she could magically transform her Acura into Fred Flintstone's foot mobile, the snail's pace ride would still transport Jan way too soon for her liking. Her phone rang again and she chose to let the call go to voicemail.

"In case you do decide after all to stop off for the tissues—you really don't have to, but in case you do—pick me up some Lifesavers, magazines—preferably *People* and *Us*—and, oh yes, I fancy some Cadbury's dark chocolate with raisins: the jumbo bar. And also mascara; I need mascara. I want the Lancôme, in black. Don't get me Maybelline. And some hand lotion; the kind that comes in a tube. The brand they use here is a very cheap one. You got that?"

Her mother called yet again, and Jan let that call also go to voicemail.

"I don't think the tail end of my message got recorded. I want you to get me moisturizer for my hands—a good brand, but not in a bottle though." Next came several beeps. "What the heck? Am I being cut off? I'm not finished yet. I'm not finished! This is making me so *meshugah*!"

Chapter Thirteen

As a distraction while she headed north past the royal palms and ficus hedges, Jan wondered how long it had been since she had spoken with Daniel, who after graduating law school had become in-house counsel to a successful high-tech firm. He was now living thousands of miles away, perhaps intentionally, but had lately seemed a little less combative toward her in their phone conversations. Jan attributed this détente to the arrival of her new grandson, Asher, which was enabling Daniel to see the world with a much broader perspective as a new father.

Her thoughts then turned to Mike, whom she imagined sitting soberly, analyzing bond rates or fretting over the market. This vision contrasted distinctly with the vision of her husband reaching for the orange juice container in the refrigerator earlier that morning. He had been leaning over so casually and wearing his blue tattersall shirt with its open collar, that it had made her heart skip a beat the same way it had when they first met. She had moved forward to hug him, but he had released her arms saying, "Don't have time. I have an early meeting with a client."

Jan called his office and greeted him with, "Hi. How's your day going so far?" Her initial upbeat tone sank to a lackluster one after she reported, "I'm on my way to Glenbrook."

"I'm pretty busy," Mike answered. The timbre of his voice was no-nonsense and business-like. "I can tell you're dreading going there again. So why not skip this one visit?"

"Wish I could, but I can't. I have to stop by the supermarket, in any case, to pick her up some things."

"Of course, you do."

There was no mistaking Mike's sarcasm, but as usual, Jan chose to ignore it. "Have you heard from Daniel recently?"

"In our last conversation—which was yesterday afternoon—we talked mostly about sports, Sunday night football, and that kind of stuff." Sounding anxious to return to what he was doing, Mike added, "I'll be sure to fill you in later."

"What about our gorgeous grandson? Is Asher okay? What is he up to now? Perhaps I'll call there this evening." Without waiting to hear a single response, Jan hastened to say, "And oh, by the way, your car is leaking oil and I want you not to meddle with the settings on my car ever again."

Mike raised his voice but not so much as if he had been at home instead of in his office. "I haven't touched the settings on your car, so don't go complaining to me about that. You're probably in a lousy mood, but it's not my doing. Have you anything else to tell me? Because I'm busy."

As she continued to speak, Jan persisted in driving behind a yellow school bus which slowed down considerably at each intersection, causing most of the cars behind her to pick up speed and switch lanes.

"I was just wondering if there was anything new with Asher," she said timidly.

"He turned over by himself in the crib," Mike offered, causing Jan's entire disposition to lighten, but just as she passed by the high school, her attention was suddenly diverted. A group of students mad-dashed their way across the street against the light, which triggered Jan to swerve her RDX into another lane to avoid collision. Looking in her rearview mirror, she could see them laughing and mocking her.

"Stupid idiots!" she called out. "Why don't you watch where you're going? They think they can live forever, those kids!"

"What just happened?" Mike asked with concern.

Jan shouted back, "They should be required to visit a morgue or sit in a few sessions of Probate Court to get a better grasp on reality." Adrenaline was rushing full speed through her blood vessels.

"Who should?" Mike demanded, his irritation rising.

Jan answered with a quivering voice "The kids I almost just hit,".

"Listen, I'm going to hang up now so you can concentrate on the road and not hit anyone else," Mike said sternly. "Unless, of course, it's your mother—that would be a completely different story."

"Ha ha, very funny," Jan shot back. "If those kids got hit, it would have been their own fault. Honestly, don't they give a damn about anyone else?" A painful thumping in her chest forced Jan to pause. She immediately regretted how frantic and senseless she must have seemed to Mike.

"I hear you," Mike said, but he sounded detached and less comforting than Jan wanted.

"I should turn around right now and spend the rest of the day staring at the waves and clearing away all this bad energy."

"Whatever," Mike uttered. "I've got to get back to work. The Dow is down four hundred, and investors are going crazy."

Jan disconnected the call after issuing a quick "Goodbye" and "I love you."

Besides her anxiety over the near-accident, it irked Jan that she had almost no time left to brace herself for the nettling unpleasantries she was about to encounter. Her mother was keenly awaiting Jan's presence at Glenbrook; a resident there for over a year and still yet to make the desired, smooth transition to her living quarters. Jan could hear her complaints echoing in her head and wondered what else would be thrown into her mother's customary diatribe. *'Nothing's any good here...the food is atrocious...everyone is dying...your shirt is creased. Do you even own an iron? Couldn't you take the time to put on a little makeup? Why didn't you buy the bigger tube of moisturizer? It costs more, but it's worth it.'*

The bus she had been trailing veered into the middle school parking lot, but Jan still chose to slow down at each corner, reining in her usual habit of zooming past the yellow lights before they turned red. She passed by arcing fronds, gabled roofs, and shopping plazas, cruising at no more than thirty miles per hour. At the junction of Jog and Seacrest, the traffic light had just turned green. Although Jan heard the horns of the impatient drivers stalled behind her, she did not jump on the gas pedal but took her right hand off of the steering wheel and pressed the FM button of the radio hoping to hear something joyful. Instead, she heard a discussion of the soaring costs of medical benefits for the poor and aging population. *That's the last thing I need to listen to now.* The phone rang again and Jan answered yet another incoming call from her mother. "No, I have not forgotten about you," she told her, wishing it really wasn't the case at all. "Yes, I'll be there soon." She stabbed the radio tuner hoping to find something more soothing for her nerves. *I'm fifty-three years old and I still have to cower to her demands like a blubbering infant!*

Without a warning, a loud, deafening *BOOM,* walloped Jan's ears. Her head jolted toward the steering wheel and a forceful tug fastened her chest to the back of her seat. Her airbag did not inflate, but the safety harness had succeeded in keeping the rest of her body secure and free from injury. Confounded and dazed, she tried to make sense of what had just happened. Gradually, she came to accept that an accident had occurred, and somehow, she was in the middle of it, guessing that a car had slammed into the rear of her Acura, propelling it forward. Jan pulled over by the curb, feeling a little shaken. She was glad that her car was still drivable. The car that hit her followed, with the other driver, a woman wearing a fancy pantsuit, screaming and ranting. "Green light means *go, lady*!" Both women set about surveying their cars for damages. As Jan checked her SUV, she hoped her legs wouldn't give way. The bumpers, doors, mirrors, and paint appeared to be in good order. Neither car had so much as a scratch or dent.

"You're lucky this time," the other driver shouted. "I had to be somewhere ten minutes ago, so I'm in a rush. I don't even think we need to exchange information. You're getting off easy, lady."

Jan thanked the woman and watched her speed away. Walking toward the driver's side of her car, Jan sensed a nervousness in her stomach and continued weakness in her legs. She was glad to sit down again behind the steering wheel and buckle up, although driving a car was typically one of her least favorite things to do. Checking multiple times in her side mirror for clearance, she slowly edged away from the curb. *No way am I ever going to mention this mishap to Mike or anyone else.* "All right; All right, I'm coming," Jan screamed to the ringing phone, as she reentered the stream of traffic.

Chapter Fourteen

Alice rose from her armchair, double-checked that neither Sondra nor any of the aides were anywhere in sight, and headed toward the brass floor lamp with its huge, pearlescent glass shade. She braced herself against the television stand and reached up on her tippy-toes to peek inside the bowl, pushing aside Bingo markers, hair rollers, chocolate kisses, a collection of safety-pins, and a coin purse.

While Alice was busily searching for her private cache of pain relievers, Sondra scurried to get to the 'Meet and Greet" before the beverages and tidbits were cleared away. Halfway down the hallway, she came face to face with Jan. "How is she today?" Jan asked.

"Oh, she's just fine. She's always just fine," Sondra reported as she continued on her path.

Jan wrinkled her brow. "She sounded awful over the phone."

Sondra called out over her shoulder, "Alice lays it on thick just for you, trying to make it look like she be dying any minute, but she's never as bad as she tries to make it seem." An elevator door opened, and Sondra quickened her pace. "I'd stay and talk some more, but I'm in a mighty rush. Rest assured Jan, before you show up, she be doing just fine. Why, that old lady sure can act!"

Jan began to cough loudly as she entered Alice's apartment. She found her mother smiling contentedly with her hands clasped behind her back, but then her expression quickly transposed into one of suffering, with lowered eyebrows and her thinned lips pulled to the corners.

"Don't tell me you're sick again," Alice whined, teetering toward her high-back chair. "Aaaaaaaaaaaaaah," she moaned.

"No, Mom, I'm not sick at all. I just didn't want to scare you when I came in. You seemed to be very engrossed in what you were doing. Where shall I put the items I bought?"

"What items are you talking about?" Alice asked, her eyes adopting the vacant gaze of an amnesiac.

"The things you asked for," Jan answered gruffly. *Don't try pulling the memory lapse game on me, you hustler.*

Alice blinked a couple of times. Jan presumed a make-believe light bulb had just turned on in her mother's skull. "I didn't ask for them," Alice disclosed. "I merely insinuated that I needed them."

Jan scowled at Alice, harrumphed to herself, and then walked briskly to the bathroom. "It reeks in here! Did you drop one of your colognes or did you spritz the entire bottle on yourself?"

Alice leaned forward in her chair, a poster child for the ingenuous and demure. "What's all the fuss about? I'm not wearing any cologne, and no, I didn't spill any either. That so-and-so Sondra must have carelessly done so as she was tidying up. Good luck getting her to admit it or pay for the damage though."

"It's enough to give me a good headache," Jan complained and flipped on the switch to the overhead fan. Above the whirring sound, she could still hear Alice grouse, "I don't see the magazines. Didn't you make a list? I specifically wanted those magazines. How could you forget to buy my magazines?"

"Sondra will put the tissues, lotion, and mascara in the medicine cabinet and your Lifesavers and chocolate in your side table for you." She called out extra loud for her mother to hear. "I've got the magazines here in this bag."

"Well, I'd better find the Lifesavers when I want them," Alice mumbled. "She has a sweet tooth, that one. All morning long I've been searching for my good nightgowns. That's why I have all this stuff strewn across the floor and bed. I'm actually having difficulty breathing now."

"It's probably due to the mustiness of the air," Jan advised.

"No, it's because I've made myself ragged looking for my good nightgowns." Alice wiped her brow with her hand and uttered, "Ach, ach." Then her voice took on a feebler tone. "I guess I could try cleaning everything up, but I'm afraid I might pass out. So, I suppose you'll have to do it for me. You know where all these things are supposed to go."

Jan's head was pounding and she was beginning to feel queasy. She sat on the toilet seat and let out a few relieving belches. "It would make more sense for you to put your things away; that way, the next time you want them, you'll know exactly where to look."

Jan waited for her mother to change her mind.

"I'm much too weak and dizzy," came Alice's response as if she had just finished crossing the Sahara on foot. It was an Oscar-worthy delivery. "I'm afraid the bending up and down will make me faint. My God, I can hardly lift myself out of this chair." Her words, accompanied by a series of pants, ceased upon seeing Jan drag herself out of the bathroom to gather up the limited bits and pieces of Alice's domain.

Alice stretched out her legs and leaned back in her chair. "Jan, it's so amazing how the years have flown."

Jan offered an "Uh huh," as she crawled on the floor to pick up $2.89 in change and then stood to place it in her mother's purse.

"I see you've got those ugly brown marks growing on the back of your hands. Isn't there some treatment you can take for that?"

Jan turned to fold her mother's lingerie, allowing this comment to evaporate, unaddressed, into the air.

"You used to be a skinny little thing, and now look at you, in your fifties, with a good ten to fifteen pounds you could certainly do away with."

"Thank you for bringing that to light."

"And now having your hair colored to get rid of the mousy gray when you used to be a natural blonde as a child."

"Yes, I certainly do that. Anything else you'd like to point out now that you're on a roll?"

"Personally, I thought you would have grown to be a little taller than you are, but I suppose being the same height as me is all right."

"Mother," Jan shrieked, "you have shrunk considerably. I am at least four, if not five inches taller than you now."

"Let's not be testy," Alice responded, stiffening her back. She delicately tapped on the recently polished nail and clasped her hands in her lap after discovering the nail was sufficiently dry. "Do be sure to arrange everything in neat piles on my chenille comforter before storing each item in its appropriate place. It comes as no surprise to me, Jan, that someone has stolen my nicest nighties." Raising her voice sternly, she added, "I warned you about what goes on in this place. These women from foreign islands can't be trusted. They talk to you nicely and all the while plan to take everything you have behind your back." Alice lowered her chin. She sunk her forehead into the palm of her hand. "I can barely hold my head up today. Look what being here has forced me to deal with. A few more months of living like this, and…" A whimper escaped her lips. "And, well, er, the end shouldn't be that far away."

Yet another brilliant acting job from the sacrificial lamb. Before releasing a rumbling burp, Jan managed to say, "But Mom, *you're* from a foreign island!"

"Don't be so cheeky," Alice admonished, sounding a great deal perkier than before. "How can you compare England to the West Indies, or East Indies, or wherever the hell these people come from? And since when did you lose your manners?"

"Hmm. I understand how upsetting losing your nightgowns can be," Jan replied. She lifted a stack of the clothes and walked toward Alice's dresser. "Now take notice Mom, of where I'm placing these things. I'll take a good look in my house tomorrow, just in case the nightgowns happen to be there."

"And?"

"And excuse me," Jan added, before releasing one more burp. "By the way, remind me to buy you a new bottle of cologne—one that doesn't have such a heavy scent."

"Yes, that would be nice, but don't bother looking in Walgreens or CVS for it. Muriel told me that they have a nicer selection of the better brands in Bloomingdale's and Saks. They have the kind with the matching pocket atomizers, which I can definitely use. Don't let them fool you into buying toilet water. It's the cologne that I wear, or better yet, the parfum will do just as well."

Yes, of course! Shall I pick you up a Givenchy gown while I'm at it?

Jan had promised herself that the visit with her mother would be limited to one hour. Each time she attempted to leave, however, Alice would find another excuse to detain her. Official-looking, business envelopes, most with glassine windows and crammed in a drawer with used tissues, needed to be opened and read; Medicare was disputing a claim, but Alice couldn't make heads or tails of the matter; and somehow, appointments had erroneously been scheduled for the same morning with two different doctors. Obviously, whoever was entering the information at one of the doctors' offices was a scatterbrain and should be fired, according to Alice. It was up to Jan to make the correction.

"Don't go yet, Jan," Alice said with urgency. "I want to show you a snapshot."

Jan, lifting her pocketbook in preparation for her departure, responded straightaway. "I've seen it already."

Alice trod delicately around her trapping device. "You don't even know which one I'm referring to. Even if you saw it already, I want you to see it again. It's the one of me with my brothers when we were young and lined up in size order; probably my most valuable possession. I can't find it anywhere."

Jan scrutinized the collage haphazardly scotch-taped to the mirror overhanging the dresser. There were photographs of graduates, babies, brides and grooms, and class groupings but not the one that Alice had wanted.

"I remember it like it was yesterday," Alice said wistfully as she flipped through a stack of photos, odd-sized, lusterless, slate-gray, black and white. "The six of us were all dressed alike, even Morris who was the oldest; my

100

mother was so proud of us. Now I'm the only one that's left alive, if you can call it that." Alice's tone grew somber and a lonely tear drop rolled down her cheek.

"I've lost every one of my five brothers and their wives too," she whispered softly, her voice choking under the weight of emotion. After blinking twice, she grabbed a scrunched-up tissue from her pocket and dabbed at her moistened eyes. "It's very lonely, Jan, to still be around while all those from my generation, all the entertainers and famous politicians, have long since departed."

Alice returned the wet tissue to her pocket and limped towards the chair by the window. After seating herself, she looked out beyond the parking lot and grassy areas below at scenes Jan presumed to exist only in the dusty reservoirs of her mother's mind. "I would have had so much more time to spend with my brothers if your father hadn't forced us to leave England when he did." Her pining for what could have been overflowed with animosity and resentment. "They thought the world of me; we had so much love for each other, and it ripped my heart in two having to say goodbye to them the night before we sailed, but your father was consumed with jealousy. It ate him up." Alice sighed, clucked her tongue, and turned to face her daughter. "Jan, do be a dear and help me out. You just have to go through my photographs to find the one I want. It shouldn't take too long, and then you definitely will be able to leave."

The forlorn look in Alice's face made Jan feel guilty. She had been in Alice's apartment for hours already, and because she had hurried from her own house without stopping to eat lunch beforehand, she was now hearing urgent, grumbling sounds emanating from her stomach. *I hope she doesn't hear my hunger pangs. If she does, she'll force me to stay for dinner. Of course, I can't leave until the stupid photograph is found. What kind of insensitive human being would I be?*

Jan removed her shoes to stand on a small table in front of her mother's closet, pushing aside pocketbooks, purses, cereal boxes, a half-filled bag of cheese doodles, and department store shopping bags. She explored the contents of each item before returning it to its previous spot on the shelf. In the box of Special K, Jan discovered packets of instant decaf coffee and Heinz tomato ketchup sitting atop the rice flakes. *I understand how much she appreciates my visits, but just how much manipulation can I tolerate? She's the one living in Glenbrook, not me. Am I not entitled to have a life as well?*

Jan proceeded to sort through all of the drawers of the side tables and the dresser, gathering up dozens of used tissues, tea bags, white-coated, moldy chocolate chips, and wrinkled Jolly Rancher wrappers. She discarded this litter along with the empty Burger King bags and French fry containers she found crumpled in the bottom corner of her mother's closet. All the while, Alice was glued to her TV set watching angry guests shouting, scuffling, and hurling licentious accusations at each other. By the time a separate plastic bag filled with Alice's mementos and additional snapshots had been located under the bathroom vanity, there was a steady stream of residents lining up outside in the hallway waiting for the elevator to bring them down to the main floor. Dinner was about to be served in the dining room, and it was highly unusual for any resident not to be seated at least ten minutes before the first course was placed on the table.

Alice turned away from the TV as a commercial for Depends was being broadcast and invited Jan in a sugary-sweet voice, "Please be my guest for dinner tonight; it gets so lonely here sometimes. Mike won't mind in the least bit if you choose to stay."

Jan was quick to shoot off, "I hadn't planned on it, and I don't know what time Mike will be getting home."

"Why don't you call him?" Alice nudged. "He can join us too, if he likes."

Jan reluctantly hit the redial button on her phone to call Mike.

"Once more, you've decided to play the sap," he complained after begging off the invitation. "Will you be able to come home after dessert or will you have to stay for Bingo as well?"

Jan told him, "No, I'll be home right after dinner." She repeated, "I'll be home right after dinner," a second time for her mother's benefit. "By the way, there's stuff in the fridge you can reheat."

Not one to enjoy eating leftovers, Mike informed his wife, "Maybe I'll eat out with a friend."

Jan wanted to ask Mike which friend, but she held back on the question. After ending the call, she felt like she was being pulled apart in two opposite directions. Paying no heed to her own uneasiness, she turned toward her mother and said, "Okay, let's do this!"

Chapter Fifteen

To Jan, Alice's pit stop in the bathroom to primp herself for the general public seemed to take forever. Fresh lipstick was applied to her lips, a little mascara stroked on her eyelashes, and her hair was pushed and poked until it more closely resembled the compact oval form it had acquired at the beauty parlor at the start of the week. On her most recent visit, the hairstylist had washed a purple rinse through Alice's hair and Alice was now trying her best to cover the dyed streaks with her natural platinum strands.

Jan heard the door slam shut and asked her mother if she needed assistance, but Alice was busily removing the white talcum powder applied to her cheeks in anticipation of Jan's visit, replacing it with blush to give her face a rosier complexion.

When Jan pushed the three-wheeled Rollator toward the bathroom, Alice refused to use it; she insisted instead on leaning on Jan for strength and support, but Jan persisted in bringing it along and dragged it gracelessly with her left hand all along the hallway. In the elevator, Alice conversed with a woman with a burgundy rose in her hair, who boarded the cab with her private aide at the interim stop.

"Natalie, you must be going on a hot date tonight; you look like a million dollars," Alice said with a giggle.

In between her shaking bouts, Natalie managed to spurt, "Alice, I'm going to the same ritzy place as you. Didn't you get the black-tie invitation?"

"As a matter of fact, I did," Alice said in her thickest English accent. "But don't think that you're the only one who can bring a date. Jan, say hello to Natalie and Rosalita."

There was a chorus of "How do you do?" and "Nice to meet you," although Jan was quite sure she had been introduced to Natalie and her aide many times before. Rosalita gave Jan a knowing nod and then proceeded to guide Natalie out of the elevator when it reached the ground floor. Alice said to Jan, "She wears a different color flower in her hair every day. I think her husband might have been a florist, and that way she still keeps him close. I tell you; we have a bunch of loonies living here." Alice stepped out of the elevator and Jan and the cumbersome Rollator followed.

The stylishness of the dining room's décor never failed to favorably impress Jan. When Mr. Dean had originally led her and Alice on their introductory tour, she presumed the design to be a replica of a salon from a grand, country French estate, but besides its European elegance, Glenbrook's dining room, to its credit, still managed to evince an atmosphere of coziness and comfort. Glass paned doors, framed in gloss white paint, lined the wall leading out to a terrace; the other walls were covered in subtle gold flock wallpaper, and the dining chairs were upholstered in shades of lemon and powder blue. At one end stood an impressive extra wide cherry wood breakfront, displaying pewter mugs, blue and white ceramic ginger jars, platters, and teapots. It was next to this breakfront that all the canes, walkers, and wheelchairs had been deposited.

As Alice and Jan wound their way around the cloth covered tables, Jan had to keep disengaging Alice's Rollator from being caught up in the tables' legs, and every one of the diners and staff were made aware of the "younger" woman accompanying Alice to her designated seat. Jan rushed to park Alice's Rollator with the other mobility aids and returned hastily to her mother's side.

"This is my daughter; the one that lives in Boca," Alice bragged with a beaming smile and better than usual posture to each set of attentive ears. "She's joining me for dinner tonight, so you all better be on your best behavior."

"Oh, Alice, you're such a doll and so lucky to have such a beautiful daughter," was the typical comment.

"Love you, babe," Jan's mother replied. "But you should see her sister: a real stunner!"

Strangers stopped Jan to shake her hand or touch her arm. "Your mother's quite the lady. She really is something," they shared. "Oh, you look so much alike." Each time, Alice would be sure to correct them. "Not really, I resemble my older daughter more."

After sliding Alice into her chair, Jan was ordered by her mother to walk over to give Muriel at the neighboring table a personalized greeting. "She'll think I told you to ignore her if you don't."

Jan returned to her mother's side with crimson splotches on each of her cheeks.

"What did she say to you? What did she say?" her mother pressed impatiently.

"She gave me two kisses—one for you and one for me—and said that you were a doll."

Alice raised her right hand, waving it slowly, barely twisting her arm or wrist. Jan envisioned her sitting in a royal coach or standing on the balcony at Buckingham Palace. After blowing a kiss in Muriel's direction, Alice whispered to Jan from the side of her mouth, "Such a bitch she is. Nobody likes her."

Alice dipped her spoon into her soup bowl and took a sip of chicken broth before motioning Mimi, an employee of Glenbrook, to her side. "How's your little girl doing today?"

"She's doing just fine, thank you."

"Glad to hear." Alice set her spoon down on the tablecloth and pointed to her bowl. "Please heat this up until it boils. I prefer my food to be piping hot, which is exactly how I like my men." Although Jan had heard this comment repeated so many times before, it still made her cringe. She felt the skin hairs bristle on the back of her neck.

Clearly amused by Alice's humor and winking eyes, Mimi responded, "Alice, you is such a riot!"

Alice had been married for forty-nine years to Norman and had hated every minute of it. When her husband passed away at the age of seventy-one in 1985, Alice had sworn off men forever. Some of the few males at Glenbrook had made the mistake of approaching her with an air of cordiality and friendship when she had first arrived, but she had reacted like a rabid animal warding off a perceived attack. This helped to make Alice a very popular figure among the female residents at Glenbrook, many of whom were competing for companionship in a field of slim pickings.

The sixty-something plates with steamed fish, boiled potatoes, and green vegetables rested in rows on the Corian countertop surrounding the half-walled kitchen in the center of the dining room. During the initial assessment visit, it had been explained to Jan that this design was meant to encourage the residents to help themselves to food at all hours of the day. Glenbrook was meant to feel like "home".

Jan noticed her mother eying the plates with an icy stare. "They better serve the entrée before it gets too cold," Alice announced unhappily. "I see those plates just sitting there. God forbid someone should move themselves to give us a meal with some *tam*, a little flavor and warmth still in it. Sometimes, I swear, I think I'm eating a picture of my food rather than the food itself."

At the dining table, Denise, whose bloated cheeks and multi-layered chins almost obliterated her peanut-sized eyes from view, was seated in her electric powered wheelchair to the right of Jan. She was wearing a dingy olive robe with a stained, quilted satin collar. Four inches of her cotton floral nightie protruded from the robe, almost touching the top of her white stretched anklets. When Jan made the mistake of asking Denise about the array of buttons on her armrest, Alice gave a sharp dig under the table to Jan's left leg. Halfway into Denise's lengthy demonstration of all the gizmos and extra features of her state-of-the art wheels, Alice pinched Jan's same leg and quietly scolded, "You should have never gotten her started. There'll be no silencing her for the rest of the meal." This was joined by cold accusatory stares emanating from the others at the table, some of whom were partially hidden by the huge paper sunflowers sitting in a foil-lined oats container, which Alice suggested should find its way to the garbage dump.

Diana was about to bite on a wedge of lettuce. Placing her knife and fork back on her salad plate, she gazed at Alice with hurt eyes. "I worked very hard on this centerpiece in the Arts and Crafts session today."

Alice, impervious to Diana's distress, —or anyone else's for that matter— took delight in fanning the flames she had just sparked. "Obviously, you didn't work hardly enough because these flowers look like a two-year-old made them."

Diving in on damage patrol, Jan offered Diana as much encouragement as she could. "The arrangement looks beautiful. I really like it. It's interesting how you used rubber bands and paper clips to hold the stems in place. Were the flowers difficult to make?"

Diana immediately perked up. "Not at all. Charlotte gave us very clear directions. This one looks exactly like the model she had us copy." If Jan discounted the lines on Diana's face and the puffy bags beneath her eyes, she could picture a much younger, more striking Diana turning heads upon entering a room. "I can take you to the Arts and Crafts room one day and show you how to do it too."

Alice gave Jan's foot a solid, hard kick, forcing Jan to pitch to her side and to send Diana a lopsided smile. Denise, however, was still deep into her narration, supplying details regarding the urine elimination tubes and blood pressure analyzers of her machine, which finally became too overwhelming even for Jan, who was remaining outwardly calm and unruffled despite her mother's needling aggression. Jan interrupted Denise just as the explanation of her battery backup system was about to begin.

"Denise, your food has been served. Why not take a break to eat and fill me in on the rest after dessert?"

To everyone's relief, Denise finally quieted down and decided to concentrate on her dinner plate, but added, "Remind me to tell you about the thrift store where your mother worked and I was the manageress."

"Yes, yes, yes. We know all about it, Denise," Alice hissed with disgust; she was one step away from full predatory mode.

Denise widened her eyes, making them just a tad less lost in her face. "How am I supposed to know if you've already mentioned it to your daughter?"

"The entire world knows about it. Once you begin, there's no shutting you up. Anyone sitting still long enough in Glenbrook has heard you tell about it, and that includes the dying and those already dead. I wish *I* were dead right now so I wouldn't have to hear those boring dissertations of yours."

Alice's last rebuff made Helen want to laugh. Jan could see her white unruly hair—controlled by a lattice of bobby pins—shake as she picked up her cloth napkin to hide her face, but it was too late; Denise was already incensed. She slammed on a lever and a whirring sound tilted her body backwards at an inclined angle. "This is why I choose to eat most of my meals in my room. You're a bunch of nasty, unfeeling people."

"Oh Denise, please don't feel that way. I would love to—" Jan's attempt to dissuade Denise from departing was aborted by a dessert fork piercing her new polyester skirt.

"Leave her be," her mother demanded. "She'll be back soon enough and will have forgotten everything that was said to her this evening."

"I feel so badly," Jan stated as Denise and her souped-up, motorized wheelchair made their way out of the dining room.

"Don't," Alice answered her with a shrug. "This is the way things are around here. You're hardly here, so you're not used to it."

"What do you mean by saying I'm hardly here?" Jan burst out. A pulsating behind her eyes caused the right one to twitch. "I'm here at least every other day!"

"Well, you're not here often enough for my liking."

Jan heaved a long, frustrated sigh and was about to defend herself when Harold, who was seated mid-room and was half of the only married couple residing in Glenbrook, let out a loud, explosive fart, which was trailed by uncontrollable diarrhea.

"Oy," Alice groaned. "I don't know how Dina has put up with him for so long. I hope he doesn't completely poop himself away before their anniversary celebration."

Unfortunately, Helen's sense of smell had not been diminished to the extent it had for the other diners and she started to gag, which resulted in an upchucking of everything she had previously digested. As Helen's retching went unabated, Alice hurriedly scooped the last drop of strawberry Jell-O and whipped cream from her bowl and popped it into her mouth. Smacking her lips, she then proclaimed it was time for Bingo and patted Jan on the arm, saying, "Let's get there early so we can get a good seat."

"Aren't you the least bit concerned about the wellbeing of your friend?" Jan asked, considerably shaken by the turn of events and worried about Helen, whose head lay in the middle of her dessert plate.

"Which friend?" Alice responded as if she had just landed from the moon and had no idea of anything being out of whack.

Jan unlocked her finger from her clenched fist and pointed to Helen. "Her: the woman who is heaving her guts out three seats away from you."

"You mean old metal-head? She's not my friend," Alice answered, maneuvering herself to an upright position while using the edge of the table for support. "She's just another body at the table. Come on, be a good girl, go fetch me my walker and let's get a move on. I'm hoping we'll get good cards tonight."

Jan rose to pull her mother's chair farther away from the table. *Stay assertive and in control of the situation*, she coached herself. "Mom, I told you before that I'd be leaving right after supper. I will not be playing Bingo." As she reached under the table for her pocketbook, she was happy to see two staff members arrive to aid Helen, clean up the mess, and wipe her face with a cool washcloth. She heard Mimi utter, "There, there" as she patted Helen's back. Jan then headed off to reclaim her mother's Rollator.

"Come on, Jan," Alice yelped as she charged boldly toward the elevator. "Just make sure I get safely up to the second-floor social room. That's all I ask. God forbid I get raped along the way." Jan had to quicken her step to keep up. When Alice came to a halt, she pounded repeatedly on the "up" button and turned to face Jan. "This is what I live with," she grumbled. "This is what I see day in day out. Ach, you should never know from this. Believe me when I tell you that there is nothing pretty about growing old."

Jan had promised herself to walk away once she had reached the bank of elevators, but as she had passed by several of the residents looking ghost-like and sickly in their wheelchairs, all of her resistance had drained out of her. "No, there isn't," Jan concurred.

"Oh, do stay for just one round," Alice cajoled, shaking Jan's arm with the persistence of a nagging child. "You'll have fun; you might even win some money."

"I don't care about the money," Jan stated, wanting to sound less spineless than she felt.

"Then care about *me*," Alice pleaded.

Chapter Sixteen

The second-floor social room at Glenbrook, as with all the other common areas, was tastefully appointed. Hand hewn walnut shelves stretched across the entire western wall, housing leather-bound vintage books, Lladro statuettes, crystal vases, a gold, filigree, wall clock, and other well-placed curios. Upon entering the room, Jan turned to Alice and remarked about a particular pair of silver candlesticks. "They look like they might be antiques, like those your mother used to use on *Shabbos*."

Alice was quick to point out, "These ones are fake; they're only silver-*plated*."

"They're elegant nonetheless," Jan replied, walking uncomfortably slowly so Alice could lead the way to the table of her choosing.

"What's the point of showing off your silver if you're not going to keep it looking nice?" Alice nitpicked. "Someone should be making sure they stay polished. I'm assuming you're keeping my mother's candlesticks in better condition than these. Don't make me regret not giving them to Maureen!" She shuffled along and called, "Hurry up over here, before someone else grabs my lucky chair."

Jan noticed the time on the wall clock was off by twenty minutes.

"Don't even mention it," Alice warned as if she were reading her mind. "Twenty minutes early, twenty minutes late: it makes no difference to us jailbirds." She tossed her walker aside and sat hastily in her preferred seat, setting her sight on the other people entering the social room. "Here they come *kriking* along," Alice noted snidely. "If molasses was human, this is what it would look like."

Jan turned her head to watch the slow-moving crowd of hopeful Bingo players file in—which included Muriel and Helen, who was looking much better and back to her old self—but was disrupted by a nervous tugging on her sleeve.

"Hurry up before the disco queen takes your seat," Alice ordered.

As soon as she was in her chair, Jan opened her wallet to extract two singles to pay for her own and Alice's Bingo cards, but Alice wouldn't hear of it.

"Put your money away," she snapped. "I don't want anyone thinking I'm cheap."

So, Jan acquiesced and watched her mother tediously count out two dollars from her booty of coins, the bulk of which being pennies and nickels. Mimi walked about the tables to collect the entry fees. When she reached Alice and Jan's table, Alice quickly introduced Jan to Mimi.

"This is my daughter—the one who lives in Boca, not the very rich one. She's joining us for the evening." Alice started off by sounding warm and friendly, but by the time she uttered, "Make sure you give her a winning card," her face was without a smidgeon of humor.

Mimi smiled anyway and answered, "You know, Alice, I like to keep the winning cards for myself. Have you forgotten that you introduced me to your lovely daughter just a few moments ago in the dining room?"

"I'm just testing you, Mimi," Alice replied jovially. "I want to see if you're keeping on your toes. It's easy to lose your mind in a place like this! And, by the way, how's your own little girl getting on?"

"She's good for now, thank you," came Mimi's reply. Mimi then asked Helen if she was feeling well enough to play Bingo and Helen responded, "I'm doing just fine, dear," as she extended a dollar bill.

Alice whispered to Jan, "I see some of her bobby pins have fallen out; let's hope she doesn't detonate." Mimi then moved on to Muriel, who opened a shimmering gold purse, handed Mimi four quarters, and mimicked Alice's request for a winning card.

"Why are you using your quarters now?" Alice demanded of Muriel. "You'll need them for the individual rounds."

"What's the big deal?" Muriel answered, arranging her Bingo cards, markers, and tangerine rabbit's foot in an orderly fashion on the table. "No need for you to go worrying on my account."

"Well, just make sure you don't come to me then when you need any."

"You're the last person on earth I would ever borrow money from!"

"What do you mean by that?" Alice challenged, rising from her chair and seeming to Jan to be extraordinarily outraged.

Muriel flapped her hands about as if she were swatting an annoying fly. "Oh, sit down, you old goat. I didn't mean anything by it at all."

Alice folded her arms. "I'll sit down when I'm good and ready."

The first game began and Mimi yelled out, "N 36."

Leaning into Jan's ear, Alice cupped one hand over her mouth and attempted to whisper again, "The last thing in the world I needed was for her to follow me to Glenbrook." Her spit landed all over Jan's cheek.

"In case you don't know, dearie, everyone can hear what you're saying. If I knew you were living here," Muriel countered, "I would have told my son to book me into The Residences at Marriott. Honestly, you act like the queen of—"

"I can't hear the numbers being called out," Helen squealed.

"The two of you: enough with the bickering!" Jan implored, using a tissue to wipe her face. "Can we all please pay attention to the game?"

Alice reclaimed her seat as she glowered menacingly at Muriel.

Several rounds of the game were played, but there were no winners at Alice's table. Following the drawing of each ball, a chorus of comments would resound about the room.

"What number did she say?"

"Speak louder!"

"We can't hear you in the back."

"Is this an 'H' round or a full card?"

Muriel reached for her rabbit's foot, stroking the fur three times in each direction. "Something's very different tonight. I can't quite get a fix on it, but it's definitely affecting our luck."

"It's not Jan's being here if that's what you're thinking," Alice snapped.

"It was the farthest thing from my mind," Muriel defended.

White-haired, misshapen Stella, who was seated next to the spinning cage, stood up and dragged her walker over to where Jan was sitting. She asked if anyone had any extra quarters to spare. Muriel stared straight ahead, Alice arranged her markers into color-coordinated piles, but Jan extended a few coins to Stella, who then left the room.

"You shouldn't have done that," Alice scolded. "Stella goes begging around the room every time we play Bingo. She's a thief."

Mimi called out, "G 54."

"Was that B 54?" Alice asked, "I couldn't hear what was called."

Muriel offered, "It was C 54. You should try turning up the volume on your hearing aid."

Jan, the referee, explained, "There is no C 54; it was *G* 54. There is no 'C' in B-I-N-G-O."

"Inconsiderate numbskulls. Keep it quiet back there!" yelled a man wearing striped pajamas.

Jan thought she saw steam coming out of her mother's ears. Alice called Muriel, "A big, old, worthless, dumb ox!"

Fearing that a barrage of insults was about to erupt, Jan's eyes darted from Alice to Muriel and then back to Alice again, but to her relief, Alice tossed Muriel a caramel Nip, which she caught and noisily unwrapped. More shushes, "no common decency", "some of us are trying to play a game!" and other such mutterings arose in the room again until Murray, who at other times looked like death warmed over, shouted out vociferously, "Bingo!" and the rest of the room booed, screeched and yelled, "*Feh*," "Yuck," and "Oh hell, no!"

"Mom, what's with the relationship between you and Muriel?" Jan asked, guiding her mother toward her apartment at the conclusion of the Bingo game. "I thought she was one of your closer friends."

"She is, but you always have to be on the lookout for a person's true nature. She drove us to a dance one night at Century Village. We had agreed ahead of time that we would leave together no later than ten o'clock, but when ten o'clock came around, Muriel was nowhere to be found. She left me stranded. Like a beggar on the streets, I had to go from car to car in the parking lot hoping some kindhearted stranger would give me a ride home."

Listening attentively, Jan asked, "Why couldn't you take the bus?"

"I didn't have my bus pass with me, so the driver refused to let me get on board. It was humiliating."

"What ever happened to Muriel?"

"I found out later that the cheap slut went home with Arnold Kofferman. Then, what made matters even worse: Muriel disappeared for the next two weeks. She didn't show up for a single Rummikub or Kalooki game. What was I to think? I pictured her in the woods with her throat slit. Degenerate men, who portray themselves as gentlemen to everyone else, do those kinds of things to unsuspecting women."

Jan tried to dismiss the vision of her father that her mother's description had evoked. Despite not wanting to, she had been drawn deeply into Alice's cliff-hanger. "And?"

"Muriel finally picked up one of my phone calls. 'Took me to the woods?' she mocked. 'Arnie could hardly shuffle his way from the living room into his kitchen. You're just a jealous old bat.' No, I told her. I place a higher price on friendship and loyalty than you do. So she said, 'Good, next time I'll remember to curtsey because you obviously come from blue blood.'"

Truly perplexed, Jan asked, "What was that supposed to mean?"

"I told her," Alice said in an uppity voice, "that she didn't know anything about loyalty because her husband fooled around the entire time he was married to her. 'Better to have a decent man cheat on you,' she said, 'than be trapped with a vicious, good-for-nothing, has-been who nobody but an asshole would've ever wanted.'"

"Ouch," Jan replied, looking straight ahead into her mother's eyes, trying to ascertain what lay hidden behind her haughtiness. "Well, she got that right, didn't she? I mean about Dad being a complete good-for-nothing has-been—not the part about you, of course."

Alice's expression revealed little. "It wasn't her place to talk to me that way," she stated calmly.

Observing her mother, Jan could imagine an invisible cloak of victimhood draped across her shoulders. "The truth hurts, doesn't it, Mom?"

"You should only know the half of it," Alice muttered bitterly, waving goodbye.

Chapter Seventeen

"You're in a codependent relationship and it just isn't healthy," Mike shouted the next evening when Jan, looking disheveled, finally appeared in the kitchen—seventy-five minutes later than what she had originally promised.

This echoed the very same sentiment he had expressed the night before, when Jan had returned home after staying for Bingo at Glenbrook and tried to tell him about Harold's mishap and Helen's unfortunate reaction to it. "I'm not in the least bit interested in hearing those gruesome details," he had told her. "Why do you even have to repeat them?" Turning his attention back to the program he was watching, he raised the volume on the TV while requesting that she not interrupt him anymore. "And don't even broach the topic again when we're in the bedroom later on. You know how I feel about that hogwash."

On this occasion, Jan announced her presence with a loud, "Honey, I'm home," as she passed through the garage connecting door to the house. Without receiving an audible response, she wondered if Mike had grown tired of waiting and chose to go out for dinner. *No, I just saw his car parked next to mine.* She subsequently found him reading the newspaper at the kitchen table but acting all sorts of impatient. His jaw clenching, repetitive foot tapping, and grumpy frown clearly indicated that he had been on pins and needles anticipating her homecoming. She approached his back to give him a really big bear hug, smack his neck with a mushy kiss, and expand upon a heart-felt sorry. "I'll try not to let it happen again."

"I've been waiting all this time to eat my dinner," he grumbled. "Although I would have bet a million dollars on you being late again. Please don't embarrass yourself and don't patronize me by brushing this situation off with an insincere apology."

"I *am* sincere about this, Mike," Jan said. "I wish you would believe me."

"There's nothing good in the refrigerator and I'm starving," Mike griped. "I had hoped to find something to stave off my hunger, but there was only cottage cheese and leftover cooked carrots. But hey, the good news is you didn't stay for Bingo again like you did yesterday." His cold shoulder dismissal made Jan's heart sink into her boots.

Jan threw her pocketbook on the floor and placed a box of Chinese take-out food on the kitchen island. The pungent aroma from the food added to the heaviness of the room's atmosphere. "The moisturizer I bought her was the wrong brand, so I had to go and change it."

"You're a practicing lawyer with responsibilities to your clients. You owe something to them and yourself, but not to her," he snapped. "She could just as well have used the moisturizer you bought yesterday; it wouldn't have hurt her."

"Evidently, this brand gives her a rash," Jan responded flatly.

"I just bet it does. And if you didn't go running to replace it right away, what would have happened?" The anger in Mike's voice did not let up.

"She would have complained on and on. It was easier on my nerves to do it this way instead."

Mike flipped the pages of his newspaper until he came across an article on the Federal Reserve. While scanning the first few lines, he commented, "I hope the food you picked up is still hot."

"Why shouldn't it be?" Jan asked, rushing to the sink to wash her hands and then rapidly wiping them on the dishtowel. "I ordered it as I was getting ready to leave Glenbrook."

Mike glared in Jan's direction. "And then you spent an additional forty-five minutes looking for her favorite earring? Please give me a break! Would her ears fall off her face if she could never wear those specific earrings again?"

"Well, she made a special request just as I said my goodbye," Jan stated quietly.

"What else is new?" Mike broke in, rolling his eyes.

"It bothered her that she had lost it," Jan continued as she set about hunting down her porcelain Chinese teapot set.

"Don't bother going all out for me," Mike called out, the edginess still clinging to his voice. "I'm skipping the tea and having a beer instead. Can you hand me a can from the fridge while you're standing right there?"

Jan took out what had been, as of that morning, a six-pack and yanked one can free from the plastic handle. She noticed the empty circles where two other cans had previously been held in place.

Mike accepted his cooled Bud Light from Jan's outstretched hand. "Every time you leave, she comes up with a new stalling tactic." He took a sip of the beer and tried to finish his article, but his face reddened and he slammed the paper down.

"The earring had been a gift from Aunt Gilda," Jan offered, lifting the small white food cartons out of the box and onto the granite countertop. Picking up the dishtowel, she wiped away sweat from under her nose and dabbed at her forehead. "I'm not disagreeing with you, Mike."

"Your mother knows full well how she's playing you, and you know it too!" Mike continued to vent. "You need to have a heart-to-heart talk with her to set this matter right once and for all. I can't believe *how many times* these *very* words have come out of my mouth. *How many times* have I begged you to do this? The situation is beyond abnormal. It's utterly intolerable."

Jan sighed.

"I've turned into one long, broken record and you, well er you, you're just broken altogether!"

Jan shoved Mike's arms aside to make a space for the placemats on the kitchen table after having asked him to move the paper aside. Mike attempted to fold the paper neatly, but the various sections combated him. He jumped up and strode away from the table, resorting to throwing the entire newspaper into the recycling bin sitting on the garage floor.

"Hey, I didn't have a chance to read that yet," Jan complained.

"Too bad; we all can't have what we want. I didn't choose to be this hungry." Mike sulked his way back to the kitchen table. "I should have never switched my dinner meeting to next week. Stupid me thought we could actually spend some quality time together. Please hand me something to munch on in the meantime."

Jan tossed him the sealed bag of fried noodles and proceeded to spoon rice and chicken into bowls. Mike ripped the bag open and all the noodles came flying out, landing on the table and on the floor.

"Mike, you should calm down," Jan cautioned. "You're not one to typically drink so much beer."

Mike pushed back on his chair. "Somehow, amazingly so, I'm not that hungry anymore. In that case, I'm going over to the gym; Gillian said she needed a ride there."

Jan sat at the table, surrounded by the scattered noodles, too upset and worn out to ask him to stay. She just didn't have the strength to drum up any more excuses about how and why she dealt with her mother the way that she did. *What does Mike think, that his running around with Gillian is going to make me change my ways?* She'd had her fill of threats and what others expected of her. *Push me one way; pull me another way; after a while, people, I'm just going to fall apart. Damned if I do and damned if I don't.*

Chapter Eighteen

For several weeks in a row, Charlotte had everyone in Arts and Crafts making centerpieces for Harold and Dina's party. Ordinarily, Alice did not like to participate in Charlotte's activities; they made her feel like she was in kindergarten. Most of the supplies involved construction paper and blunt soft-grip scissors. The cutting and pasting reminded her of the projects her grandchildren had made when they were little, brought to stick on her refrigerator door, but were tossed in the trashcan the minute the grandchildren departed. But these special centerpieces were going to adorn the tables for Harold and Dina, who had married as lovebirds in 1943 and were now celebrating their 60th wedding anniversary. Alice enjoyed counting the couple as her friends and was happy to be a part of their celebration.

Helen, Muriel, and George were already seated in the hobby room sorting out the materials when Alice joined them. George looked at the empty chair next to him and then regarded Alice with apprehension.

"I'm not going to bite your head off, George," Alice said as she plopped her rear end down. Charlotte looked up to see if there was a disturbance and Alice responded that they were all behaving like angels, so not to worry. In assembly-line fashion, the group took turns twisting yarn around the stems of artificial flowers and arranging them in transformed decorated milk containers, spray-painted in silver. Even Alice had to admit that the overall effect was pretty.

Rumors had spread throughout Glenbrook that Harold and Dina's son, the rich one who lived in Canada, had made arrangements for the food to be prepared by an outside caterer. Suddenly, several of the residents began to reclaim the appetites that had eluded them for many years.

"I heard it will be surf and turf," Helen told Muriel. Muriel responded that she heard it was filet mignon with a shrimp cocktail appetizer. "Either way," Helen confirmed, "it's going to be a fancy-schmancy party."

"Barry, the one who lives in Toronto, is not sparing a single expense." George added in his two cents. "He's flying the entire family in from across the United States so they can all be together."

Sondra, Mimi, and several other staff members had set up rows of bridge chairs in the second-floor social room, and a florist was hired to decorate a makeshift *chuppah*. The Rabbi who conducted Friday night services at Glenbrook had been invited to officiate at the ceremony in which Harold and Dina were going to renew their vows. Silver and white streamers stretched from one end of the room to the other, and flameless candles were placed on every table and available nook.

***

Alice raved to Jan over the phone the next morning about the extravaganza. "It was almost as regal as Princess Di's and Prince Charles' affair."

"That much hoopla, huh?" Jan would have rather stuck needles in her eyes than have to listen to more details of the anniversary celebration. She started to chip away at the nail polish on her thumb.

"Yes. Elegant but tastefully done," Alice boasted. "Even I was impressed. They also served lobster linguini; some sticky rice dish they called risotto; a Caesar's salad *with* the anchovies, but another Caesar's salad *without* the anchovies for those people who don't like them."

Jan, scraping the nail polish on her other thumb, issued, "Oh, wow."

Alice related how stunning Dina looked, wearing an ivory, poi de soie dress with a lace collar; how she walked down the aisle without so much as a cane, holding onto Barry's arm; how suave Harold looked in his tuxedo, even though it was a rental, it still looked very chic; how everyone in the audience was given a single white rose to hold—smelling like it had just been picked; how the men were given matching yarmulkes to wear— she had pocketed one for Mike; and how absolutely delicious and refined the banquet was that followed.

"Did I tell you about the Rabbi?" she babbled on. "His sermon was so touching; we were all *kvelling*. Chanted the blessings like an opera star, he did." She added that she would save the following week's newsletter for Jan to see, for it was sure to be jam-packed with photographs that Charlotte scurried around taking of the event. "And the best part, for which you will surely thank me, is that I grabbed a centerpiece for you to place on your kitchen table, before Charlotte recycles the parts for another project."

Jan found Alice's level of excitement to be unnervingly cloying, even more irritating than her everyday abrasiveness. "Did you forget that I have that ceramic bird bath there now?" she asked, working on eliminating the nail polish from both her pinkies.

Alice, still pumped from the celebratory event, didn't give a hoot what Jan had to say. "This centerpiece is so much nicer than the one you've got. Nicer than any ones they've made here before. They could be sold on Worth Avenue or on the Miracle Mile; that's how upscale they are!"

"But the bird bath was a souvenir from the trip Mike and I took to Spain," Jan said, struggling to stand her ground. "We love that piece. At least I know I still do."

Jan and Mike had squabbled right before Mike had left for the office that morning, and Jan, still feeling deflated, regretted answering yet another one of her mother's calls. While Mike was eating his cereal, he had let it slip that his companion from the previous night's business-related dinner had been Gillian McVey. Jan had immediately hurled such words as 'suspicious,' 'inappropriate,' and 'on the prowl' at him, but Mike had told her she was just being ridiculous and accused her of being sexist. Jan answered she would not have been sensitive to any other woman, just Gillian McVey. "Didn't you just have lunch with her?" she had asked. "What do you think people are going to think?"

"I don't worry about what other people think," Mike had said before retreating to the bathroom to brush his teeth.

"I promise you Jan," Alice pressed on, "you'll love what I have for you more. Your house will look like Queen Mary's Rose Garden in Regent's Park," to which Jan responded, "I'm going to have to look further into this."

"The bird bath has run its course. Such a *tzimmes* you're making over a little, dated knickknack. My flowers will look more beautiful. Listen to me, you know I have good taste. I'll have it ready for you when you come by later today."

***

The euphoria from Harold and Dina's festivities at Glenbrook was short lived. Ten days after the grand celebration, medics were called in the middle of the night. Harold had awoken to pee and found Dina lying face up on the sheets, soaked in urine, with her eyes wide open. Her skin was a grayish blue; her body was as stiff as month-old licorice. There was nothing he could say or do to revive his beloved bride of sixty years. He kissed her cheek and whispered, "I'll be seeing you soon, babe," before the medics wheeled her away. One of the nurses called Harold's nephew, who lived nearby in Fort Lauderdale, to apprise him of the situation. They had last spoken at the anniversary party, waiting in line for their turn at the buffet table. The nurse then helped Harold pack a bag with a few essential items and sat with him in the first-floor lounge until his relative arrived. The night-time housework crew immediately set to work making the apartment presentable for whenever Harold would return.

At breakfast that next morning, the news was well circulated that Dina had suffered and died from a heart attack. The memorial service was to take place the following day in the very same room where the wedding ceremony had been.

Alice put down the spoon with which she had been eating her soft-boiled egg and raised her reading glasses to her forehead so she could better seek out Harold in the dining room; she wished to extend her condolences to him in person, but he was nowhere in sight. Muriel, Sophie, and Helen were also seated at Alice's table, nibbling on their rolls and oatmeal while they chatted about the weather. The tall brocade drapes had been pulled back by the windows and French doors to allow the morning sun to lighten up the room, but all the chandeliers above the tables were still turned on. "Old people like to know and see what they're eating," Alice had once explained to Jan. "We don't need mood lighting; we need plenty of light so we can make sure no one is trying to poison us."

Sophie postulated there might be a morning shower coming their way and that the outdoor jewelry sale scheduled for eleven o'clock might have to be canceled.

"Oh no," Muriel moaned. "I placed a two-stranded white beaded necklace on hold after I bought the matching earrings last week. We can't have them cancel the jewelry show. That would be a disaster. That necklace was *to die for*."

As a young single woman, Muriel had been a model for a dress manufacturer in Manhattan's design district. After a short flirtation with her employer, she became pregnant, and the two were married before their first child was born. This many years later, she had still retained her slim runway figure and shapely Sophia Loren lips, which she refreshed incessantly with dramatic, deep-red lipstick. However, not all the parts of her body were held together as tightly as they had been in the past. At Glenbrook, she was never seen without her face fully made up and her white, short-clipped hair teased meticulously into a bouffant.

Alice, slicing the crust off a blueberry muffin, turned to Muriel. "That necklace was pretty, but not enough to kill yourself over. I'm sure you'll be able to find one just as nice. But, of course, if you really want to be in Dina's company, then we can surely make the arrangements."

"The earrings matched the necklace perfectly. I'll never be able to find one equally as good," Muriel pouted. "I spent over an hour picking that set out. Are you telling me now that I wasted all that time?"

Alice shrugged and popped two loose blueberries into her mouth. "As if you had something else much better to do."

"Having nice things to wear still matters to me, as it should to you."

"When they bury you, I'll make sure you're wearing something especially nice with the appropriate accoutrements. I'll tell the mortician to take extra time and effort to fix up your face. You'll look better than ever."

Muriel thrust her chin into the air. "Too bad you won't be around, dearie. I will have buried you first."

"Ladies, ladies," Helen jumped in. "You're like two pecking hens in a barnyard. Please give it a rest. They won't cancel the jewelry sale, even on account of what happened to Dina. They'll probably just move it indoors. It's business as usual around here no matter what."

Muriel studied the reflection of her nose in a compact mirror, patting it with a cosmetic sponge. "You'll have to wait in line," she advised Alice, who was searching about the room.

"Excuse me, what exactly do you mean by that?" Alice demanded.

"Didn't you notice all the activity taking place in the kitchen earlier this morning? It was a real cook off! The women were running around crazily just the same as if it were Penney's department store giving away all their merchandise for free. Eggs, flour, cheese, and milk went flying off the shelves."

"I don't take notice of those things," Alice divulged.

"Now, they're all waiting in the hallway for Harold to return to his apartment," Muriel continued.

"It's too early to sit Shiva."

"He's not sitting Shiva," Muriel corrected her. "Charlotte has to keep disbursing the crowds. Their causing traffic jams for the wheelchairs."

"I don't understand why the people are lined up to begin with."

"Alice, how did you get to be so naïve? *Only the women are lined up!* They've got their casseroles, kugels, and pies already made because Harold is a single man now."

Alice raised her eyebrows in puzzlement. Turning toward Helen, she said, "I've never heard of such a thing. Have you?"

Helen responded that such a display of insensitivity toward Dina turned her stomach, to which Alice warned, "For heaven's sake, don't go throwing up again."

"This will be very entertaining," Muriel chimed in. "Like watching a reality show on TV. What's that one called, *The Bachelor*?"

"The wife's body hasn't even been buried yet!" Alice said with disgust, but then added, "In a place like this, I guess no one can afford to wait."

Chapter Nineteen

Sondra poured herself a cup of coffee from the full carafe sitting next to the refrigerator in the kitchen, making sure not to pick up the one with the decaf label. After placing the milk container back in the fridge, she emptied the contents of two packets of sugar into her Styrofoam cup while uttering "Lordy, Lordy, oh my" and then slipped four more packets into the pocket of her shirt uniform. Longingly, she eyed the two plates of pastries and shortbread biscuits perched on the counter, but after the talk she had with Mr. Dean about the refreshments not being intended for the staff, Sondra tried to exercise some restraint. The icing on the cheese Danish, however, looked so sweet and enticing that Sondra began to salivate at the thought of biting into its soft crust.

No matter how hard she searched Alice's apartment that morning, she had been unable to locate her hiding place for the last remaining chocolate chip cookies—she suspected that Alice hadn't finished off the most recent batch quite yet. Alice sure kept finding the most unlikely places to hide those cookies and cakes and was still just as reluctant to share them with anyone else. Despite not being shown any real appreciation for what she did, Alice's daughter kept supplying Alice with the most delicious home-baked treats for the entire time Alice had been living at Glenbrook.

Just shortly before entering the kitchen, Sondra had encountered Mr. Dean escorting a visitor on a tour, so she figured he would be making the rounds throughout the facility that morning. He had been in a closed-door meeting with the maintenance crew right before that, which Sondra wished had lasted a little longer, giving her more time to grab the treat she'd been eyeing. Glancing around to make sure no one was watching, Sondra lifted the protective glass lid over the plate and grabbed the Danish, shoving the whole pastry quickly into her mouth. A red-checkered dishtowel was sitting on the counter, and Sondra wet a corner of the cloth to scrape away any telltale crumbs from her uniform. She then ran to an unoccupied table in the corner of the dining room and emptied one more packet of sweetener into her coffee. After gulping down the last chunks of her cheese Danish, Sondra took a rare moment to relax and leisurely sip her drink.

Sondra was feeling worn out and beaten up from the demands of her morning shift, which had begun at 5:30 a.m. that morning. Already each of her residents had to go potty or else have their night-time Depends changed, everyone had to have their meds administered, many of the bed linens had been soiled and had needed to be changed, and several residents had needed assistance with their grooming and dressing. It seemed to Sondra that the list of her chores was never-ending.

It felt so good to be finally sitting and resting her legs. She was especially grateful for the slides of Denali National Park being shown in the social room, which all of her charges were attending. Even Alice, who had resisted most lectures and demonstrations, had overcome her stubbornness and acquiesced to viewing this documentary. It had taken Sondra eight trips—forward and backward and up and down the elevator while pushing or pulling a wheelchair or guiding along a walker or cane—to get everyone where they needed to be before the slide show began.

To Sondra's chagrin, in forty-five minutes the process would have to be reversed all over again, only it would be lunchtime and everyone would be more cantankerous and less willing to wait in an orderly line. For some reason, getting to the dining room and reaching their meals early was a high priority for the residents of Glenbrook, and so with much impatience and belligerence on the part of the residents, a safe procession into the dining room was almost always impossible to achieve.

Sondra checked the recently missed calls on her cell phone and her voicemail messages, half hoping to see Delmont's name. Her son was a sophomore in an upstate college on a football scholarship. Lately, though, he had been complaining a lot about the coach getting on his back about his excess weight and for skipping some of the practices.

"Don't you go on and do something stupid to lose that scholarship money, Delmont," Sondra had cautioned. "I'm working hard enough to be keeping you there, and we need every penny that comes in extra."

During Delmont's last call, he had sounded like he was high on weed and he kept on telling her to send more cash.

"I need it!" he had yelled.

Sondra purposefully refrained from suggesting to Delmont that he contact his father for some financial support. The last time she had made such a reference, Delmont slammed down the phone and Sondra hadn't heard from her son for three months, giving her way too much to worry about. Even self-absorbed Alice had noticed the frown permanently plastered on Sondra's face.

"Are you on a special kind of diet?" she had asked. "You're not so chipper anymore. Here put a few of my coffee toffees in your pocket; they'll do you some good."

Sondra sometimes worried that she alone was to blame for her son being the way he was; after all, she had given him the name Delmont, which meant "From the mountain…being strong in material matters, determined, and stubborn." She had hoped this would have given him a sturdy foundation to make up for the one that should have been provided by his father but never was. *Why, once Delmont got his mind set a certain way, there was no derailing him—not one iota.* She very might as well have called him "mule head" or "jackass."

Whenever Sondra spoke with Delmont, he would either say he was in a hurry, seem highly agitated, or act overly laid back. During this past call, much of what Delmont said came out slurred.

"All's I'm saying," Delmont had implored, "is that the rent's coming due, and I need the money to pay for it." Delmont's voice tapered off so quietly at the end that Sondra had to ask him if he was still on the phone.

"Yeah. I still here."

"You're there all right, Delmont, but I think your head's in some other dimension. What did you do with the money they gave you? You were supposed to pay the rent with that money."

"Mom, you never went to college so you don't understand the expenses I've got coming at me. If they kick me out of these digs, then I might as well just quit the school and find me a real job."

"No. Don't do that, Delmont," Sondra had begged, raising her voice. The prospect of her son leaving school for good upset her to no end. "You promised me to stay in school until graduation. Our deal was that if you didn't get picked up by a professional team, then at least you be able to get a job coaching gym for younger kids, but you have to come up with grades higher than D's on your transcript for that."

"I can't handle you getting all ballistic over this. Try and keep it cool 'cause you bringing me down real fast. There's nothing wrong with getting D's as long as I get credit for the courses I'm taking."

Sondra had taken a few deep breaths and tried to calm herself down before responding further. "Well, I don't know too much about that."

"Well, I do; I want you to be proud of me, Mama."

"I am proud of you, son."

"Then help me out here. Send me some more money so I can do what I gotta do. You've been working a number of years at that place now. Isn't it time that you got some sort of raise? Don't let them folks take advantage of you. You hear me?"

Sondra could hear music in the background as Delmont rattled on about his wants and must-haves. Then she had heard some females talking followed by their laughter. Delmont had told Sondra, "I have to go; I have some things to take care of."

"Delmont, you be sure to stick with your studying now! You do that and I'll speak with Mr. Dean about putting a little more money in my paycheck each week." Sondra knew she had no chance in hell getting a raise out of Mr. Dean. There were plenty of available care workers that could take her place. They'd even work for less than what she was getting. No, she wasn't going to jeopardize her job, but no way was she going to share this fact with her son.

"Like I told you already, I need to pay my bills."
The tension in Delmont's voice was palpable. "It's only
right they pay you what you're worth. Please send money as
quick as you can."

Sondra worried constantly about Delmont. She had
seen what happened to the other kids in the neighborhood
where she lived. There were just too many gangs, much too
much crime, too much drinking, and too many drugs. The
Reverend Johnson usually talked about these problems in
his sermons on Sundays in church, but no one else appeared
to be listening or taking the Reverend seriously except for
Sondra and a few of the other women sitting alongside her
in the pew. Where she was seated there were a lot of
"Amens" ringing out, along with "Yes Siree," "Hallelujah,"
"That's right," and "Thank the Lord," but people in the back
pews were not being as vocal. Many of the attendees were
Spanish, French, and Creole-speaking migrant workers who
were not just there to pay their respects to the Lord on the
Holy Day but to share in the salads, ham, and chicken dishes
that were part of the communal meal. For some of these skin
and bones people, it was the only decent food they would
eat all week.

She had tried talking to the Reverend about Delmont
when the two of them were alone, but the Reverend had his
mind focused on other things, and Delmont most certainly
wasn't one of them. Sondra was afraid to risk losing her
friendship with the Reverend. Most of the men she had
dated were too poor, too slaphappy, or too untrustworthy. A
lot of these men were tall and skinny with missing teeth and
jutting jaws that spoke of malnutrition and hungry days, but
Reverend Johnson, he was just as rotund as Sondra and
loved his food to the same extent that she did. She admired
the way he dressed in fine shirts and fancy ties, always

138

having a silk handkerchief tucked into the breast pocket of his suit jacket. Sondra felt desired and cherished when she was with him. He had a way of making her feel important and feminine all at the same time. He kissed the protrusions on her ears, her engorged nipples, and the folds in her belly while praising God for the sumptuousness bestowed upon her.

"I sure do find you sexy, my Bahamian princess," he had declared during one of their trysts at the Big 8 Motel in downtown West Palm Beach.

"And I sure is happy to hear that," Sondra had replied, planting her puckered lips on his receding hairline. "Seems to me you like your women any which way you can get them."

The Reverend had grabbed hold of Sondra's rear end in each of his two hands and said, "No matter how much I have here, it's never enough. It wouldn't faze me none to have double the amount," as he had pulled her closer into his embrace.

"Your wife's all prim and proper with slender bones and a tight ass. It's no wonder you be roaming and chasing some other brown sugar to quench your thirst."

The grin stretching across the Reverend's puffed-out cheeks had abruptly disappeared, making Sondra immediately regret bringing up the reference to his wife. He shoved her off to his side as he sat up. "My wife is an overbearing imperious witch. As much as I love serving the Lord at this church, I'm having a hard time tolerating Mildred's rules, her accusatory eyes, and constantly nagging tongue. She forgets to leave the principal part of her at school when she comes home. Makes me feel like I'm always doing something wrong and about to get my ass kicked into detention." Softening his expression, he looked toward Sondra with a tilted head. "What if I were to call you up sometime and tell you to meet me at such and such a place with your belongings packed in a suitcase? Would you do it? There's no reason why the two of us can't be spending more respectable time with each other. Would you be willing to go with me?"

Sondra, thrilled by this request, gave her reply in the form of a big wet kiss.

The Reverend slid his pudgy fingers down Sondra's shoulder and onto her thigh. "That's a mighty fine way to say yes. I've got one hour left before Miss Mildred walks through our front door and starts demanding dinner on the table. How about we make the most of these few minutes?"

Since the very first day she had attended services at the church five years earlier, Reverend Johnson had been its spiritual leader. Sondra took comfort in knowing that he wasn't going anywhere that she was aware of, but now she was overjoyed with the prospect of running away with him. At the age of forty-two, she still had a lifetime ahead of her, and she wanted *that lifetime* to be shared with *that man*. She certainly didn't want Delmont's situation to drive a wedge between her and the Reverend at this juncture.

For sure, it had not been easy raising a boy like Delmont on her own. His daddy, Mr. Raymond, although comfortably well off, hadn't been much of a help at all. She'd left him back in the Bahamas with his wife and six other children, and had taken the thousand dollars he had given her that was meant to cover an abortion in the States. At first, he had asked her to get rid of his baby, but Sondra wouldn't hear of it, so she took his money and promised not to involve him in their child's future, sending photographs at various stages of Delmont's life to Mr. Raymond's business address, a place she knew only too well, with its dust-collecting stacks of papers and fancy furniture to be polished.

Sondra's mama had known all along what was going on and judged Sondra a fool for the choice that she had made. "Not going to be easy to attract a man with another man's seed growing in your belly," she had cautioned. She was swaying in her rocking chair on the porch of her timber framed house, while Sondra leaned against the outside wall, snapping peas out of their pods. The front door was slightly ajar, revealing the one room with a row of bare mattresses and a rickety dresser. "A thousand dollars is letting him off too easy. If you had spoken to his Missus, you would be getting more out of dem. And once the child is born, who is going to support you? You and your baby walking around in rags with your bottoms hanging out, and him with his fine house and fancy clothes living a mighty grand and respectable life. You a rich lady with fortune bags dat I'm not aware of?"

"My mind's made up, and that is that," Sondra had declared. "I'm gonna have this baby and love it to bits. Show him how a real mama is meant to take care of her children."

Sondra's mama shook her head from side to side. It was swathed in a knotted, red and yellow headwrap. Wells of purple hung below her tired, glazed-over eyes. Folding her arms, she pointed her chin at her daughter. "I's can't help the lumbago dat runs in my bones and keeps me from moving around like regular folks. I done the best for you dat I could. None of dose rich American ladies is gonna hire a cleaning lady with a screaming baby on the job. If you thought you had it hard before, you be in for a big awakening."

As Delmont matured, his resemblance to his father had become more and more astonishing. Sondra had not held back in telling him the truth about his daddy. He knew his name, where he lived, the details of his other family, how she had been hired as a maid to tidy up Mr. Raymond's office but that it had led to additional services being provided as well, and the agreement Sondra had made specifically regarding their child. Mother and son had bumped into Mr. Raymond at a grocery store in Nassau one Christmas when they were visiting Sondra's family. She had sent Mr. Raymond a short note in advance, telling him where and when they would be. "Delmont does not know about this note. I've got no expectations about you coming to see him, but just in case you have the inclination, I want to give you the opportunity to do so," she wrote.

Delmont was still a high school student then, and his father had been visibly impressed with the appearance and demeanor of his strapping son, claiming their encounter to be purely by accident.

"And what a wonderful surprise this has turned out to be!" Mr. Raymond had exclaimed, taking a hold of Delmont's hand and giving it a strong shake. "I wish that I could take you home and introduce you to my wife and other children, but that would be too disrespectful to them. Boy, you do understand this, don't you?" He had handed Delmont his business card attached to an envelope filled with hundred-dollar bills, but Delmont handed it right back to him.

Delmont's lips had quivered, as his head shook from side to side. "No, sir; that's not what I want from you." Sondra could have slammed Delmont's body into the soda freezer and thrown a crate of soda pop cans over his head for exhibiting too much pride when their circumstances had been so dire. Raising Delmont had been quite a challenge and Sondra would not have hesitated one second to accept that offer. How many nights had she come home swollen and worn-out from sweeping out store fronts after a day of cleaning houses only to fall into bed for a mere few hours before starting the routine all over again? That money could have gone a long way paying for shoes, jackets, books, and even bread. Lord only knew what an appetite a growing boy such as Delmont had, not to mention how much she would have relished taking a day off from forever moving about on blistered feet.

To her knowledge and continued disappointment, neither Delmont nor Mr. Raymond had been in touch with each other since that one and only meeting. It didn't seem fair to her at all that there was Mr. Raymond with so much wealth and Delmont wanting no part of it. She had close to nothing, but Delmont had no problem taking that from her and even asking for more. *But just how much more could she keep on giving?*

Sondra could hear the rattling sound of dishes and cutlery being distributed in the kitchen. She heard the oven and refrigerator doors being opened and shut and was surprised to see how many of the tables in the dining room had already been set. Dreading that her too short of a break had come to an end, she determined from the face of her digital watch that just four minutes remained before she needed to be upstairs gathering up the lunch bunch. She rose and then fell back down to her seat. With more exerted effort, she tried to lift herself to a standing position again but was once more unsuccessful.

Sondra thought about the few things she had already taken here and there, but Lenny-boy had just paid her pennies for that stuff. Grudgingly, she considered going for

143

the better things. There had to be a valuable old watch or some real gold bracelets lying around. She might even have to start digging into the jewelry cases; perhaps she'd find a diamond brooch or two. Those old ladies loved those baubles, and Lenny-boy's eyes would light up with the prospect of getting his hands on *that* merchandise.

She hated having to steal, but wanting Delmont to have a better life had become her utmost priority. What else was there to do? Sometimes, the old folks hadn't even noticed anything was gone—and if they did complain, it wasn't real hard convincing them that their stuff was just hiding somewhere else. However, Sondra wasn't one hundred percent sure this would ring true this time around with the more important pieces. In any case, it was a risk she felt she had to take.

Dear Lord, Sondra prayed silently, *"you knows how tired I am, and that I keeps on working real hard and dedicated-like with the unaccommodating body you gave me. These people ain't short for nothing; they've got their meals and snacks and entertainment all waiting for them from morning 'til night. The lucky ones even have relatives come and spend some time with them. We all knows this is the last stop. They ain't needing what I'm taking. It ain't harming anyone; I'm just helping Delmont out so he can stay on the right track. You yourself can see how easy it is for Delmont to slip. I don't wanna have to identify his sorry-ass body in some morgue the way that Lucinda had to do with her son, the way he went into a street fight and never came out of it.*

With her eyes still closed, Sondra felt a darkness fall over her and she shivered.

"How much longer you going to be at this table, hon?" Mimi asked, standing at the edge of the table. "I got to have my settings done so's I can start warming up the sweet rolls. I don't want to intrude on your privacy, but I do have my job to do and besides, you know you're supposed to have gotten yourself upstairs already."

"I'll be out of here real soon. I promise," Sondra told Mimi. "Just give me a second or two more. I have something on my mind that needs clearing. If yous can start setting up the plates instead, I'll be very grateful. In fact, I'll do the Bingo calling for the rest of the week."

Mimi left and Sondra continued with her prayer. "I've known enough misery; I sure as hell don't need that added to my burden. I knows you gave me my extra bumps on my ears as a punishment. I can live with them. Old mean-tongued Alice calls them 'cauliflower ears'. I'm plenty used to people talking about me behind my back, but she's got the nerve to speak that nasty right to my face. 'Is that why you wear a straight-haired wig all the time?' she asks. 'Or are you trying to imitate a white woman? If that's so, you're not fooling anyone. I wouldn't wear earrings on the days you're working here, if I were you,' she says. 'It would draw attention to your cauliflower ears and there'd be a whole lot more puking, and we've got plenty of that already!'

"Sometimes Lord, I want to get a hold of that woman and shake her really hard to put some decency back into her, but I guess it's too late for that. She'll be meeting you soon enough for that I guess."

Sondra opened one eye and surveyed the room. She saw the plates lined up on the Corian countertop waiting to be served, and Mimi, standing guard over them, patted her wristwatch and indicated to Sondra to get a move on. Sondra raised the pointer finger on her right hand.

"One more second; just one more second," she mouthed in Mimi's direction.

Mimi shrugged and yelled out, "Please move soon. Mr. Dean's finished his tour and is heading this way."

Sondra had known Mimi, who came from the Dominican Republic, for two years now and had never heard a cross word come out of her mouth. She was one of the sweetest, most obliging women she had ever met. Her husband, Edwin, was a decent man too, one of the rare ones. He held a steady job spraying pesticide with a landscaping crew. They had a little four-year old girl, named Brianna, who suffered from asthma. Edwin was able to bring Brianna to work with him when her wheezing and coughing kept her home from school, so Mimi didn't have to lose pay at Glenbrook. It wasn't the best of solutions, but it was the only one they had.

Sondra's final words came out in rapid succession. "Before I get to my last request, I need you to watch more carefully over Mimi's Brianna. See if you can send extra healing her way. They're good people, but you probably know that already, *being that you're who you are.* So I'm also asking you now, Lord, to give me the strength to get myself up off of my chair and help me move my blubber in the direction of where it now needs to go—especially before Mr. Dean catches sight of me and calls me one of those lazy good-for-nothings!"

Chapter Twenty

By the time Sondra reached the social room, the slide presentation had already ended and many of her people were irritable and anxious, hoping to be escorted as soon as possible to the lower level for their midday meal. As not even the slightest deviation from the customary schedule was ever tolerated well at Glenbrook, Sondra's overdue presence was greeted with many hisses and boos. Amongst the roar of the angry comments, which included "Where have you been?", "What took you so long?", and "Good, she's finally showed up!", Sondra heard Alice declare, "Give the poor girl a break. People the size of a whale can't move that fast."

Choosing to ignore the last of Alice's many put-downs, Sondra shouted, "Yes. Yes, I knows you're hungry. I'm here, aint I? You'll be eating soon enough."

"What's on the menu for today?" James called out from the corner of the room.

"Meatloaf and fried tilapia are your entrée choices, and there's either beef consommé or chicken noodle soup for starters," Sondra responded. The cook did a pretty good job preparing each one of these dishes, and from the excitement in the room, Sondra could tell that the residents were happy with the selection. The belligerent atmosphere began to calm down and Sondra proceeded to guide groups into the elevator four at a time.

Once all the courses had begun to be served, Sondra took her leave of the dining room. She stood a little while outside the arched entranceway, assuring herself that the muted chatter of the room and the clinking of the silverware indicated that everyone was engrossed in their meals. She was hoping for a good fifteen minutes without any interruption as she made Alice's apartment her first destination.

She's got some nice things that her fancy daughter Maureen gave her for her last birthday; I just got to find out where the old badger hid them. This morning, I pulled out clean towels for the bathroom racks so I knows there was nothing in the vanity. In her bra and panties drawer there was nothing else but some gum wrappers and old cough drops. Might be something in the side table though. Filthy stinking dirty tissues! I tell her over and over again that tissues are not to be used again no matter what. "Yous get as many as you want all the time; what you gotta save the ones covered in snot for?" I ask her, but she just stares at me like I'm accusing her of some terrible crime.

***

Seated at her usual table in the dining room, Alice pushed aside her uneaten meatloaf to complain, "This Mexican seasoning is making everything taste way too spicy," and refused the alternative tilapia because, "it had such a nasty odor; the people all the way in Kings Point in Delray Beach are turning their noses up from the smell." Having requested double servings of dessert to make up for her forced starvation, she guzzled down bowls of rice and chocolate puddings with her portion of cake and swiped off three maraschino cherries from puddings on a tray waiting to be served.

Leaving her dining mates, she informed them she'd be seeing them all at the Bingo game, but they should be prepared to lose. "I don't have the patience to sit around forever waiting for you to chew up these gas-inducing meals."

Denise reacted by snarling at Alice, but Helen remained pleasantly smiling, which made Alice realize she hadn't heard a word she said. "What difference does it make what I say?" she confronted Denise. "People are either too deaf or too old to care."

***

After finding nothing noteworthy in the closet, Sondra stealthily approached the standing lamp in Alice's apartment to examine what Bingo winnings had been hidden there. She was so busily rummaging through the contents of the glass bowl, however, she failed to notice Alice leaning on her walker at the foot of her bed.

"If you tell me what you're searching for, I can tell you exactly where it is." Alice's offer cut the air like the falling chunk of an iceberg.

"Oh," Sondra gasped as she swiveled around to face Alice. "I was just taking advantage of this free moment to do some housekeeping."

"It seems to me like you were taking advantage, but not to clean."

Sondra alternated between whistling and singing "la-la-la" as she approached the side table. "Well, that's just what I was doing," she informed Alice before straightening a pile of magazines, and then rolled the top one to sweep a bunch of dirty tissues into a plastic supermarket bag. As she tied the loops of the bag into a knot, Sondra stopped whistling and took Alice to task for not placing her dirty tissues in the trashcan. "I've told you a million times already; now, why is that too difficult to remember? And why are you up here anyway?"

"I came to get my lucky poodle that I tie around my walker," Alice said, ignoring the reference to the tissues. "I want it with me for the Bingo game this afternoon. It must have fallen off this morning. Have you seen it?" Alice would not take her eyes off of Sondra, who was trying her utmost to seem undaunted.

Sondra resumed singing her "la-la-la" as she scanned the carpeted areas and pulled the curtains away from the wall, finding the miniature stuffed animal caught in the folds of the drapery.

"Here you go," she said, forcing a smile on her face. Feeling relieved, she tossed the pink fluff to Alice. "Now you can go down and finish your meal."

Alice chose to sit on her bed instead of leaving.

"Do you want me to tie the poodle around the handlebars for you before you go?" Sondra's words came out saccharine sweet.

Alice sat rigidly, remaining cool and stoic. "No thank you. Sondra, you're pretty anxious to have me go, aren't you?"

"Alice, yous don't want to miss dessert today," Sondra said with immoderate gusto. "They're serving devil's food cake, and I know how much yous love that." She extended her arms to assist Alice to an upright position. "Want me to bring you back to the dining room?"

Alice dug in her heels, folded her arms, and in no uncertain terms stated, "No. I do not. That will not be necessary."

"Suits yourself, then." Sondra resumed her affected humming as she headed toward the door. At the end of the hall, she announced, "Well, I guess I'll just leave you here alone while I go tidy up some of the other residences."

"Didn't find anything worth keeping yet?" Alice asked snidely.

Without turning around, Sondra answered, "I'm not sure what you're referring to."

"I think you do. It looked to me like you were looking awfully hard for something to steal."

Sondra rotated to face Alice. "Are you accusing me of committing such a terrible act because I'm a black woman?"

"Don't throw race into this," Alice said with disgust. "I stood here watching you go through my things not with the intent to clean them up, but to take something. I saw you. The color of your skin has nothing to do with it."

"You're mistaken," Sondra yelled back. "Your mind's playing tricks on you, Alice."

"It isn't to your advantage to raise your voice the way that you just did. I don't get fooled so easily. I may be old, but I am not crazy or hallucinating. If you don't lower your voice and stop acting so offended, then maybe we can work something out. If not, you'll just have Mr. Dean to tell your story to."

Sondra held still while Alice tapped her fingers on her arm. "My patience is running thin, Sondra." She pulled her walker closer. "Tell me what's going on that you have to go stealing my crap. Why would you risk losing a job that gives you a steady income? Does this have anything to do with your good-for-nothing son?"

Sondra shrieked, "Delmont's a good boy. Let's be keeping his name out of this," but she erupted into tears at the mention of her son's name.

"You're not doing such a great job of convincing me that Delmont isn't connected with what's going on here," Alice announced. "I met him when he came here late one afternoon searching for you. Tall, muscular, and athletic, he was. I wouldn't want to bump into him in a dark alley. He seemed to be desperate, so I figured he needed a much-needed handout. He's a good-looking boy; I'll grant you that. But to tell you the truth, right away I pegged him to be a real *schnorrer*. I even told Jan that I thought he was a con artist, but she told me I have a habit of judging people way too harshly. 'Not this one,' I told her. 'I'm right on the button with this guy. As God is my witness, you'll see that time will bear me out.' And it has, hasn't it?"

Sondra sighed, taking in only a half of what was being said and feeling too weak to fully defend her son. "Yes, Alice. You is so smart. You called it just like it is. All young black men have something devious on their minds; that's why everyone in the whole wide world needs to be afraid of them. *Is that what you want to believe?*"

Alice looked Sondra in the face. "I'm not going to lie and say there isn't some truth in what you just said."

Sondra threw up her hands. "I was being sarcastic, Alice. *Sarcastic!* There's no proof for what you're thinking. It's all based on falsehoods and prejudices." She caught herself from delving further into the wrongs of society. Mr. Dean would surely be on her case for that, and where would that get her? Actually, no place different than where she was, right then and there. "Now, if you don't mind, I have my rounds to make. There's plenty left in the day that be needing my attention. I'm not going to stop you from doing what you gotta do." Her voice broke. Another stream of tears spilled from her eyes.

"Sondra, please take that tremendous load off your feet." Alice indicated for Sondra to sit beside her. "Do something smart for a change and come park your gigantic ass next to mine." It surprised Sondra to hear a sliver of kindness come out of Alice's mouth, as backhanded as it might have been.

There was a heavy jolt on the mattress as Sondra plopped down next to Alice. Alice placed her arm around Sondra and said, "Tell me how much you need and why."

Sondra sucked up the mucus flowing from her nostrils, dabbing her cheeks with the tissue Alice handed her. "Don't worry, it's a clean one," Alice said in response to Sondra's hesitancy.

"Delmont is not into doing bad, but he says he needs more money; that's all there is to it. I gives him more money, and then he says he needs even more money." Sondra's explanation came out punctuated with a sequence of sighs, sobs, and sniffling. "I've got him up in that school and that's where I want him to stay. If and when he graduates, then he'll get himself a decent job and have a decent life. That's what I pray for every sweet day of my life."

"So, he needs the money for legitimate reasons?" Alice peered directly into Sondra's eyes.

Sondra's entire body shook as she nodded her head. "Yes, ma'am. That's what he tells me, and I have no reason to suspect anything else. Contrary to what you want to believe, I knows Delmont to be a good boy."

"So you take items from the various apartments here and sell them?"

"I'm truly ashamed to admit it, but yes I do." Sondra swallowed. "I don't grab everything that I see, just one or two pieces that I don't believe will be missed that much. You can tell Mr. Dean and have me fired, 'cause I'm confessing all to you now. I didn't think I'd be causing so much hurt to the residents, but from my point of view, it's like I'd be saving my boy's life."

"I had a son once," Alice whispered so quietly that Sondra needed to repeat the words she thought she heard.

"You had a son besides having Jan and Maureen?"

"Yes," Alice admitted, her face agonizingly grim.

Sondra, somewhat startled and a little hesitant to press Alice for too many details, decided to proceed slowly. "Where's he at now?" she asked timidly, but she had to move within an inch of Alice's face to hear Alice answer.

"I think he passed away."

"Off in Vietnam or the Gulf War?"

Alice's eyelids shut tight. "No, nothing like that at all."

"You don't know if and when your son died?" Sondra asked incredulously.

Alice grasped her walker, arose as abruptly as her delicate body would allow, and announced, "I'm going downstairs to join the others. I suggest you come with me. I do not intend to mention any of this to Mr. Dean or anyone else."

Sondra took this as a cue that the discussion had ended. "Thank you; I do appreciate that," she said wholeheartedly.

"Starting tomorrow, Sondra, we're going to try to figure out a better way to get you all the money that you need. Don't you worry, something will pop up. I'm very good at coming up with fail-proof game plans. We just need to bide our time; let's hope it'll be sooner than later."

Chapter Twenty-one

In preparation for Thanksgiving, which was being celebrated at the end of the week, Charlotte had stretched a four-foot banner across the wall outside Mr. Dean's office. The banner was covered with decals of various sizes, the largest of which was a gold and earth toned cornucopia; next to which was a turkey wearing a top hat, and then there were pencil-colored images of little Indians and pilgrims dotting the empty spaces. "Happy Thanksgiving 2003" was painted across the bottom. Alice repeated to everyone in Arts and Crafts that she did not celebrate Thanksgiving in England, to which Muriel replied, "Yes we know, but you're here now, so give us all a break and finish gluing on the rest of the feathers; they're making my nose itch."

Early Wednesday afternoon, the day before the holiday, Charlotte had requested the work crew rearrange the red brocade sofas in the living room to form a semi-circle facing the fireplace hearth. Additional chairs were brought in to accommodate an expected large crowd, as a musical recital had been planned for the holiday festivities. Charlotte had assigned Helen and Charles the job of distributing photocopied song sheets for the sing-along part of the program to the residents and guests as they sauntered in while she climbed a step stool to hang the "Welcome Strings Alive" sign from the mantel. Alice had begged off participating in the production of this sign, as she claimed that construction paper, glitter, and magic markers were too frou-frou for her liking. Three chairs facing the audience were set up for the trio of string musicians, all of whom were students from the County Music and Art High School.

Having arrived a few minutes earlier, Jan mingled among the many residents gathered in the living room as she waited for Sondra to escort her mother and others down for the event. When the elevator door opened to reveal the bustling activity, Sondra announced merrily, "First Floor, everybody out!"

"Are you feeling all right?" Jan asked after Alice hobbled to her side, looking like the grumpiest of the seven dwarfs.

Kneading the sides of her head, Alice cried, "Today's not a good day for me." She tugged at her collar and rubbed her elbows.

"Why not? Are you sick? Why are you so antsy?"

"My arthritis is acting up again," Alice responded with a sigh. "My knees ache. I've got pains everywhere. I have heaviness on my chest. I have ringing in my ears. How else do you think I should act with ailments like these?"

"I'm sorry to hear all that, but you do smell rather nice, though. Are you wearing the Estee Lauder cologne I bought you?"

"Yes, I am," Alice replied grudgingly. "It's all right; nothing to write home about."

Jan pointed to some unoccupied chairs close by. "Well, I like it. Let's sit down." *Ungrateful wench. I should have poured bathroom spray into a fancy bottle and given her that instead.*

"No, I'd rather be in the back in case I come over poorly; I wouldn't want to cause a scene and draw attention away from the show, as amateurish as it may be. It won't be easy seeing over the ridiculous head pieces some of these idiots are wearing, but I'm willing to make the sacrifice."

As Jan took hold of Alice's elbow to guide her toward the rear of the room, Alice halted to gain Helen's attention. "What am I, chopped liver? You didn't give me or my daughter a *Playbill* yet!" A foghorn would have sounded less intense. Helen, wearing a beaded headband, quickly obliged, and Alice tossed the sheets of paper on an empty seat in the last row.

"Aren't you even going to look at it?" Jan asked.

"Why bother? There'll be music, we will all clap, you'll disappear at lightning speed, and then the rest of us will be able to eat our gobble-gobble dinner. Why don't you stay? It'll be my treat."

Jan indicated she would give Alice's offer some thought, but as soon as Muriel seated herself on the unread programs, Alice turned toward Muriel, ignoring Jan completely. Muriel and Alice gabbed about the weather, the toughness of the lemon sole served at lunch, the skimpy portion of strawberries, the stupidity of a *Wheel of Fortune* contestant from the previous night's show, and an upcoming trip to the Parker Playhouse in Fort Lauderdale, while Jan busied herself looking about the room. Several minutes passed and a boisterous buzz began to arise as an agitated Charlotte came rushing by on her way to the parking lot.

"Plan, plan, plan. That's all I've been doing for weeks on end," Charlotte muttered as she checked her wrist watch. "Nothing's going according to schedule. The trio should have been halfway into their first selection by now, but they haven't even shown up yet." Some of her newly permed curls began to unravel down her cheeks.

On her return to the living room, Charlotte was approached by an anxious looking Mr. Dean, who offered to contact the music director at the school. As he walked toward his office, he kept bending down to pick up blue and red feathers that had fallen to the ground.

"Well, you can assume there isn't going to be any performance today," he reported back to Charlotte. "The minivan had a flat tire just two blocks from the school's campus."

Charlotte removed a green feather from Mr. Dean's suit collar. "They should have called me ages ago to let me know."

"Yes, that would have been the courteous thing to do, but these are kids, and they don't think that way at all." He rubbed the tip of his nose briskly to dislodge a sticky, red feather that had taken up residence there while a blue feather wafted into Charlotte's hair.

"Uncivilized: that's what this world is coming to," Charlotte complained, scratching her head. "No one cares about manners or about being polite anymore."

The noise from the living room was growing louder. Many of the headbands and *Playbills* were being thrown on the floor. "You can theorize as much as you want about the bleak future of the universe," Mr. Dean warned, "but you need to turn your attention to the natives, who are becoming alarmingly restless as we speak. There's still an hour and a half before dinner, so do conjure up something to keep them from rebelling."

Charlotte proposed bringing everyone to the second floor for an Arts and Crafts project.

Overhearing Charlotte, Charles lamented, "I don't feel like making paper baby dolls." Sharing the bad news with the rest of the residents, he shook the balance of unused *Playbills* in the air. "Everyone, you might as well throw these in the trashcan since there'll be no concert today."

There was an outpouring of remarks, illustrating the disappointment and confusion in the room.

"Oh dear."

"What a pity."

"I was so looking forward to hearing that performance."

"What the heck is going on?"

Muriel turned to Alice and asked if she wanted to take a taxi ride to the Indian casino.

"I can't," Alice replied. "I'm stuck keeping my daughter company. Who even knows if the casinos are open on this holiday? Then again, why would the Indians celebrate the day they all got massacred?"

"I'm here because you pleaded with me to be here," Jan reminded her mother.

"Well that was only to hear the concert," Alice responded. "Now that there isn't going to be one, you might as well just get up and leave. You're not going to want to make some stupid doo-dads that belong in a kindergarten class."

"And by the way," Jan added, "Thanksgiving is a time to express gratitude and reflect upon the spirit of brotherhood and cooperation." *Something you know nothing about.*

Mr. Dean walked over to the "Welcome Strings Alive" sign and announced, "May I have your attention, please? We are going to relocate to the upstairs social room in an organized manner."

The residents responded with a ruckus of bad-tempered complaints.

"All this for nothing?"

"Will they cancel Christmas as well?"

"I'd rather be watching Maury Povich."

"It has been upsetting," Mr. Dean added, "but please help us to work around this situation as best we can."

Jan, understanding full well what it meant to feel hopeless, couldn't help but feel sorry for the residents being shepherded and maneuvered like a flock of sheep after having waited in good faith for so long for a concert that was never going to take place. Mimi and Sondra went through the aisles trying to calm the most disgruntled.

How about letting them stay in place, engaged in a stimulating discussion instead of subjecting them to some infantile diversion? Most of their minds are still in pretty good shape. Anyone can lead it; even I. No, I can't. Don't get up. Just keep sitting; this isn't my problem. Oh, what have I got to lose?

Jan took to her feet and skirted past three parked wheelchairs, stepping over several walking canes to grab the middle seat facing the audience.

"What's she doing?" Muriel asked.

"I've no idea. She's tone deaf, so I doubt she's got the audacity to sing," Alice answered. "I sincerely hope she doesn't make a fool of herself and embarrass me while she's at it."

"What do you think?" Jan asked no one in particular, but loud enough for everyone to hear. "Do you think the performers should have called to let us know they were stranded?"

"Yes, of course," Muriel replied. Her sentiment was echoed by mostly everyone present except for Alice, who sat silently and appeared to be shocked by her daughter's actions.

Jan continued. "Do you believe that our society has changed for the better or the worse?"
This time, no one answered. "Well, are our children less polite than the way you were taught to be?"

"You're darn tootin!" someone shouted. "It's the damn television giving people license to act like ruffians."

"Who said that?" Jan asked the audience, and Harold raised his hand to take ownership of the statement.

For the next fifty minutes, Jan led the discussion, trying to engage as many of the residents as she could. She heard further comments from Muriel, Denise, Natalie, Joe, Morris, and several others. Helen added that children used to be afraid of their teachers and that they didn't use to speak back to their parents or principals. Charlie said that a good spanking didn't hurt anyone and that now no one could dish out a decent punishment because they were all afraid of a lawsuit.

Alice sheepishly raised her hand. "Miss, I have an observation to contribute."

Jan didn't understand why her mother was calling her "Miss." It was the first time she had chosen to participate, and Jan wasn't sure if she should recognize her as "Alice" or "Mom."

"Yes, the lady in the red and white striped shirt. Do you have something to add?"

Alice pointed to herself and Jan confirmed, "Yes, you!"

Taking the time to enunciate each syllable with perfect elocution, Alice said, "When I was a little girl, we didn't speak unless we were spoken to."

Jan answered, "Ah, thank you. Things have certainly changed since then." *Shoot me now, why don't you?* She then glanced around the room and asked, "Anyone else care to comment?"

Notwithstanding Alice's dig, Jan received nothing but raves for her spur-of-the moment exchange—so much so, that both Charlotte and Mr. Dean both approached her to consider continuing such a program on a regular basis.

Charlotte recommended the future sessions take place upstairs in the lounge area by the fireplace. "Hey, I've even come up with a great title. We'll call your program 'Fireside Chats.' What do you think?"

Mr. Dean proposed that Charlotte add the activity to the Daily Events Flyer for the next week. "That is Jan, if you're amenable,"

"I'm not properly qualified," Jan protested. "And, even if I agreed to do so, I couldn't consider starting until after the New Year."

"What you did was absolutely perfect," Mr. Dean exclaimed with over-the-top enthusiasm for such a milquetoast personality as his. "I could tell how much everyone enjoyed it, and what's more, I refuse to take no for an answer."

Charlotte gave Jan a warm hug and said, "I'll set it up for Thursday afternoons beginning in January. I might be overly optimistic, but I'm pretty sure we've got a winner here!"

Chapter Twenty-two

Besides being one of the busiest times of the year, when everyone in South Florida seemed to be hosting an end-of-2003 celebration, the calendar in Jan's Palm Pilot was crammed with entries sending her in all sorts of directions. Arranging for guest speakers for an exhibit on the Holocaust, planning a weekend retreat for the synagogue, and overseeing the repaving of her community's roads were among the many activities vying with her legal work and her incessant running back and forth to Glenbrook.

Rarely was she not rushing about, but when she could find a moment to relax, her thoughts invariably gravitated to the frostiness escalating once more between her and Mike. It troubled Jan just how aloof and less affectionate her husband was becoming.

I'm the one who has to initiate a hug or kiss. I'm the only one calling to say "hello." I'm the only one wishing a "good night" or a "good morning" or asking "how has your day been?" It's never ever the other way around. Mike's taking more trips, attending more seminars, eating out more dinners and lunches, and claiming all the while it's all to do with his business. Business, my ass!

Before climbing into bed one evening, Jan decided to confront Mike, who was already under the comforter and flipping through the pages of his photography magazines. She asked if there was anything out of the ordinary causing him to feel bothered or more perturbed than usual. "Was it something I said? Did I offend you? Are you under a lot of stress at work?"

Mike's attention was centered on the camera ads, and he issued a lot of unrevealing "No's."

"Whom have you been having dinner with so much?" she asked, trying to sound nonchalant.

"Not one person in particular," he answered, eyeing the winning entries from the *Best Shots of the Month*.

"What about lunch? I noticed you haven't been brown-bagging it for a while."

Mike turned a page and mumbled, "Same old, same old people: a lot of wholesalers and brokers."

"What about Gillian McVey?" Jan inquired.

Mike started to read an article on zoom lenses and answered, "What about her?"

"Does she fit into any of those categories?"

"Why yes. I guess she does," Mike said, fully engrossed in the article.

"How many times?" Jan asked, her voice taking on urgency. "How many times?"

"How many times what?" Mike asked without looking up.

"How many times have you gotten together with Gillian McVey?" Jan tore the magazine out of Mike's hand and threw it off the bed.

"A few times," Mike offered but his reaction was far more controlled and less enraged than she would have anticipated.

If nothing out of the ordinary is going on and Mike is above suspicion, then why didn't he become more furious over what I just did?

"Please go and get me my magazine back. I haven't finished reading it," Mike requested. "You're acting like a spoiled child, by the way."

He's acting too deliberate. I can tell he's purposefully pacing himself, trying to not let any of the truth leak out. He's still so good-looking at fifty-six; it's obvious that Gillian is out to nab him.

Jan jumped off the bed and retrieved the magazine, but she wouldn't give it back to Mike until he supplied further details.

He acknowledged their get-togethers had been haphazard and completely innocent. Gillian was an insurance broker with lots of leads for Mike's financial practice; he had been hoping their friendship could be mutually beneficial. As far as the photography club to which Mike belonged, it had been purely coincidence that Gillian had signed up as well. With regard to spending too much time at Gillian's house, there was a high-hat that had burst all the way up on a fifteen-foot ceiling, a kitchen cabinet door had fallen off its hinge and was hanging precariously over her tiled floor, and her generator needed to be started and checked out periodically. He just so happened to be passing by the mall when her son needed to be picked up and he didn't mind running into Publix to grab a dozen eggs at the same time.

"Just how stupid do you think I am?" Jan asked, her hands bent at the waist and her elbows projecting pointedly outward.

"Right now, I'm sorry to say 'very stupid,' because your imagination is running wild with preposterous ideas. It doesn't become you."

"That's some poker face you have on," Jan replied. "I can't tell if you are lying or not."

"I'm not a liar."

Jan took note of his blue, oversized sleep shirt, the one they had picked out together while rummaging through the clearance rack of an outlet store. "I'm worried about us," she announced.

"Oh? That's a shocker! I've been warning you forever how unhappy I've been. You haven't seemed to care before."

"So what's next then?" she asked, feeling crushed and alone.

"Perhaps it's time to see a marriage counselor. Will you agree to that?"

"Why *that* route, Mike?" Jan shrieked. "Are you all set to leave me for Gillian? Arranging your ducks in a row, huh? Complying with the mandatory step for a Florida divorce?"

"I'm not going to say the thought has never crossed my mind, especially when you behave like this."

"Like what?"

"With overblown theatrics; acting like a raving lunatic! How many times have I warned you that I'm reaching my limit?"

Neither Jan nor Mike were able to sleep peacefully that evening, and they were barely civil to each other the next morning, dodging bodily contact in the bathroom and at the breakfast table. Jan felt as if her entire world was collapsing. She wasn't sure if she wanted to go on living if it meant Mike would no longer be a part of her life. When Mike backed up his car from the garage to go to work, Jan ran to tap on his window.

She heard the news blasting from the Audi's radio. "Go ahead and make the appointment," she called out, pushing back on the extended branches of an elephant plant. Afraid she hadn't been heard, she was relieved to see Mike give her a thumb's up. Jan retraced her steps on the driveway but forced herself not to look in the direction of Gillian's house.

Chapter Twenty-three

Despite his laidback disposition, Rick, the marriage counselor, took copious notes. It seemed to Jan that he was writing down a lot more of what Mike was saying than any of her comments. She and Mike were sitting at opposite ends of a brown leather couch; Rick parked closer to the window in a tan club chair. Wearing denim jeans and a pale blue Chambray shirt, Rick looked right at home. Jan thought, *If he wanted to be viewed more professionally, he should have taken a position right smack in the middle instead of being on Mike's side of the room.* She wondered if Mike and Rick already knew each other. *Perhaps Mike has previously told Rick that the marriage is over and our meeting today is just a mere formality.*

"So, let's begin by one of you telling me how you met," Rick said.

Mike turned to Jan and said, "Okay, you can start."

"We met quite unexpectedly at a party in my junior year of college," Jan explained. She followed this statement with a brief description of their marriage, the birth of their son, and their subsequent move to Florida.

"That's the black and white version," Rick commented. "Can you provide a little more color? We have plenty of time."

Jan continued. "I thought he was a quiet, kind, strait-laced guy who was very chivalrous—which to be honest, absolutely infuriated me."

"Why is that?" Rick asked, tenting his fingers. His manner of speaking appeared to Jan to be nonconfrontational, making him easy to talk to.

"Because I had grown up with a father who was cruel, callous and aggressive. That's what I had erroneously equated with masculinity and I thought that there might have been something deficient in Mike in terms of his manhood."

Rick leaned back in his chair. "And yet, you were still attracted to him?"

Turning to face Mike, Jan answered, "Yes. In the beginning, Mike's actions made it seem like I was something of value, and that made *him* seem desperate. But as we continued to date, something inside kept telling me he was the right one. He had shown me unconditional love— something I had never known before and sorely needed. I came to love him very much and still do."

"So, would you say Mike provided you with a safe emotional structure in which to thrive?" Rick asked.

"Absolutely. He showed me he was someone I could trust; not an easy thing for me to do. He had me convinced he would always be there."

Rick slid forward. "And you don't feel that support or trust is there now?" He scribbled something on his pad, which Jan wished she could see.

"No, I do not," Jan answered sadly. "I don't trust that Gillian woman either. There's something going on between them." She eyed Rick to see if these words were being recorded as well.

Mike crossed his arms and shook his head vehemently. "There's nothing's going on between me and Gillian," He was about to say more but Jan cut him short.

"Rick, let me tell you: There's been way too much 'Hi, Mike; when you coming over? Can you fix my door? Can you fix my garbage can? Oh Mike, what well-built muscles you have. How do you like my new boob job,

Mike? Ooh, I baked you a cake, Mike.'" Jan hoped Rick was taking ample notes on this part, capturing the essential points. She glanced sideways at Mike and caught him distorting his face in disgust. *Perhaps, I went a little too overboard just then, but most of it is true.*

Mike explained to Rick that since Gillian's husband was stationed in Ethiopia as a subcontractor for the army, he was just being neighborly and helping her out, which took Jan by surprise because she had assumed all along that Gillian was a divorcee.

"You were helping her out by taking her to dinner?" Jan attacked. "That's the sort of thing we should have done as a couple."

"Rick, she sells insurance. We've been discussing ways to refer business to each other," Mike defended.

Rick allowed for a few more minutes of bickering and then said, "The volleying back and forth is helpful, but I would like to move on."

Jan felt like she had been roughed up in a rock tumbler. Mike, remaining calm and collected, cleared his throat, and Rick flipped over a page on his legal pad.

"So," Rick proceeded, "Am I right in saying that there is also tension in your home because you cannot agree on the level of care that is needed for Jan's mother?"

"Yes, without a doubt," Mike answered.

Jan closed her mouth and breathed in through her nose, letting the air fill her lungs. After exhaling slowly, she concurred, "Yes, that is a fair assumption."

"Okay then," Rick offered with a reassuring smile. "We all appear to be on the same page. So, Mike, tell me why you're so upset with the current arrangement."

While Mike recited a litany of complaints, Jan scanned the titles on the bookshelves. "My wife is unnaturally obsessed with her mother. She has made everything else secondary to that. Like a magnet, she is continuously drawn to where her mother resides, and then finds it impossible to break free. This has been going on for almost forever."

"Only it really is necessary nowadays," Jan interrupted, hoping for an endorsement from Rick. "You hear all about the abuse that goes on in these places, and it's best if a relative makes a frequent appearance to deter it." She shifted to the edge of the cushion. "Iris's father was in a nursing home and developed the most atrocious bedsores because he wasn't receiving adequate care. Sharon's another friend; her mother went wandering off from a different home and was missing for days. Someone has to be an advocate for my mother, and unfortunately, it has to be me."

"Yes, but you're more her dishrag," Mike argued. "You're not much of an advocate for anyone."

"That's spiteful," Jan accused.

"It's the truth!" Mike answered. "Glenbrook is simply not providing substandard care. There is no abuse going on there." Turning to Rick, he added, "She thoroughly vetted the place beforehand."

"You two are doing great so far," Rick said, "but I'd prefer that you converse with each other and not look to me for input."

Disregarding Rick's request, Jan informed him that in parts of Asia and Russia, taking care of an aging parent was required by law and not just a moral obligation.

"It's me you're supposed to be talking to," Mike announced. "By the way, here's a newsflash: we live in America. You can tell us both: was she ever such a wonderful mother to you? How about to Henry? Did she humiliate you every chance she could?"

Jan remained silent.

"So, what's so difficult about treating her in the same vein?" Mike pleaded.

Jan's phone began to vibrate. She had turned off the ringer when she first sat down.

"I'm sorry, but I have to take this call; it's from Glenbrook," Jan said.

Mike threw his arms into the air. "See? What did I tell you?"

The staff nurse from Glenbrook was calling to notify that Alice had ingested too many aspirins. She was inquiring as to how Alice had obtained the aspirins, as her drugs were solely administered in the vacuum-sealed packs under Glenbrook's control. There was some concern that Alice may be developing an addiction.

"Are you aware your mother has been trading toiletries for medication with other residents?"

"No."

"Are you aware your mother has been buying medicines from other residents?"

"No."

"All of her medications are supposed to be restricted to the blister packs we supply. We found loose Valium, Ambien, and Lexapro wrapped up in tissues and stuffed into pockets of her clothing, but we're pretty sure that this one incident involved only aspirins. Have you been supplying your mother with her own aspirins, contrary to the regulations on the commitment documents you signed?"

"No; not at all. Is my mother going to be all right? Where is she now?"

"She was examined by the doctor on call. His advice was to allow her to rest and to keep her well hydrated. She'll be fine in a few hours or so. In the meantime, can you please ascertain where the pills came from? We'll continue our investigation over here."

As soon as the conversation with the nurse ended, Jan shared the nature of the call with Mike and Rick.

Flipping her phone from one hand to the other, she asked Mike, "You don't know anything about those aspirins, do you?"

With embarrassment very much evident on his face, Mike admitted, "Actually, yes I do; that little sneak! Last Friday night after dinner, she started to cry when you were out of the room. She said she had the most terrible headache and asked for Tylenol or Advil. I gave her a half empty bottle of pills and then she begged me to give her a few more in case the headache came back in the middle of the night."

"Why did you do it, Mike?"

"She didn't stop sobbing; she looked so pitiful that I really felt sorry for her."

"Uh huh. What was that you said about not letting her manipulate me?" Jan turned toward Rick and said, "I'm sorry, but I have to get over to Glenbrook. This is an emergency situation—it can't be helped."

Rick uttered, "Of course, I understand, but before you go can I count on your commitment to work with Mike on this particular issue in the future?"

"Yes, most definitely," Jan answered, grabbing her pocketbook and slinging it hastily over her shoulder. She leaned over to kiss Mike goodbye before running to her car.

Chapter Twenty-four

Jan drove over to Glenbrook to check in on her mother, but stopped off first to meet with the nurse, informing her of Mike's culpability with the aspirins. The nurse's station on the second floor was the size of a closet but large enough to house a desk, chair, and a small Christmas tree with one strand of twinkling lights. Although the nurse was sympathetic to the scenario that Jan portrayed, she did issue a stern warning, indicating there would be consequences in the event of a reoccurrence. From the nurse, Jan learned that Alice was still asleep, and as of the latest examination, appeared to be out of any immediate danger.

Jan took her time walking in the direction of her mother's apartment, girding herself for the onslaught of conflicting emotions that this last medical mishap would resurrect. Passing through the third-floor lounge, she came across Helen, Denise, and Sophie, sitting by the lit, oak-encased fireplace where "Merry Christmas" and "Happy Chanukah" banners hung from the mantle.

When she had first noticed an infrared fireplace installed on each floor at Glenbrook, Jan thought it a silly mistake in the design concept, given the tropical climate in which Glenbrook was located. *If it's hot and humid here for much of the year, why would anyone want to sit in front of a pretend flame radiating a ton of heat? These old people can't possibly be fooled into believing it's freezing cold outside, so what gives?*

Jan had since come to realize that while much of Florida's youth walked around in shorts for most of the year, its elderly population tended to be clad in sweaters while complaining of persistent chills. She now appreciated the coziness of the hearths and the inviting ambiance they created in the social rooms—with or without their heat features being turned on.

Sophie and Denise were seated in their wheelchairs, but Sophie was positioned higher off the ground, as her wheelchair was bulkier and less automated than Denise's. A black and white mesh tote bag filled with knitting needles and skeins of blue speckled yarn sat on Sophie's lap. Both women suffered from severe diabetes and were transported to dialysis treatments on a regular basis. Even though Sophie had lost a kidney to the disease, she did not have to be taken to the hospital as frequently as Denise. The first time Denise was taken away on a stretcher, Jan lined up with everyone else at Glenbrook to wish her well. The second time, Jan was there along with the others to send her off with the same fanfare. After a while, however, Denise's comings and goings—which were separated by extended hospital stays—were no longer deemed newsworthy and no one could really account for her presence or absence much of the time. "She could be in the hospital, she could be having her hair washed, or she could be on the moon," Alice would say in response to Jan's probing. "Even Mimi and Sondra don't have a clue as to where Denise is right now, so how the hell should I know or care?"

Jan took a seat on the velvet couch next to Helen and answered the other women's enquiries about Alice's status. Jan could tell they genuinely cared about her mother's well-being, which struck her as odd; they obviously didn't see Alice the same way she did. The conversation moved on to accents as Denise related how the customers at the thrift shop used to love hearing Alice speak. "It made the store seem very classy," she declared. "Your mother was a wonderful salesgirl. She could sell the biggest piece of junk,

174

suckering people into believing it came from a palace or a castle."

"Unfortunately, she thinks her accent gives her license to say whatever's on her tongue," Helen shared, "but I let most of what she says roll off my back." She was dressed in a grey pleated skirt and a mauve cashmere twinset that was trimmed with seed pearls.

"Are you going somewhere special today?" Jan inquired.

Helen replied that her sciatica was bothering her so she was "staying put."

"Well, you look awfully smart for someone going nowhere."

"This is how I was taught to dress, Jan. No t-shirts or dungarees were ever allowed in my wardrobe when I was growing up."

Jan's curiosity was piqued. "Where else did you live then before moving here to Florida?"

"After graduating college in Iowa, I travelled a lot, never living in any one place long enough to call it home. I've been all around the world and then some."

"So, when you married was it to a military man?"

"No," Helen answered with a chuckle. Her eyes glistened and a warm glow spread across her cheeks. "My husband was a pilot who worked for an oil company. That's why we were always on the go, enjoying countless adventures. It was a wonderful life and a wonderful marriage. Once my sons were born, though, I stayed home to take care of them and let my husband do the gallivanting on his own."

That's what my husband's doing all right, Jan thought. *Gallivanting!*

Sophie, in a squeaky, high pitch, asked Helen how she could be so trusting.

"I didn't have a choice. That was the way things were back then. You accepted your lot in life and did a lot less grumbling than the younger ones do now."

Helen, as sweet and as deferential as you are, you wouldn't have taken too kindly to Gillian McVey either.

"It's true. Our lives were harder, but we made less noise about it," Denise concurred.

Jan asked Denise if she ever married.

"Absolutely; I married the love of my life. We were childhood sweethearts. Haven't you ever seen him when he comes visiting?"

Jan responded in the negative.

"He took care of me as long as he could," Denise answered, shrugging and cocking her head to one side, her voice weakening, "and then we agreed it would be best for me to move in here. No point in his dying ahead of me from the strain my illness was putting us through." Jan tried to focus on the lilac peonies printed on the nightgown sprouting out from under Denise's cover-up while Denise swallowed, shutting her eyelids.

Turning to Sophie, who had begun to unravel a string of wool from a ball of yarn, Jan asked, "What about you? What kind of marriage did you have?"

"He was a tailor who worked in the back room of a cleaning shop shortening hems, letting out seams, sewing on buttons, and hating every minute of it." Sophie touched the lapel on her jacket. "This is just one of the many clothes he made for me. If you look close enough you can see the buttons and the buttonholes don't match up. He just didn't have his heart in what he did."

Jan asked why he didn't quit and try some other field.

"Because," Sophie answered, "that's what his father had done as well as his father before him. Sam didn't know any other trade. After he came back from the war, we were lucky he had some way to make a living. It put two kids through college, camp, and braces, and when he finished paying off the last semester's tuition he was diagnosed with pancreatic cancer and died three months later."

"Oh, I'm so sorry," Jan said, hoping to sound appropriately sympathetic.

"I like to wear this jacket as much as I can. Of course, your mom mocks me plenty for it, calling me a 'poor little ragamuffin on wheels.'"

Jan pressed her lips together, attempting to conceal the repulsion she was feeling for her mother at that moment. She reached forward to tap Sophie's knee. "I'm sure she doesn't mean anything by it." Speaking to all three women, she added, "You all have such interesting, albeit somewhat sad, stories to tell."

Helen took Jan's hand in hers. "You should have been here last year when Geraldine was still alive; she was the oldest survivor from the Titanic and told us things none of us had ever heard before. More than what was in the movie even!"

"And what about our Holocaust survivors from the Nazi camps?" Denise contributed. "They have altogether different stories to share."

"And you should see how their children dote on them," Helen added, squeezing Jan's hand. "There's nothing they wouldn't do for their parents—especially after all the unspeakable misery they experienced."

"I wouldn't want to trade places with those kids," Denise said. "They have it plenty rough; feeling guilty for every little thing they have in life, knowing that their parents' lives were filled with so much horror."

Sophie shook her head and commiserated, "You see? No one goes through life unscathed."

.

Chapter Twenty-five

Jan reached her mother's apartment and met Sondra standing outside the door. Sondra was sporting a new floral tunic over turquoise scrub pants. A flashing Santa Claus pin was affixed to her collar and a pearl snowman swayed from each of her ears. With a bright orange, curly wig topping her head, Sondra informed Jan that Alice was doing okay but in a deep sleep.

"Do you think my mother was trying to kill herself?" Jan asked as she waited for Sondra to find the right key to open the door.

"Not at all. Uh-uh; your momma's still got plenty of life left in her," Sondra responded. "She complains about her headaches all the time but is too impatient to wait between doses. The doctor's checked her out plenty, and you know the MRI and CAT scans showed nothing at all. She just be thinking if she take a whole load of them at one time then the headache won't ever come back at all."

"She shouldn't have gotten her hands on that many aspirins at one time," Jan stated.

"I knows she shouldn't," Sondra agreed, appearing upset. "I knows this sounds like a crazy time to tell you, Jan, but you really don't have to be here as much as you are. Take a break; it would do you some good, and it wouldn't hurt Miss Alice 'cause I'll still be here to take very good care of her. I knows it doesn't look that way given the circumstances now."

Jan placed a consoling hand on Sondra's shoulder. "You're not to blame at all. Mike gave my mother the pills. She can be sneaky."

"I wouldn't be expecting that kind of behavior from your husband," Sondra said.

There are a lot of things I wouldn't be expecting him to do.

"He's always acting so right and proper whenever I sees him," Sondra added.

"Well, you can never be a hundred percent certain of what any person is capable of doing, can you?"

"Ain't that the truth," Sondra agreed while playing with the keys on her keychain.

"Why do you have her apartment locked?" Jan asked.

"I didn't want the maintenance crew going in there and disturbing her. They're going around changing the A/C filters, and hers can be done some other day."

Jan nodded. "That makes sense. Thank you for being so considerate."

"They wanted to call your sister Maureen to come as well. I hope I didn't do wrong by telling them it wasn't necessary. I figured you'd call her if you wanted to. She hardly comes at all, and it don't seem to bother Miss Alice that much."

"Well, Maureen travels a lot and she helps plenty in other ways."

"Jan, maybe you should do more traveling and less visiting around here too. Why don't you take a quick look at her and then you can be off?"

The elevator doors opened and two repairmen exited carrying tool boxes and air conditioner filters. As they walked past Sondra and Jan, Sondra asked the men if they had finished replacing filters on the third floor. One of the men explained that all the apartments would be completed that afternoon. "We'll be making the rounds again, though, changing all the broken light bulbs."

Jan peeked in on Alice while Sondra continued to speak with the repairmen. She discovered Alice fast asleep and covered up to her chin, looking quite the cherub. Maureen's words from the past trickled into Jan's head:

"Our mother is not as vacuous or as fragile as you think. Jack and I are in absolute agreement on this. We'll do what is necessary to keep her alive, fed, and clothed, but beyond that neither of us is interested in doing more. She doesn't deserve more than that."

When she returned to Sondra, the men were well on their way to the end of the hallway. Jan asked, "Did you ever feel driven to do something you wish you could stop—almost like a bad habit but more complicated than that?"

Sondra's response flew out of her mouth. "I certainly do, especially when it involves Del—" but then she clammed up tight. She angled her body against the wall for support. "I'd say sometimes I do and sometimes I don't, but right now, I'd have to say that my feet sure are growing tired of supporting what's on top of them."

"It's very, very complicated for me," Jan admitted ruefully. "I feel compelled to help my mother almost to the exclusion of doing anything else."

"That's a mighty heavy burden to have on your shoulders," Sondra said.

Just then, Helen slipped by in the hallway on the way to Harold's apartment. Lowering her voice, Sondra told Jan, "In case you didn't know, Helen and Harold are now a pair; them two have moved in together."

"Good for them," Jan exclaimed, temporarily expressing a glimmer of joy. "It looks like Helen is doing her own fair share of gallivanting."

"They make a really cute couple." Sondra giggled. "Every time you be seeing them together, they be holding hands and smiling. Some of the other women are mad 'cause Helen got a hold of him and they didn't."

"The others will get over it soon enough," Jan assured Sondra. "Although, Maureen blames my mother for staying in her marriage and has never gotten over it. She believes Alice preferred to have our father beat up on us instead of her."

"And what you be thinking about that, Jan?"

The keychain Sondra had been tossing from one hand to the other fell to the floor, so Jan quickly stooped to grab a hold of it, but Sondra told her, "It's all right; I got it." Sondra wheezed as she bent over and Jan lent support to Sondra's elbow as she rose back up. Sounding out of breath, Sondra asked, "Do you believe that, Jan? You think it didn't hurt your mama to know yous all was being beat up on?"

Jan tried to explain about the cultural limitations of women in England when Alice married Norman. She talked about the Battered Spouse Syndrome and how powerless her mother must have been.

"I sure don't see your mama as a powerless woman," Sondra commented, still panting. "Hon, if we're going to be talking a while, I might consider sitting on the floor, but I'm not so sure I'd be able to get off my butt again. How about we park ourselves in the two chairs by the elevator?"

As she and Sondra strolled toward the elevator, Jan considered how often she had been slighted or offended by her mother's actions. She pictured her mother laughing in her face, telling her how ugly and goofy she looked.

Huffing and puffing, Sondra took her seat beside a potted poinsettia plant wrapped in red foil for the holiday season. She fanned her face with a handkerchief and then

182

dabbed under her chin. "I should buy only the cotton uniforms from now on because the polyester ones retain way too much heat. Now, where were we, Jan? Yous was saying your mama was a powerless woman."

"She had no idea how to parent, not having any formal education and such," Jan said, and then wished she could take it back because Sondra's face became contorted.

"There's plenty of good, hard working parents in this world who do mighty fine with their children even though they don't have no formal education." Sondra took a gulp of air and then carried on. "Ain't that something that comes natural to most people? I have a son just like you do, Jan. Didn't take no parenting course to raise him, did you?" Her eyes flashed open and then closed into tight slits, making Sondra's irritation even more conspicuous.

"No, I didn't take a parenting class," Jan revealed, "but it hasn't been so wonderful in the mother/son department at my end." She hoped this confession would convince Sondra they were both on the same side. "How about your relationship with Delmont; what has that been like? It must have been difficult raising a son as a single mother, if you don't mind me saying so."

"I've had my challenges," Sondra answered, inching her butt forward so she could lean further back in the chair. "It's plenty hard for a young black man in America to get ahead." Her expression turned gritty and determined. "You got to worry about things no white mothers have to worry about. Bad enough there are street gangs and such, but you also got to worry about run-ins with the police and how they'll treat your boy, even if he ain't done no wrong."

"The jails are overcrowded with lots of young black men, most of whom I don't believe are guilty," Jan contended.

Sondra nodded and said, "That's what I'm talking about. I don't want my Delmont to be one of those statistics."

"No. Of course you don't," Jan said. "I wouldn't want that either for Daniel. No mother in their right mind would want to see their child harmed in any way."

The elevator doors opened and Jan recognized Sydney Penofsky hobbling out with his aide, Clara, assisting him. Clara asked Sondra if the maintenance crew had finished with Sydney's apartment because he needed to take a rest. Sondra gave Clara and Sydney the go ahead.

"So's you don't sees your sister that much, huh?" Sondra asked. "I gather she don't have much to worry about in the money department."

Jan told Sondra about the comfortable life Maureen enjoyed with her husband, Jack, and about the professional careers of their children.

"Seems to me her kids turned out mighty fine," Sondra said. "I hope I can say the same for my son one day."

Jan wished her own family was not so spread out across the world, and she was just about to express this sentiment but then thought better of it. *Didn't Sondra leave her family in the Bahamas? Didn't she have one of her sisters living in Boston and a brother in Texas? And where was her son Delmont? Up in some northern school and very seldom here.*

"I sees my sister, Ambrose, every time I goes back to the Bahamas and she comes here to Florida every six months."

"Yes, you introduced me to her that one time." Jan smiled, recalling Ambrose's affable personality.

"I'll tell you something: she sure is nuts about Alice. Spent an entire afternoon with her, fixing up her hair and doing her nails on account of that's what Ambrose does in Freeport."

"It sounds like you're very proud of her," Jan commented with enthusiasm.

"I sure am," Sondra acknowledged, her face beaming. "She's a successful business woman with her own beauty parlor shop. Ambrose has as much flair for making money as she does for knowing what's in fashion. Last time she come, your mother and her were talking up a storm, laughing like little sassy girls enjoying a splash in the ocean with nothing else on their minds to worry about."

The elevator doors opened again and Charlotte stuck out her head. "Anyone here seen Mr. Dean? I'm looking for him; he's not picking up his cell phone."

Both Sondra and Jan shook their heads and Charlotte reentered the elevator, holding back the door from closing after she spied Clara hurrying toward her. "I'm just running down to fetch a snack for Sydney," Clara explained.

Sondra eyed her watch and tapped Jan on her knee. "Come on now, Jan. I need you to pull me up. It's time we both check in on your mother again." The two women ambled down the hallway toward Alice's apartment, walking arm in arm.

Chapter Twenty-six

When Thursday, January 8 rolled around, Jan pulled a pair of beige pants and a cream blouse out from her closet, trying her best to project a professional appearance. She topped off the outfit with a navy blazer, brown spectator pumps, a pearl necklace, and gold earrings. As she drove her usual route to Glenbrook, she sang along with a Golden Oldies tune playing on her car radio, and was neither perturbed nor grateful when a slow driver forced her to miss the green arrow signal to turn onto Seacrest Road.

In preparation for her first Fireside Chat, Jan had spent considerable time reviewing several Bible passages. She believed that most of the elderly people would be familiar with the personages from the Old Testament, and the challenges these characters had faced would be a good stepping stone for a discussion.

Jan's father had been very much schooled in Judaic studies and considered himself quite a scholar in this regard. Without having made a personal commitment to observing the rituals, he had been highly critical of anyone he considered to be a traitor to his faith. Paying honor and respect to the elderly and one's parents was a theme Norman had repeated often in his rants, despite his distancing himself from his own parents at a very early age.

Beginning when Jan was quite young, Norman had regularly subjected her to his fanatical, religious instruction. "Now get this into your head: you must always obey me. I am your father, and as such you do as I say. You've heard of Sodom and Gomorrah, haven't you? They were evil. They sinned. They were tortured and destroyed. Disobey me, and God will surely do the same to you."

While continuing her research on the internet, however, she had gravitated to the narratives of Eve, Rebecca, Leah, Esther, and Tamar—all of whom had used deception or feminine wiles to achieve their goals. As Jan had read about their tales of trickery, she learned that these matriarchs had all been portrayed as implementing the goals of divine will.

Curiosity had then led Jan to investigate further about the mythical femme fatales throughout history, and as she did so, she had become more and more unnerved. These notorious women had employed charm, lies, or coercion to captivate and hypnotize their victims into compromising, dangerous, and deadly situations. They were the "dark ladies", spider women, and evil seductresses who immobilized and mummified their prey. Utilizing tools that worked best for them, they had gained powers society had previously denied them.

Why, Alice Block, you fit right in with these heroines!

Jen had then become fascinated with a black and white illustration of a female superhero squatting in a spider's web that popped out from an array of Google images. The more she had stared at that particular image, the more she couldn't decide if it depicted a figure on the prowl or one who had been caught.

It really could be either one of us! You, Mother, lying in wait to attack or defenseless me, already entrapped. Sooner or later, this paradigm is going to have to shift. Somehow or other, one of us is going to have to leave that web. It can't be impossible to do. For sure, I don't want to be the one stuck in it forever.

After scanning through the notes saved from her research, Jan had decided to dump them all into the trashcan. *No, I'm not going to give my time and energy to perpetuating these myths; they serve me no benefit at all.* She chose instead to let the group determine their own subject matter for the inaugural Fireside Chat.

Mr. Dean waved to her through his office window as she walked towards the building from her parked car. When she strode into the lobby, she found him standing by the staircase, shorn of its sprays of evergreen, hanging stockings, and red velvet bows from the holiday season.

"Everything is ready and waiting upstairs," he informed her. "Fifty folding chairs have been set up on the second floor." Jan found this number to be a little daunting.

"No need to worry," he told Jan. "We estimate there'll be closer to ten participants for your first Fireside Chat. It's not easy getting old people to try something new. Really, don't expect any more than this. The folding chairs had to be set in place for this evening's activity."

Pointing to the wingback armchair in front of the fireplace as the place where she was "to park her butt," Charlotte told Jan, "You can see we have some early buyers already." As more residents trickled in, Jan distributed sheets of trivia she had prepared. "This is just a fun exercise for us to start with," she advised.

Thirty photocopies of the trivia sheet had been made, but within seven minutes, a good thirty more people were left wanting a copy. Mimi had to volunteer to run to Mr. Dean's office while Sondra led a stream of three wheel-chaired residents into a spot in the corner of the room.

***

On her way to the discussion group, Muriel had stopped by Alice's apartment so the two women could walk into the Fireside Chat together.

"I'm not going," Alice told her friend in no uncertain terms.

"Why not, for heaven's sake? It's your own daughter! Don't you want to be there to support her in this?"

"No, I don't!" Alice declared. "Why the hell do I have to make a special appointment to chat with Jan? I get to speak with her any time I want."

"Suit yourself," Muriel replied, hurrying off and hoping not to show up too late for a comfortable seat up front. By the time Muriel arrived, however, every chair in the room had been occupied. Several staff members were settled on the windowsills while others were seated cross-legged on the floor. At last count, there were seventy-three people in attendance.

***

The topics that were covered included the proper way to raise one's children; movie stars from the thirties, forties, and fifties; what "bluing" meant with regard to the laundry; how difficult life must have been during the World War years; and whether there was too much sex and violence currently being shown on the television. Mimi and the other staffers had just as much to say on these matters as did the residents, and on several occasions, Jan had to ask everyone to hush up. "Don't worry; everyone will definitely have a chance to speak," she told them.

Muriel raised her hand and Jan called on her. "You're not remembering the olden days so honestly," Muriel said to the crowd as a whole. "You're painting too beautiful a picture. It used to be dreary, the clothing was bland and heavy, our options were more limited, and life today is so much more fun!"

Many in the room were anxious to dispute Muriel's claims and so they raised their hands, vying for Jan's attention.

In the meantime, Jan had not taken much notice when Charlotte, at the beginning of the session, had stepped behind Jan's chair to plug in the infrared fireplace so burning logs could provide a nice visual backdrop for the talk. By mistake, however, Charlotte had set the heat output at its highest level.

Thirty minutes later, the simulated flames had been glowing non-stop and the radiation on Jan's back was becoming almost unbearable—her underarms were drenched and her forehead was sopping wet. She wished she could remove her jacket, but was embarrassed by the sweat stains on her blouse. She checked her watch and wondered if she could tolerate yet another half hour under the intense heat.

"Is the air conditioning on?" Jan called out to the staff members.

"Sure is," someone in a pastel pink uniform replied.

"Well, can someone kindly please find the thermostat and lower the temp?"

"We're not allowed to touch those things; they're off limits to everyone except Mr. Dean," the staff member said.

"Is there any way then that we can get in touch with Mr. Dean to do so?" Jan asked with urgency.

Sondra volunteered, "I last saw him by Gladys's apartment, but that was a while ago. I can page him, if you want?"

Jan replied, "Yes, please!"

Jan noticed that Irving, whose wheelchair was parked close by and who usually could barely manage to lift his fingers from his lap, had become fidgety upon hearing Muriel's statement so Jan granted him the opportunity to speak. While Irving croaked out his thoughts, Jan dipped down into her pocketbook and found her travel-sized package of tissues. Unfolding the first tissue, she dabbed her face, worrying all the while if little clumps of lint were going to adhere to her newly moistened makeup. As soon as Sondra caught Jan's attention from the back of the room, Jan realized her concern was not unfounded. Sondra had been waving her arms and motioning for her to brush each of her cheeks.

The audience did not seem to sense any discomfort on Jan's part—or they just didn't care; they were all too pumped up from participating in the stimulating activity. Jan searched the room and observed that no one had fallen asleep, no one was drooling on their chests or sleeves, there were no audible snores, and there was not one measly mention as to when the next meal was going to be served.

One of the residents shouted, "Irving, you've got to speak louder; I can't hear what you're saying."

"He can't speak any louder," someone from the front row yelled back on Irving's behalf. "He's talking as loud as he can."

"Well, he shouldn't have been called on then," a disgruntled woman screeched.

"Don't be so quick to judge," some other woman new to the debate rallied to Irving's defense. "He's recovering from a stroke. It's a miracle Irving's able to say anything at all."

Jan leaned forward in her seat so she could better understand the gist of what Irving had to say.

"For those of you who could not hear Irving, he said, 'How could things possibly be any better today when most of us are not in any condition to enjoy them? We should all be doing our living while we can, regardless of the times.'"

Arthur rose by his chair. "I'll stand so none of you will have a problem hearing me."

The sentiment of "Good going Arthur," was repeated around the room.

Arthur continued, "I understand how Irving feels. Many of us feel that way quite a bit, especially from year to year, as we get older and feebler. But aside from that, you've got to admit that the world used to be a much gentler, kinder place."

***

As Arthur talked on about how much more wonderful the music was in his time, Alice was hunched over two boxes of Girl Scout cookies, taking turns sampling from the Samoas and Thin Mints in Gladys Smith's apartment. After having been both surprised and relieved at how easily she had been able to slip in unnoticed through the unlocked, entry door, she had needed to sit right away on the first available chair to rest her palpitating heart and allay her nerves. *Ooh, this is really quite exciting. I haven't felt this alive in ages. I don't know why I didn't do something like this a lot sooner.*

She counted herself lucky in two regards: not one staff member had stopped her in the hallway, and she had discovered the two boxes of treats waiting on a folding tray right next to the chair where she had needed to take a short rest. "Thank you, Gladys. Those were delightful."

Alice scanned the various items and pieces of furniture displayed in Gladys' room. *The first thing I'm going to do is grab the shitty brown dress Gladys loves to wear all the time. She looks so deplorable in it. I'm actually doing her a big favor by taking it away. Tomorrow, I'll throw it in the dumpster outside the kitchen in case Sondra agrees it's too shitty to hawk.*

Alice wiped roasted coconut flakes off her lap and clasped her hands together. *Now on to the closet and to finding where Gladys' Bingo money is stashed.* Leaving her walker aside, she half-darted, half-hobbled her way around the bed, credenza, curio stand, and TV, placing objects and cash into the shopping bag she carried, all the while giggling nervously. On the floor in a corner behind an armchair, Alice found a freezer bag with lots of little bags inside. After picking it up, she decided it was probably full with packets of sugar or artificial sweetener and returned it to its resting place. Moving along, she cautioned herself not to take too many things from one place the first time out, but she came to a halt before a pair of lilac anodized aluminum earrings hanging from a jewelry case. *When was the last time you wore these, 1980? Ooh, you sexy, sexy thing. Will you really miss them?* Alice struggled to grab hold of a tune beginning to play in a far-off section of her mind. *'Yesterday, I was a lonely person...now, you're lying close to me, making love to me...ooh, you sexy, sexy thing, ooh, I believe in miracles...I believe in miracles...and...and... I can shimmy...I can shimmy like my sister Kate.'*

Alice's internal songfest was interrupted by the phone ringing, which gave her a start. As her heart skipped a beat, she debated running into the closet in case someone came to answer the call. She tried talking herself out of a panic, pretending to be a commanding officer bolstering his troop's confidence before leaving the bunker. "Don't lose it now, old girl; that'll be the worst thing to do. Remember, you're British and we British must muster on!"

She stood still, holding her breath and listening for footsteps as the phone continued to ring. "I'll just stick with the story I rehearsed if I'm discovered." Alice peered toward Gladys' bathroom and contemplated running in there quickly. She suddenly had to pee badly. "No, I shan't attempt it. I don't want to be caught with my knickers hanging down."

The phone died down, but after a pause it began to ring again. "She's not here, you idiot—whoever you are! If she didn't answer the first time, why do you think she'll answer this second time around? I should pick up the phone and give you a bloody-good talking to."

But thinking better of it, Alice gathered her walker and shopping bag and slipped out of Gladys' apartment, passing by a maintenance crew on her way to the elevator. She started to hum several discordant notes and managed to fling a skip into her walk every now and then. "I'll tinkle in my next break-in before I conduct my other business," she said with self-assurance. "Ooh, you sexy, sexy thing. This is quite fun. Sondra, you don't know what a lucky girl you are to have such a selfless, gallant friend as me."

***

Since Mr. Dean had failed to respond to his pager, neither the thermostat nor the fireplace had been adjusted to Jan's satisfaction. She had continued to sweat profusely throughout the entire Fireside Chat inaugural session. Ralph was now moralizing on what the entire audience had already agreed was immodest, tasteless clothing worn by the younger girls of today when Jan observed Alice slip unobtrusively into the social room. *Mother, you sure can move quickly when you want to.*

Alice headed straight over to Sondra and whispered something in her ear, which caused Sondra to first appear shocked. Sondra looked quickly at Jan and then back at Alice, her expression reverting to one of terror. Pulling her lips back, she manufactured a broad smile and surrendered her seat to Alice.

While issues of indecency, drugs, alcohol, and the damages from cigarette smoke were being debated, Sondra attempted to find an empty space against the wall large enough for her to lean against. Jan continued to lead the discussion, trying her best to overcome her roasting discomposure and ignore her mother's Cheshire Cat's grin. Never before had Jan seen Alice sit so tall in the saddle, radiating such a beam of immense satisfaction and pure, unadulterated joy.

Chapter Twenty-seven

"Miss Alice, what yous gone and done?" Sondra asked in a half-whisper after shutting the door to Alice's apartment. She was on her last shift of the day, dispensing meds, and making sure her residents were tucked in comfortably for the night. Earlier, while the dinner meal was being served, she had tried to make eye contact with Alice, but Alice kept looking back at her as if Sondra was a total stranger.

"Uh huh," Sondra commented to herself as she had placed a plate of à la carte blueberry pie at each setting. "You'll figure out who I am real soon, if I gives you too small a scoop of vanilla ice cream. I know you sure can act, but you likes your sweets more!"

"I'm in here, Sondra," Alice called from behind the bathroom door. "I'm counting out our booty."

"Now you hush up about this," Sondra said with urgency. "Open up this door so I can see just how much of a mess you be getting yourself into."

"The door's unlocked. I can't wait to see the look on your face when you see just how much I managed to grab my very first time around."

"I ain't seen you yet, but I can tell you be gloating when I have a feeling you should be repenting. This has been your first and very last go-around."

"Hold your comments until you can see just how successful I was," Alice excitedly advised. "I feel so exhilarated. If my legs would let me, I'd be doing somersaults up and down the hallway."

"Yep, that's an excellent way to keep quiet about what yous been up to!" Sondra pulled the door open and gasped out loud as she entered the bathroom, her goggle-eyes revealing her astonishment over the massive accumulation of objects and cash piled up in the sink. She immediately fell back a step, hitting the towel bar on the wall.

"What do you think, Alice? That nobody gonna miss any of the stuff you took? You've got enough here to fill an entire warehouse. People will surely be noticing just how much of their stuff is missing. This is gonna lead to a whole lot of trouble for you and for me! Lordy, Lordy, Lordy, just what am I gonna do now?" Sondra raised her eyes and her hands toward the ceiling. "Help me, Lord. For sure, I'm in a boatload of trouble."

"Hold your horses; hold your horses," Alice yelped. "There's no need to panic. There's no need for you to turn into Mahalia Jackson. I was very, very careful. Nobody is going to suspect me of doing anything wrong."

"That's exactly right, 'cause they're gonna suspect me of doing the stealing," Sondra said angrily. "I'll lose my job. No one will ever hire me after this, and Delmont will have to quit school. Some mess you got me in, Alice!" Her legs took turns tapping uncontrollably. She covered her mouth with her hand as her eyes darted to the side, up, down, and over to the other side of the bathroom. "Let me think now. What am I going to do? What am I going to do?"

"How can they fire you if you were in the discussion group the entire time?" A smug smile puffed up Alice's cheeks. "You have the perfect alibi."

Upon hearing Alice's latest remark, Sondra began to calm down. She tilted her head as she contemplated the plausibility of the cover story. "Hmm. I need to think on this," she said under her breath, but then she quickly became agitated again, flexing her fingers and stomping back and forth in an effort to shake off her jitters. "Alice, has you put the stopper in the drain?" she squealed with alarm. "We don't want any of the rings falling in the pipe, and then we'll have to get a plumber to unclog your sink and everyone will find out what you've been up to."

"Sondra, I'm no dummy," Alice said, leading Sondra to the toilet seat to sit down. "Yes, I put the stopper in first thing. You've got to relax about this; I'm telling you, it was like taking candy from a baby. I know that nothing I took is going to be noticed. I was very cautious; a dime here, a nickel there. Fortunately, it all adds up to a nice chunk of change." She stretched out her arms. "Take it as I am giving it to you: free and clear and with a full heart."

As Sondra began to fill her pockets with the jewelry and money, Alice watched with delight. "Just this one time, but no more. This is it; I mean it!" Sondra stressed.

"Your uniform is going to bulge out too much, and not just from your thighs and *tuckus,*" Alice cautioned. "Take a shopping bag; it will be less conspicuous. I'll give you the one from the Dollar Store but not the one from Macy's. It's more realistic that you'd shop at the Dollar Store. You don't want to draw more attention to yourself than you already do."

"Okay," Sondra exclaimed, concentrating on placing every last piece of the stolen objects into the bag as Alice hovered over her. "So now we each have something to hold over each other's heads. We're even. There'll be no more talk about what yous took, or about what I'm gonna do with it."

Alice extended her right hand. "We're partners for a good cause. Let's shake on it."

"No, we ain't partners, Alice," Sondra said. "I don't know what you got cooking up in your head, but we're not in this together. It's stopping right this minute. Do you hear me?"

"What about Delmont?"

Sondra started to walk out of the bathroom and turned her head to say, "Delmont's my problem, not yours."

Following after her, Alice called out, "He needs your help—you said so yourself."

Looking straight ahead, Sondra opened the door to exit the apartment and stated fervently, "I'll handle it myself."

"I'll handle it with you," Alice called again, rushing as best she could to keep up with Sondra.

"He's my son and my problem!" Sondra declared, genuinely troubled by Alice's persistence.

Alice tottered along. "But you may not be in the best position to help him the way I can," she beseeched.

After taking several steps in the direction of the elevator, Sondra spun around and placed the shopping bag on the floor, hoping to finally conclude the discussion.

"Alice, I don't fully understand why you're doing this. Are you bending over backwards just to be nice or are you trying to make amends for some mistakes you made with your own son? For the last time, I'm telling you that I'll take care of my personal business by myself from here on out." Her voice was steady and determined.

Alice placed a hand over her chest and grimaced as if in pain. She struggled to say, "This could be the big one! From the bottom of my weak, failing heart, I want to help you, Sondra. Why do you have to make things so difficult?"

"Don't pull that fake heart attack on me, Alice. You knows better than that. I'm looking at you square on and I knows you're just fine."

"You can't blame a kid for trying."

"You're certainly not a kid, and there definitely is not going to be anymore trying." Sondra double checked that they were absolutely alone in the hallway and said in her sternest tone yet, "Look, I did something wrong and I got caught. That was God's way of telling me to change the path I was on."

"That's just it," Alice said with too much animation for Sondra's liking. "You see, the way I look at it, God delivered you into my hands. You have too much to risk continuing the way you were, but I don't. I'm on my last leg, my very last dime, my next to last breath, or however that *fershinkiner* expression goes. What are they going to do, hang me from the gallows? Don't take away my last hurrah, Sondra, I beg you. It's for a good cause. The ends justify the means; do you get my drift? *Fershtay*? Look, I'll repeat it in English: do you understand what I'm telling you?"

Frustrated, tired, and ready to give up the fight, Sondra replied, "Alice, you don't have to speak so loud like I'm some foreigner."

"Good," Alice responded, nodding happily. "Then it's settled. We're partners." She approached Sondra, hugged her tightly, and kissed her arms because that was the highest part on Sondra she was able to reach.

Sondra put her arms around Alice's waist to keep her steady. "We're not partners," she uttered on a sigh.

"We have an orally binding contract," Alice announced into Sondra's bosom.

Sondra gently pushed Alice away. "I got to go. I don't have time to stand here debating this with you no more." She picked up the shopping bag again and told Alice to go back to resting in her apartment.

"All right. All right. We'll table the discussion for another day. How's that for proper business talk, partner?"

"The next time we meet, we're going to permanently break up this partnership you worked out in your head that I never agreed to. Yous got that?"

Alice reversed her direction and braced herself by using the handrails on the walls as she returned to her apartment to watch TV. "Make sure you get a good amount for the silver chain necklace," she whispered. "It's a good quality. Muriel treats herself very well."

Chapter Twenty-eight

Jan had not sought out Alice's opinion nor her approval for conducting the Fireside Chats at Glenbrook, but she did mention it at the following late-afternoon counseling session she and Mike attended with Rick. As was their routine, she was seated on the couch next to Mike. "You're a glutton for punishment," he muttered, shifting farther away.

"Do you want to discuss this rationally? Rick told us we need to express our true feelings to each other."

"That's easy to do: I'm plenty pissed with you right now," he answered.

"But I am doing these people a service. If it can help some of the residents, why not? I like to do good wherever I can." Jan's effusiveness could have earned her the Good Samaritan of the Year award.

"That's not your job," he commented gruffly.

"You didn't see how their faces lit up. Mike, it was as if someone were breathing life into them again."

Mike maintained a steady focus on Rick, tapping his fingers on the armrest.

"You should have seen them, Rick," Jan continued. "They were able to share their stories without someone rolling their eyes, biding their time, or taking small steps in the opposite direction."

"Not your responsibility," Mike interjected.

"Well, I'll see how it goes next Thursday. I have to be there anyway to check up on my mother." Jan edged closer to Mike. "This is something entirely different than before. Isn't it, Rick? I've only agreed to give an hour's talk once a week."

"Exactly one hour too much," Mike objected. "While you're accomplishing 'your good,' you are tossing everything that we've created together down the drain. Your mother is a bigoted, self-centered, manipulative woman who doesn't really care a shit for you or anyone else."

Jan's eyes watered; her nose began to run. "This isn't just for my mother; it's for everyone at Glenbrook."

Mike clenched his jaw. "I'm going out to get gas for the car. Sorry Rick, but I need a break from this crap. I have some last-minute things to see to at the office anyway."

As soon as Mike departed, Jan gathered her pocketbook and rose to leave as well.

"Why not stay, Jan?" Rick offered. "You look a little distraught. We can continue to chat during the time remaining."

Jan had no intention of staying in Rick's office. As she made her way to the door, she told him, "I'm here at Mike's suggestion only. I'll come back when he does."

"I'm sorry to hear that," Rick said. "Please know that I'm here for the both of you. I'll be available whenever you have a need to talk."

After Jan ate dinner alone that evening, she sluggishly cleared off the table, placed the dirty dishes unsystematically in the dishwasher, and sauntered to her bathroom to take a shower, put on her pajamas, and watch a movie on the television. *At least this time, it'll be one of my choosing.*

Jan did not take kindly to cold showers, and on this occasion, she waited before entering the stall until the water ran nice and hot. She squirted an ample portion of body wash onto the loofah, making sure to scrape every inch of skin on her entire body. It was like she was erasing rather than lathering. Next, she vigorously shampooed her hair and heavy-handedly massaged her scalp with conditioner. It wasn't until she was in the middle of the final rinsing-off stage did she allow herself a moment to relax and catch her breath. The water, now reduced to a more acceptable, lukewarm temperature, cascaded over her. *This feels so good. I wish I could stay here forever. Goodbye hot flashes. Goodbye to all the have-to's and should-haves in my life; I almost feel free again.*

Making sure not to fall on the slippery wet tiles, she grabbed a hanging towel to wipe her eyes. *A few more minutes and then I'm out of here*, she promised. The water drops slid down her hair, which was far longer than in its drier, curlier state. Thinking about her earlier interaction with Mike, she began to get upset all over again. *Why do I always have to act like such a fool? In so many ways, he's right and I'm wrong.* She thought about the awful events that had gotten her into the hopeless quagmire that now defined her life. Her reminiscing carried her back all the way to when she was seven years old and was still being referred to as Janice.

She remembered herself as the little girl pouting in the backseat of her family's brown and beige sedan as it made its way to the Brighton seaside. What misfortune it had been to be stuck sharing the day with the fuddy-duddy Aunt Gilda and the excessive, headache-inducing fragrance she loved to wear. The heavy scent had filled the close quarters they were riding in with sickening fumes. Why couldn't she have gone with Henry and his friend to the funfair instead? She had been told that there was no more room left in that car, but she would have been happy to sit on someone's lap. Maureen, her older sister, always seemed to be granted the most freedom; she had been allowed to stay at home all by herself, plum out refusing to have Jan tag along, and no one had forced her to change her mind.

Uncle Morris and her father, both wearing their tweed coats and grey felt hats, had sat upfront. The smoke from her father's cigarette and Uncle Morris's pipe contributed to the unbearable noxiousness of the air. Aunt Gilda, plump and short, grinning with pride at the new fur stole wrapped about her shoulders, took up most of the room in the back seat by the far window, leaving little space for Janice's mother and herself. Janice had to squeeze her arms inward just to fit.

From the minute the car had pulled away from the curb, Janice had begun to sulk. She kicked her legs until her father's roar came bellowing into her ears, warning her to change her attitude lest she be dropped off at the side of the motorway. "And you'll have to find your own way home in the pitch black, with no one to help you."

She had decided instead to count the letter boxes and roadside signs that were passed along the way. After reaching a figure between thirty-five and forty and growing tired of the exercise, she thought she heard her mother beg, "Norman, you've got to stop the car. Oh, it hurts so bad."

Turning away from the window, Janice had noticed rivulets of blood streaming down her mother's legs, staining the bunched up, seamed stockings and garter belt gathered at her mother's ankles. Slabs likes those of cows' livers, commonly displayed in butcher shops, were now oozing out from under her mother's knickers.

Janice continued to gape as Alice clenched her teeth and drew her knees closer to her chest. A chorus of beeping horns from the surrounding traffic were not loud enough to drown out her mother's screams, as more blood poured out beneath her legs.

Janice's eyes darted from her mother's cringing face to what was being ejected from her mother's vagina. Aunt Gilda inched forward sideways, uttering, "There, there," as her sister-in-law feverishly attempted to cradle her pelvis. Neither Janice's father nor Uncle Morris had turned around, each maintaining a steady focus on the road ahead and continuing to exhale smoke, as if no drama was taking place at all. Then her mother had murmured that it was over, but Janice did not budge an inch, frozen and incapable of moving even if she had wanted to. Janice's arms were fixed firmly across her chest; her legs felt like they had been stiffly glued together.

Her father next parallel parked the car into a snug spot on a crowded market street. Janice observed him depart from the driver's seat, slam his door shut, stomp on his tossed cigarette butt, traverse the pavement, and enter a nearby sweet shop. Feeling quite astonished but also a little bit secretly pleased, she wondered if he was going to buy a bag of sour gumdrops. Through the rear rolled-down window, her father handed Aunt Gilda a newspaper—his only purchase—which Janice recognized as the same daily paper delivered to their home.

Aunt Gilda and Alice set about gathering up all of the bloody objects and depositing them into the newspaper, which Aunt Gilda had since spread open upon her lap. Janice sat mesmerized, trying to convince herself, *those are not little body parts. Those are not teeny weensy baby arms and legs on top of the "Funnies" page.* Aunt Gilda fully covered and compressed the bundle and handed it back to Janice's father through the window, which he then dumped into an overloaded trashcan sitting next to a bus stop. Aunt Gilda took a hairbrush out of her handbag and moved some errant strands away from Alice's forehead. She kissed her

206

cheek, leaving an impression of ruby-red lipstick. After returning the hairbrush to her cosmetic bag, Aunt Gilda produced a pair of black leather gloves from the zippered compartment of her handbag. "Put these on," she had said to her. "They will make you feel like more of a lady."

Before returning to the car, Janice's father had ordered her to join him and Uncle Morris in the front seat. "Get out! Get out now!" he had commanded. It took three times before Janice comprehended he was shouting at her. Her father pulled open the door where Janice was sitting and yanked her arm. "Come on then. Move yourself. We're in a hurry, you dim-wit." As Janice took her place, wedged in between her father and Uncle Morris, she caught Aunt Gilda whisper to Alice, "At the very least, we didn't have to use a knitting needle." The reference left Janice even more perplexed. Not one adult in the car had considered it necessary to explain to the little girl what she had just witnessed.

***

Jan turned off the water and stepped out of the shower onto the mat by the sink. Ordinarily, she would have wiped the glass enclosure with a squeegee, but her mood had now turned sullen and she didn't have the energy. Starting to shiver, she wrapped herself in a terry-cloth robe and sat on a stool facing the mirror. Her once buoyant attitude had been replaced by a weighty sadness. *Now there's the fat, old, fart that I'm more familiar with. I bet Gillian doesn't have such a flabby belly.* She stared at her own unsightly image with resentment and blotted her hair with a hand towel. *It's no wonder my sex life is nonexistent.* Combing through the few remaining tangles, she pondered the volatility of joy. *It can be so fleeting and deceitful.* Once more, she began to reminisce.

This time, her recollection brought her on board the *Queen Elizabeth* as it was sailing across the Atlantic Ocean to America. Ten-year-old Janice along with the rest of the Block family had been travelling for two and a half days when they encountered an extremely severe storm, which was later designated to be one of the worst to hit the eastern coast of the United States.

Strong gusts had attacked the ship, causing it to vehemently rock from side to side as pelting rain bombarded the portholes and decks. In spite of the inclement weather, Norman had led Janice outside to the upper-most deck permitted for passengers, where they had been blown about with the deck chairs and tables, becoming drenched through and through.

Jan pictured the stiff English, sturdy, leather brogues her younger version was wearing on the ship that day—the ones Norman required her mother to purchase before leaving London. *As goofy as they looked, those "concrete boots" probably helped keep me anchored and from falling overboard.*

It had been at that perilous moment that Norman chose to impart the most essential of his life's lessons to his middle child. With his right pointer finger wagging dogmatically within inches of her face and his left hand bearing down forcibly on her shoulder, it was as if Janice was locked in a vise. He told her that under no circumstances was she ever to lose her British accent.

"No matter what, do whatever is necessary to hold onto it. Mark my words; this is absolutely critical! *Do you hear me?*"

Janice was not aware that she spoke with an accent and failed to see the crime in losing the British one that she supposedly had. Nonetheless, her father had asked a question, which required to be answered. She tried hard to have her "Yes sir" be heard above the thunder of the crushing waves.

"Furthermore, your only purpose in life, Janice," Norman continued, sounding no less ominous or cold-hearted than a hungry wolf about to charge at a trapped deer, "is to take shit from everyone else in your family."

Her father grabbed onto her other shoulder with his right hand, his grip digging into her flesh. The image of the scariest, meanest, fairy tale ogre came into her mind. She fought to control her trembling, lest it irritate her father and lead him to call her "Stupid, little crybaby," in the same manner he had often called her in the past. The fear that he might have been contemplating throwing her off the ship was very much in her mind. Then he stared directly into her face and concluded by saying, "Don't for one minute forget any of what I'm telling you. You are to carry my words with you wherever you go for the rest of your life. You are a nothing. Nothing at all. A piece of shit. That's it. Absolutely nothing! That was the sole purpose for which you were born. It is the only reason you are here. It is the only reason why we let you be a part of this family. You are a servant to us. You are to do whatever we tell you to do. You will obey our commands no matter what. You are to keep all of this to yourself. Never tell a soul about it. Do you understand what I'm telling you?"

As Norman persisted with his threats, little Janice kept envisioning the dead baby in the car from the Brighton outing. She was terrified that her father might chop her up, roll up her bloody parts in a newspaper, and then throw the package into the ocean. The taste of acid now rose in Jan's mouth as she remembered what had happened next.

Norman dragged Janice through narrow passageways and down stairwells in the direction of their cabins. When they temporarily stopped at the main lobby area and the doors of the lift opened up, Janice uncontrollably vomited into the cab. Fragments from her breakfast landed on shoulders, heads, and walls. The stench had been horrid, as were the looks on the other passengers' faces. In the midst of all the confusion, chaos, and disgust, Norman, had hurriedly taken his exit.

"You son-of-a-gun! What a bastard you were to have done that to me," Jan called out into the air, stepping unenthusiastically into her pajamas and slippers.

For seemingly forever, Jan had been cursed by the memories of the fateful car ride and the terrifying trans-Atlantic voyage. She had not shared details of these events with another living soul. In her later teen years, Jan's older sister, Maureen, finally spilled the beans about what had been her mother's abortion, which their father had masterminded and singularly desired.

"He didn't want to have any damaging evidence found close to home," Maureen had related. "What was done was illegal, and they could have both gone to jail."

"Poor Mom," Jan had sniffled.

"Everything always had to be carried out according to Dad's plans and say-so. Mom wanted so much to keep that baby. I could hear them fighting about it for weeks on end."

"Poor Mom," Jan had repeated with so much sorrow and infinite empathy for her mother that it almost swallowed her up.

Chapter Twenty-nine

To Alice's way of thinking, it would be impossible to ever be found guilty of stealing at Glenbrook. Were she to be caught red-handed, trespassing in another resident's apartment, Alice's planned strategy was to feign utter confusion, and thus have the incident chalked up to old age and memory loss. She was confident her performance—in which she would incorporate mostly imbecilic behavioral traits—would eliminate the need for any further inquiries.

From her perspective, absentmindedness and batty brains ran rampant at Glenbrook. Like a highly contagious, potent stomach virus that contaminated every host in its path, each person who had been given a life sentence at Glenbrook eventually became smitten with the ailment of idiocy and grew dumber and more incapacitated with each passing day.

What had at first been a major source of irritation to Alice was that the apartments had all been constructed with a cookie cutter approach, diminishing the concept of originality, leaving no room for the expression of character, and creating living spaces that were mostly dull and boring. "Where was it written," she used to ask, "that old people have to live so blandly?" Now, however, the monotonous duplication worked its way well into Alice's scheme.

"And what makes matters worse," Alice used to bellyache to Jan, "is that everyone's lackluster furniture seems to come from the very same nearby Sears. That's where their relatives more than likely ran in to hurriedly purchase a modern, print ensemble in the identical washed-out tones of peach, teal, and tan with sprigs of ferns in the background. Why does everyone's furniture have to be cut from the same cloth and upholstered over bamboo legs that belong in a screened-in patio? All because some daughter or nephew felt it necessary to substitute some musty threadbare pieces and unceremoniously discard them into a dumpster despite their original owner's desperate pleading not to."

To which Jan would often reply, "Maureen got rid of your cut velvet couch and chenille armchairs. I had nothing to do with it."

How could Alice possibly be blamed for venturing into the wrong apartment when on each and every wall was the almost indistinguishable cluster of nostalgic memorabilia commemorating the highlights of the past seventy to ninety years' worth of family get-togethers and rites of passage that surely had to be put on view as an entrance requirement before gaining access and admission to this Glenbrook club—the one to which no one in their right mind would ever really want to belong?

Inside each of the virtually impossible to tell apart residences, Alice reasoned, was the same old-person smell with its matching air, void of energy, hope, or expectations, hanging heavily with sentiments of regret, remorse, heartache, and fear. These homes were mirror images of each other, as were their skeletal, ground-down, no longer useful occupants, and so Alice was smugly confident in the plausibility of her ironclad excuse. One of the weirdest things she had discovered during her hunting expeditions, though, was that many people kept their packets of sugar or artificial sweeteners in freezer bags on the floor in the corner of their apartments. It was a reoccurrence that kept her baffled, but, then again, who was she to question this practice? She alternated between her shoes, bathroom vanity, and underwear drawer to store her own Sweet'N Lows.

The administration certainly hadn't paid attention or given much heed to any of her previous complaints regarding missing items before; why would they bother to question Alice's supposed slip-up in taking a wrong turn and misappropriating someone else's trinkets? Mr. Dean, Charlotte, and their entire entourage would never suspect the truth behind Alice's actions.

As far as what she took, well those senile victims were probably too far gone to notice anything had even gone missing. And seriously, what difference did it really make if she was found with a necklace or earrings from another person's home? Come to think of it, what did it mean to possess anything of value at this late age? Absolutely every object including one's own body were on loan, and the rental periods for all of Glenbrook's inmates were nearing their completions. No. No one in their right mind would ever suspect that oh-so-posh Alice could be or would ever choose to be a thief;

Over a period of six weeks, she had been reveling in these secret escapades, and this had certainly added spice to an otherwise drab, uneventful life. Now, she awoke each morning with her head spinning with plots and plans as to which direction she would start off on her daily prowl. *Third or second floor?* she would debate as she squirted Crest toothpaste on the bristles of her toothbrush. Before rinsing and spitting into the sink, she would wonder, *Start with the west or east wing? Avoid the nurse's office, although there's never anyone in there.* As she picked up her partial dentures from the overnight cleaning solution, she would consider, *I noticed in the dining room that Shirley was wearing a decent pearl necklace. I hope she's left it out in plain sight on her dresser. I'll start at the end of the hall with Shirley's place and work my way down to the smaller studio apartments to pick up the loose coins tossed into the obsolete ashtrays and plastic containers.*

As she marched with her Rollator down the hallways, she would try to temper her own enthusiasm—it was causing her to walk faster than her body was actually capable of moving. *I hope Jan has an especially long session planned for today. Forget about photocopying pages; she should bring along encyclopedias of trivia when she comes.* She would pull open drawers and yank hangers along closet rods with specific articles in mind she had seen someone wear or had heard them boast about. *Mary was bragging about a cashmere sweater her daughter-in-law bought her yesterday. Hopefully she hasn't removed the tags yet.* She would hide her loot with so much glee and excitement that she oftentimes forgot where she stashed it. *Sondra does a good job of making believe she's annoyed with my undertakings, but she sure does grab those pickings in a hurry—way before I can even say "Bob's your uncle!"* On her very last go around, she scooped up one of the ever-present freezer bags because she was running low on her own stash of sweeteners.

Before Alice engaged in this life of petty theft, much of her focus had been on finding fault with everyone and anything associated with Glenbrook. Among her many grievances, however, the one she had felt most keenly about was the loss of control over her own destiny.

During much of her marriage to Norman, Alice's wants, thoughts, feelings, choices, and aspirations had become inconsequential. One of the sweetest rewards that had come out of Norman's dying was Alice's liberation, which she grew to appreciate from the very first evening she was sprawled out across her double sized mattress and worry-free about having to share her bed with someone she considered an insensitive, despicable creep. For too many years she had been forced to live under Norman's thumb, lacking the courage to flee from his grasp and always too scared to let her own voice be heard. When Norman had thrown her youngest child—her handsome, immensely adored son—out of their home, Alice felt too helpless to do anything other than obey Norman's command. Oh, how she wished she had had the strength and stamina to stand up to that tyrant. If she had been armed with a dagger, she would have sliced Norman in two at the very moment Henry packed up his things and walked out the door.

Alice had tried to surreptitiously keep in touch with her son but was afraid that Norman would find out and punish her for it. Her husband had his sadistic ways of keeping her in check, and there were some battles Alice was smart enough to know that she had less than a snowball's chance in Hell of winning. Maureen used to provide snippets about Henry's activities in San Francisco, but after a year, Maureen's source of information had dried up.

"Make calls," she had told Maureen. "Go there in person and see for yourself," she had begged, but Maureen had her own family to take care of and a jet-setting lifestyle sending her in the opposite geographical direction to deluxe ski and spa resorts in Europe.

About two years after Henry's coerced departure, Maureen had finally agreed to fly to California. After a week-long attempt to get in touch with her estranged brother, she had managed to trace Henry's whereabouts to a particular commune not too far from the Berkley campus. She met with as many people as she could on her trip, but no one at that commune could pinpoint Henry's latest address. She had heard horrid tales about his out-of-control drug use and run-ins with the law, which had caused her to be miserably despondent and ill to her stomach. After a day's recuperation in her hotel room, Maureen handed members of the commune calling cards, already printed with her name and phone number, should any more information about her brother be discovered or come to light. When she returned home, she had shared with Jan and her mother how gutted and dejected she felt. "But we should all keep believing he is still alive and well." However, not one additional lead or phone call ever arose.

Jan had made a similar trip six months later, distributing her own contact information but also failing to ascertain Henry's location or status. Both sisters were hurt and terribly disappointed Henry had declined to make any further contact with them.

Alice worried constantly about Henry. Many nights in the privacy of her bedroom, she would cry herself to sleep. When Norman entered the room, he would always make some derisive comment about Alice's tear-stained pillowcase or the tossed, used tissues littering the floor, but that did not deter him from forcing himself on her.

***

Approximately twelve years after Henry's departure and out of the blue, Jan received a phone call from a woman she had given her contact information to in California. The woman, named Josie, had been packing up her clothes and personal items for a move to Chicago and came across Jan's card in an old Rolodex.

They hadn't been speaking for more than a minute when Josie said, "What's happening in Chicago is a disgrace. Too many cities nowadays are being segregated. African-Americans are being subjected to more violence and injustices every day, but the politicians won't stop fighting amongst themselves long enough to do something about it. Blacks and whites, Republicans and Democrats, they're all at war with each other. I say it's finally time to turn things around!"

"Please tell me again how you knew my brother," Jan had said, her patience growing thin as the young woman rattled on.

The woman, stopping short, asked, "Are you a Democrat or a Republican?"

"Why is that relevant to what you have to tell me about Henry?" Jan snapped.

Paying no heed to Jan's climbing anxiety, Josie had then demanded to know, "Would you vote for a black mayor?"

"I prefer not to discuss my political affiliation," Jan said. "I vote for character and policies; I don't care about race or religion."

"Henry told me his sisters were decent. If you're really one of them, then I guess you are."

"I assure you that I am Henry Block's sister," Jan stated, desperately hoping to move the discussion forward.

"Oh yes, you're the other sister, not the rich one." The woman had swallowed noisily after taking a swig of some liquid. "I put a lot of time into tracking you down. This isn't the original number you handed out."

"No," Jan acknowledged. "My husband and I have moved since then, but I'd be happy to compensate you for your efforts. It was very kind of you to persevere and find me."

"Henry was a good guy," Josie had continued. "I'm doing this for his sake and all the men he worked with. I'm not asking for anything from you."

217

"What kind of job did Henry have? Did you work with him?"

"Henry and I had reached San Francisco just about the same time. The city back then was crawling with young people. Each of us was shacking up in Polk Gulch 'cause that's where the rent was really cheap." Jan heard a *glug-glug-glug* and Josie smacked her lips.

"Please go on."

"It was fantastic! The music was unbelievable, and there were tons of pot everywhere. You'd be standing on the street minding your own business when a band would suddenly start playing on the corner or there'd be an amazing, impromptu parade come along, celebrating the beauty of the universe. Love, food, and drugs—all could partake—and you'd end up right smack in the middle of it. One continuous, never ending high. It was really something all right!"

"How long did my brother stay at Polk?" Jan pressed.

"Not that long. He was really digging that scene, but then he got heavy-duty into the peace movement. Henry told me your sister and her hubby had sent him money, but he didn't want to take it anymore because it was tainted. He claimed it helped escalate the Vietnam War."

Jan was confused. "But how?"

"That money was the product of capitalistic greed, profiting from killing machines let loose in Southeast Asia."

"My brother-in-law worked long and hard and plenty good hours for that money."

"Hmm. Henry sure didn't see it that way. When he moved into the farm commune, he made a point not to send his family his forwarding address because of it."

Jan discerned the pop and click of a bottle cap being pried off. "My family has never stopped worrying about him. If you can, please tell me more."

"After a few years, Henry got tired of farming. There was constant bickering at the commune where he was at. All those petty jealousies, you know? This guy was into that girl, but *that* guy was into *that* girl. You follow? He met some college students at a party in Haight-Ashbury, who got him interested in living in the city again. They were the ones who introduced Henry to Castro and the work of Harvey Milk. It seems to me, Henry was always trying to reinvent himself."

Jan was both astonished and feeling tremendously proud. "Henry was involved with Harvey Milk? Was he there when he was assassinated?"

"I'm not sure if he was still working with him at that time. Um...Henry started getting into a whole new scene at some point, and that's going to be a little harder for you to digest."

"I want to hear it all."

"Well, Henry's new hangout became the area between 18th and Market Street. Have you heard about this place before?"

"No, I'm sorry I haven't."

"I'll 'splain it to you then, but this is where it starts to get gritty." Josie had paused to take another swig. "He cut off twelve inches from his ponytail and started dressing in really tight denim jeans and black boots. Do you get the picture? The guy I had met in tie-dyes and pastels ceased to exist. I mean that figuratively. Now, he hung around the kind of clubs filled with male strippers. He was looking to get high. He was also looking for hook ups for sex. That really wasn't my thing. You know? I like it both ways but

I'm fussier about where it comes from. I didn't see him any more after that."

Jan tried to remain calm. "So, you can't tell me with any certainty what happened to him after this period of time?"

"I do know exactly what happened to him—it's not very pretty at all. Are you sure you really want to hear this, though?"

"Yes."

Josie gulped down a considerable amount of her drink before proceeding. "Henry's body was covered in rashes and sores when it was found in an alleyway. He was transported to the city morgue in early 1984. Since the public administrator had been unable to trace Henry's identity or any of his assets, the medical examiner arranged for Henry's cremation within weeks after he had been found."

"He was just thirty-one years old," Jan had cried, nausea overcoming her. Her blood withdrawing from her face. "And you know this because…?"

"Word got around. AIDS was killing everyone then. I lost a shit-load of my friends. Paranoia was running rampant. If it was someone you knew who died of AIDS, you made out like you never heard of him before. Like I said, you kept your distance—especially from the cops and the authorities."

"Thank you so very much for telling me this," Jan struggled to say. Her throat choked up, tears raining down her cheeks. She silently vowed to never share any of these horrific details with Alice.

***

Not for one minute did Alice ever doubt that Delmont was manipulating his mother, even though she had no proof to back up her assumption. His constant demands for money for what he claimed to be legitimate school expenses were, according to Alice, an ineffectual cover-up for crooked mischief that he had no business getting himself into. When it came to scamming, Alice was one of the best, and since *it took one to know one*, she believed Delmont's actions to be underhanded and completely self-serving. *Wasn't there a photograph of a black man on the nightly news program every time a crime was reported in Palm Beach County? Why would Delmont be any different from the rest of the rotten bunch? The first and second set of robbers at the liquor store had been black too, although, Norman's fatal run-in happened to be with white guys. Most people probably assumed that was just a freakish, oddity. Let them think what they want. I know better!*

She had caught Sondra stealing, and, therefore, Alice reckoned Sondra's son had to be up to no good as well. *It ran in their blood.* Nevertheless, and in spite of the preponderance of signs bearing witness to Delmont's unworthiness, Alice felt strongly compelled to assist Sondra in supplying her son with the cash he so fiercely needed.

Alice wanted Delmont to graduate college. She hoped Sondra could one day be proud of the grown man Delmont would become and that Sondra would believe she had done her absolute best in raising him. It was just a fraction of what she would have hoped for Henry.

Perhaps there was someone out where Henry had lived who might have helped him get to where he needed to go, just as she was doing now for Delmont. Alice tried to take comfort in this as she slipped through the hallways, darting in and out of the unlocked units and grabbing whatever goodies she thought would translate into enough money to satisfy Delmont's implacable demands.

Alice had long surrendered the notion that Henry was alive and would someday call or make an appearance at her front door. For a fleeting moment, Alice had even imagined that Henry might show up for Norman's funeral, despite Maureen's and Jan's insistence that it would not and could not ever happen.

"He'll surprise us all," Alice had persisted.

"You've got to give up the idea of ever seeing Henry again," Jan had said. "It's just never going to happen."

Taking her signal from Jan to jump into the conversation, Maureen had added, "No, he won't, Mom."

"You don't know that for sure," Alice had declared, staring straight ahead. "Miracles do happen. I finally got rid of your father, didn't I?"

Chapter Thirty

It was the third time that week that Alice had called Jan and asked her to buy more Depends. Twice already, Jan had pulled her car alongside the curb and ran into Glenbrook, hastily shoving a newly purchased box into the hands of a staff member who would commit to delivering the package to Alice's apartment. On the third go around, however, Jan brazenly questioned the authenticity of Alice's need.

"Are you eating them? Is someone stealing from your reserve? Have you forgotten where you stored them?"

"Don't be such a wise guy. How could I possibly miss seeing such big boxes in my little apartment? Don't you know how mortified I am to keep on asking for these?" After hearing Jan agree to make yet another trip to Costco later that day, Alice pressed, "Don't wait too long. Go as soon as you can."

"Mom, believe me, Costco will not run out of Depends," Jan answered. "Why on earth do you need so many? Are you selling them?"

Unfazed by Jan's spot-on accusation, Alice pranced through the rising action of her script, barreling full steam on to the climax. "For your information, missy, I keep shitting myself. If you were here more often, you would be able to see for yourself. The muck goes all over my body; all over the bathroom mat; all over my sheets and carpet. I have to lie on the floor like a six-month-old, like a complete nincompoop, while Sondra cleans me up, and she doesn't go around second guessing me either. She's an absolute angel, that woman; I'd be dead ten times a day if it wasn't for her!"

"I'm truly, truly sorry," Jan apologized. "I feel so ashamed for ever doubting you. I had no idea you were experiencing this horrible discomfort. Does the doctor know about this problem?"

"Of course, he does!" Alice yelled.

"You can stop being so upset, Mom. I'll definitely bring you more Depends this afternoon."

Alice hung up the phone and took an extended bow while cheerily announcing to Sondra, "Well, that should bring us in a few more bucks." Having skipped breakfast in the downstairs dining room, she was still dressed in her nightgown, which she had covered with a matching floral robe.

Sondra, hovering by Alice's side, shot her an unmistakable look of disapproval. "Tsk tsk. Have you no shame? That was downright nasty, Alice." She handed her a cup of water and pills to swallow. "As much as Delmont's fooling around gets my goat, I always want to do right by him. Plenty of people in this world will to try to bring him down, but I surely won't be one of them." She shook her head from side to side. Her shoulders and torso convulsed with an exaggerated shiver. "I feel all dirty inside having heard what you just said. You had no business disrespecting Jan that way. No siree."

Alice gazed up at the ceiling, scratching her chin vigorously with her sharp nails. "Well then," she replied, "that's just one of the many differences between you and me, isn't it?"

"You were much too hard on Jan just then," Sondra admonished. "Why do you lay it on just for her?"

Alice swallowed her pills and placed the cup on the side table. "Enough already; just put Jan to rest for now." She opened the top drawer of her side table and pulled out a sandwich bag. It was filled to the brim with earrings. "I've got something much better to talk about. Take a look at these juicy tidbits from two trips worth of my treasure hunting. Quite a number of Delmont's textbooks can be bought with these, don't you think?"

"Put that back where you keep it hidden," Sondra directed sternly, in a voice that allowed for no misinterpretation.

Alice giggled nervously at the frown Sondra was wearing. "Oh, oh. I feel a lecture coming on. You should be overjoyed by what I'm doing, but you're acting like a grizzle gut today."

Sondra's countenance did not soften. "You have no problem pouring on your sweetness for your oldest child, Maureen, and she's hardly ever here. Why, I've never heard you once say you love Jan, and that poor girl runs rings for you."

Alice returned the bag of earrings to its hiding place, closing the drawer with a resounding thud. "Oh, do give it a rest! Enough. Enough. The reason I treat Jan the way I do is because of religious reasons. I don't want to give her a *Kina Hora*." She sat on the edge of her bed, which Sondra had just finished making, none too pleased that her performance had been so ill received.

"*Religious* reasons you say?" Sondra lodged her hands on her hips and tilted her head, emitting a smirk of disbelief. "I don't even know what a *keenahorra* is."

"Yes. It's part of a little-known Commandment. You have to be Jewish to understand."

"A Jewish Commandment? That's mighty suspicious sounding, if you don't mind me saying so."

"Oh, okay then. If you want to know the truth," Alice spouted out. "Maureen and Jack are loaded, and they're very generous with me. I have to be nice to them or my life support will be cut off. Without their backing, I'd be homeless on the street."

"Jan would never allow for that and you knows it!" Sondra picked up a trashcan from the corner of the room to dump its contents in the garbage bag receptacle outside the apartment door. On her return, she straightened out a pair of Alice's shoes, tossed haphazardly on the floor, while Alice tapped on the flabby skin of her upper arm,

"Sondra, did you know that some women have this excess ugliness removed with plastic surgery? I should have done so ages ago."

Sondra took a deep breath and scowled at Alice. "There's nothing wrong with your arms. If it bothers you then wear long sleeves all the time."

"Other women in Glenbrook have turned into chunky frumps, letting their figures go, but I've truly managed to stay svelte," Alice bragged.

"Yes, Alice; you're a real looker all right!" Sondra bit down on her pulled-in lips. Her tolerance for Alice's baseless conceit was about to boil over. "I started my day with countless elevator rounds, helping people get to their exercise classes or physical therapy. You chose to stay in bed all morning long like the spoiled madam you is when you could be strengthening your muscle tone and flexibility. Why not give it a try? It would give you something positive to look forward to instead of looking for ways to take advantage of your own daughter." She gazed at Alice hoping for a fitting reaction, but Alice's expression turned as blank as a store mannequin's, sending out the message *nobody's home so leave me alone.* "You've got to stop this stealing and selling business and the finagling with Depends and such. I've seen how you come to life with all of these actions, but they're not doing your heart or your soul any

226

good. You've gone from bad to worse lickety-split. Don't be forgetting who you're messing with, Alice. I sees you for what you are. Jewish Commandment; my ass!"

Sondra walked over to the side of the bed. "You know what Mimi told me this morning, Alice?" she asked quietly.

"No. Why would I know that?" Alice answered. "Am I supposed to know everything that's in Mimi's head?" Alice reached across the comforter to pick up the remote control before kicking off her slippers and swinging her legs back onto the bed. She turned on the television.

Sondra brought her face within inches of Alice's ears. "Well, I'm going to tell you 'cause it concerns your interests, as well."

Alice continued to stare at the screen as she rapidly changed the channels "Why do they always have to broadcast their advertisements at the same time?" she complained. "It's not like this in New York."

"It's exactly the same in New York," Sondra corrected.

"Are you going to tell me they are serving frozen fish in the dining room?" Alice asked. "I know that already."

"Mimi and Rosalita are starting to worry about their jobs," she said in an even more hushed tone than before. "And mine might be at risk too."

"Why is that?" Alice asked out loud, not respecting the atmosphere of secrecy Sondra was trying to create. "Glenbrook can't be running out of money to pay your salaries. They charge a fortune for us to be here!"

Sondra whispered, "'Cause Mr. Dean is concerned about a lot of robberies taking place.

Plenty of folks are reporting not being able to find what they want, so Mr. Dean's starting to seriously investigate the situation."

The color drained from Alice's neck and cheeks. Her head bolted away from her pillow so fast that Sondra had to jerk backwards to avoid being bopped on the nose. "You almost gave me a heart attack just then!" She paused for a moment to regain some strength, smoothing out the fabric of her robe by her legs. "I'll just have to take a little less on my next rounds, and I'll pace them out more."

"No you won't!" Sondra yelled after jumping back up to an erect position. "You have to stop completely! This ain't no joke, Alice. Me and the others could lose our jobs over this, and we don't have no rich family to support us if that happens."

"Like I do," Alice said with a sneer. "Well, that's exactly why I have to keep taking what I do. I'm the good one who's helping you out. Think of me as an updated version of Robin Hood."

Sondra strode determinedly toward the door. "That's it; we're finished for now. There's no talking sense into you, today. As I've told you before, count me out of your schemes. I'm done with them!"

"So, you're not going to take anything more from me?" Alice asked haughtily.

"No, I ain't—and I mean it!" Right away, Sondra regretted how loudly she had uttered these words. She quickly checked the hallway for anyone passing by. "This has been going on much too long. I thought you would get tired of sneaking around and grabbing things after one month or two, but this is way too absurd. My God, we're into month three of you being a law-breaking, good-for-nothing robber. I hoped that once the thrill wore off, you would go back to being the old Alice."

"I don't want to be the old Alice. I'm old enough as it is," Alice howled. "There wasn't any fun in that!"

"The stealing has to stop! Do you hear me?" Sondra yelled. She took one or two long breaths and then said, "All right, we got to take it down a peg or two. Let's both calm down, okay?"

Alice's response was, "Well, er…well, we'll see," but it came out more singsong than earnest. "We've got to make sure Delmont makes it through to his senior year, don't we?"

"This ain't no more about Delmont, or you, or me. From now on you can go and partake in the Glenbrook events just like the other folks do." Sondra stooped to pick up a set of dirtied towels. "Go and hear what Jan has to say at her Fireside Chats. She's got a whole following coming to see her; she's become quite a celebrity, answering legal questions as well and not charging a single nickel for it."

Alice went back to flipping through the stations on her TV, trying her best to tune Sondra out.

"She's doing those folks a whole lot of good. Last week, they even ran out of space and had to put more chairs in the hallway."

"That's a safety hazard," Alice commented as she fluffed out a flattened part of her hair with her fingers.

"Alice, it don't surprise me none that you be the one to point that out without having anything else nice to say."

Sondra exited the apartment, leaving Alice deflated, deprived of her single justification for her crime spree.

"I'll prove to you that you're making a big mistake!" Alice called to the closed door. "You'll be sorry. I know you will be. Wait until you see the next batch of goodies I collect. Your tongue will be hanging out the way it always does. You'll change your mind in a heartbeat and will be begging me for a handout. Yes, you will. I know you will!"

Alice's anger toward Sondra spilled over to the dining room, social room, and wherever the two women happened to be sharing the same space. At lunch, Alice would accidentally-on-purpose drop her napkin beyond reach of retrieving it, spill her tea or coffee, send back her "too cold" dishes, and complain about the "too small" or "too large" portion sizes. On some days, she would eat slower than a mouse, forcing Sondra to wait longer than usual for Alice to finish every last crumb before being able to finally clear the table and move on to her other chores. Alice would shoot her stares, sneers, smirks, and unspoken messages of hate, which resulted in half-scoops of ice cream, slivers of pie, crumbled cookies, and broken brownies on Alice's dessert plates.

For revenge, Alice would intentionally aim outside the bowl when she had to use the toilet. "I had an accident. I couldn't help it." She would fake her apologies while Sondra hunched over on her knees and scrubbed away at whatever mess Alice had caused.

"I bet you do feel sorry, Miss Alice. I don't doubt that one bit," Sondra would mutter. "Hmm, it must be scary losing control over all your faculties the way that you are. Old and decrepit. What could possibly be next?"

Chapter Thirty-one

Alice was alone in her apartment and changing the channels on her television, hoping to watch a soap opera or talk show, when a news bulletin flashed across the screen. The Palm Beach County Sheriff, tall and serious in his hunter green uniform, was standing behind a podium flanked by a trilogy of governmental flags. A large five-pointed gold star spanned the wall behind him as he held a freezer bag with lots of little bags inside, raising it higher for the benefit of the camera crew. The bag was identical to the ones she had found on her clandestine travels within Glenbrook and had presumed to contain sweeteners, which caused Alice to perk up and pay attention to what was being said.

"This is a major coup for our department," the sheriff announced. "We have successfully raided a local mill engaged in the production and distribution of heroin. Four people have been arrested and authorities have seized 80,000 individual doses of heroin in addition to bricks containing fifteen pounds of heroin."

Alice stared at the TV. "Holy crap! Oy Gevalt."

"We believe this narcotics ring is responsible for 59 overdoses, 27 of them fatal. The amount of heroin found could have killed tens of thousands of people."

Alice repeated, "Oy Gevalt." As quickly as she could, she jumped off her bed and maneuvered her way to her closet. Fueled by the excitement over this latest news, she had no need to use her walker. As usual, there was a total mess on her closet floor. Leaning on the closet door for support, she lowered herself gradually, emitting several grunts and puffs, until she came to a sitting position. Like a woman on a rampage, she then flung shoes, pocketbooks, cereal boxes, and empty fast-food containers aside. *Please tell me I didn't use any of it yet. But I would have known then, wouldn't I? Sondra, you better not haven't taken any for yourself. Holy crap! I can't believe it. I can't believe it. What's that stuff doing here anyway? Do all those residents know about it? How come it was in their apartments?*

She threw her bag of photographs so hastily aside, many of the snapshots spilled out onto the floor. Becoming a little light-headed, she paused a short while to regain her equilibrium. Next, she dug into jacket sleeves and pants' pockets, sunhats and music boxes, until she came across the freezer bag she had pilfered, stuffed into a Macy's shopping bag. It looked just like the one the Sheriff had held up.

Alice's next action was to make sure her front door was locked. Leaning on the closet door with both hands, she managed to hoist herself up. The flurry of activity had been exhausting, so she took in some necessary breaths to bolster her strength. Her legs were shaking as she walked first to the front door and then back to her bed, gripping the freezer bag firmly all along the way. After she dropped onto her bed, she was able to get a closer look at the more-than-likely contraband. Counting out ten of them, she noticed the tiny bags inside were really just folded wax paper. *I have a bundle of 10 bags, just like the Sheriff on the telly.* She opened up one of the bags and studied the brownish, white powder. It had a pungent, vinegary smell. *Well, this sure isn't Sweet'N Low or Splenda, I'll tell you that much.* She considered dabbing some powder on her moistened finger and placing it on her tongue, but then thought better of it. *I've got to tell someone about this, but who can I tell? Jan? Mr. Dean? They'll want to know how I happen to have it.*

What possible story could I cook up? They'll find out about my thefts and what I've been up to. I can't have that at all! What about telling Sondra? No! She could be in on the drug ring. Maybe that's why she stopped being my accomplice. I could have been too much of a liability. Maybe, it got too much for her to handle. Well, in any case, she'll now have her hands full clearing up my closet and the mess I made this morning.

Alice placed the freezer bag in back of the drawer where she stashed her other loot. *For the time being, I'm not telling anyone about this. I'll try and forget all about it.* She picked up the remote control and flipped through the stations, dodging the commercials until she could find the Jerry Springer show, Maury Povich, or something just as raunchy.

Chapter Thirty-two

While Charlotte was busily decorating the lobby for the 2004 July 4th bash Glenbrook was hosting that coming weekend, Jan tapped on her shoulder to comment about the lineup of residents outside Mr. Dean's office.

"What's going on today? Are they giving away freebies?"

"Oh that," Charlotte uttered. She was wearing a self-made Uncle Sam hat that had fallen over her eyebrows. "It seems some of our residents are missing more items than usual. Mr. Dean is compiling a list, trying to get to the bottom of it." Charlotte pushed the poster board brim toward the crown of her head.

"That's too bad," Jan said, perusing the queue of agitated seniors. "My mother complains a lot about missing items, but they always turn up somewhere or other."

"Yes, that's usually the case," Charlotte agreed, sprinkling glitter on the daily menu markup where she had squirted dots of glue. She closed the cap on the glitter stick. "Still, we don't want the folks getting more riled up than they already are. We don't want them becoming more afraid and distraught over memory loss. My own mind is a sieve. I'd forget where I put it if it wasn't already sewn on."

"I know what you mean. That's why I have lists in every room of my house."

"Lists?" Charlotte repeated as she rubbed her fingertips free of the glue and red specks. "I have lists, I have string on my fingers, I have notes sent to my email, but none of these gimmicks seem to work."

Jan glanced at her watch and started moving away. "I'm sorry, but I'm already a little late. I've got to run upstairs for my Fireside Chat."

Charlotte pointed to the staircase. "It's in the large lounge upstairs, in case you've forgotten. You'll recognize it behind the curtains of crepe paper I hung earlier and by the gung-ho crowd waiting inside."

Many of the arranged folding chairs were already occupied by the time Jan took her place at the head of the lounge. As was her custom, she now doublechecked that the heat switch to the fireplace had been turned off before she sat down.

Surveying the area, Jan was impressed with the array of red, white, and blue balloons and the miniature American flags placed artfully about the furniture. She greeted the attendees with either a wave or a smile, until she came across her mother's reserved and unfriendly face parked in the middle of the room between Muriel and Helen. Alice had not shown up since the tail end of the very first Fireside Chat. *What is she doing here? When I delivered her supplies, she hadn't mentioned a word about attending this afternoon. Oh crap, I hope she doesn't make a scene or cause trouble.*

By the time the lounge had grown full to capacity, Jan had already distributed a quiz sheet and pencil to each individual present. A buzz arose in the room as the audience began to tackle the questions, prompting Jan to call out, "I grant you that some of these might be tricky, but it will prove more fun if you try to tackle them on your own."

Jan heard Natalie confess to her neighbor that she couldn't remember the last name of Fred Astaire's dance partner and would appreciate a little help. Murray asked if anyone knew which movie starred Edward G. Robinson and

Bette Davis, and Miriam refused to share with Mimi the name of the 1943 Broadway show written by Cole Porter in which Ethel Merman enjoyed top-billing. Denise wanted to know if it was Frigidaire or Maytag that had made the first home installed freezer. Although Alice had immediately tossed her sheet of paper aside, she was actively assisting Muriel in filling out her answers. It was pleasing to Jan to see how engaged and excited everyone had become with the exercise.

After reviewing the quiz results and identifying the freezer manufacturer to be Sub-Zero, to which most people commented, "I've never heard of that one," Jan steered the conversation towards issues of modernization and matters of technology. Arthur yelled out, "We've come a long way, baby!"

Jan asked how many in the room owned a cell phone, but only the staff members raised their hands. Arthur again yelled out, "Nobody talks to each other anymore. I don't want to talk into a tiny little device like Dick Tracey did. I want to see the expression on a person's face; if they are sad or happy about what I've just said, then I want to know it. Do you remember the silent films, when the entire story was played out through the actors' eyes?"

"Oh please, that wasn't acting," Alice shared with Muriel. "Those films seem utterly ridiculous now."

Helen stood up and offered, "My grandkids sit talking into their phones at the dining table—even when we're all gathered at a restaurant. I think it's deplorable. My father would have given me a smack on my *derrière* for such rudeness." Harold squeezed Helen's hand, leaned over, and gave her a peck on the cheek after she sat down, which spurred Alice to whisper to Muriel, "Those lovers should take it outside."

Jan acknowledged a woman she had not met before, whose brunette-hair was pulled back into a bun and whose raised hand displayed a large pearl pinkie ring. "I feel like I don't fit in anymore. It's a completely different world out there than what I'm used to."

Alice looked again at Muriel and asked, "Who the bloody hell is she?"

Muriel reported, "Her name is Esther and she just moved in on the ground floor."

"In Alberto Monti's place?" Alice inquired, to which Muriel responded, "uh huh."

"Jeez, he just died a few days ago," Alice exclaimed.

"No, it was actually three weeks ago," Muriel corrected.

"They move them in and out quickly enough around here," Alice noted.

"Hush up, you two. With your mumbling, I can't hear a thing anyone else has to say," a man sitting directly behind Muriel complained.

Alice twisted her torso sideways to address the man. "I suggest you mind your own business then and stop listening in on our conversation."

When it was Denise's turn to speak, she commented that the concept of "family" or "quality family time" wasn't the same anymore. "And family isn't just what the Republican Party wishes for us to believe it is."

Someone in the back row called out, "Well, the Democrats aren't any better. Most of their male candidates are caught with their pants hanging down in some other woman's boudoir."

"Let's try to keep politics out of this discussion," Jan hastily requested.

Denise was anxious to add more on the subject. "I don't think families are the same as what they used to be. Most young women go to work either because they have to for economic reasons or because raising children is just too darned difficult. Women's Lib has sent a lot of women up the corporate ladder, but I don't believe so many of them are that happy. The year may be 2004, but no, Arthur, we have not come such a long way, baby!"

"Does she think she's running for office?" Alice asked no one in particular. "Denise, that was some speech; you've got my vote, but how about moving on to a juicier topic?"

Denise, choosing to ignore Alice's snub, continued with her train of thought. "Kids today are being raised in overcrowded daycare centers or in their own homes where the televisions are glorified babysitters and the caregivers are ignorant people who don't even speak a word of English." An audible shuffling of feet followed this last remark, and some staff members chose that moment to depart the room.

Alice leaned into Muriel's side and whispered, "Is she talking about the ones that work here at Glenbrook?"

The same person in the back row as before called out again. "You don't even have to be married to have kids. There's nothing holy about it anymore."

Arthur volunteered, "Well, you've also got queers hoping to get married and have babies as well. What kind of families would you call these?"

It seemed many people had an opinion to express about this matter, and the decorum in the social room completely fell apart. Amid the turmoil, Muriel shared with Alice that she heard Esther's son was a homosexual.

"What's the difference if someone is gay or not?" Alice responded, her tone far from pleasant and her eyebrows slanted so close together they left hardly any space between them. "Do I care what someone does behind closed doors? No, I do not and neither should anyone else. Muriel, you're a malicious yenta who should keep her damn mouth shut!"

Amid the ensuing chaos, Jan went about trying to regain control of the group. She called out, "May I please have your attention? Please, let everyone calm down. Let's not get carried away," and then resorted to flicking the overhead lights on and off. She heard some frantic cries related to a possible earthquake, hurricane, or fireworks and then called out, "Nothing terrible is happening. I turned the lights on and off to get your attention. I'm sorry to tell you but the session has ended. We've run out of time."

"You should have said something," Alice said to a very flustered Jan after she made her way to the fireplace wall—most of the others had shuffled past her in the opposite direction. Before leaving, Muriel stood by the doorway waiting for Alice, but Alice had waved her on. "I'll catch up with you downstairs. Save me some potato chips and a diet coke from the refreshments, if you will."

Now the mother and daughter were standing in the empty lounge, face to face. "You're not very good at this," Alice denounced. "It's very stupid how you're handling it."

"What would you have liked me to say?" Jan countered. Already feeling bent out of shape and exhausted by the disintegration of the Fireside Chat, she did not take kindly to her mother's additional censure.

"You should have said something in support of gays getting married," Alice argued.

"Oh, really?" Jan replied in a manner she knew was far too smart-alecky for Alice. "I didn't think that was of concern to you. How well do you keep abreast of this topic?"

"I watch the evening news. I read the newspapers," Alice declared.

"I thought the only paper you read was the *National Enquirer*."

"There's nothing wrong with gay people enjoying the same rights as everyone else," was Alice's retort.

"I'm glad to hear you say that," Jan commended. "You're revealing yourself to be quite a liberal proponent. You need to keep in mind that this is Florida. This is where Anita Bryant fought an ordinance banning discrimination against gays in the 1970s and won. This is the state where gay couples can never adopt children." Jan felt a throbbing in her temple, and became aware of a strain fermenting around her eyes. She would have liked to swipe her mother's presence away with the swoosh of her arm.

Alice raised her chin. "There's no need to act so *snooty*, trying to poke fun at me." An inflexible rod of steel, she continued to bate Jan with a vindictive undertone. "You should have said more on that particular topic. It's a disgrace that you didn't." For some reason, these words hit Jan like a one-two punch.

"Mother," Jan voiced with contempt, "I don't believe you are in a position to judge me right now or to accuse me of poking fun at someone." She flitted around the room picking up discarded flyers and tossed pencils, hoping her mother would take the hint and disappear like the others already had. Stooping to pick up the remnants from a white shattered balloon, Jan knew what she was about to shout out would be hurtful, but she said it anyway. "And while we're on this topic and talking about judging people, why didn't *you* ever try to get in touch with Henry? How could you have *thrown* him out of your home in the first place?"

Alice began to topple, but she grabbed hold of her walker, backing up to increase the distance between herself and Jan. Her faltering indicated she had received a damaging blow. "Things were different then. I did the best I could, given my circumstances. I made the decision that seemed right at that time."

Jan turned to look Alice in the eye. "Your son was gay, and you disowned him because of it. That's what I call a disgrace! No one in their right mind would ever consider that the right thing to do. As a mother, you failed him miserably."

Alice's body stiffened, cementing her to the ground. "And how did you treat your own son when he was just a boy?" she pounced back.

"Fine. I treated him just fine," Jan said defiantly, massaging her cheekbones and forehead.

"That's not what he said when he would come crying to me. 'My mother's a jerk…she's always on my case…whatever I do it's never enough…she's suffocating me…I hate her.'"

"He was just going through a stage then. All boys do," Jan defended. "But Henry's death was a direct result of your actions." Jan paused to gather her composure and inhaled slowly. Thrusting her right finger at Alice's face, she chopped the air and screamed, "You killed Henry!"

"Is my chest bleeding?" Alice cried. "I just felt a knife stab right through to my heart. How nasty and vicious you can be! Just like your father, you are. You, more so than the others. You think you just inherited his brains? Well, you're just like him: sadistic, spiteful, narcissistic, cruel, and bitter! Don't forget sick and crazy!"

It was as if a lock on Alice's true emotions had suddenly sprung open. Accusations, insults, and vulgarity spewed out of her mouth, revealing a fury that had been compressed, submerged, and hidden over a lifetime.

"I hate you! You're a heartless bitch! You don't think I notice how you resent having to come here? Too high and mighty to be seen with the likes of me? You're nothing. Nothing at all! I never wanted you from the get go. You belong in the mud with the muck and slime. I don't need you. I never did," she shouted. "I wish I could drop dead right in front of you so you'd know along with everyone else that you were the one to kill *me*!"

Jan's eye strain had now developed into a full-fledged pounding headache. She could feel her heart racing a mile-a-minute. Somewhere, she had once read if someone was insulting you, the best thing to do was erect an imaginary shield all around your body so the barbs bounced off of the shield and did not penetrate any further. Alice's words, however, came hammering down on top of Jan's head, pounding her into the ground and rendering her completely incapable of forging any effective defense. The condemnation that she was a nothing, a repetition of her father's most vile denunciation, was tantamount to being mercilessly kicked after having fallen from the top of Mount Everest.

"You know," Jan yelled, summoning whatever strength she could in order to retaliate, "it was a good thing you aborted that other baby. Otherwise, it would have been one more sorrowful, wretchedly unhappy child that you would have brought into this world only to suffer from your neglect and ignorance. Too bad you weren't dumped in the garbage can along with the fetus!"

"How dare you say that to me? How dare you!" Alice shrieked, holding onto her walker with all of her might. "I never wanted you. I wished you were never born. I tried to abort you too, only it didn't work." She inhaled deeply, the air making a harsh grating sound. Her lip curled; her nostrils flared. "And when you were a child growing up? You were a waste of my time. An undesirable deformity. A valueless non-entity!"

Everything inside Jan felt trampled and raw. She fell into the chair next to the fireplace, dizzy and disoriented. *What has been my legacy from Alice and Norman Block? What did they bestow upon me? What were their gifts?* "Murdered fetuses and hemorrhaging blood," she lashed out. "Hatred, abuse, self-loathing, misery, constant fear, constant guilt, constant shame, and, yes, don't forget intimidation and domination. Thank you, Mother. Thank you for being one of the shittiest parents in the entire world."

"Why don't you pack up your fancy, oh-so-important briefcase and go home now?" Alice's voice came out icily cold. "You don't belong at Glenbrook, and I for one never want to see you here ever again. Get out!" She hoisted her walker in the direction of the exit and stormed off.

"Amazing how fast you can propel yourself when you want to, Mom," Jan shouted after her. Alice glanced over her shoulder and flipped a middle finger, surprising Jan that her mother even knew the meaning behind the gesture.

"You need to take lessons from some of the other women here on how to age gracefully." Jan continued to yell but the door of the elevator had already closed with Alice securely tucked into its compartment.

"You're a nasty, crotchety old bag," Jan muttered, not caring if anyone else heard. *You delight in portraying yourself as the victim in life, but I know full well how downright mean and sadistic you really are. I know how far you'll go to get rid of something that you really don't want. Your "doll" friends should know some of the real stories about you. Perhaps I'll talk about Izzy at the next Fireside Chat when we explore the notion of pet therapy. They'll be eager to learn about how you decided against drowning your dog but took him instead on three different bus rides so you could ditch him in a far-off neighborhood, hoping he'd be hit by a car.*

As Jan descended the central staircase, she thought some more about Izzy. *Aren't dogs supposed to be smart? How come Izzy beat my mother back to her home and waited for her by the front gate? Didn't he know enough to stay away?*

Chapter Thirty-three

Sondra lifted a dried tea bag from a pile of discarded papers and placed it in an empty mug to bring back down to the kitchen. Before heading for the door, she turned to Alice, seated by the window and staring out into space. "What's the matter, Alice? You be looking mighty low today. Do you want me to take your temperature?"

"I'm not sick," Alice was quick to report, albeit lethargically. "You don't look so hot yourself."

"Then why you moping and looking like somebody be giving you a good talking to?" Sondra approached Alice and placed her hand on Alice's forehead. "I noticed you didn't finish all your fish and chips at lunch today."

Alice pushed Sondra's hand away. "I don't need you to spy on me in the dining room, and I don't need you now to check my temperature," she said with renewed vigor. "What you just said about me, I could throw right back at you. You're trying mighty hard to mask some kind of sadness, but your eyes are speaking the truth."

"Say what you want; I was just being hospitable."

Alice looked about her room, twiddling her thumbs. "I was going to give you all the *People* magazines I just read, but now I've changed my mind."

"I read them all already."

"That's right. You sneak into my room when I'm not around, eat my cookies, and read my magazines," Alice accused.

"Who's the sneak around here?" Sondra asked, eyes popping wide open. "Don't you go accusing me of doing what I don't be doing no more." She sat down on the mattress and took hold of both of Alice's hands. "Now you tell old Sondra what really be going on with you today. Did you get caught stealing? I need to know the truth."

"It's a long story. Don't you have other work you should be seeing to?"

Sondra took note of a tear forming in Alice's eye and said, "I'm seeing to you; that's my work for right now." She handed Alice a package of tissues. "Come on, sugar; tell me what be troubling you."

"I'll tell you if you tell me first."

"Fair enough," Sondra agreed. "I'm sad today because I spoke to Delmont this morning, and he told me a friend of his died from overdosing on tainted cocaine. There, I've got it off my chest; I don't want to say any more about it. Let's move on to you."

"It was the fish and chips."

Sondra couldn't hold back from laughing. "I'm sorry, hon. That's what got you so upset? Today's lunch menu?" Her face broke out into a wild, explosive laugh. "And I even saw to it you got two cherries on your ice cream sundae, being I was in a kinder mood and tired of this cat and mouse game we been playing."

"No, you idiot!" Alice yelled. "The fish and chips reminded me of an incident from long ago."

Sondra attempted to rein in her chuckles. She extracted a tissue from the package she had given Alice and dabbed at the corner of her watering eyes. "I see. Well, er, you just go ahead and fill me in on everything that happened so long ago to be making you as upset as you are now."

The very last time when Norman had come to the hospital to retrieve her, Alice was more reluctant than ever to leave. She was just seventy years old at that time—already feeling old, but what did she know then? "Someone should have told me that when you get to be 90, which is what I am now, *that's* when you really know what feeling old is all about! ".

"I always appreciated how considerate everyone treated me there," she relayed to Sondra. "People handled me with respect—actions sorely missing in my personal life."

Sondra nodded, listening full-heartedly, and then decided to add, "Yes, everyone be needing to be treated with respect."

"Anyway, as our car entered the parking garage of our Forest Hills apartment building, I happened to ask Norman, 'What have you been up to lately?' I said it as casually as if I were asking him about the weather."

Sondra sat patiently for Alice's story to unfold.

"Norman was startled by the inquiry, and that of course made him angry. 'What's it your business?' he asked all mean-like. Well, I don't know what got into me then, being so bold and all, but I told him that I'd had enough of his prancing around the apartment in nothing more than a robe and feeling sorry for himself all day long. 'Why don't you get a job?' I asked him."

Sondra contributed, "White men, black men; they're all cut from the same cloth."

"Norman couldn't believe that I actually had the audacity to speak to him the way that I did, and he yelled at me again, 'I'm the head of this fucking household and I make the decisions around here. Who in the bloody hell do you think you are?' Pardon my French, Sondra."

Sondra said, "Go on, Miss Alice, and don't be feeling like you have to apologize for the language you use."

"I told Norman that there were tons of listings in the newspaper. He was so intelligent and had such a great mind; he could have been an asset to any business that hired him. Well, the blood vessels in Norman's forehead began to pulsate like an unattended teakettle about to blow its whistle. He placed a heavy foot on the gas pedal, causing the car to dangerously lurch forward into its spot. I saw the concrete wall through the windshield coming right at me; I was petrified."

Sondra bit her bottom lip. "Did you crash into that wall?"

"No, thank God. The next thing Norman did was leave me in the car without saying another word, but he made sure to slam the door plenty hard behind him."

Sondra leaned forward, her curiosity piqued. "What did you do then, Alice?"

"I felt so weak. The car had been left extremely close to a support column, which stood right smack in the middle of my door. I had to clumsily inch my way out of my seat and it was exhausting. I huffed and puffed all the way to the bank of elevators where I could rest against the wall and wait for the empty cab doors to slide open. By then, Norman was nowhere in sight."

Alice went on to describe how the elevator had brought her up to the seventh floor without making any stops and she had been so thankful and surprised to have found her apartment door, with its tarnished copper '7B' centered on its façade, left ajar.

After trudging inside, she placed her pocketbook on the floor by the foyer, expressing a heavy sigh of resignation with her unfair lot in life—loud enough, though, for Norman to hear wherever he was hiding—and then she headed straight to the kitchen to make the *mamzer* his dinner.

"After all that, you made the bum his dinner?" Sondra asked incredulously.

"I was too afraid not to," Alice stated.

"He beat you? That dirt bag beat you right out of the hospital, Alice?"

Alice trembled. "No, not really; he just beat me once when we were much younger."

Sondra's head shook up and down. "But you was in fear that he'd do it again?"

"I lived my entire life in fear. In any case, a short while later, I called him to the kitchen table to eat a sizzling pile of fish and chips, which was his favorite."

Sondra acknowledged the reference to the fish and chips. "I guess this is the point your story's been leading up to."

"Norman neither responded to my call nor made any appearance in the kitchen that evening, 'Don't think for one minute that I'm wrapping up your meal and putting it in the fridge for you to enjoy later on,' I told him."

"No siree!" Sondra cheered.

"So I threw the entire contents of his plate in the trashcan."

Sondra shrieked, raising both her arms into the air. "High five me, girl."

It took Alice a while to figure out she was meant to slap Sondra's hands, but then she complained, "Ahem. My voice is drying out a bit." She made several attempts to clear her throat and pointed to her dresser. "Sondra, be a dear and hand me some Nips from my candy dish, please."

Sondra rose. She stuck her hand in her pocket and brought out a roll of tropical fruit flavored Lifesavers.

"Here," she said, tossing the pack to Alice, "suck on these instead; they will help coat your throat." Alice took the top pineapple candy and offered Sondra the next in line, which was red. Sondra placed it in her mouth.

"Watermelon or strawberry?" Alice asked as she chomped on her candy.

"Watermelon," Sondra answered as she sat down, her eyes daring Alice not to make a saucy comment. "Now don't you go breaking your teeth on that candy. It's meant to dissolve!" Alice suggested that they switch places so she could recline on the bed, so Sondra helped Alice to the bed and then seated herself on the chair.

The two women took some time to savor the sweetness in their mouths. Alice downed her third Lifesaver, which was coconut, and went back to her recital.

"'You can sulk all you want,' I said, getting back to the scene I was telling you about, 'but I'm not playing into your temper tantrums anymore.' Even I had been stunned by my newly found bravery. Norman screamed, 'You can go fuck yourself!' pardon my—oh never mind. That night I slept on the couch in the living room. We didn't speak a word to each other the next day. I'm still feeling a little peckish, Sondra. Want to share some of Jan's cookies?"

Sondra answered in the affirmative, so Alice directed her to behind the bathroom door, where her floral fleece robe was hanging. "They're in a Ziploc bag in the inside left pocket." Sondra came back holding the bag, which she extended to Alice. Each woman took a cookie to munch on.

"You see, Maureen, Henry, Jan, and I had all been used to Norman's silent treatments," Alice began again. "These were actually preferred to his vehement tirades, but on this occasion, Norman peppered his behavior with a lot of nastiness. He had hidden the car keys and pulled out all the phones from their wall jacks. If I wanted to see or speak to anyone, it meant that I had to walk several blocks to the nearest phone booth or take public transportation. Don't forget: no one had cell phones back then."

Alice took two more cookies and indicated to Sondra to do the same. "Wait one minute," Sondra said, and she ran to the bathroom again, coming back with a pitcher of water and two paper cups. "Just in case we're thirsty."

"Maureen and Jan took turns visiting me and tried convincing me to seek a divorce," Alice proceeded, "but I wouldn't hear of it. I thought I was too old for that. What would have been the point at that time of my life? I felt too sorry for him to leave; he had no one else."

Sondra poured the two cups of water and handed Alice her drink. "I know it's easier to preach than to do. Your daughters thought they were making sense at that time. I know plenty of women miserable with the men they got, but then they be just as miserable when they're not with them anymore."

"Two weeks later, Norman came and asked me if I was good and happy."

"Oh, he did now? And what did you tell him?" Sondra asked.

"I had returned home on a Thursday evening from the boutique, where I used to work, at 10 o'clock that night. Under normal circumstances, Norman would wait in his car outside the store in order to drive me home, but for the last two weeks, I had to ride the subway."

Sondra shook her head in disapproval.

"'I'm fine; thank you very much!' I told him. 'Well, you should be feeling even finer now,' he said. 'Norman, I'm tired; it's been a very long day. I'm not up to solving any of your riddles,' I told him, and then he said, 'I'm starting tomorrow as manager of the liquor store on 63rd Drive in Rego Park, so you can finally put an end to all of your nagging and complaining.'"

"That was wonderful news," Sondra exclaimed.

"That's what I said. 'That's wonderful news,' I told him. 'I hope things work out for you there.' So that's when the iciness between us began to temporarily melt away."

"Hmm," Sondra exhaled, "that's some story, Alice."

"The punch line is that working in the liquor store was what got Norman killed."

"Oh, I see," Sondra admitted, swallowing her saliva. "That must have been just something awful to live through. Some wounds ain't never going to heal, Alice, and it's better not to keep picking at 'em either." Sondra made several attempts to arise from her sitting position. "Oh, oh, my legs are rebelling and have gotten all stiff on me," she groaned. "Give me a hand up, won't you?"

Alice rolled off her bed, taking her time to become fully erect, and then did her best to assist Sondra to a standing position. As she pulled on Sondra's hands, she asked, "Is this what they call 'the blind leading the blind'?"

"Whoa. I can hear my bones creaking," Sondra announced. Her uniform was disheveled and puffy pouches appeared under her eyes. She stifled a yawn.

"You should go take a nap somewhere," Alice advised. "And it wouldn't hurt you to lose a few pounds and exercise more."

Sondra regarded Alice with a blank stare. "I sees a hint of a worried look on your face so I be assuming you be talking from your heart this time out of concern for my well-being and not trying to go back to being nasty again likes you were before."

Alice nodded. "Yes, I do care about you, but that's only because I need you here to take care of me." A tee-hee escaped from her lips.

"I've got to go and do some of my other errands now," Sondra told her before allowing a second yawn to escape. "Unfortunately, napping is always out of the question, but I would be happy to hear you tell me all about that liquor store some other time. Why don't you turn on your television and watch *Jerry Springer*; the program is just about to start. If you're lucky, they're be a whole lot of hair-pulling and name-calling going on, just the way you like it!"

Chapter Thirty-four

After Alice was ready for bed the following evening, she asked Sondra to stay a little longer so they could continue their chat from the day before.

"I already stayed longer than I wanted to, trying to find your green nightie that you hid in a shoebox," Sondra told her. "I'm mad enough that I've wasted so much of my free time on account of you."

"I didn't hide it there. You must have put it in the shoebox when I wasn't looking," Alice insisted.

"Uh huh. That's right," Sondra answered, vigorously nodding her head up and down. "I was terribly afraid you might steal it from yourself."

"Come," Alice beckoned, "Give me a few more minutes of your time."

"You ain't too tired? I already gave you your sleeping pills."

"I didn't swallow them yet." Alice opened her right hand to reveal two little white pills pressed into the creases of her palm.

"How'd you manage that?" Sondra asked with astonishment. "I swear I watched as you swallowed all of your medicine."

"I'm very good at faking some things," Alice admitted with a grin. "You should have seen me when I had sex with Norman."

"Alice, yous a riot, all right! I'll stay for fifteen minutes but no more. I have an appointment to meet with someone later this evening, so's I need to do some fixing up beforehand."

"With a man?" Alice asked giddily, sounding too much like a fourth-grader discovering her best friend had just been kissed.

"Yes, with a man," Sondra confirmed.

Alice snickered. "Did you find him on a black dating service?"

"No, I did not. He's someone I happens to know personally, for your information."

"Good, you'll be a lot safer that way."

Sondra pulled a chair next to Alice's pillows and turned off the overhead fixture. She then switched on the lamp by the bedside table, casting an amber glow into Alice's room. Sondra sat down, bending forward to be included within the circle of light. "Okay, let's hear what you got to tell me,"

Alice sat with her legs outstretched in front and her back leaning against two stacked pillows. Her multi-freckled chest sank below the scooped neckline of her green striped nightgown. It almost seemed to Alice like she and Sondra were two young friends at a sleepover, sharing their most intimate secrets; oh, how she relished having Sondra's undivided attention.

Alice talked about the first few months Norman had worked at the liquor store; how he had thrown a young customer out onto the street for being barefoot. Another time, he got into a heated discussion over which company made the oldest and best Scotch. That customer had insisted it was a Macallan, but Norman, who didn't like to be challenged on any subject, argued it was a Dalmore, calling the customer, "An ignorant piece of shit," and two minutes later, shoved *him* out the door."

Sondra mentioned, "I never heard of either whiskey; they must be way too rich for my blood. Norman didn't care too much about customer loyalty, huh?"

"One evening Norman was particularly ruffled over a run-in with his co-worker, Jake," Alice continued. "The dispute arose when Jake took a dig at Norman's clothing. When Norman told me exactly what Jake had said, I couldn't believe my ears."

Sondra tilted her head closer to Alice.

"Jake said, 'I'm guessing you polished your oxfords a million times to get that shine; too bad your ugly mug is what everyone else is going to see in them.' What stopped Norman from punching Jake in his face right there and then for being so insolent, I'll never know. He belittled and berated me for saying a lot less than that, I'm telling you, Sondra."

"I bet he did, hon," Sondra concurred.

"Fast with the comebacks, Norman then asked Jake if he was borrowing his daughter's plimsoles. 'If you had any sense in that lump of wood you carry around on your shoulders, you would know they belong in a gymnasium but not in a place of business. Why don't you go home to change and come back when you're not looking so much like a fag?' Jake didn't like hearing what Norman had to say. He raised his fists, ready to strike, saying, 'I'm gonna teach you something useful—'"

Sounding keyed-up and self-congratulatory as if she had found the main clue in a murder mystery, Sondra cut Alice off. "That's where he done your old man in?"

"Who?" Alice asked, losing track of her place in the story.

"Jake. They got into a fight and Jake iced Norman. Jake killed Norman." Sondra clarified.

"No, you silly goose. That's not how it happened," Alice corrected.

"Well, what happened next?" Sondra said, tapping her foot and becoming testy about the time.

"Jake told Norman, 'They're called 'sneakers' in America. When you gonna get with the program?'"

"And?" Sondra asked.

"And what?" Alice responded.

"And how did Norman die in the liquor store? That's what I'm sitting and waiting to find out all this time, all the while I have a nice hunk of a reverend man waiting *for me*. Alice, tell me the rest of the story and don't you go be beating around the bush none no more."

Alice, taking note of Sondra's reference to the reverend, went on to tell her about the robberies in the liquor store, describing how Norman had yelled out, "Scum bags!' after the very first one."

"Yes'm. I bet he did," Sondra replied.

"After the second hold-up," Alice told her, "he said, 'I'm going to quit. I've had enough of that shit.' I begged him not to, seeing we needed the money so badly. I just thought he shouldn't go overboard and wear his fancy things to work. That gold watch of his would certainly catch the eye of someone up to no good. Well, for that he whip-lashed me with his tongue."

Sondra reached over to pat Alice's wrist.

"Norman didn't quit his job, but he got a gun instead."

Sondra's tone turned serious as she took hold of Alice's hand. "Guns sure are a nasty business. I've seen plenty of them and plenty of the damage they've done, tearing flesh apart as well as families, crippling legs, killing little kids and good earnest folk, and landing way too many misguided hot heads, foolishly believing they were stronger and knew better than anyone else, in jail. Yes'm; guns sure are a nasty business."

"Well, you've certainly made it quite clear how you feel about guns, Sondra. Why not get yourself a soapbox in Hyde Park and ramble on over there, if you've got any more to add. If it's alright with you, I'll go on," Alice said.

"Okay, 'Miss You-can-mock-me-all-you-want.' I'm done talking. Now, *you have* less than two minutes to wrap this story up."

"In the third robbery, Norman's gold watch was taken as well as all the money. See, Sondra, I wasn't so stupid after all, was I?"

"No, you wasn't," Sondra reassured Alice.

"Jake had called out to Norman, 'Just give them what they want, please!' but Norman reached for his gun. He thought he knew better than anyone else. He had such a swelled head, swaggering everywhere he went, just like John Wayne in the movies, my husband was. Only he wasn't one bit like John Wayne. 'Fuck you,' Norman called out. I'm not apologizing for the curse words this time. You know it's not really me that's saying them; it's what Norman was saying."

"I thought we cleared this up yesterday," Sondra reminded Alice.

"Yes, we did. Anyway," Alice concluded, "Norman got shot, and he died right then and there."

"I'm sorry, Alice. It must have been very difficult for you at the time," Sondra commiserated.

"No. It was wonderful," Alice admitted, looking at Sondra sideways to see how she would react to such a peculiar confession. "I could finally feel free from that horrible man. He was like my prison guard. At his funeral, I stood respectably solemn, especially so with the men from the liquor store standing there in their finest Sunday suits and winter coats, looking so visibly upset and expressing so much concern for me and my family. Not one person could have guessed just how happy I really was inside; just how well things had actually unfolded. Had I been alone at the gravesite, I would have danced a jig like a *Wizard of Oz* munchkin celebrating the death of the wicked witch. For me, it was a true celebration!"

Chapter Thirty-five

For the balance of 2004, Jan had to make a concerted effort not to pull her car into the Glenbrook parking lot on the days she drove eastbound on Seacrest Road from State Road 7, returning home with her assignments from Susan Walsh's office. Mike had been astonished to see the observances of Labor Day, Rosh Hashanah, and Yom Kippur pass without any reference on Jan's part to her mother.

"She's not coming for dinner?"

"No."

"You're not stopping by there?"

"No."

Without spending excessive hours with Alice, Jan was now keeping herself busy with a multitude of assignments that ranged from drafting simple wills, making court appearances, filing motions and pleadings, and meeting personally with many of her clients. This new schedule with its freed-up time slots was also allowing her to participate in an interfaith coalition, which had recently formed in response to the genocide occurring in Darfur.

During some of her case consultations, it would pain Jan to see the disillusion painted across her clients' faces whenever they sought to exclude their family members out of their wills. She heard countless stories about how this son didn't talk to that son, how this child had lost a ton of money on a lame venture, how a wayward grandchild had become a drug addict, or how an ex-son-in-law had secreted every last cent in a contested divorce.

"If they didn't think my Seder was important enough to attend, then I'm not leaving them my money."

"They didn't even think to send me a Christmas card! Why should I bequeath them thousands?"

"He invested his half in the stock market and made a fortune. Why shouldn't his sibling get more to even it up?"

Time and again, she would ask herself, *where does the acrimony come from? What purpose does it serve? What happens to the rosy expectations people have at the start of their lifetimes, when they're making their plans as well as their babies? Where do they disappear to?*

After the big showdown, Jan refrained entirely from contacting her mother, assuming the staff at Glenbrook would be sure to notify her should a true emergency ever arise, although she told Mike her mother could rot and die in place without Jan ever wanting to see her again. Just the other day, however, while she was at work, she received a phone call from Mr. Dean, who had first assured her Alice was doing just fine. "She's just as cheery and charming as always," he told Jan, who had been grimacing silently in response.

As a courtesy, Mr. Dean was calling to make her aware of possible thefts being reported at Glenbrook. He was not sure if items were being stolen or misplaced, but he wanted her to be on guard, reporting anything unusual or suspect she might notice during her Fireside Chats.

"Oh, I'm sorry if Charlotte hasn't told you yet, but I've taken a hiatus from the Fireside Chats. There won't be any more for a while." Jan did not believe a further explanation was warranted.

"That is too bad," Mr. Dean offered, sounding genuinely upset. "I know how much everyone here looked forward to that activity."

"Just so you know, my mother had been complaining plenty about things being stolen from her apartment. Once, she had gone on and on about nightgowns she previously insisted I take home for safekeeping and had forgotten all about. Practically all of her so-called stolen items did eventually turn up again."

"Yes, I understand that's a strong possibility— especially given the age and condition of most of our residents," Mr. Dean replied, "but recently, I am receiving many more complaints than usual. We hire from a bonded company and all the staff are fully vetted, but still, I can't take the residents' concerns too lightly. I'm trying to keep tabs on the matter without alarming the Glenbrook community as a whole. If I can't get a handle on what's really going on, though, I will have to notify the police. My preference is not to do so, however. Please forgive me, but I have another call I need to take. Don't be shy about stopping in my office to say hello on your next visit."

"I'll do that," Jan said politely before ending the call. "Don't hold your breath until then," she added after placing the handset back on its receiver and hurrying off to the restroom.

Jan had been unhappily suffering from a bad case of the runs ever since she experienced the major confrontation with her mother. Erratic panic attacks, brought on by as little as a slight change in climate, would jolt her into scurrying for a bathroom to relieve her pain and discomfort, even in public venues such as supermarkets or department stores.

It had not helped Jan any to have to pass by Gillian's house each and every time she was following the route out of her community. Gillian, with her cute, perfect figure, would be gardening; Gillian, with her straight, thick shiny

262

hair would be sweeping; Gillian, with her non-flabby waistline and cellulite-free backside, would be fetching the mail; Gillian, with her long slender legs, would be walking her golden retriever; *Oh, what's that? Gillian isn't around? Oh, that's right: Gillian and Mike are attending a financial forecast seminar together*; and Jan, coming up short in every comparison to Gillian, would have to delay whatever trip she was intending and make a U-turn right back into her house, bolting over steps and through doorways to reach the nearest lavatory.

There wasn't a single trip taken on the turnpike or I-95 where Jan had not urgently pulled over onto an exit ramp to use a bathroom or dash through a restaurant searching frantically for the door labeled "Ladies", "Women", "Gals", "Dames", or "*Senoras*". On more than one instance, she had taken the plunge to enter the "Gents" out of sole desperation, hoping that the urinals remained unoccupied.

All of Jan's medical tests—of which there had been many—failed to identify a specific physiological ailment. The blood work, colonoscopy, and endoscopy revealed no abnormalities, but Jan was now weighing a lot less than she previously had. Jan pooh-poohed Mike's suggestion to visit Rick to discuss her predicament. "He's your guy, not mine," she maintained.

Throughout all of this turmoil, Mike moved into the guest room, claiming he wasn't getting a decent night's sleep due to Jan's running back and forth to the toilet. Jan suspected that this was just a convenient excuse. She would worry incessantly about when Mike's divorce papers were going to be served and would drill him: "Have you contacted a lawyer yet? Have you hired someone I know from Boca? Are we going to keep the financial division amicable and fair? Does Daniel know about us?" Mike would just stare back at Jan, throw his hands into the air, and stomp away.

"Well, you're stringing me along and it isn't right," Jan would yell. "Lawyers charge by the hour, and you're dissipating our marital funds by dragging this out."

Chapter Thirty-six

Shimmying in tune with the upbeat *Boogie Woogie Bugle Boy of Company B*, Charlotte dispensed tongue depressors, paints, string, and odd-shaped buttons to the few people at the work tables in the Arts and Crafts room. It was an overcast, rainy day outdoors, and Charlotte was doing her best to liven the mood of the participants. She had on a canary yellow T-shirt, with the word, SMILE, printed in black across her chest, and blue jeans, splattered with a rainbow of droplets. "Come on you guys, get with the rhythm. Tap your feet or move whatever muscles you can. Let's get this party started!"

Entered into the 1.30 p.m. time slot on the activity sheet was a choice of *Simon Says* or fabricating "Home Sweet Home" plaques for the residents' front doors. Despite Charlotte's racing through the corridors earlier in the day, trying to drum up enthusiasm, attendance at each of the two pursuits was minimal. Mimi had to bring her two only *Simon Says* enlistees to Charlotte's post because the game was short-lived with so few players, and one of the enlistees had her arm in a cast. The bulk of the residents could be found watching television or snoozing in the first- floor lounge.

CBS had just finished airing *The Young and the Restless,* and *The Bold and the Beautiful* was about to come on the screen, although, hardly anyone facing the television was paying too much attention. Without the *thing-a-ma jig,* someone had to get up and walk over to the TV set to change the channel or raise the volume. Those capable of accomplishing these tasks didn't feel like doing so; "We pay good money to be here, so why do *we* have to *do* the work?"

was the general sentiment expressed by the grumpiest of the old fogeys. Many of the non-sleeping residents had been frisked down, their pocketbooks and walkers searched, their seat cushions upended, and their blanket throws tossed aside, but the *blasted thing-a-ma jig* could not be found anywhere. So much hustle and bustle was involved in this endeavor that outsiders might have assumed it was a planned treasure hunt scheduled on the Daily Events Flyer. The day before, however, Mr. Dean had confiscated the remote control when two of the male residents came to fisticuffs over the right to keep it in their lap. Mr. Dean, employing a senior version of Time-out, had requested that each man relocate to a different area in the facility, and then announced the remote control would be returned when it could be permanently affixed to a wall, a fact no one in the lounge seemed to recall.

Sophie was knitting a pastel cap for her newest grandchild. Her wheelchair was to the side of the sofa, where Muriel was stretched out in slumber land, emitting a low-frequency, mumbling snore. Joe, discontented about not being able to watch his beloved *Fox News*, had tried his darndest to dislodge Muriel to see if the *thing-a-ma jig* was hiding under her fanny, but Sophie had defended Muriel's right to sleep uninterrupted, a gesture Joe did not take too kindly to.

"Leave her alone," Sophie warned, "or I'll jab you with one of my knitting needles." At that moment, Mimi had scurried past on her way to the front entry door, causing Joe and Sophie to turn their attentions. Sophie called out to say, "Good bye," and to offer Mimi an umbrella, but Mimi, contrary to her usual practice, darted out into the parking lot without uttering a word. Joe, forgetting what all the fuss had been over, sauntered back to his chair to catch some ZZZs.

Charlotte later learned from Mr. Dean that Mimi's child had been admitted to the hospital with severe breathlessness, a symptom resulting from a major asthma attack. Mr. Dean had cautioned Charlotte to keep the information close to her chest. "The doctors don't know if she's going to pull through or not."

The staff at Glenbrook did their best to suppress the news, but suspicion arose when some other caregiver had taken Mimi's place in the dining room.

"How come Mimi's not serving tonight?" Alice asked directly of Sondra the first night that Morrisa brought her lamb chop and baked potato to the table.

Sondra's rehearsed response slid off her tongue. "She had something to take care of."

"How come Mimi's not calling the Bingo numbers?" Alice asked the second night, her eyes squinting and inquisitive.

This time, Sondra was a little hesitant before she spoke. "Morrisa is taking over some of her duties. Mimi's still busy with *that thing*."

"What thing?" Alice's voice shot up. She rose and drew Sondra to the corner of the room, out of earshot of the other players. "*That thing* has nothing to do with the robberies, does it?" This time, her voice was hushed.

Sondra crossed her arms, becoming a whole different person, angrier and less patient. "Alice, this is Mimi's private business and *not in the least bit anything to do with your business.*"

"Well then, was she arrested?"

"Arrested?" Sondra's head jolted forward in disbelief. "What are you talking about Alice? Why would anyone want to arrest Mimi?"

"You don't know?"

"No, I don't know, and shame on you for suspecting anything like that. Women don't come any nicer or more upright than Mimi."

Alice peered into Sondra's face, but all she could read was Sondra's anger over Alice's insinuation.

"How come Mimi didn't take our lunch order?" Alice asked Sondra the third day. "I miss Mimi's chirpy disposition. Morrisa looks too disinterested, like she doesn't care at all. I sent back my carrot soup to be heated up, and it came back just as cold as before. I don't appreciate the lack of attentive service I'm receiving at this dive. What's going on here?" Alice was downright annoyed to be left out of the loop, even if it was none of her affair. "Don't we have a right to know?" Alice spotted a tear sliding down Sondra's cheek before she walked away without having addressed Alice's nosiness.

At dinner that evening, a typed note appeared on every table, sharing the status of Mimi's child's illness. She had bronchial constriction and poisoning of her lungs. Her condition was critical and prayers would definitely be appreciated. The temperament at Alice's table grew somber. Brianna and her family appeared to be on everyone's mind. Helen could be heard whispering, "Dear God Almighty," and Alice kept repeating, "*Oy Gevalt.*"

For the next few days at Glenbrook, there was more moaning, more crying, more listlessness, but a lot less complaining. Personal discomfort was taking a back seat to nervousness over the ordeal that Brianna and her parents were facing. Fewer dishes were sent back to the kitchen for being over-cooked, under-heated, or too tough. The upbeat music generally pumped into the dining room and lounges from the sound system had been switched to classical, more serene selections. Charlotte's pasted smile evolved into more of a frown and her stride lacked its peppy spring. Residents were calling it quits and going to sleep in the evening, earlier and earlier.

A collection was taken up to send money and food to Mimi and Edwin, the idea seemed to have sprung contemporaneously from several like-minded, well-intentioned individuals. Even Sophie, who most often appeared to be lacking in sufficient funds, managed to find some loose change in her apartment to contribute. Sondra delivered these gifts to where Mimi and Edwin lived. The rental, in a low-rise building in East Boynton Beach, was in the same development as Sondra's own apartment. Mimi and Edwin looked like they had run emotional marathons, fatigued and gaunt, but they sent their thanks for the outpouring of love and concern.

Frequent comments such as: "Have you heard?", "Have you heard anything?", "I hear it's touch and go.", contributed to an uneasy undercurrent of continuous chatter throughout the rooms and halls of Glenbrook. The residents were advised by Charlotte and Mr. Dean, "When we hear something, we'll absolutely let you know. We'll send out a bulletin of sorts."

"A tragedy seems so much worse when a young child is involved," a melancholy Alice expressed to Sondra. She had awoken from a nap when Sondra entered her apartment to tend to some light housekeeping.

"It's true," Sondra agreed, gathering used towels for a wash but moving in slow motion. Brianna's near-death was zapping the energy out of her. "There's no greater pain than the loss of a child. Alice, yous knows about that. I imagine the pain never goes away."

Alice rubbed her eyes. "Better to take ten of us instead of one of her," she shared with an aching heart.

"We've lived plenty, but that little girl is only first starting out. If God would make such a request, I don't doubt that every resident at Glenbrook would volunteer to take her place." Since Brianna had been hospitalized, Alice had been so distraught, she had even refrained from her daily robberies.

When Alice slipped into her chair for lunch the following day, Helen threw the most recent bulletin onto her place setting. "Did you hear the good news?"

Alice's posture sprang up with restocked optimism. "I hope you're going to tell me something wonderful about Mimi's little girl. If not, I'll sue you for almost giving me a heart attack!"

"Yes. Yes. Read the note," Helen gushed. "She's been released and is on the way home with her parents."

Diana shrieked, "She's breathing normally again."

"*Danken Got*!" Alice said, with a mountain-load of relief. "*Danken Got*! That means 'Thank God' for you goys at the table. Helen, don't get too overly excited. Remember your sensitive stomach. Diana, take a deep breath. You look like you're in a tizzy; you could pass out and end up in the hospital, yourself." It took Alice less than a nano-second to revert to her former, deprecating ways.

The doctors had determined that exposure to pesticides had greatly aggravated Brianna's condition. Since Edwin had no choice but to continue working in his same capacity at the landscaping company, for the few days Brianna needed to rest at home, Mimi was provided with paid leave, but alternative plans would have to be made for any reoccurrence. When Brianna did finally return to school and Mimi resumed her position at Glenbrook, Alice was within the closest circle of well-wishes who hugged and kissed her as soon as she entered from the parking lot. Charlotte had staked a position by the window and have given the more ambulatory residents the heads-up when to start mobilizing.

Later in the afternoon, there was a special "Meet and Greet" organized to toast to Brianna's continued good health. Red and white wine, gouda cheese and crackers, and potato chips were served. Glen Miller's band, saxophones, clarinets and muted trombones, could be heard reverberating from the speakers. The lounge was fully occupied, but Alice did not attend. Her foraging sorties did, however, continue as before.

Alice had decided to scout out Esther's apartment. She had not been inside since it had belonged to Alberto. During the last Fireside Chat, Alice had noticed the fancy ring Esther had worn and wondered what other specimens of fine jewelry were ready to be picked. Walking at a fast pace, she bumped into Mr. Dean in the hallway.

"Where are you off to Alice?" he asked.

"The restroom," she answered, "but I'm in a rush because I don't want to miss too much of the party."

"I don't blame you," Mr. Dean offered with a smile.

"Shouldn't you have called it quits for the day by now?"

"Yes. I wanted to be here for some of Mimi's Meet and Greet. I'm actually on my way now to the parking lot. Good night."

Alice opened the Ladies Room door but was surprised to find Mr. Dean continuing in the opposite direction to the parking lot. She purposefully did not pass all the way into the restroom. Looking over her shoulder she saw him enter Esther's apartment. *That's not the parking lot. What's he doing there?* Shortly thereafter, he exited

Esther's apartment, walking directly to the lobby and then on toward his car.

The modifications Esther had made to Alberto's apartment greatly impressed Alice. There were decorative chair rails, cove moldings, dark hardwood floors, and an eclectic selection of tasteful furniture sitting atop an antique Persian rug. Sheer, white, full-length voile curtains hung at either side of the windows. The one hanging to the right was swaying ever-so-lightly. Alice wanted to take in the beauty of the surroundings before harvesting several items for her collection, but she couldn't gauge how long the Meet and Greet would last. She did, however, notice a freezer bag way in the back on the floor behind the moving curtain. *Another one of those? I wonder if Esther knows about this? Perhaps that's the source of her wealth?*

On her way back to the lobby with several dollar bills and a silver bracelet jingling in her pocket, Alice passed by a maintenance crew and asked them if the party was still in force.

"Sure is," one of the men answered.

She headed back to the lobby but turned around just in time to see the maintenance crew head into Esther's apartment. *That apartment seems like a very a busy place today.*

Chapter Thirty-seven

On the day Jan arranged to meet Sondra and her sister, Ambrose, for lunch, Jan purposefully skipped breakfast, limiting her intake to glasses of room temperature water. Ambrose wanted to discuss some legal issues, which involved giving money to her nephew, Delmont, preferring the funds not be dispersed until certain restrictions had been met. Jan suggested establishing a trust and proposed a meeting in her office, but Sondra thought it nicer for the three women to gather over lunch instead.

Even though Coco's Jungle Café was located in a shopping center not too far from Glenbrook, Jan was the first to arrive at the restaurant. Ambrose and Sondra, appearing not too long afterward, were escorted by the hostess, wearing a safari hat and cargo pants, to the corner table two feet away from a stuffed five-foot gorilla hanging onto a bunch of fake bananas. Ambrose, whose hair was pulled back in a chignon, radiated sophistication in her pale pink, silk blouse adorned with rhinestone buttons, while Sondra lumbered behind in her maroon uniform and thick-soled nurse's shoes.

"I hope you've been making small talk with that mighty fine, good looking hunk while you've been waiting for us, hon," said Ambrose, pointing to the gorilla as she pulled out her chair. "I can tell he's interested in you 'cause he's looking straight at you."

"Hush now," Sondra chastised her sister. "Jan don't know you well enough to tell if you're kidding or not."

When Jan stated that she was terribly insulted, Sondra shot her sister a look of disapproval.

Ambrose's red polished lips broadened to reveal a pair of attractive dimples and a row of bright white teeth. "She's pulling your leg, you doofus."

Sondra squeezed her pocketbook between the table rim and her chest and tut-tutted as she the read the menu. Ambrose gaped at a herd of giraffes painted across one entire wall of the restaurant and at a hanging net filled with plush chimpanzees and zebras. "Somebody definitely went whole hog on this jungle motif, don't you think?"

"Stop your looking around and decide what to order. Not all of us can be on vacation," came Sondra's abrupt response.

Ignoring Sondra, Ambrose announced, "If this were my place, I'd paint the walls pink and white, the same as my beauty shop."

"Those are girlie colors," Sondra protested.

"I'll have you know that pink, being upbeat and positive, is known to stimulate energy and confidence. Meanwhile, I'm getting the heebie-jeebies from this superficial wilderness. Jan, how would you decorate this place if it was yours?"

"I'd use mostly blues and lemons to create a Country French theme, just like the dining room in Glenbrook. I think they did a really nice job in pulling that off."

"And what about you?" Ambrose poked Sondra with her elbow, diverting her sister's focus from the laminated menu.

Sondra answered without hesitating, "I'd get rid of every single stuffed animal for sure. Ain't nothin' cute about them. They're dust collectors and unsanitary. Why who knows the last time anyone gave them a really good cleaning?"

"Well, I suggest you should still keep the gorilla and his bananas for yourself," Ambrose advised her sister, who was now looking puzzled. "That way you'll always have something to cuddle up to at night and not get too hungry while you're at it."

Sondra crossed her arms and forced a mighty cold death stare in Ambrose's direction. "What I tell you, I tell you confidentially," she whispered.

The waitress approached the table just as Ambrose began to spin her knife in circles. After the three women took turns giving their orders, Sondra picked up Ambrose's knife and placed it back in its initial spot on the table. "Did you know that Jan painted that beautiful picture of flowers hanging in Miss Alice's room?" she asked.

"Yes, I did. Alice told me herself," said Ambrose. Turning to Jan, she added, "I can tell you love colors. There's nothing dull about that piece."

"I do love colors," Jan confessed. "I actually get very emotional over them. I don't just *see* them; I *feel* them. There's so much more to a color than what's being reflected on a surface."

"That's exactly like what I was saying before," Ambrose concurred.

"Please don't take this the wrong way," Jan continued, "but it bothers me all the time to be called 'white.'" Sondra shifted in her chair and glanced questioningly at Ambrose. "Those race and ethnicity questions on surveys and applications really get my goat. Why should I check off 'white,' when I'm not white?"

"What are you then?" Sondra asked.

"You feel more comfortable, hon, saying you're Caucasian?" Ambrose piped in.

Jan extended her arm on the table. "You see, my arm isn't white. There's pink, brown, beige, blue. Just like neither of you are black." Jan pulled one arm from Sondra and one from Ambrose to line up next to hers. "From an artist's perspective, I think the color of your skin is far richer and more beautiful than mine."

Sondra tilted her head sideways and uttered, "Mmmm." She tried to remove her arm back to where it sat before, but her sister used her other hand to keep it in place. Ambrose twisted her own arm to reveal her palms and to study the various tones. "Yes Jan, I can see where you're coming from."

"I see burnt umber, sienna, and hazel in your arms," Jan continued. "Now I ask you, which color is really esthetically the more beautiful one?"

"I never thought to look at it that way," Sondra admitted.

"It's not the way the world sees it," Ambrose complained.

As plates of chicken, salad, and turkey burgers were served, the three women discussed what needed to be done to set up the trust for Delmont. Once the details of the legal matter had been decided, the conversation then switched to fashion, hairstyles, and how Ambrose had learned her trade during the years she spent growing up in New York.

"She got to live in a nice fancy place," Sondra commented with an unmistakable tinge of resentment.

"Aunt Tyeisha gave each of us girls the very same offer. So, Sondra darlin', you can remove that pout immediately. You just chose a different route than I did."

"I *chose*?" Sondra exclaimed.

"Water under the bridge," Ambrose said. "I don't want to hear how mistreated you were, getting the raw end of the stick, 'cause then we'll be here 'til Doomsday. Let's move on."

Sondra stabbed her fork into her food and chewed noisily. When Ambrose tried to pinch a fry from her plate, Sondra picked up the bottle of ketchup and poured a whole load of sauce on the fries, followed by a ton of salt.

"Why'd you go and do that for?" Ambrose asked.

"That's how I like 'em. If you want some, order your own."

Jan motioned for the waitress' attention but had to go running hastily to the bathroom. Upon her return, she saw a new order of fries sitting before Ambrose, but Jan was too fearful to eat anything on her own plate. After apologizing to Sondra and Ambrose, she went on to mention about a rally she was organizing to help raise funds for Darfur.

"It's being held this coming weekend," Jan informed them. "Perhaps you can both attend?" The sisters each looked at Jan with glazed eyes.

"Is that another one of your charity groups?" Sondra asked. "Jan also spends her time working for civil rights, finding the cure for cancer, and feeding the poor," she informed Ambrose.

"Is that so?" Ambrose's face perked up with interest. "Ain't you the busy, busy lady!" This warranted a kick from under the table and a menacing look from Sondra. "What? What did I do wrong?"

"The Darfur rally has to do with an ongoing genocide," Jan explained. "Hundreds of thousands of innocent people in parts of Sudan are being killed."

"And this is going on right now in Africa?" Ambrose asked. "I had no idea."

"Neither did I," Sondra echoed.

"It's too bad, but I won't be here, hon," Ambrose shared apologetically. "I'm going home to Freeport tomorrow, but I'll be sending you some money after I get back. Even going to start a collection' in my beauty parlor for the people suffering from this awful genocide."

Sondra told Jan she had to see how the rest of her week went before she knew if she "be coming or not."

To Jan's surprise, Sondra did show up at the rally held at the Armenian Church in Boca Raton that Sunday afternoon. She had entered the auditorium at the same exact time as Susan Walsh. Jan walked over to greet the two women and introduced them to each other. Before Susan departed to join her friends, she shared her plans to further expand her law practice and hire more attorneys based upon the continued growth and success the practice was enjoying. Jan offered her congratulations while Sondra stood silently by her side.

Honorees and guest speakers began to assemble on the stage as a garbled "Testing, testing, testing: one, two, three," emanated from the microphone and surrounding speakers. Jan indicated to Sondra the program was about to begin and invited her to sit in the front row, but Sondra preferred remaining in the back of the room.

"How comes you never mentioned before you worked for a black woman attorney?" she asked Jan.

Mystified by the question, Jan answered, "Why should I have to?"

"Just thought it would have come up sometime; that's all."

"It never occurred to me," Jan stated, somewhat confused. "I don't tell you about all the white people I work with either."

Although it had been a nightmare for Jan and her committee to settle ahead of time on an appropriate seating arrangement for the dignitaries— sworn enemies as well as, in some cases, members of the opposite sex needed to be kept apart—they were pleased by the participation from many of the houses of worship in Palm Beach County. Despite their many differences, the clergy did rise to the occasion and succeeded in delivering a united, urgent plea for peace and intervention in Darfur. At the end of the rally, Jan approached Sondra and noticed the tears in her eyes.

"And you as a white—I mean pink, beige, and blue Jewish woman—really cares about this, huh?" she asked Jan. "I was greatly touched by everything I heard here today. The rabbis, priests, ministers, and nuns all be coming together and speaking so beautifully. I'll have to tell Reverend Johnson about this too, and see if he'll say a little something about it at our church. Such terrible things happening to women and children. Men being murdered and women raped. How come I never heard a word about it before?" The expression on Sondra's face demonstrated she was genuinely troubled.

"That's what we have to do: inform every person we can about the atrocities so we can try and put a stop to it."

"Amen," Sondra said, handing Jan a check written out for one hundred dollars.

"Are you sure about this? This is a lot of money," Jan commented, hoping not to insult or embarrass Sondra. "It is more than generous of you."

"I want to do this, Jan. Please take the money. It's important that I do this for many reasons."

Chapter Thirty-eight

The following Monday, as Jan was on her way to Delray Beach to argue a motion in Family Court, she had to make an unwelcomed thirty-minute pit stop at the Walgreen's bathroom on Military Trail. Jan called the judge's clerk to say she was stuck in traffic, but the clerk was not sympathetic to her ordeal.

"We're expecting you to be on time," the clerk insisted, making Jan feel so pressured and defeated she considered flushing herself down the toilet. *I can't go on like this anymore. Something has to give!* Each time she attempted to exit the drugstore's bathroom, however, within seconds she would have to dash back.

Exhausted and drained, her next call was to Rick's office, and she was grateful to schedule an immediate appointment. After that, she placed a call to Susan Walsh's office to see if an attorney could substitute for her court appearance, but no one was available. Once more, she communicated with the clerk and finally succeeded in obtaining a different hearing date.

After the greetings and formalities had been dispensed with, Rick, who was looking his usually relaxed self in jeans and a lilac polo shirt, suggested Jan fill him in with some background information. He asked about her childhood. "What kind of little girl were you? Did you have a lot of friends? How did you fare in school?"

Jan lowered herself into the corner of the couch and explained how she used to feel unbearably shy all of the time, to the point that she melted just hearing her name called in attendance. She didn't really have too many friends. This she attributed to her disfigurement.

"Disfigurement? Rick asked.

"I was told repeatedly how ugly I was by my parents; they made me believe that I resembled Quasimodo or worse. As a result, I always felt like an outsider."

Even though she had excelled in her studies, Jan had hated every minute being in school because her classes were always too structured and stifling. "I never felt like I belonged there or anywhere else. There were many days, I just stopped going to school and wandered off on my own."

"And how did your parents react to your truancy?" Rick asked.

"They didn't. It didn't concern them in the least."

"I take it your parents did not have a hands-on approach to your education. Talk to me about your father. What kind of man was he?"

"I have a million and one stories I can tell you about him," Jan shared. She spoke in a controlled, unemotional voice, having revisited these childhood narratives in her head, over and over again, trying to make sense of them all.

"I'm here to listen," Rick responded with a smile as he opened a new file on his laptop and began to tap on the keyboard.

"He was born in the early 1900s to a poor Orthodox Jewish family in a very gentile neighborhood in Nottingham, England. His father was dictatorial and often violent. His mother was a hard-working woman who exhibited zero compassion for her son. At the age of thirteen, my father supposedly ran away from home."

Rick looked up as he typed. "Why do you say supposedly?"

"Among many of his faults, my father was also a pathological liar. How do I know anything he ever told me was the truth?"

"Did he ever tell you he loved you?"

She shook her head and sighed. "Not once. Not ever."

Jan described the vagabond life her father had adopted in London at a young age, surviving on petty thievery, craps, and poker games.

"He met my mother at a tea dance in September 1934; she was pretty but also a naive nineteen-year-old. Apparently, he made a concerted effort to be on his very best behavior. He wined, dined, and proposed to my mother within the span of three months.

"Unlike the gentleman he initially pretended to be, however, he began to criticize and argue with her in public while snidely belittling her friends. She started to have serious misgivings about the marriage, and a week before the ceremony was to take place, she returned his engagement ring."

"It sounds like her instincts were correct," Rick offered, closing his laptop and leaning back in his chair. "What happened next?"

Jan cleared her throat. "My father threatened to jump off a bridge."

"And?"

"Unfortunately, my mother caved in to the pressure." Looking directly into Rick's eyes, Jan added, "I hope I don't shock you by saying that we would have all been better off if she had allowed him to jump."

"You haven't shocked me," Rick stated. "I doubt, though, that your father would have followed through with his threat."

"That's probably true," Jan responded with a shrug. "He wasn't much good at following through on most things."

Rick reopened his laptop. "Please continue."

"For much of her married life, my mother was miserable as miserable could be. Her only respite came during the war when my father was sent to Africa." Raising her elbow onto the arm of the couch, Jan propped her chin in the palm of her hand.

"Are you feeling okay? Do you need to take a break?"

Jan swallowed and assured Rick that she was fine. "All this running non-stop to the bathroom has really taken a toll on me."

"Let me get you some water." He rose and walked over to a small refrigerator next to the window, returning with a bottle in his hand. "How do you know your mother was so miserable in her marriage?" he asked.

After taking a drink, Jan placed the bottle on the cushion next to her. "Although my mother would say she was too stupid and didn't understand most things, she didn't hold back on constantly telling me why she hated her husband. Believe me, there wasn't a single, lurid detail she bothered to omit."

"How did you feel when you heard this?" Rick asked while intently studying Jan's face. "Have you any idea how much this influenced your own feelings toward him?"

Jan straightened her posture, folding her arms across her chest. "I absolutely hated my father, but I had plenty of my own reasons."

Jan divulged how all of her father's many businesses had failed and how he had continued to borrow money from the banks, extended family, and friends, defaulting on all his loans. A bad gambling habit eventually eroded whatever balances remained in his personal accounts. So, in 1960, at his urging, the family emigrated to the United States to find a better life. Maureen was twenty-two, Jan was ten, and Henry was eight-years-old.

Once in America, however, money continued to remain scarce. Alice had no choice but to take a job as a salesgirl in a boutique, working long hours in order to pay the rent, put food on the table, and clothes on her children's backs.

"My father attributed his failures to his wife and children's lack of vision," Jan theorized. "I figured this is probably why he screamed and berated us all the time."

"Was he physically abusive as well?" Rick asked, adding to his notes.

"No," Jan answered abruptly, her face reddening. "I do have some painful memories of inappropriate touching at a much younger age; molestation to be more accurate."

Rick looked up, waiting for Jan to expand upon this revelation. After a few moments of awkward silence, he asked whether she wished to discuss those incidents further.

Jan responded wearily, "Not right now and only if you believe it to be essential, but I do have to pardon myself to make a visit to the restroom if you don't mind."

"Of course," Rick said, handing her a key attached to a six-inch heavy wooden bar. "I keep losing the keys, so I came up with this as a solution. People have no problem remembering to return this one."

After rushing back to Rick's office, Jan made a point of dropping the key loudly on his desk. "You see; the system really works!" he said with a chuckle. He had poured himself a mug of coffee and offered Jan a hot beverage or more water. She chose a mint tea from his selection of teabags and then described how Norman had spent most days reading newspapers and watching TV, wearing nothing more than a short terry bathrobe, which would become unfastened more often than not.

"It was as if our family had a different set of rules than everyone else. If Maureen, Henry, or I dared to contradict any of our father's lies, there was hell to pay. He would explode if anyone challenged his authority."

Jan paused to sip her tea and regarded the artwork and certificates on the walls. Her eyes came to rest on a Calder-like mobile suspended in a corner by the window. The steel wires and varying black leaf shapes danced rhythmically in the air.

"I hadn't noticed that when I was here before. I like it; it's sort of like poetry in motion," she told Rick. "I could sit and stare at that all day long."

"At the end of a busy day, that's exactly what I do: lie down on the couch and stare at the mobile until I'm sufficiently relaxed," Rick shared. "You were going to tell me some more about your father?"

Jan took another sip of tea, licked her lips, and said, "I was terrified of him—we all were. He was an absolute monster."

Chapter Thirty-nine

Jan was surprised to see Rick wearing a suit and tie when she arrived for her next appointment. As he loosened the knot around his collar, he explained he had attended an early morning funeral and didn't have time to change. "Sorry to keep you waiting, I just need to get more comfortable." Jan studied the mobile while Rick took off his jacket and draped it around his chair.

"No problem," Jan replied. "Take all the time you need, especially since I'm not sure what we're supposed to talk about today."

Once seated, Rick gathered a pen and pad from the side table and said, "We're not *supposed* to talk about anything, but we can pick up on the discussion begun in our last session. How about you tell me more about your father? If that's okay."

Jan leaned against the back cushion of the couch, placing her hands on her sweatpants "I can do that. I see you're taking manual notes today. I'm concerned your hand might grow tired; there's quite a bit to tell."

Rick informed Jan that he had left his laptop at home. "Either method works for me." He rubbed his hands together slowly. "You were saying?"

Jan had so many hair-raising incidents to share, she didn't know where to begin, but she rattled off a slew of them in no chronological order.

"My life always felt like a helter-skelter, never-ending, death-defying rollercoaster ride," Jan admitted glumly. "When it was his turn to learn how to drive, I warned Henry never to let Dad teach him. Though, that experience would have been relatively minor compared to what he eventually had to endure."

"Your father was all about seizing power and maintaining absolute control," Rick stated solemnly.

Jan reached for the bathroom key and hurriedly excused herself, glad to be wearing sneakers so she could sprint.

When she returned, Jan recounted how her mother had publicly embarrassed and humiliated her most of her life, making Jan her scapegoat. As a little girl, she was abandoned in playgrounds, on crowded London streets, in market squares, in department stores, in the underground's cavernous tubes, and on the top and bottom tiers of double-decker busses. Time and time again, Jan would examine her body, hoping to find the gross abnormality that had devalued her being in the eyes of her parents and had made them hate her so.

As Rick listened, providing encouragement and comfort at the appropriate times, Jan became more trusting and less tense. She was finally able to open up about her mother's abortion, her father's mid-Atlantic threats, and other painful episodes of her past.

"There's no question at all you've been traumatized and abused," Rick advised. "Each event would have been enough to do substantial damage, but taken as a whole, Jan, your survival skills are remarkable."

"In between high school graduation and college, when my mother was in the hospital again—that was like her second home—I summoned up the strength to tell my father I was afraid of him. He was in our living room, watching the nightly news.

"'You're lying. You're talking rot,' he said. 'What a nasty, little shit you are. You're a spoiled rotten bitch. Get out of here. Just get out of my sight, you filthy piece of shit!'

"From that moment on, I was 'dead' to my father, which really suited me just fine. It allowed me to evade his constant bullying, but that was also when I started sleeping around with lots of guys, smoking pot, and dropping acid. I suppose that was my inane way of getting back at him."

Rick lifted a pitcher from the coffee table and poured water into a glass, which he handed to Jan.

"I loathed feeling like shit all the time," she said sadly.

"Can you describe to me how you mostly feel nowadays?" Rick asked.

"Whatever I do is never good enough. I am exhausted. Trying to please everyone is exhausting. I don't want people to think of me only as a piece of shit. I've adopted every disease, famine, and injustice in the world as my own personal cause all the while being my mother's primary support and caregiver. It's so terribly depleting. It seems like the weight of the world is forever on my shoulders."

"I hear you," Rick said.

Jan went on to explain how in college she earned a full scholarship and the opportunity to attend a prestigious art school in Europe. It had been her childhood dream come true.

"That's pretty impressive. What happened?"

"No surprise; my mother fell ill again and ended up in the emergency room with another supposed heart attack. She begged me not to go, saying Maureen was too caught up in her own life and Henry was just a young boy. If I didn't stay close to home, she was afraid my father would kill her."

288

"There it is again. Your family's history of emotional blackmail," Rick remarked.

"Naturally, I felt sorry for her. Of course, I stayed and ended up meeting Mike. Don't get me wrong, I love Mike very much, but I've always felt like I missed out on something really special."

Throughout a period of two months, Jan maintained a weekly schedule of conferring with Rick, always keeping the cumbersome key by her side until each session ended, as her urgent restroom calls still persisted. Rick cautioned her not to expect an overnight recovery.

"It probably won't be cataclysmic," he warned. "One day, when you are feeling healed, safe, and secure, you'll suddenly notice that your ailment has just disappeared. It's no accident that you're suffering from gastro issues. Besides the blatant references to 'shit,' your symptoms are strongly connected to your mother's abortion as well. It's almost like the scenario you described is being repeated over and over again."

While her therapy proceeded, Jan indulged herself by taking slow drives along A1A, parking at whim in lots adjacent to the beach so she could spend moments reading a novel in the company of washed-up crabs and jellyfish or being mesmerized by the waves. She took time off from preparing legal memoranda and court documents to meet a friend for lunch, stroll at the mall, or work out at the gym. With Rick's coaching, these activities soon became part of her weekly routine as Jan learned how to become selfish, but in a good way.

On her last visit, Rick taught her, "We are all victims of childhood dramas—some more perilous than others, and in your case very extreme—but at some point in our maturation, we must be willing to put these unhealthy dramas to rest. A lot of what you were doing up till now is a reflection of your inner child seeking the recognition that you as a little girl never received."

Rick discussed the effects of child abuse on self-perception and interpersonal relationships, touching on such topics as responsibility and blame.

"Children cannot accept deficiencies in their parents, so they blame themselves for any abuse or maltreatment they receive. You totally bought into the premise that you were severely damaged goods, whereas it was your parents who were the damaged ones. In hopes of receiving some love or validation, you then allowed yourself to be manipulated by your mother.

"In that same vein, you are pushing Mike away now because you don't believe deep down you are worthy or deserving of his love. With so much ingrained mistrust, it is easy for you to accept the notion that he is betraying you."

"But Rick, what about this Gillian then? I didn't dream her up. Every time I turn around, she happens to be wherever Mike is. He's in her house, he's in her garage, he's in her yard. Given her looks, there's no way Mike isn't attracted to her."

"Mike has sworn to me and you that he is not having an affair. I, for one, believe him. He's not a pathological liar like your father was. In all this time Jan, has he ever left you? He's expressed his dissatisfaction and unhappiness with the state of your marriage, but it seems to me, he has stayed by your side throughout it all."

Jan rubbed her forehead and fought to keep from sobbing. "I suppose he has."

"Listen," Rick continued, "your mother is never going to evolve into what you wish she could be, so it has to be within your control to end the absurdity."

"I wish I could confront her with the truth of how I feel," Jan stated, her voice choked,
"but she's quite an old lady now. Having suffered so much sorrow and abuse already, I couldn't do that to her."

"Then how are things ever going to change?" Rick asked. "Jan, you need to forgive your parents for their inadequacies. It's time to let go of the anger."

"It was their fault my brother Henry died! How can I ever let go of that?"

"That may or may not be so. For your own wellbeing and the sake of your marriage, it's time to forgive them and yourself. Really, Jan, you're a great woman; I'd like to see you be free of all this shit. As a professional, I don't usually speak in these terms, but in this case it surely fits."

Chapter Forty

Several months had passed since the fierce confrontation with her mother, her private visits with Rick, and her last conversation with Gillian, who Jan had spotted in a mini-mini skirt and tank top walking arm in arm toward the tennis courts with a much tanned, well-built, muscular hunk of a man. Jan had hoped to drive by the couple unnoticed, but Gillian had waved Jan's SUV down to introduce Jan to Jeremy, who had just returned to the States.

Jeremy offered Jan a strong handshake after she rolled down her window. "It's really nice to meet you," he said. "I look forward to being your neighbor."

"Thank you," Jan responded, not sure if she meant it.

"I've already met Mike," Jeremy continued. "I can't thank you enough for everything you've done for Gillian and our Kevin."

"No need to mention it; anyway, it was more of Mike's doing than mine." *Did Jeremy ever suspect something was going on between Mike and Gillian as well?*

"Yeah, the guys on the base ribbed me a lot about Mike. 'Just how much is he helping your wife out?' and 'Just exactly what needs is he seeing to?'" Jeremy blushed and looked down. "Well, you can imagine the rest."

"Are you kidding me?" Gillian had pushed her way closer to Jan's window, shoving Jeremy aside. "Your husband couldn't have been more of a gentleman. That's what I told Jeremy—not that I had to. He couldn't have been less interested in me. I've had other men hit on me, but not Mike. You've certainly got a winner there, babe."

Jan had gawked at Gillian, wondering if she was putting on an act for her and Jeremy's benefit. *She's never struck me as deceptive before. Empty-headed, yes, but not treacherous or deceptive. I doubt whether she can act this well; after all, she's no Meryl Streep or Alice Block, for that matter. Could it be she's speaking the truth?* It was as if all the lights had suddenly and finally been turned on in a previously darkened room. Soon after this meeting, Jan's wrongful supposition about Gillian and Mike became an embarrassing aberration of the past.

"Perhaps I should go visit Daniel," Jan said wishfully as she and Mike sipped hot decafs in a local Starbucks. "I know it's been raining a lot in Seattle, but I think it will do me some good, especially spending time with Asher. Daniel and Emily might not mind me visiting them now." Jan hadn't seen her grandson since he was born, and the notion of hugging and playing with the seventeen-month-old excited her to no end.

"Considering your history with Daniel, maybe you should choose a different getaway instead," Mike advised, blowing short breaths across his cup. "How about going to a B&B in Mount Dora?"

"Things between us are a lot better than they were before," Jan replied. "I hardly call him at all."

Mike added half a packet of sugar to his drink. He was about to take another sip, but stopped. "I'd love to go with you, but I have a load of appointments lined up with prospective clients. There's no way I can be out of the office right now, but please check this out with Daniel and Emily, making sure they're on board with the trip before booking your flight."

"Naturally," Jan agreed, breaking a buttered bagel in half and handing Mike his share. She looked around the coffee shop and remarked how crowded it had become. This was their mid-week date night, and they were scheduled to hit the movie theater after eating their snack. The date night had been suggested by Jan as part of her conscientious effort to spend quality time with her husband, to which he had more than willingly agreed.

Jan hated herself for the harm that had been caused to her marriage throughout the years. *Hadn't Mike tried to warn me over and over again? If only I had been in a healthier state of mind to listen to him.* She felt truly blessed to have such an unwavering partner, who loved her as much as he did.

Mike bit into his bagel and reached over to wipe a crumb from Jan's cheek. "If you go to Seattle, I hope you will be able to have a good talk with Emily so she can get to know you better. She might even provide you with some sound advice. I bet she's heard plenty about you already from Daniel."

"I'm going to keep this visit nice and light. Emily doesn't need to be dragged further into our messy business. Even though she's a social worker, she's entitled to leave her job at the workplace."

"*I* didn't deserve to be dragged into your business!" Mike declared, placing the last of his bagel in his mouth. "Just in case you don't plan on continuing with this cold treatment of Alice for all eternity, while you're away I might have to arrange for a contract killing. By the time you come home, all our problems will be solved."

"Then I'll have to visit you in jail," Jan teased. "By the way, you can cut down on your devilish grin. It's a little too over the top." She tossed back her head and laughed.

***

When the afternoon for her Seattle flight arrived, Jan stalled leaving the house until she was absolutely positive that she was sufficiently blocked up with Imodium. Nervously, she focused on looking through the passenger window of Mike's car, hoping to convince her brain and her emotions that they were no longer in charge of her intestinal functions. Fortunately, they reached the departure terminal without incident.

***

Sondra entered Alice's apartment to take her blood pressure and replenish her medical supplies. She discovered Alice seated with her back to the window with the *Palm Beach Post* stretched out across her lap.

"Good, you're here," Alice said with more enthusiasm than was typical of her nature. "I have something to share with you."

With her set of keys dangling from the pink plastic coil at her wrist, Sondra began to stack the blister packs in the medicine cabinet, not really caring if she heard Alice's news.

"I think I saw something in the newspaper about the church you go to," Alice said excitedly. "Here." She shuffled across the length of her apartment in her slippers and extended the local section of the *Palm Beach Post* to Sondra, whose curiosity was just slightly aroused.

Sondra was busy counting out the Coumadin and Crestor tablets so she tossed the newspaper on the toilet seat. "Is the article about the Sunday picnic?" she asked, keeping her eyes focused on the prescription summary she held in her other hand. "Alice, you're getting low on your sleeping pills. I've got to remember to refill that order pretty soon."

Alice suddenly began to scratch her arms. "Don't you dare let me run out of those pills," she begged, her voice sounding amply agitated. "I'll be climbing the walls in the middle of the night if you do. And guess who I'll be calling to keep me company then?"

"Take it easy. Take it easy. You're actin' like a junkie in detox. I says you're getting low, not out of them!"

Halting her scratching, Alice shuddered. "No, it's a lot juicier that that."

Sondra looked up and noticed Alice staring back at her with a sardonic expression on her face. "What you be talking about now? What's a lot juicier?"

"Just take a look on the top of page two," Alice said impatiently. "It seems that the Reverend Johnson has left his congregation in the lurch. Didn't show up for services; skipped out on both a wedding and a funeral he was supposed to officiate at; and he's missed every one of this month's choir practices."

Sondra sensed the blood rushing to her face and tried not to appear too alarmed. "Obviously, there's been some sort of mistake. I know the Reverend and he would never do such a thing." She reached for the newspaper, shaking her head from side to side.

"*How* well do you know him?" Alice asked.

"Well," Sondra answered succinctly.

"How well?" Alice badgered, sounding more like a prosecuting attorney than a little old woman. "I need to hear all the details you got. Just open your mouth and let it all pour out."

"*Very* well," Sondra responded. "I'm sure this has all been a mistake, and this paper will have to print some sort of retraction. Is that well enough for you?" She opened the newspaper to its second page.

Alice folded her arms across her chest. "Well, you know what they say about these black ministers? All that tribal worshipping, hallelujahing, shouting and jumping around, putting on more of a show than what goes on in real churches."

"Here we go again," Sondra muttered to herself, only this time she made no attempt to disguise her disgust with Alice's generalizations. She scanned the headlines until the words *Minister Missing From Local Church* grabbed her attention. It pained her to read farther down the column and into the smaller print. "Stop right there, Alice, before you dig a bigger hole than you already have. I don't know for a fact that the Reverend did anything wrong. Maybe he's sick or had to go somewhere real quick for a very devout cause. Black churches worship the same God as do white churches, as do the Jews in your synagogues. Color of skin makes no difference when it comes to Christianity or any other faith."

Alice bobbed her head. "Naturally you would say that. As a woman of color you're not looking at things objectively. Anyway, he's run away."

"That don't mean nothing," Sondra said defiantly, the newspaper rattling in her hands.

"You can read about it yourself. It's all there in black and white. He's left his wife and has run away with a floozy from the church. That doesn't sound kosher to me. Does it to you?" A broad smirk spread across Alice's face, puffing out her cheeks like a chipmunk's and squeezing her eyes into little slits. "It seems he had quite an entourage of mistresses. Black men, white men; they're all the same. Not one of them can ever be trusted."

Steadying herself against the rim of the sink, Sondra felt like the bathroom walls were starting to tumble down on her. She worried that she was about to faint.

Alice moved quickly to her bed. "Come over here," she said with urgency, patting the edge of her comforter. "You look like you've been struck a nasty blow." But Sondra just stood glued in her place, looking visibly distraught. Alice came back to Sondra's side, putting her arm around Sondra's waist. "Come. Walk slowly. I'm worried about you. Take one step at a time. Please come sit on my bed just for a little while until you feel your strength come back. I didn't realize the news would hit you so hard."

She led Sondra to the bed and Sondra lowered herself. "Don't worry about creasing the bedspread," Alice advised as she pushed candy wrappers and magazines onto the floor. "The cleaners can undo whatever mess you make."

***

Mike took it upon himself to drop in on Alice at Glenbrook on his return trip from the airport, just to make sure "she was still alive and kicking." No matter how evil he and Jan perceived Alice to be, neither of them had the heart to totally abandon her at this late stage of the game. Despite not originally wanting to, he had actually come around to Jan's way of thinking in this regard.

"We're better people than she is," Jan had told him. "If we become just as cruel, then she wins. The abuse will continue with us."

He found his mother-in-law in fine spirits, walking and yakking with her friends as they entered the social room to play Bingo. Alice gave him a genuinely warm hug, locked arms with Mike, and insisted that he join her for the game, to which Mike replied, "I'll stay for one or two games, but no more."

"Such a treasure this man is," Alice professed to Muriel as she and Mike reached her usual table. "For me, he can do absolutely no wrong."

Muriel's comment, "And so handsome too," made Mike want to blush. "How come I haven't seen you around here before?" she asked.

"He's a very busy man," Alice informed Muriel, sliding half her markers in front of him. "He has more important things to do than hang around with our lot. He's a CPA; that means he's a certified public accountant."

"I know what a CPA is, Alice," Muriel said with indignation. "I even used one when I lived in New York. Now that I'm in Florida, my son takes care of my taxes for me."

"Your son is a *goniff*," Alice pointed out. "Mike here is a professional."

Muriel threw her good-luck rabbit's foot on the table. "My son is not a thief, thank you very much.

"Be careful how you treat your precious rabbit's foot," Alice mocked. "It might break and you'll be left with just its toes—a sure sign of a curse if I ever heard of one."

Muriel winced.

"Okay," Alice granted, "*goniff* may be too strong of a word. I take it back. Your son is a *shyster* businessman. Everything *my* Mike does, however, is done according to the letter of the law."

Muriel raised her voice. "And you're insinuating my son doesn't?"

"You told me yourself how he stole the company away from his partner."

Muriel threw her hands into the air, Alice's face beamed with the joy of victory, and Mike shifted uncomfortably in his seat.

"It's a pleasure to meet you," Muriel said, addressing Mike. "I know your wife *very well*. She's a *doll*; *such a doll*. Only she hasn't been here lately, and *I for one* sorely miss seeing her." Alice swung around to face Mimi, who was standing by the window.

"Jan has told me how lovely you all are," Mike responded. "She's away on a trip; otherwise she probably would have been here herself. So in that case, I would love to treat you lovely ladies to your Bingo cards." He reached forward to retrieve his wallet from his pocket.

Alice muttered, "And she should stay away," before calling out to Mimi, "We want only the winning cards at this table. We've got a live one here, and he's paying!"

Immediately, Stella propped herself up on her walker and headed straight to Mike from across the room, catapulting Alice into grabbing Mike's hand and warning him to keep his money in his pocket until it was time to pay.

"He's already taken, so don't get your hopes up," Alice cautioned Mimi, who had neared the group, extending her arm to shake Mike's hand. When Mike suggested Mimi give Stella two cards as well, Alice's mouth took a downward turn, making her disapproval obvious to everyone at the table. Mike handed Mimi a ten-dollar bill, and she went to fetch change from the cash box. Upon her return, Alice introduced Mimi to Mike all over again.

"This good-looking guy is my daughter's husband, Mimi. Keep your hands off of him; he's my hot date for tonight."

For a split second, Mike considered telling Alice that they had already been introduced, but he had learned such reminders might be disorienting and upsetting to the one doing the forgetting. However, he wasn't entirely sure if Alice's duplicate introductions were attributable to memory

300

loss or whether she was purposefully putting on an act to elicit a laugh or gain sympathy. Mimi winked at Mike and returned to the ball-calling setup.

To Alice's delight, Mike was the first person to call out "Bingo" that evening, although he had been hesitant to be declared a winner, hoping that one of the residents would grab the honor first. "You've got it! You've got it!" Alice screamed in his ear and could not have been prouder. Her glee quickly soured, though, when Mike donated his winnings to the next round's prize. As soon as Natalie won the next Bingo, she came over and gave Mike such a wet sloppy kiss that Alice warned, "When you go home be sure to scrub your face very well; venereal disease runs rampant around here."

"I've heard about the high jinx going on in this place, but I strongly doubt venereal disease is something I'll have to worry about. Mom, it's been fun, but I'm heading home now. It's been a long day."

"Before your go, take some candy with you. They're delicious." She grabbed a handful of sweets from her pocket and pushed them into Mike's chest. "Take them. They'll look better on you than on me."

Mike gently shoved her hand away. "No thank you. I'm good."

"Take them; you'll enjoy them later," Alice insisted.

"No, really. I'd rather you keep them for yourself."

Alice dabbed at her eyes with a scrunched-up tissue. "Mike, you're hurting my feelings."

Mike accepted the bundle and gave Alice a hasty kiss on her cheek. When he stood up and pushed his chair aside, it made an unfortunate grating, creaking sound. The noise set off a disturbance in the room, causing some to call out "What's going on?" and "Is the ceiling falling?" while others attempted to adjust their hearing aids.

"With too much excitement, this crowd goes berserk." Alice yelled out, "Don't you worry it's not the end of the world, you bunch of misfit *meshugenahs!* Go on, Mike; go on home and drive safely. I appreciate you coming by. Don't be such a stranger in the future."

"I'll tell Jan I saw you and that you're doing just fine," he responded.

Alice tightened her lips. She lowered her head, stacked her coins, and then popped a caramel crunch in her mouth.

Chapter Forty-one

The contrast between the flat open spaces of South Florida and the quaint, hilly neighborhoods of Seattle did not go unnoticed by Jan as her plane descended onto the runway. She had initially been disappointed with her middle seat assignment; afraid she might be constantly upsetting her fellow passengers by crawling over their laps mid-flight, but she managed to watch two movies, *Sea Biscuit* and *Love Actually,* without a single interruption. When she disembarked, she found herself to be relaxed and in good spirits.

Daniel had stationed himself to the side of the luggage carousals in the Arrivals area, and as soon as Jan saw him, she was immediately struck by how closely he resembled his father. It wasn't just the style of his hair or piercing eyes. Daniel's clothing, mannerisms, and posture made him a duplicate of a younger version of Mike. In a cream, plaid shirt and khaki pants, Daniel stood with his arms folded, looking pensive and resolved. Jan wanted to throw her arms about her son and smack his face with a million kisses, but instead she pecked him on the cheek and uttered a not too gushy, "Hi there."

As Daniel pulled his mother's suitcase while guiding her to the parking lot, Jan kept reminding herself not to fuss over him. *Why isn't he wearing a jacket? It's cold outside. Has he seen to that mole on his chin?* Mistakes of this nature had been made by her in the past. *He used to say I was overbearing and a "much unwanted pain in the neck!"*

"You've got to give me more space," he used to complain. "Won't you cut me some slack? Please get off my case! *Mom*! Enough already!"

In preparation for Jan's visit, Daniel and Emily had cleared out their spare bedroom in their spacious Queen Anne condo, giving Jan a comfortable place to stay with a beautiful view of Puget Sound. Despite the daily rainfall, the lack of tropical sunshine, and Daniel's subdued treatment, Jan was glad to be with her son and his family. There seemed to be more energy in the air, for the age of the residents in this neighborhood was at least two generations removed from where she and Mike were living in South Florida.

As both Daniel and Emily enjoyed successful, full-time careers, Jan adhered to the nanny's schedule for her time to be with Asher. She also tried to afford his parents the opportunity to be alone with their son at the end of the day.

Wearing layers of long-sleeved sweaters and jackets, which she savored, she navigated the parks and small urban squares in the mornings, —even on the gray, wet days, which were more often than not—grabbing a bagel and coffee at the corner Starbucks or buying fresh fruit from the local market. Back in South Florida, Jan would be in and out of her car all day long, but in Seattle, she delighted in walking everywhere. Used to sudden, muggy, heavy downpours on the east coast, Jan chose to keep her umbrella closed at times so she could feel the gentle mists of rain tapping on her face. Each day, she was surprised how far and for how long she could venture away from her home base, a pleasing signal that her irritable stomach issues were in remission.

In the evenings, she would stroll by the many local restaurants and bars, boisterous and alive with music and performers reflective of a young hip culture. Occasionally, she would come across men walking hand in hand or sitting at a sidewalk café sharing an intimate meal. She liked to imagine seeing Henry's presence at these scenes. *But he would be so much older now. What would he have looked like all grown up?*

One evening, Daniel saw to Asher's bath and nightly routine, allowing Emily and Jan the chance to chat. They were seated in the living room, decorated sparsely in monochromatic tones of taupe and steel unlike the warm hues of Jan and Mike's preferred palette. It took Jan a while to get physically comfortable, but she soon found Emily someone with whom she could easily converse.

Jan sank back on her cushion and lost herself in a cloud of sadness. "I've come to realize that booze and old age bring out the worst in people, especially if they were nasty to begin with," she shared with Emily. "I doubt that my mother was ever the warm or nurturing type."

Emily brushed her bangs away from her eyes and tucked her wavy, chestnut hair behind her ears. "That's a shame. I'm sorry to hear that."

"I could go on and on about her, but I don't want to bore you." Jan felt a lump rise in her throat.

Emily picked a chewy caramel from a box of chocolates on the coffee table and offered the box to Jan. "Don't tell me they're too fattening," Emily said. "Daniel brought them home yesterday and you'll be doing me a really big favor by eating some."

Jan smiled. "In that case," she said, "I'm *happy* to oblige." She placed a cappuccino truffle on her tongue, letting let it melt in her mouth.

"Now that you've come out of retirement, you don't seem *that happy* to be back at work," Emily observed.

"I'm not," Jan confessed, fidgeting with the button on her cardigan. "I don't love being a lawyer. What I really want to do is paint."

"Then why did you choose to go to law school in the first place?" Emily asked. "That was an awful lot of hurdles to jump over to get somewhere you really didn't want to be."

Jan opened and closed the button repeatedly until she rubbed her hands together and placed them between her thighs and seat cushion. "Yes, it was, and I regret having done so. I believe that I was trying to impress my father, stupidly supposing it would boost my sense of worth in his eyes." Jan reached for another truffle. "These are so delicious. Maybe you should put the box away before I finish them off—and don't you dare tell me that I would be doing you a *mitzvah*."

Emily took a second caramel and rose to place the box in the kitchen. She came back carrying a tray with two glasses of iced tea. "I am *just* your daughter-in-law, but I believe you should be doing whatever makes you happy."

"No. Please do not ever say that again," Jan urged, squeezing Emily's hand with her own. "You're definitely not *'just'* my daughter-in-law." Emily and Jan gave each other a warm hug. "I wish I could hug Daniel this way too."

"Why couldn't you?" Emily asked, looking surprised. "You should hear the way Daniel talks about you sometimes." Jan's parting lips gave testament to her astonishment. "Yes, we both know how much he regarded you as a drag when he was younger, but he talks plenty to me about your accomplishments and how proud of you he really is."

Little drops formed in the corner of Jan's eyes. "Seriously? I guess that's easy for him to say from afar but not when I'm up close and in his face."

"No, that's simply not true." Emily neared Jan and spoke softly. "Don't ever let him know I told you so, but he really does admire you."

Daniel heard laughter arising from the living room and cautioned the two women to "Keep it down in there. I don't want you waking Asher up. Is that too much to ask?"

"You're the one who went and married such a wonderful woman," Jan called to him. "We're having fun together."

"Guilty as charged," Daniel admitted. "Just lower the volume a bit, okay?"

***

Glenbrook regularly performed quarterly fire drills in compliance with Florida State Regulations. When a fire drill was to be carried out, the staff tried to inform most of the residents ahead of time, despite wanting to conduct a test in the most realistic environment as possible, but consideration also had to be given to the age and frailty of their residents. No one wanted anyone dying from a heart attack unnecessarily.

Although advance warnings of a 2 p.m. fire drill had been placed on every table in the dining room, on all of the bulletin boards, and in the weekly newsletter, Alice had simply put it completely out of her mind.

Immediately after they finished eating their Shepherd's Pie, smashed peas, and trifle, the occupants of the dining room were led into the social room to watch *The Sound of Music*. Alice was amazed at how quickly the residents grouped themselves into a disorderly queue, considering that most were disabled.

"What are you rushing for?" she asked each passerby. "You've never seen a nun sing before? You, David!" she called out to the man pushing his way ahead of a woman on an electric scooter. "It usually takes you an hour to move one inch. Slow down. You'll hurt yourself."

"Such a fuss for a film that's been around almost as long as I have," Alice announced to no one in particular. "So, it has mountains, singing, Nazis, and a man who falls in love with a girl. What's the big deal? For the life of me, I don't see why it's so special."

Alice purposefully complimented Charlotte as she entered the social room. "Is that blouse your wearing new? You look like a million dollars today!"

"Why, thank you Alice," Charlotte responded, pleased to be the object of one of Alice's rare positive remarks. "You be sure to grab one of the snack bags and enjoy the movie."

"I certainly will," Alice replied. "I can't wait to see the escape scene at the end. It's my favorite part."

Alice stayed in place until her name was confirmed on the attendance sheet, but as soon as Charlotte left the room, she rose to leave as well. *I'll tell them I'm going to make pee-pee in the little girl's room if anyone should ask.*

High on Alice's agenda was making a call from another resident's phone, so she chose David's apartment as her first scavenging destination. Ever since she had learned of Delmont's friend dying from illicit drugs, her discovery of the heroin-filled freezer bags had weighed heavily on her mind. She still did not know for sure who was involved, but she had watched enough episodes of *Miami Vice* to harbor suspicions of Mr. Dean and the maintenance crew. Too often, she had witnessed them going in and out of empty apartments within moments of each other, too involved with their own undertakings to question why she happened to be floating around in the same vicinity. Mr. Dean, who always had his briefcase in hand, was the first to enter. Soon after he made his exit, the workers would walk in. Not one freezer bag ever showed up in a corner or on the floor by the time she had made her own secretive entrance. There were just too many coincidences to ignore the implication.

Alice figured it was up to the police to examine Mr. Dean and his crew to determine what connection, if any, they had to the drug ring. Her performance on the call was a stellar one. It could have easily been Ethel Barrymore talking to the intake officer. Keeping the conversation short, Alice refused to give her real name, wrapping up her anonymous tip with the line, "That's all there is—there isn't any more to say!"

Once the call was terminated, Alice stood in front of David's closet. Knowing that he customarily wore a different shirt every day, she was taken aback by the array of stacked shirts, neatly arranged in coordinated columns— blue ones, beige ones, striped ones, solid ones, short sleeves, long sleeves, every color under-the-sun ones. *Such a dandy dresser you are. Too bad you'll run out of days before you get to wear these many shirts. I would gladly take a few but men's clothing doesn't move so fast down at the thrift shop.* Moving on from the closet, she hoped to grab a gold or silver tie clip or some cufflinks to be sold as holiday gifts at the thrift shop. *Light stuff, David. Where do you keep your light stuff? It's not so easy trekking back and forth to the thrift shop at my age. If you were considerate, you would have had some small shiny metal objects sitting right out front in full view.*

She pulled open the drawers in David's dresser and rifled through a stockpile of socks and boxer briefs. When she discovered a stash of nudie photographs and *Playboy* centerfolds, she couldn't keep herself from laughing. *I wish there was someone I could tell about this. What a dirty little rascal this David is; a real pervert!* At the very bottom of the drawer was an opened package of black lace panties. *Still getting it up, are you, David? I'll never be able to look at you the same way again.* Alice grabbed a dollar bill and some quarters from a leather jewelry box on top of the dresser and then made her way on to Natalie's apartment, where she was stupefied to find herself in a blossom-filled Shangri-La.

Natalie had decorated her home with heaps of colorful, plastic Hawaiian leis, draped around the bed posts, across the tables and chairs, and circling the dresser mirror. The walls were spotted with rubber-banded stems of dried roses, hanging upside down at different levels of the drying process. *I guess you really loved your man.* For a split second, Alice reconsidered taking anything from her. *No, she's got more than enough with her own Garden of Eden and her picture-perfect memories of her marriage. What more could she possibly ever want or need?*

When the alarms started sounding, the administrative staff and nurses were, true to their schedule, assembled at an on-site assessment meeting. Charlotte reported to Mr. Dean that all of the residents, excluding the bed-ridden ones, were in the middle of watching the Von Trapp children sing *"So Long, Farewell"* in the social room and were about to be guided expeditiously to the patio area. All of the nurses, aides, and nurse practitioners systematically arose and hastily headed to their assigned posts, where they would gather up their charges to bring them to their *Point of Safety* stations. While the evacuation process was taking place, Alice was swaying to her own unmelodious tune, digging through Natalie's furniture and searching for some more buried treasure.

Sifting through necklaces, filtering the fake ones from the real gold, she became bothered by the harsh, piercing *whoop, whoop!* of the fire alarm blasting on every floor. *Oy, why do they keep having those stupid fire drills? I'm just going to ignore it altogether and finish up with my business. I doubt whether they'll notice I'm not with the others.* But then came the sound of running in the hallways and an urgent knocking on every entry door. *All right, all right. Don't panic,* she told herself. *Just walk out of here as natural as can be. Stick to the story. Stick to the story.*

Alice shoved all of the chains back under a pile of undergarments and rushed to exit Natalie's apartment, but a leg of her walker hooked onto a lei tied to the bed frame, sending her equilibrium out of kilter. Alice went flying to the floor.

If Rosalita had not taken it upon herself to double check that Natalie was not in her apartment but included with the group on the patio, she would never have discovered Alice spread-eagled and sobbing on the artificial grass rug. She acted swiftly. "I'm going to press the emergency button first, and then I'm coming right over to tend to you, hon." Rosalita knelt by Alice's side and gently patted her shoulders. "Hush. Hush. Help is on its way. It will be all right. Let's keep you nice and still until the medics arrive."

Chapter Forty-two

Jan was crawling on the floor with Asher playing peek-a-boo when Mike called her cell phone.

"I wasn't sure if I should call you about this," he said, sounding nervous. "It seems you're in far better shape now—health-wise—than when you first left, so I was reluctant to tell you the news, especially since you're scheduled to return to Boca in two days."

"What news? What's happened?" Jan blurted out. She picked up Asher, telling him, "Nana will play with you again soon, sweetheart," and placed him in the Pack n' Play. "What's going on, Mike?" she asked into her phone, afraid that she might have to run full speed to the bathroom. *You can handle this. Think of something pleasant, something sweet and safe and loving, like Asher's smile.* "Is it my mother? Is she back in the hospital again? What is it *this time*? Was it a heart attack or a stroke?"

"Nothing like that at all," he informed her. "She fell again."

"Oh, I see." A familiar sense of desolation and powerlessness pressed Jan further down into the seat cushion.

"It happened at Glenbrook during a fire drill. Everyone seemed to be running in a different direction so the details are a little sketchy. They brought her to the hospital to run a full array of tests and x-rays to determine the extent of her injuries."

"I want to say that I'm sad, but I can't." Her voice was weak, but surprisingly deliberate. "Don't get me wrong; I don't want to see her suffer. I don't like to know that anyone is in pain, but right now, the truth is that I'm feeling kind of numb about the situation. Does this make me an ogre; an undeniably repulsive creature?"

"No, it does not," Mike assured her. "I know you and the kind of person you are. Please don't judge yourself too harshly. But wait, there's something else."

"What? Is it about her again?"

"No. It's more scandalous than that."

"And she's not involved?"

"No. This is *really* big news, though. The police came to Glenbrook and arrested Mr. Dean and a couple of the maintenance crew."

"What for heavens for?"

"Drugs. They were buying and distributing heroin from some huge drug ring. Information about the arrests has been broadcast all over the internet, television, and radio."

For a split-second, Jan thought she had misheard Mike, but then the reality of his words sank in. Watching Asher bang on a toy bench of wooden pegs, her mouth fell open. "I can't believe it! Mild mannered Mr. Dean? Oh my God!"

"Someone from Glenbrook's corporate headquarters in Lake Worth called our house, inviting us to a special meeting. I went there yesterday and met the newly installed director, Georgia Okeke. You'll like her a lot. She assured everyone at the meeting that the residents were safe, and the staff were doing their best to minimize the impact from the arrests."

"I sincerely hope they're handling this matter appropriately."

Mike assured Jan that Ms. Okeke, a recent immigrant from Nigeria, seemed to be a savvy, no-nonsense, super sharp woman, who appeared to have Glenbrook totally under control

As soon as Jan hung up the phone, she called the airline to switch her flight to the very next one available and began to pack her clothes. Daniel and Emily, upon hearing the news, agreed to hurry home so they and Asher could drive Jan to the airport. Amid the traffic congestion and commotion of people streaming every which way, Jan bid her farewells on the sidewalk, making sure to give each family member a heart-felt hug and generous kiss.

"I'll call Dad with the particulars of your flight," Daniel promised. "Be sure to send our love to Grandma when you see her."

The flight east was easy and direct, and Jan was happy to see Mike waiting by the curb when she walked out of the terminal in Fort Lauderdale.

"Let's go straight to Glenbrook," she directed, wheeling her suitcase to the rear of his Audi.

Mike hoisted the case into his trunk. "You've just come off a really long flight. Why not go tomorrow and give yourself a chance to rest up from the journey?"

"I'm fine. Really. I want to gather some of my mother's things. She'll be wanting her nightgowns, lipstick, glasses, and pocketbook."

"Aren't you jumping the gun?" Mike asked. "I realize your mind's fixed on visiting her right away, but they've set her wrist and she'll probably be in the ICU for a while, in which case she won't be allowed to use any of that stuff."

"Mike, I know this routine. Even if she were dying, my mother would want her personal items with her. How did she look when you saw her in the emergency room?"

"I only saw her for a few minutes before they took her away. Jan, there's no reason for you to be overly alarmed. Please don't let your mother's mishap cause a relapse in your stomach condition."

"Don't worry about that. I think I finally have that issue licked."

"She didn't look great," Mike continued, "but she didn't look the worst that I've ever seen her. She looked how you would expect her to look."

***

Jan heard voices stemming from the television in her mother's apartment and discovered Sondra on her mother's bed, looking like she was just about to doze off. Sondra's shoes sat on the floor next to a tote bag, which Jan hoped was packed with all the items she had specified in her phone call.

Sondra hurriedly jumped up, brushing her head against the headboard and dislodging her wig off to one side. Looking visibly shaken, she shifted her weight from one foot to the other while trying to avoid Jan's eyes. "I'm finishing these off because they've gone stale and your mother has no recollection of where she'd last hid them," she told Jan. The reference was to a freezer bag containing the last remains of the chocolate chip cookies Jan had previously baked.

"I didn't mean to scare you just now," Jan apologized as she walked towards Sondra. "Don't worry about the cookies; you don't have to eat those. Why don't you throw them away and I'll make you fresh ones once things calm down?"

"No need to do that, Jan. These still taste plenty good." Sondra picked at the crumbs lodged in the creases of her uniform and dropped them into her mouth. "I'll vacuum the ones on the floor after you leave."

"You first might want to adjust your hair," Jan advised, trying to not sound too critical. "It's facing the wrong way."

Sondra headed toward the mirror.

"Were you with my mother when she fell?" Jan asked nonchalantly, pretending to peer out the window so Sondra could fix her wig without discomfort.

"No, unfortunately, I was in a meeting."

Observing Sondra's reflection in the window, Jan saw the wig had been returned to its proper position. "Oh, was my mother by herself when she was visiting with Natalie?'

Sondra fidgeted with her wig again.

"No, I don't think so. I mean, she might have been. I wasn't there, so I really can't say for sure." Sondra kept tugging on the back, front, and sides of her wig.

"I think your hair is looking fine now," Jan advised. "It's sitting perfectly on your head."

Sondra's arms dropped to her sides. "Well then. I'll just turn off the television and be on my way."

Jan watched Sondra push a button on the remote but then unexpectedly sit down on the bed. "Sondra, you have a look on your face like you're trying to hide something. You've always been above board with me before. What's the story?"

"Ain't no story at all," Sondra stated, rubbing her hands together. "Your mother fell in Natalie's apartment. That's all there is to it."

"But Natalie wasn't there. From what I understand, there was a fire drill going on."

"Uh huh. That's exactly it." Sondra's words came out much louder than necessary. "Everyone was running about getting to where they were supposed to be. Your

316

mother was probably just confused and went into the wrong place."

"My mother's apartment is in the west wing on the third floor, and Natalie's apartment is on the second floor in the east wing. My mother has never been that confused before."

Sondra shimmied her way off the bed, stooped to pick up Alice's slippers, and headed toward the closet. "Old people be getting like that. You got to expect these kinds of things."

Jan thought Sondra had stalled an extra-long time after placing the slippers in their proper place before coming back to where she was standing. "Sondra, you have that look on your face again. Has my mother been diagnosed with Alzheimer's? Has she developed dementia, and I don't know about it?"

"No, ma'am."

"Did anyone intentionally hurt her that you know of?"

"No, ma'am!"

"You're not covering up for some of the staff? Is that nasty business with Mr. Dean connected somehow with this?"

"No, ma'am; I'm not covering up anything. Nothing like your hinting at goes on at Glenbrook—that I know of. That drug dealing caught us all off guard for sure."

"I'm sorry. It sounds like I'm badgering you; I don't mean to. It's just that I'm naturally very upset."

"Sure you are. And you must be tired and all after your long trip."

"Yes, I am. Thank you so very much for the help you've already given," Jan announced while reaching for the tote bag. "I really appreciate it."

Sondra grabbed the bag ahead of her but wouldn't let go of the handles.

"Thank you again, Sondra, for putting these things together," Jan reiterated. "I'm going to take them to the hospital now."

Sondra's grip did not lessen. Jan considered yanking the tote bag away, but then she noticed Sondra's bottom lip purse. It began to tremble. Sweat appeared across Sondra's forehead as a steady stream of tears flowed from the corners of her eyes. Before long, Sondra was bawling her heart out and Jan was trying her best to console her.

"Sondra, everything is going to be all right." She led Sondra to sit back down on Alice's bed. "My mother's been through this kind of thing many times. You probably have to deal with these tragedies every day, and the emotions keep building up. Or maybe, it's the situation with Mr. Dean. It must have been very upsetting with the police, the arrests, that whole drug scene, and now having to adjust to a new administrator. I understand how troubling everything might seem. You just keep on crying as long as you have to."

Sondra shook her head and said, "Yous don't understand. It's not like that at all."

"It's okay," Jan said as she massaged Sondra's back. "If and when you're ready, you can tell me what's making you so upset."

"It's all my fault," Sondra bemoaned. "It's my fault that your mother was in Natalie's room; well, not really, but in a way it was."

As Sondra's shortness of breath evolved into a period of hiccupping, Jan handed her a couple of tissues and waited patiently for Sondra to be able to clarify her confession. All the while, Sondra would not lessen her grip on the tote bag.

Just as Sondra announced, "Alice was in Natalie's apartment so she could steal things for me," Jan's phone rang. She would have preferred to have ignored the call, but then she realized it was Mike and he was probably concerned why it was taking her so long. She answered Mike's call and hastily informed him she couldn't speak, everything was okay, and she would be down in the parking lot soon. Jan then turned to Sondra with widened eyes and a look of bewilderment and asked, "Did you just say that my mother was stealing?"

"Yes."

"And that she was stealing for *you*?" Jan dropped down on the bed next to Sondra.

Sondra gave Jan a full detailed report of how Alice had caught her in her room taking things and why. She then went on to reveal how Alice had elected to adopt Sondra's problem as her own cause and how she went about stealing from the others, even after Sondra had begged her not to anymore. This elicited not only a frown from Jan, but she flopped her head all the way down to the comforter, spreading her arms apart and uttering, "This is absolutely f-ing unbelievable! My mother's a common thief."

Sondra stretched back, leaning on her arm, so she could face Jan. Even in her less frenzied state, she still kept squirming to find her balance so that the mattress bounced about like a rowboat in turbulent waters, inducing Jan's body to jerk up and down.

"If you don't keep still, I am going to throw up any minute," Jan complained.

"I'm sorry. I'll lean against the headboard and that'll be better." Sondra pulled herself to a sitting position. "Jan, please don't be so quick to judge your mama like that."

"How can you say that?" Jan yelped. "She's a horrible, horrible person, and you're no perfect saint yourself."

"No, I ain't. The Lord knows I ain't. But Alice has lived through some nasty, mean business, what with your father tormenting her and such. I don't walk in her shoes, and she don't walk in mine, so I'm not going to be the one to judge her."

"Was she behind all of those additional thefts being reported to Mr. Dean?"

"Yes."

"Didn't anyone else wonder what my mother was doing in Natalie's apartment at the time she fell?"

"Not with all the confusion of the fire alarm. No ma'am. It kind of got forgotten. Rosalita didn't think twice about it."

"Who the hell did she think she was? What could possibly have gotten into my mother's head? She's conniving and amoral. I hate her. She hates me. Now we're even. I'm going to wash my hands of her for good."

Sondra bent over so she could make eye contact with Jan. "Oh hon, she don't hate you none."

"Sure she does."

"She's very proud of yous, Jan," Sondra said gently. "Told me so herself; you being an independent woman who can stand up for yourself and how you married such a fine man who's your equal—someone who respects you and treats you so nicely. She been living through you like that word they say 'vikerously.'"

Jan threw out the word "vicariously" to Sondra, but her mind was racing in a million different directions.

"Yes, ma'am."

"What the hell do I care about that now? What she did was wrong; plain outright wrong. And you too! Although I have a little more compassion for you, Sondra."

Sondra shook her head. "I don't deserve that."

"Well, what am I supposed to say or do now?"

"She's not all bad; yous got to know that."

"Yes she is. Water sinks to its own level. I used to believe that my father was the rotten egg, but my mother was just as awful." She sounded more than furious.

"Once I stopped' being her accomplice, Alice hid everything she took in a box in the bottom of her closet," Sondra shared. "Once a week, she'd take the bus to the thrift shop and donate them things she stole."

"That doesn't make her actions right," Jan shouted.

"No, it doesn't, but it might interest you to know that the thrift shop is run by the people who give aid to victims of domestic violence," Sondra added. "She done lots of other good stuff too. She took a torn skirt from Denise's apartment and sewed up the hem without telling her about it. She left bags of Brach's sucking candies on all of the nightstands and replaced the dirty, worn down toothbrushes with new ones, right out from the package from CVS. She called Ethel's daughter to tell her that Ethel wasn't eating enough and that the daughter should look into it, and anonymously sent Flossie flowers after her nephew died. For Charlotte's daughter's wedding, she paid ahead of time for Charlotte to have a manicure and pedicure without letting her know it was her that did it. When Archie Silbert died, she waited in the room with his dead body laid out on his bed until the funeral people came so his spirit wouldn't have to be alone and uncared for. There's plenty more acts of kindness that your mama did, but I've said enough for now."

Feeling like the wind had been knocked out of her lungs, Jan lay motionless, thinking about her mother's evil deeds with Sondra's words going around and around in her head.

"I never seen you so unstrung like this before," Sondra said, stroking back Jan's hair and patting her arm. "I'll just be staying close by your side, while you'll be doing your best to remain calm."

"Stay calm? How can I stay calm? What is there to stay calm about? I listened to all that you said, Sondra, but I don't believe any of it is sinking in. I'm still in shock from the very idea that my mother was a crook! I feel nauseous again; like I'm going to faint." Jan rocked her body from side to side.

"You're not going to faint, so don't go having that on your mind as well. I sees the color's come back to your face. Yous was a little white just then, er, paler pink and less beige, but now you're not." Sondra kept her eyes on Jan. Trying not to shake the bed too much, she clumsily slid to the floor. She walked over to the couch and carried two cushions to the foot of the bed. "Just keep on breathing slowly," she coached, raising Jan's legs to rest on the stacked cushions. "No need to get hysterical."

"I can't stay here forever like this," Jan uttered between exaggerated breaths.

Sondra placed her fingers on Jan's wrist to check if her pulse seemed regular. "Just a little while longer, sugar, and then it'll be safe to let you go."

A few minutes passed and Jan sat up, sliding her feet off the cushions and lowering them to the ground. "I'm fine.

322

I just didn't see it coming. What you told me hit me like a ton of bricks."

Sondra assisted Jan to her feet. "Glad to see you've calmed down. There's one more thing, though, Jan."

Jan faced Sondra with trepidation, looking visibly upset. "I'm not going to faint or throw up. I just want to hear what you've got to say while I'm sitting down. And tell it to me quickly because I don't want to give any more time for this kind of garbage." She sat herself back onto the bed, trying to preserve every ounce of strength she had left.

"No, it's not anything like you're thinking," Sondra said meekly as she took out a folded check from her shirt pocket and handed it to Jan; what Jan saw left her aghast.

"Three thousand five hundred dollars? Am I reading this correctly?" Jan barked with astonishment. "Is this so you can clear your own conscience: giving me more money for Darfur?" Jan attempted to return the check, but Sondra tilted her hand forward to stop her.

"It's from Ambrose," Sondra stated softly, her expression doleful and pained. "It comes right from a good place. She be sending me this to give to you. True to her word, she took up a collection in her shop. People were very generous when they heard about the situation. They got together and done something good. Please Jan, let the money do good. Those people in Darfur need the help."

Jan swallowed, took a few more deep breaths, and placed the check in her pocketbook. Wearily, she told Sondra, "I will definitely get in touch with Ambrose to thank her for this kindness. In the meantime, if and when you speak with her, please extend my gratitude and tell her that the money will go to buying solar cookers, which are essential to increasing the safety of the younger girls and women."

Sondra nodded. "I'll be sure to tell her that." She then released the tote bag into Jan's care. "Your mother will be wanting these things. Please take them to her and send her my love. I only ask that you give me a little notice about what you decide to do as far as I'm involved."

Chapter Forty-three

The floor nurse directed Jan to the last section in the ICU and cautioned her that the patient was still under the influence of anesthesia. Jan quietly pulled the privacy curtain back and tiptoed over to the chair at the side of her mother's bed. All she could see were her mother's drooping jowls and sparse white hair sticking out from under the hospital blanket.

Just under the surface of Alice's skin were a network of veins and capillaries and a pattern of crow's feet branching horizontally from the corners of her eyes towards each of her ears. Jan eyed the path of age spots and the chalky complexion the wrinkles crossed and tried vainly to connect this image to the younger model of the woman she had adored as a little girl. The woman she had so often longed to be embraced by.

"If I close my eyes tight, she'll put down that mascara wand, or pencil lip liner, or pancake sponge and come over to hug me and give me really big kisses," Jan used to pretend, but Alice would complete her makeup routine, walk out of the room dressed to the hilt, and often leave the affection-starved Jan stranded with her unfulfilled wishes, believing she was unworthy of ever being loved.

Wearily, Jan kept waiting for Alice to budge just a little, but the mass beneath the blanket continued to hold its beleaguered shape. She busied herself by taking note of the instrument panels, drip paraphernalia, heart monitor, and other sterile medical equipment—all of which had been familiar backdrops in the many hospital rooms and triage areas in which Alice had sought temporary shelter or restoration. From time to time, as Jan surrendered to the exhaustion from her flight and the shock of Sondra's revelation, her eyes closed and she fought to open them again to remain attentive.

A male nurse entered the room to change the IV drip bag, and Jan smiled appreciatively. *My father would have had a field day tearing this man apart because he's doing "women's" work. Naturally, Norman would have presumed him to be gay.* Jan regarded the transparent intravenous saline solution. *Clear and simple; just what we need to sustain our lives. Why do we have to go and muddy it all up?*

After approximately forty-five minutes, Jan was resigned to leave. She turned on her cell phone, having been instructed to shut off all mobile devices upon entering the ICU. She read a fresh email message sent from Mike, whom she had driven home before coming to the hospital. He suggested she call it quits for that visit, get some rest, and return the next day feeling more refreshed.

As Jan rose, her mother opened her eyes and feebly asked, "Why are you leaving so soon? You just got here."

"I've been sitting here for three quarters of an hour," Jan stated benignly. "I didn't even know you were awake."

"Well, I was," Alice griped, her tone none too weak.

"The entire time?"

"For most of it."

"So nice of you to tell me," Jan said, remaining deadpan as she sensed the taste of acid rising in her throat. *Me and Izzy, dumb and dumber; we just keep coming back for more of the same.* "How do you feel?" Jan asked without a hint of care in her voice.

"Like somebody threw me from a building," Alice struggled to say.

"Once the anesthesia wears off from the surgery," Jan offered, drawing upon her vast experience of Alice's former procedures, "you'll start to feel a little better."

"That's when the pain will set in," Alice moaned.

"That's when you'll ask for medication and will probably get hooked on that as well," Jan responded, tongue-in-cheek.

"When I die, Jan," Alice said, looking up at the ceiling and sounding tired and fearful, "I don't want to see Norman again."

"I can understand that. None of us do. You won't have to," Jan assured her mother. "You'll be with your parents and brothers."

"Well, just to be on the safe side, I want to be buried in Florida; that way it'll be less likely that I'll run into Norman."

Making no attempt to disguise the disdain she was feeling, Jan said, "I'm sure that can be arranged. Or better yet, you can steal yourself a plot of land in whatever cemetery you choose. Why not take a mausoleum or two? One for your coffin and one to use as a hideaway for your stash, or 'swag' as you might say in your fancy British vernacular."

"I'm going to ask Maureen and Jack to make all of the arrangements for me."

"Yes. Of course, you will. You go ahead and do that."

Alice twisted her head to face Jan, her lips parting as if she lost her battle to contain an excruciating pain. "But what if Henry is there? What am I going to say to him?"

Jan was speechless. She sat back down in the chair, her feet tapping.

"I sent him money, you know. Stole a little each week from my household money that your father gave me."

Jan peered back at her mother, repressing any thoughts of mercy. "Evidently, stealing runs in your blood."

"The mingy buggar was cheap with everything," Alice continued, pausing to take a deep breath. "But I managed to put a little aside that I would give to Maureen, and she'd send it off to San Francisco. Told her not to tell Henry it was from me. I didn't want to give him an excuse to send it back." As Alice labored to roll onto her side, she softly asked Jan, "When did you find out he was gay?"

"He told Maureen and me. He had asked to meet us at a sandwich shop when he came home on a break during his freshman year at college. 'Just the three of us,' he kept repeating. I hadn't been at all surprised; neither was Maureen."

"Yes, there was definitely something overtly feminine about him," Alice said with a sigh.

Jan shifted her legs, crossing them at the ankles. "Henry chastised me for whispering to Maureen about the way the waiter hovered over him, eyeing him with more than just casual interest, but Henry was so naïve; he just didn't realize what was going on. He accused us of being childish."

"What did he say exactly?" Alice questioned, her voice growing stronger.

Jan folded her arms, the toe of her right shoe kept knocking against the floor. She looked around the room; her anger toward her mother filling every nook and cranny of it. "It's been these many years and we're first discussing this *now*? Do you *realize* just how many times you shut me up when I had broached the subject of Henry *before*?"

"I was wrong. It was too painful. Please, I'm asking you now; tell me what Henry said." Alice's head dropped to her pillow, a wilted flower begging for water.

Jan exhaled slowly. "He didn't say anything about that," Jan continued, her frame of mind strained, devoid of its original feistiness. "We beat him to the punch and *told him* that he was gay, and then he wanted us to explain how we knew when he really hadn't known for sure until quite recently. Maureen responded that it was a feeling she had, to which Henry wanted her to supply a more detailed explanation. He asked, 'Do I walk funny? Do I talk differently? When did you first suspect?'"

Alice was paying attention to every word coming out of Jan's mouth, hardly breathing between sentences. "My poor baby," she said ruefully, and then motioned to Jan to go on.

A new patient was brought into the cubicle next to Alice. Jan could hear curtains being drawn, the shuffle of feet, the patient call out in pain, and orderlies being dispersed. "Don't pay too much attention to any of that," Alice advised. "They roll in and out of here like clouds. The storm will pass over soon enough, and we'll either have a corpse lying next door, someone in a coma, or an incoherent, delirious maniac."

Jan was about to ask her mother why she consistently sought refuge in hospitals then, but her mother stated, "Compared to them, my life seems like paradise. Jan, don't stop now. Tell me more."

Gazing at her mother's hand, painted purple from the needle jabs and resting atop the blanket, Jan remained fixated on the patch of tape holding the IV in place. She reluctantly resumed. "Henry asked us if we had said anything to you or dad, and Maureen shouted, 'What are you, crazy?' I told him that it was his life and his responsibility alone to inform you, if and when he completely lost all of his marbles and chose to do so."

Alice said, "You should have prevented him from telling us anything at all. Things could have turned out differently perhaps."

"I didn't believe it was mine or Maureen's place to get involved—unless, of course, it had become necessary to do so. We told him that we would take our cue from him, and that we were there to help whenever he needed us."

"You were his older sisters. You should have stopped him. You should have done more!" Her voice became elevated to a shout.

"It doesn't surprise me that you're trying to place the blame on me," Jan protested, her tone laced with anguish and bitterness. She counted to three under her breath, throwing in "Asher's sweet smile" between each number. *Okay. Alright. That's all water under the bridge.* To Alice, she said, "If you don't lower your voice, I will leave immediately."

Emanating from the hallway was a cacophony of background noise consisting of loud beeps and buzzing alarms. "I want you to hear me over this racket! They expect patients to sleep or get well in a place like this?" Alice then quietly pleaded, "Please, please, Jan. Tell me everything you know. I need to hear this. See? I'm not yelling anymore."

Jan cleared her throat. She searched through her pocketbook for a package of gum, popping a spearmint tablet in her mouth before picking up where she left off. "Maureen tried to advise him not to say another word about it. 'Dad is not going to be kind, considerate, loving, or understanding,' she warned. 'He isn't any of those things in the best of times.'"

"You can say that again," Alice interjected.

"I'll continue, if you let me," Jan offered, unable to completely shake off her peeved state. "Maureen told Henry that Dad was homophobic and she was seriously worried about what his reaction would be. 'You're up at school,' she advised. 'Continue to live your life the way you want, and just don't let them know anything about it as long as you can.'"

"Maureen was using her noodle," Alice again interrupted.

"Yep. She's always right."

"What, she's not?"

"Anyway…"

"Anyway, please continue."

Jan purposefully omitted the part where Maureen had cautioned Henry to "Be careful. Be very careful. Neither one of us wants you taking up with the wrong kind of people, and by this I mean people that will take advantage of you or *abuse you*." This last statement had fallen heavily on the table, and none of the siblings issued additional comments until the food was served, with the exception of "pass the salt" and "is there any ketchup left in that bottle?"

"Neither of us knew then that returning to school was no longer an option for Henry. As you well know, against our advice, Henry did decide to sit down that evening and engage in an honest, gut wrenching discussion about his newly confirmed sexual orientation with you and Dad. Later, in a frantic phone call to me, all the painful details of that confrontation came spilling out."

"It was awful, Jan. Just awful," Alice said. "If I could have killed your father that day with my own bare hands, I would have."

Perhaps you should have. Anything would have been better than what you did: rolling over and playing dead like a helpless, lame dog. Jan spat out her gum into the tissue she grabbed from the overbed table and rose to toss it in a trashcan.

Alice kept her sight glued on Jan until she reclaimed her seat, "And what happened next?"

"For days in advance, Henry had been practicing what he was going to say, but he found it hard to zero in on just the right words. He thought about saying, 'I prefer boys over girls' or 'I'm more different than any of us realized' or 'I've had an affair with another man.' My heart went out to him. He was my sweet, sometimes pain-in-the-butt brother, but Henry didn't make himself gay. He was born that way. He shouldn't have had to explain anything about himself or his particular sexual preference to anyone. No apologies were ever necessary."

"What difference would it have made what words he chose to say?" Alice posed plaintively. "Norman would have reacted the same no matter what."

"Any of those options would have been a trigger to make Dad go berserk. I'm thankful now that he didn't own his gun then," Jan stressed.

"Not that the bastard didn't threaten to shoot Henry. We were sitting on the sofa watching the TV when Henry walked into the living room looking extremely nervous. Your father called out really sarcastic-like, 'For God's sake, don't come begging me for more money 'cause I haven't got any for you. You should be pulling your own weight around here just as I did when I was your age. Don't think

I'm going to pamper you like your spoiled American college friends."

Jan gritted her teeth and spouted, "Ugh, I hated him so much!"

"Henry told us that he wasn't there asking for money, so your father said, 'Well, hurry up and tell us what you want. The commercial's almost over.' Henry began really slow, explaining about how he felt and what he had discovered about himself. His left leg was shaking a lot, and he couldn't get it to stop. Then, like a wild lunatic, your father threw one of the decorative pillows from behind his waist at the corner standing lamp. It sent the lampshade flying and the stand crashed to the floor."

"What a jerk!" Jan said bitterly. "What were you doing all this time?"

"I immediately scooted off of the couch and rushed to clean up the mess, but your father reached over, grabbed me by my hair, and pulled me back down again. I swear, his voice could have been heard hundreds of miles away. He turned to Henry with a look of intense revulsion. 'You're a filthy liar,' he shouted. 'I'm ashamed and disgusted by you. You turn my stomach. Unless you take back everything you just said I want you out of my sight forever!'"

"No big surprise there. What did you say?"

"I was crying, naturally, and I begged your father to remain calm. He screamed, 'Calm? Are you so much of an idiot that you didn't understand what Henry is telling us?' I said that I had heard everything. 'He's a fucking pansy, Alice,' your father yelled back at me."

"He called him a *pansy*?" Jan's jaw fell open and her eyes widened. Her horrified reaction was spiked with abhorrence for her father.

"Not only that, he said to Henry, 'From this moment on, you're dead to me,' and to me he said, 'Alice, he's dead to the both of us! I'll make the arrangements to sit Shiva for the queer.' Those were his exact words." Alice could no longer hold back her tears and she wept like her heart had been wrenched out of her body.

Jan turned her head toward a jostling of the curtain and saw that a nurse had pulled back the flap to get her attention.

"We're monitoring your mother's blood pressure," the nurse said softly, "and we're noticing a steady rise. Just to be on the safe side, I'm asking you to leave. No need for alarm, but we're going to sedate her so she can get more rest."

Alice swallowed the pills the nurse handed her and said to Jan, "It hurts a lot not knowing exactly how and when Henry died. Did he have a proper burial? Did anyone say *Kaddish* for him? I don't know if he hated us up until his last breath."

"Yes, well, don't think about that now. You need your strength to recover from your fall."

"I know he died," Alice blurted out through her sobs, "because I dreamed about it one night. He came to me as if he was no longer a person and just a spirit. He kissed my forehead and I tried so hard to hold onto him, never wanting to ever let him go. He said that he was now happy and forgave me and that he was freer than he had ever been before. I'm glad that he's in a happier place, but I shall never be able to forgive myself. I'm afraid to die, Jan. When God takes me, I'm going to be punished."

Jan regarded Alice and succumbed to the immense pity and grief she was feeling on both of her mother's and Henry's behalves. "Hush up now," she offered softly as her

334

own tears flowed freely down her cheeks. She dabbed her mother's face with a clean tissue. "Try not to think about these things. You have to concentrate on getting stronger."

Alice motioned Jan closer. "God knows we killed that other baby too," Alice whispered into her ear. "It would have been a healthy baby if I had carried it full term and the baby would have lived. Your father wanted it dead, not me. He said he was too old to have another child to take care of. I tried to convince him that we could work it out, but he wouldn't listen to me. He gave me pills and said, 'Swallow this like you would aspirin for a bad headache; it'll be over before you know it.' I knew I was doing something wrong. I knew what I was doing was illegal. Every time I walked by a policeman, I was terrified he'd haul me into jail. No matter how horrible God's punishment is going to be, it can't put me through more sorrow and dread than what I've lived with my entire life."

"Rest up, Mom. Try thinking about something else. You should see how beautiful Asher is. He's gorgeous, and so clever—a real combination of Daniel and Emily. I'll show you the photographs when you're able to sit up."

Alice attempted to smile. "Right from the moment Daniel was born, Jan, you were an excellent mother; not like me. You did things I never could. You were so much smarter than me. I saw how you helped Daniel in school and got him involved in sports and clubs. My words were worthless when it came to those things, but you still turned out just fine. Just fine." Alice's voice trailed off into a murmur. Jan could see that her mother wanted to say more, so she leaned even closer to her face and heard her say, "Jan, will you ever be able to forgive me?"

Alice closed her eyes and fell back to sleep. Jan wondered how much of her mother's praise was influenced by her drugged condition. She kissed her forehead and whispered, "I'll be back tomorrow. Your lipstick and things are in the closet. Of course, I forgive you." Alice nodded, and Jan, shattered in more ways than one, walked down the corridor to go home.

Chapter Forty-four

Jan stopped by the hospital again the next day after having some of her clients' documents recorded at the courthouse, and was pleased to find Alice, her left arm in a cast, sitting up and watching the television in an assigned hospital room. Alice's complexion was no longer as anemic and pasty as it had appeared the night before. Her hair looked like a comb had been pulled through it. As Jan moved a chair closer to the bed, Alice grabbed an opened bakery box from the overbed table with her good hand and offered her daughter a cookie. The box wobbled as Alice's right hand shook. Through her parched throat and dry lips, Alice struggled to enunciate, "They're *rugelach*. Take one; you'll enjoy it. They sent these over from Glenbrook; such dolls they are over there."

Jan said, "No thank you. I had a full breakfast this morning."

"Jan, please don't worry about the calories. I want you should taste how absolutely delicious they are. This little pastry won't add that much fat to what you've already got."

Jan gaped at her mother, taking in her fragile condition. *As weak as you are, you still manage to dig!*

"Take one please," Alice cajoled. "The raisin/nut combination is delicious." Alice picked up a *rugelach* and placed it on a napkin, her hand still shaking. "Here, now you can go to town!"

Jan accepted the pastry and said, "Those dolls at Glenbrook saved your life."

"And don't I know it!" Alice agreed. "And I heard that everyone seems to like Mrs. Okeke, who has taken over for Mr. Dean."

Jan bit off a walnut from her rugelach. "Oh, you know about that, do you?"

"Muriel couldn't wait to tell me that she's a foreigner."

"Yes, as are we all," Jan replied, cutting off Alice before she shot off more flak in that regard. "Did you have any idea of what Mr. Dean was up to? He being a fellow lawbreaker and all?"

"Absolutely not!" Alice replied sharply. "Enough about that. Jan, I want you to tell me some things that have been on my mind. You want a drink? You want anything else?" Alice turned off the television with the remote. "Ach; they play nothing but commercials in Florida." She motioned to Jan to pass her a cup of water with a bent straw sitting in it. Jan continued to hold the cup as her mother took a sip.

Jan asked her mother about the condition of her left hand, and was informed that several bones had been broken at the wrist. No other physiological damage had been detected.

"What is it you want to know?" Jan asked as Alice nudged her to remove the cup.

"Everything else that you know about Henry. Please don't hold anything back." Alice talked slowly, as she kept getting short of breath. "I want to learn as much as I can. Start with the night he left us. I know he went to Maureen's from our apartment. What did he say? What did she tell you about it? Tell me," Alice implored, lying back down against her pillow, her eyes focused on Jan's lips.

Jan extended her legs and brushed the sides of her face with her palms, reaching past her ears to rake through her hair with her fingers, and then locked her fingers behind her head. "You're sure you really want to get into this now?"

"Yes, I do," Alice said, nodding.

"Do you remember that I was active in protesting the Vietnam War in those days?" Jan began. "Well, my home was filled with anti-war workers preparing for a rally, so when Henry called, Maureen and I decided it was better for Henry to head out to Bellmore to stay with Maureen. He grabbed the next train heading east to the South Shore, and Jack met him at the station."

"He must have been terribly, terribly upset, my poor boy," Alice uttered, full of compassion and pity.

"Henry told Maureen and Jack in detail about the altercation and how Dad had overreacted."

"Overreacted? He was a raving lunatic!" Alice spat into the air.

"Henry said that Dad told him he was revolting, that what he did was unnatural and against everything holy."

"Those were his exact words," Alice whispered.

"Dad told him to 'Get the hell out of my home, and don't ever come back! I don't want to ever hear from you again—and you can say goodbye to your mother too. You won't be seeing her or talking to her as long as I'm alive.'"

Jan observed a stream of tears rolling down Alice's cheeks. Leaning in, she asked, "Are you sure you want me to go on with this? Maybe I can tell you the rest when you are feeling stronger and better able to handle it."

"I can handle it now," Alice responded decisively. "At the time, I was so confused and upset; I didn't know what to do. I remember shivering in the corner of the sofa and then I ran into my bedroom to hide under a pile of blankets. I could hear Henry gathering his clothes. He opened my bedroom door and peered in at me, but I laid perfectly still. I didn't know what to say to him. The next thing I heard was the door slamming and Henry was gone. I want to know what happened next. How did he look when he arrived at Maureen's house?"

"Very drained and agitated," Jan complied. "He kept saying 'It just isn't fair,' over and over again."

"It wasn't fair, and it wasn't right—not by any sane person's standards," Alice concurred. After exhaling a crestfallen sigh, she added, "That boy couldn't hurt a fly."

"Henry did not sleep very well that night. He rose early the next day, set the breakfast table, and collected the newspapers from the driveway," Jan continued. "Once Maureen and Jack entered the kitchen, he revealed his plan about heading out to San Francisco. He also told them about a relationship he had up at school." Jan stopped speaking, hesitant to provide further details that might embarrass her mother.

"Go on. Everything; I want to hear it all," Alice urged.

"He told Maureen and Jack how he felt like a lost sheep when he first arrived at Buffalo. He couldn't find a place where he could fit in. He went to fraternity parties and attended a few dances, even met some girls, but nothing ever clicked. A few times, he eyed some guys on the dance floor and wished he could be with them instead. Jack became uncomfortable listening to this part, so he offered to leave for work, but Maureen and Henry shouted him down.

"One day, when Henry was sitting in the Ratskeller restaurant in the student union eating a pizza and listening to music on his transistor radio, a young medical student named Dave approached and asked if it was alright for him to sit at Henry's table. Henry said the man was handsome."

Alice closed her eyes. "I'm not sleeping. Go on."

"Henry said his legs felt like Jell-O and he must have been blushing when he told Dave it was okay to sit. He pushed aside his books to make a clear spot for Dave's tray. They spoke about Smokey Robinson and Sonny Terry and Brownie McGhee."

"Who are those people? Are they homosexuals?" Alice asked, her eyes fluttering open.

"No, Mom; they're musicians."

"Oh," Alice acknowledged, closing her eyes again.

"Well, um, Henry went back to Dave's place." Jan took a peek to see if she could read Alice's emotional state, but Alice's face just looked tired, revealing nothing else.

"After discussing music, movies, and politics, Henry spent the night at Dave's apartment. They slept together. It was the first sexual encounter for Henry, and he thought that he had fallen in love." Jan checked Alice's face again for a reaction, but there was no visible one.

"Henry stopped going to his classes, and he and Dave were together a lot." Jan purposefully omitted telling Alice about how the two men had met in alleyways, restrooms, and the back seats of cars to screw morning, noon, and night in between Dave's seminars, labs, and clinics. Despite failing all of his own classes, Henry had been euphoric, continuously stoned, and in heaven for the following three months. He had done everything he absolutely could to please Dave, and his daily existence had become totally subservient to Dave's beck and call, making it impossible for Henry to pay heed to the warning signs of Dave's eventual waning interest.

Alice's right eye opened and shut.

"Henry moved in with Dave. They became a couple. Henry was very happy," Jan told her.

"How long did it last?" Alice asked.

"A few months," Jan answered.

"I'm surprised *that* long," Alice commented like a street-smart know-it-all. "I'm guessing that Dave eventually grew tired of Henry and kicked him out. That's how those kinds of relationships go." Jan's lips parted. Her eyebrows rose a notch. "Dave obviously met someone new," Alice continued. "Gay people go from man to man to man, but Henry was probably too naïve at the time to realize it."

Jan considered debating her mother on the generalities and stereotypes she had just conjured up, but dismissed the idea. "Dave told Henry he had become boring, and Henry begged to stay, but he eventually packed up his gear and bought a ticket on a Greyhound bus heading to New York City. This was when he first got in touch with Maureen and me. Henry had completely misjudged how virulent Dad's reaction was going to be after hearing his confession. He had never counted on support from you, but he never anticipated being cut off from you for good either."

These last words made Alice flinch. As best she could, she tried to roll on her side, but the cast impeded her movement. Falling back on her pillow, she asked, "What else did Henry tell you that time the three of you met?"

"He said he had reached his limit on being emotionally horse whipped by Dad, and that it had been going on forever. He couldn't take it anymore. He was also tired of seeing you demeaned all the time."

Alice began to whimper. "He used to ask me all the time, 'Why do you take it? Why do you always just stay and take it? You could walk out of your marriage. You truly could. Another woman would have done it ages ago.'"

"What would you say?"

"I told him he was too young to understand and he would tell me, 'I can see very well what is happening. Our lives would be so much better without him.'

"'Hush, Henry,' I would say. 'You must respect the man; he's your father.'"

"Yep, that was your go-to line," Jan stated angrily. "I'm surprised you also didn't mention that you stayed for the sake of peace in the home."

"*Bayit Shalom*," Alice whispered.

"What peace was there ever in our home?" Jan uttered with disgust. "Anyway, Henry complained that Dad had been breathing down his neck, issuing a whole load of demands, and making him feel like a prisoner all the time."

"He did it to all of us," Alice conceded.

"He felt inadequate and incapable of ever fulfilling Dad's expectations. He said he wasn't macho enough for him. Mom, are you getting tired? Do you want to try sleeping for a little bit?"

"No, I'm doing okay. Please finish with what you have to say," Alice said, stifling a yawn.

"Henry was never into sports like Dad was as a kid. Dad didn't stop ribbing him about his hair when Henry grew it long. Dad told him, 'I don't care if this is how the Beatles wear their hair. No one in my family is going to look like a putz or a Teddy Boy.'"

Alice muttered, "Henry looked so much like Norman. You would think it would have made Norman treat him better than he did. It's almost like it made it worse."

"When Henry wore T-shirts, Dad complained he looked like a scumbag. Whatever music Henry listened to, Dad called it 'awful blasting noise' and purposefully scratched all of his records."

"He did that?" Alice asked quizzically.

"Yes, he did that and plenty more. He called him 'an ignorant oaf' for studying French instead of Spanish and 'a complete and utter embarrassment' because he got the lead in a musical in high school. He told Henry that he would split his head in two if he ever found him with a joint, but he had no problem with him smoking cigarettes or getting drunk because that was a manly thing to do."

"How come I know none of this, Jan? I was there when all this happened."

"Because you really were never there!" Jan yelled. "You chose to stick your head in the ground, telling us all the time that you were too stupid to do anything else. You hardly spoke at all then." Jan's voice was becoming choked up, and she considered getting up and leaving the room.

"What could I have done?" Alice cried. "What could I have done?"

Jan stared at her mother, attempting to regain her composure. A nurse knocked on the door and stuck her head in to check that everything was all right. After her mother told the nurse, "Yes, we were laughing at a joke," Jan arose and took thirty steps in each direction down the hallway before reentering the room and taking her seat again.

"I'm glad you came back. I was afraid you had left," Alice disclosed.

"Just call me 'Izzy,'" Jan replied with the mindset of someone surrendering.

Alice, looking confused, asked Jan if she wanted another *rugelach*. After Jan declined, Alice asked for a drink for herself, so Jan supported her mother to a sitting position and held the cup with the bent straw close to her mother's mouth.

Alice thanked Jan and reclined on her pillow. Jan took up her former position on the chair next to the bed. "As you were saying," Alice prompted.

"When he joined CORE, Dad accused Henry of doing it just to spite him. He would yell, 'Those black people are lazy; they could get jobs like everybody else' or 'those Commies have to be wiped out' or 'the government of the United States of America can do no wrong, period, and all hippies are filthy scalawags.' Dad loved to throw his weight around, and it was mostly at me or Henry.

"Henry was very hurt by Dave. He thought the relationship was really beautiful, and it turned into something nasty and sordid. He came home looking for comfort and solace, and ended up being thrown out like he was less than dirt. He told Maureen and me that he couldn't go back to college because he didn't want to ever see Dave again, and besides that he no longer had matriculated status."

"I never knew that he did so poorly in school," Alice moaned. She glimpsed at Jan but then turned away.

"What did you know, Mom? What *did* you know?" Jan's voice crescendoed. She took some deep breaths before resuming the rest of Henry's saga.

"Maureen tried to talk some sense into him. She told him that things have a way of working out for the better and that most people experience a tragic first love.'"

Jan thought she heard her mother murmur, "Yes, love can turn out to be very tragic."

Jan checked the dry erase board on the wall and noted it was soon time for another dose of her mother's medication. "I'm going to wrap this up so you can get some rest."

"I promise I'll go to sleep as soon as you're done. Please, please finish," Alice begged, her voice groggy.

"Mom, Henry went to California because he wanted to be with other free spirits and nonconformists. He needed to be in a place where he could finally live his life freely. He wanted to go where no one knew him so he could start off fresh and be totally honest with himself and others.

"Maureen tried to counsel him by saying, 'Henry, you're young. You've just had your heart broken. Maybe now isn't the time to make such a drastic decision. Please don't give up on a college education.'

"Jack, echoing Maureen's sentiments, chimed in, 'It's very important to get that degree. You'll need it for the rest of your life.' Knowing that Dad would cut off any financial support for Henry, Jack offered to cover the tuition and board for any school Henry chose to transfer to."

Jan stood up and straightened out the pillow, sheet and blanket on the bed, tucking Alice in so she would be more comfortable.

"He's a good man, that Jack," Alice maintained in a whisper. "He always has been, right from the start when he helped to pay our hospital bills. What did Henry say to them?"

"Unfortunately, Henry had made up his mind. He told them, 'It's the 70s and a new age, and California is the place to be. I'm leaving tomorrow. Some other dropouts from my school are heading that way, and I'm hitching a ride with them. I've already arranged it.'

"'Who are these people? Maureen asked. 'Do you know enough about them? They could be draft dodgers—' but Jack cut her off. 'Well, you be sure to stay in touch so we can send you a little something from time to time, just to keep your head above water. And try not to give up on that college degree; I'm with your sister on that one.'"

"And then he left," Alice said sadly, closing her eyes and wrapping up the scenario, but Jan still had one more comment to make.

"Maureen tried to get Henry to delay his trip until he was less emotional. She proposed that he stay at least three months at their home, just to build himself up before heading west. She wanted Henry to be sure about what he was doing. Jack, however, had tugged at Maureen's sleeve, signaling for her to stop talking. 'He's made up his mind,' he told her. 'You have to stop sounding like a worrywart. You've done all you can. You're not his mother.'"

Chapter Forty-five

Alice returned to Glenbrook after spending five more days in the hospital. When Jan brought her mother home, Sondra was waiting in the apartment ready to give Alice a loving hug and an exceptionally warm reception, but she had difficulty making eye contact with Jan. Jan decided to address the problem straight on.

"I want some assurances from the both of you that your deviant behavior has definitely come to an end," she stated in her sternest voice. Wasting no time, Sondra ran to the library tucked into the second-floor social room and returned with a bible, eager to swear an oath before Alice and Jan that she was done taking for Delmont's benefit—or for anyone else's as far as she was concerned. She swore up and down ten times over that she'd be walking on the righteous path from here on in. Alice was quick to add, "And you should promise to go on a serious diet while you're at it."

"And mother, what say you?" Jan said, turning to face Alice, who had her arm still in a cast, supported by a navy and white Hermes scarf tied around her neck—courtesy of Maureen and Jack.

"I'm over it," Alice acknowledged. "Kaput. Finished. *Finito.* No more. Jan, I promise you. I'm on the straight and narrow, even if my life goes back to being boring as hell, which it most definitely will."

As soon as Jan and Sondra had left Alice alone in her apartment, the first thing she did was to rid the hidden freezer bag of its contents, flushing the heroin down the toilet. "You could have brought me in a pretty penny in my heyday, but now, I'm a changed woman, on the up-and-up. I think it's best that we go our separate ways."

Accordingly, Jan chose not to expose Sondra's and her mother's wrongful deeds to anyone at Glenbrook, hoping that these past misdemeanors would go undiscovered. She also suggested that Charlotte search for another facilitator if she wished to continue the Fireside Chats. Intending to make the most of her freed-up time, Jan cleaned off her old brushes, purchased a new easel and a variety of art supplies, and resurrected her passion to paint.

In the weeks to come, Jan could not be too sure if her mother had truly relinquished her life of crime, or if the cast about her wrist impeded her flexibility for rummaging and, therefore, unwillingly caused her to withdraw from further thefts. In spite of these doubts, Jan now approached Alice with a greater softness in her heart. She wondered if this new-found attitude was vaguely connected with her forgiving her mother during the first night's visit at the hospital.

Despite Alice's assertion that the van transportation was more than adequate, Jan sometimes accompanied Alice to see her doctors for her follow-up visits and subsequent x-rays. She learned from the orthopedist that in spite of Alice's advanced age, her bones would mend with time and the cast would eventually be removed.

"Jan, I don't need you to come with me," Alice would stress. "I understand you have plenty of other things on your schedule."

"Mom, you'll be stuck in the waiting room forever until the van comes back to pick you up. Why not give me a call at the end of your appointment? If I can, I'll be there for you."

***

There were many days that Alice did ride the van and not just for her doctors' appointments. On several occasions, she would join Muriel, Helen, and the other women for jaunts to the casino, specialty restaurants, and the movies. Although her dexterity was limited, Alice also helped her friends prepare decorations for the 2004 Christmas/ Chanukah/Kwanzaa holiday season. Despite some subtle changes to her personality, Alice's crusty sense of humor remained intact. "Kwanzaa? I never heard of such a holiday. What religion celebrates Kwanzaa? Is it a new religion? *Just what the world needs is another religion.* They make up names for these new things all the time now. Before you know it, there'll be a Happy Eskimo Day or a National Observance Day for Wild Salmon."

"What's so terrible about finding something new to celebrate?" Muriel asked.

Arthur, busily gluing red berries on shiny paper for a special lunch menu, said, "I'd rather celebrate holidays I've never heard of than dwell on what's going to make me miserable and unhappy."

"I agree with you Arthur," Helen commented. She was pinning foam snowmen to a poster board.

Alice stood to survey the progress of work around the table and called out, "Doris, don't be so skimpy with that wreath. People will mistake it for a bagel!"

While ribbons, construction paper, and paper flakes were being cut and pasted, Charlotte buzzed around her Arts and Crafts participants. She gave each of them hugs and pats on their backs and marveled at their projects before rushing to the office on the lower level to get more glue.

"She's such a doll, that one," Doris chimed in.

"Yes, she's wonderful," echoed Helen and Muriel, who immediately crossed pinkies, said "Jinx" at the same time, and waited until someone called out one of their names.

Arthur obliged them quickly by saying, "Helen, Muriel, you're free to go."

"Do you know that when Charlotte got divorced," Doris asked of no one in particular as she traced pictures of reindeer, "that her daughter, who was just a teenager then, went to live with her ex?"

"Really?" Helen inquired.

"How come?" Elaine asked, intrigued by the tidbit of gossip.

Murray volunteered, "Charlotte don't seem like a drug addict to me."

"Being an addict isn't the only way to lose custody of your kid," Alice corrected Murray.

"Oh no?" Murray seemed perplexed.

"We should ask Jan," Muriel offered.

Alice hastily rejected Muriel's suggestion. "Leave Jan alone; she's got enough to do."

"Well, it just seems odd that someone as nice as Charlotte would end up without her daughter living with her," a baffled Elaine posited.

Muriel was tying a red ribbon around a green metallic box. "Helen, can I borrow your finger please?"

Helen placed her finger on the ribbon so Muriel could finish making a bow. "Sometimes people are nicer to strangers than they are to their own family members," she said, "For some, it's easier to love people from afar."

"What does that mean?" Elaine asked as she threaded candy canes through tinsel ropes.

"Well, Charlotte's often very nice to us, but perhaps she was horrid to her family," Helen answered.

"I had a husband like that," Alice confessed. "To everyone else he was as impressive as the Lord Mayor of London. Everywhere he went, people gushed over him with praise; that's when he wasn't hollering his head off. To me he was a terrible bastard."

Muriel glanced over at Alice and gave her a reassuring nod.

"Maybe she didn't used to be so nice, then she changed, and now she is," Alice added.

"People don't typically change," Arthur commented. "Helen, please pass me more of the candles; I'm ready to set up my next menorah."

"A leopard doesn't lose its spots," Murray stated, mirroring Arthur's sentiment.

"I think all things are possible," Alice concluded as a beaming Charlotte reentered the room with a tray filled with Elmer's glue and a box of donuts.

As part of their corporate marketing plan, Glenbrook was hosting another big shindig to welcome in the New Year. Invitations had been sent to all of the surrounding retirement communities, and a big crowd was anticipated to share in the "Hello 2005—All Day Long Buffet."

Charlotte made a point to inform her Arts & Crafts group how delicious the food was going to be. "After all, we have to present ourselves in the best way possible. We're hoping these guests become our future residents."

"In that case, you should keep the overhead lights off and the table lamps dim," Alice teased. "That way, you'll be able to put on a good show and the visitors will be none the wiser."

"The free food always brings in the freeloaders. They come in droves," Helen complained to Arthur. "Just watch how the women are going to shovel rolls and cold cuts into their pocketbooks."

"I'm going to station myself by the after-dinner mints," Arthur announced. "For some reason, the men tend to grab fist-loads of them faster than you can say 'Jiminy Cricket.' We usually run out of mints and the sweeteners with the first bus full of visitors."

"I still insist that it would be a hundred percent better if we screened out the snowbirds from coming to our party," Alice said specifically for Charlotte's benefit.

Charlotte informed Alice that this would be an impossible task.

"That's too bad," Alice responded, "because they bring with them all the germs from up north. You mark my words, there'll be coughing and sneezing all over the chafing dishes and salads. They'll go home with their bellies full and leave us with nothing but the dregs."

Arthur proposed getting protective shields. "Like they have at those all-you-can-eat places, like the ones in Sweet Tomatoes and the Golden Corral."

Charlotte picked up a wicker basket and went about the room collecting the finished decorative pieces. "Regretfully Arthur, there's not enough in our budget for that, and Alice, we can't have anyone being such a gloomy grouch during the holiday season. Do try to be a little more festive."

"If you make it to my age, Charlotte, and I hope you do, let's see just how charming you're going to be." Using her fingers to pull back her lips, Alice stretched her top lip above her gum line and squeaked out, "Am I looking cheery enough for you?"

Chapter Forty-six

For several days after the New Year's party, Alice had not been feeling too well, spending many of her days in bed. Sondra suggested that she make an appointment to see Dr. Patel, who made his rounds at Glenbrook every Friday.

"Dr. Patel talks in a sing-song and his face reveals nada, nothing, zero emotion. What good is he going to do me?" Alice grumbled while pushing the off button on her remote control. "Firstly, I don't understand a single word he says, and secondly, I just have a slight cough. Who even knows if the schools in India teach the same kind of medicine that we have here?"

Sondra had brought in newly cleaned sheets and towels and was restocking Alice's shelves. "It's worrying me that your cough be taking so long to get out of your system," she called from the bathroom. "And by the way, Dr. Patel attended Harvard Medical School."

"In that case, it's very suspicious that he isn't on Park Avenue or in Palm Beach making millions," Alice struggled to call back. "Tell me, Sondra, since you know so much, why does the TV in Florida only have crappy shows and too many commercials?"

Sondra poked her head out of the bathroom door and said, "Dr. Patel is a smart, kind man who be knowing his stuff. You should go see him."

"Sondra, when you're this old, it's not just sex that takes longer. I'm sure I'll get better eventually."

Alice laid her head against her pillow and Sondra, worried, came to take her temperature again. "If your fever doesn't break soon, I'm going to insist you see Dr. Patel even before he comes here. I'll take yous to his office even if I be driving you there myself."

Sondra checked that there were enough boxes of tissues, bags of lozenges, flasks of tea with honey, jars of Vick's vapor-rub, and Tylenol, all positioned far from Alice's reach.

"My headache's coming back. Sondra, please give me two more aspirins," Alice begged.

"Now, don't go crazy eating up the Tylenols like you used to, Alice. We want your cough to get better and not you going through hallucinations and withdrawals like a junkie. Let me know what you'll be needing and I'll be quick to give it to you."

Alice summoned all the strength she could to complain, "Are you a dummy or what? I just said I had a headache and needed two aspirins and you've given me nothing!"

"Hon, you can have those in thirty minutes time, but not before," Sondra instructed, pulling back the top part of the sheets and blanket. She gently placed her hands on Alice's shoulders. "Here, let me give you a massage and see if it helps alleviate some of the pain."

"Ooh, that feels good," Alice sighed. "Make sure you keep your hands away from my boobs, though. Are you sure you never worked in a strip joint or massage parlor?"

"Always with the wisecracks, aren't you? Better you keep quiet Miss Alice, and let me be doing my job."

"Thank you," Alice said with sincerity. "That feels very good. It's helping me to relax a little. Sondra, there are some things that I would really love to give you. It will give me great pleasure if you accept them."

"That's all right, Alice. I'm okay with what I got right now."

"No. These are a few of my personal belongings that I know you could use and enjoy. I'll tell Jan that I gave them to you, so nobody will accuse you of taking them."

Sondra shifted to massaging Alice's arms and hands. Her movements were slow and considerate of Alice's debilitated state. "Why don't you keep them for now?"

"No; I want you to have them. I know what I'm doing. You've been simply wonderful to me. Your heart is almost as big as you are." Alice lifted her head to get a better view of Sondra. "Well, maybe not that big!" She smiled and then succumbed to a coughing episode.

Sondra brought Alice to a sitting position and braced her back. After the coughing ceased, she handed Alice a cup of water. "Drink a little at a time. You need to stay hydrated, and it will help soothe your throat."

Alice returned the cup and Sondra cradled her back down onto the sheets, making sure her head rested comfortably mid-center on the pillow again.

As her eyes began to tear up, Alice told Sondra, "Your unlimited kindness has humbled me. It truly has been an honor to be your friend. I say this with the deepest respect for the person you are."

"I love you Alice; you know that."

"I love yous too, Sondra."

***

At 11:30 in the evening, Jan and Mike received the call that once more Alice had been admitted to the hospital, and that she was now diagnosed with pneumonia. Jan was shocked and dismayed to hear the staff doctor's other prognosis. He had greeted her in the hallway, outside the entryway to the ICU unit. Jan peered through the window of the door and perceived a flurry of activity involving a policeman and several male nurses taking place on the other side. She hoped her mother wasn't involved in the fracas.

"Your mother's lungs are inflamed and full of fluid," the doctor related as he removed his surgical mask. "Furthermore, her kidneys are malfunctioning; we are recommending a course of dialysis at least four times a week, for approximately three to four hour sessions." The doctor turned from Jan to Mike, locking eyes with each of them as he conveyed the severity of the situation.

"Has my mother agreed to this?" Jan asked.

"No. Right now, and understandably so, she's in no condition to give her consent," the doctor shared. "Are you a Health Surrogate on your mother's behalf?"

Jan opened her pocketbook and extracted a folded, yellow, mailing envelope. "Yes. I have the papers with me."

"Does she have a DNR as well?"

"Yes. It's all in the envelope."

"Good. You can hand those papers in at the nurse's station."

"But what about the pneumonia?" Jan asked. "What is the procedure for treating that?"

"There's nothing more the hospital can do for your mother other than to keep her comfortable on antibiotics." He spread open his hands. "The dialysis would help prolong her life by a few months, possibly as much as a year."

"And otherwise?" Jan inquired.

The doctor shrugged. "It's hard to say, but she probably has just another month at most." Leaning forward, he gently placed his hand on Jan's arm. "I know this is a lot to take in."

Jan glanced down at the floor and then directly into the doctor's eyes. "What quality of life are we talking about, doctor?"

"That's not for me to say. I can only tell you what treatments are available; the ultimate choice will be your mother's or yours to make." He studied Jan's face. "I would like you to confer with her about the dialysis; the centers are modern and friendly environments. Each patient's chair comes fitted with television, music, and Wi-Fi. They can even arrange for transportation back and forth to Glenbrook." An orderly passed by and the doctor handed him some written instructions.

Jan rested her head upon Mike's chest as he drew her closer to him and pledged, "We'll get through this; we'll face whatever lies ahead together."

"I'm not going to force her into dialysis," Jan said with conviction. "That's no life for her."

Mike, indicating his agreement, asked, "Don't you think we should get Maureen and Jack's opinions on this as well?"

"Yes, of course," Jan responded. "I doubt that my mother will be able to go back into Glenbrook; they don't allow residents this ill. We'll have to look into nursing care or have her come stay with us."

Overhearing Jan's last comment, the doctor advised, "I'd prefer that she initially go into nursing care. I'd feel more comfortable with an onsite medical team 24/7 and her receiving readily available pain medication through IV."

"I don't want my mother to suffer from a lot of pain, doctor," Jan requested.

"Pneumonia is called the old folks' friend because it allows for a dignified end to life. Most of those suffering from pneumonia lapse into a state of reduced consciousness and then slip away peacefully in their sleep, but I must warn you that your mother's body will be filling up with fluid as her kidneys will be able to handle less and less."

Arrangements were made for Alice to be brought to the nursing home that shared the same campus as the hospital. She was given a private room, and Jan furnished it with as many of Alice's personal belongings that she could fit into the one dresser and small closet. Jan hoped her mother would not wonder about the items that had been packed into garbage bags and donated, but only after Sondra had been given the opportunity to choose whatever she wanted.

Jan and Mike had sorted through Alice's photograph collection and picked the ones most representative of Alice's entire family. These Jan taped to the walls over the dresser and around Alice's bed.

Sondra made a point to visit Alice every day during her free time. She straightened her bed linens, accompanied her to the bathroom, brushed her hair, moisturized her hands and legs, and otherwise just kept Alice company. Alice, however, was nowhere as animated or as sassy as she had been before.

"I brought you your lucky pink poodle, Alice. I'm placing it over here so it be watching over yous when I'm not here."

A feeble "Thank you" drifted out with Alice's constricted breath.

Sondra pressed her lips gently on Alice's forehead. "Hush. Don't try to speak; just get your rest."

Alice raised her skeletal hand, wrapped in bulging veins and purple bruises, to grasp Sondra's arm, mobilizing all the strength she could. "Come closer. Bring your lips closer to my mouth, Sondra."

Sondra obeyed.

"I did it," Alice confessed in a whisper.

"Yes, you did," Sondra agreed softly. "Now, try to get some sleep."

"No, you don't understand what I'm telling you." Alice gasped for air.

"You need to conserve your energy. Close your eyes. I'll sit by your side, even if you doze off."

Alice struggled to release her words, pausing to sigh between syllables. "I arranged for that third robbery."

"Close your eyes, Alice and get some sleep. You don't know what you be saying now."

Whenever Sondra passed the nurse's station, she intentionally directed a comment to the nurse in charge, just to let it be known that someone was paying close attention to Alice and expected her to be treated well. Each time she said her goodbyes, she gave Alice a long, affectionate hug as if it would be their last.

Very slowly, Alice's body began to engorge with the fluid that her kidneys could not process. Her clothes could no longer fit comfortably, so Jan bought her warm-up suits made of stretch material in extra-large sizes in three different colors. When Alice could no longer wear her shoes, Jan purchased men's slippers. As each week went by, Jan would have to purchase the next size up until the extra, extra-large open-backed scuffs were also no longer big enough. Jan took pains to remove any information relating to the size. Often, she wondered if Alice was aware of the true nature of her condition. *How much does she realize? Does she know that she's dying?* If Alice did fully comprehend her situation, she never spoke a word about it to Jan.

Bingo was played in the nursing home each afternoon. Jan tried to join her mother once or twice, making sure to fix her stray curls, apply color to her lips, and add a little blush to her cheeks before they departed Alice's room, but Alice took no joy in partaking in the activity. After Jan wheeled Alice into the recreational room, Alice looked around and became even more depressed.

"What's the point? I can't hear the numbers that are being called out," she told Jan, but Jan believed that Alice really didn't want to see herself in as bad condition as those about her.

Three weeks later, Jan was notified that Alice was in a coma and had been transported back to the hospital. Jan and Mike then made the calls to everyone else in the family, indicating that Alice's death was imminent.

It had been quite a while since all the members of Jan's family had been gathered in one place. Unlike the idealized families portrayed on TV and in the movies, Jan's family did not convene frequently to celebrate holidays; no one wanted to make the arrangements or had deemed such an assembly worthy enough to push aside plans for a ski vacation, cross-country hike, or Mediterranean cruise. There seemed to be a lack of connection among the cousins and toward their aunts and uncles, which Jan attributed to the diseased root of her family tree, stemming from Alice and Norman's ill-fated marriage. Henry's expulsion was like a branch snapped off in a perilous storm, causing the tree to wither further and grow even more septic.

Nevertheless, Maureen and Jack, and their two children, Aaron and Jacqueline, and Daniel took whatever actions were necessary to fly to Boca Raton as soon as Jan shared the news with them. Within a few hours of each other, they filtered into the ICU area where Alice was resting. It bothered Jan that Alice's grandchildren could make the effort to see her when she was dying, but couldn't be bothered when she was well enough to enjoy their company. She shared this with Mike, but then added, "But it is much better that they're all here than not at all."

"It's not our place to judge," Mike advised.

Maureen and Jan each held one of their mother's limp and almost lifeless hands. The rest formed a circle around Alice, everyone holding the next person's hand.

Jan spoke first. "Mom, we're all here with you now. I've brought your lipstick and your hairbrush. They're on the nightstand next to you."

Maureen approached her mother and said softly, "You can now go ahead Mom and join your brothers and your parents. They are waiting for you. You can go in peace. You can go with all of our love. We love you dearly."

Each person took a turn expressing their love and wishing Alice a peaceful, loving journey. The group stood in the circle for quite some time. Alice's face was without expression; her body lay completely still. Jan expected the heart monitor to cease recording the presence of a pulse. She looked questioningly at Maureen, who was just as perplexed.

The staff doctor entered the room and expressed his condolences, but Jan said that her mother hadn't died just yet.

"Actually, she passed several hours ago."

"That's impossible," Jack stated softly. "We've been observing her heartbeat and pulse; the beeping and graphic patterns never stopped." The confusion that Jack expressed was shared by everyone in the room with the exception of the doctor.

The doctor explained, "The activity you've seen on the monitor has been from your mother's pacemaker."

Daniel and Jacqueline began to laugh.

Jan looked at Maureen with resignation. "Even in her death, Mom managed to pull one over on us."

Mike hugged Jan and said, "She did remain a fantastic actress all the way to the end."

Chapter Forty-seven

Each time Jan passed by the pylon sign of Glenbrook's main entrance on her way to a scheduled meeting with Susan Walsh or on her way back with a briefcase full of files to research, a slight tug pulled at her heart. Ever since her mother had ceased to be a resident there, Jan had refrained from visiting the facility. Whether driving east or west along Seacrest Road, she would notice the new white slat rocking chairs on the porch, the redesigned flowerbeds, and freshly blackened parking lot, and would wonder about how many of the apartments inside had been spruced up as well. *Just how many of the old people that I knew are still there, or have they also all passed on by now? Collections of stories, memories, and bothersome ailments just keep constantly moving in and out of Glenbrook. Life is surely a revolving door there.*

Jan had tried to stay in touch with Sondra; they last spoke at the funeral parlor at the end of the service for Alice.

Sondra kept dabbing at her tear-filled face with a sopping wet, man-sized handkerchief. She held onto Jan tightly and repeatedly told her how much she had adored Alice. "Your mama was really something all right. She was tough as nails and had a mean side that kept me on my toes, but I suspect her saying them unkind words was a way to keep her own self from getting hurt again, considering the load of hurt she was already carrying around with her. When it was just her and me, we'd get to talking and I learned a lot about your daddy and how he was. Alice used to tell me stories that made me shiver and feel sorry for her circumstances, but Alice also had a really big heart, and that's what I'm going to remember most about her."

As Sondra squeezed Jan's hand, Jan's other hand squeezed the package of tissues that Emily had slipped into Jan's pocket, but that package remained unopened throughout the service and the internment. In fact, Jan never did shed any tears after her mother's death; she did, however, regret never having had a completely honest discussion with her mother to dispel the erroneous perceptions and unfulfilled expectations they each had harbored toward their relationship.

Sondra went on to share details about her new work assignment as a baby nurse. "It's harder on my ass and legs, especially during those middle of the night feedings, but much easier on my emotions when I don't have to keep saying my goodbyes at a cemetery." Two weeks after Alice's funeral, Sondra went to Chicago, and this was the last that Jan had heard from her.

Sometimes, during the days that followed the funeral, Jan was concerned that she might have turned into a terrible, cold, uncaring human being. She questioned whether the others in the family believed she had been so overcome with grief and remorse that she couldn't emote or let go of her sadness, but that was not the case. For Jan, the overpowering pressure of being responsible for her mother's well-being was finally over, and she understood that her mother was finally where she had hoped to be: at peace and with the spirits of those whom she most truly loved.

On the afternoons when she wasn't reviewing a file—which typically involved an adoption, a Temporary Restraining Order, or compliance with mandatory child support guidelines—or when Jan wasn't painting in a studio with a local artist group, she would set off to meet Maureen, who had purchased a vacation unit in a hi-rise condo close to the Florida shore. Jan and Maureen had made a commitment to renew their sisterly bond, sampling different dining venues to accomplish this goal. At these lunches, Jan would be animated as she described the cases she was working on, and Maureen would listen intently.

Mike had been the one to show Jan the value of her law degree and had urged her not to be so quick to throw it all away. "Use your brains to help others," he said. "You know firsthand how destructive a dysfunctional family can be. With your skills and credentials, you can help people rebuild their lives."

Jan never stopped wondering about Norman's outrageous behavior and if there may have existed some process to have curtailed it. *But he would never have acquiesced to any kind of treatment, viewing it as an affirmation of inferiority. What made him want to be so angry all the time? Did he realize how much he was hurting each of us? Did he care?*

Henry had come the closest to being the most forthright and daring in his communications with Norman. Had he not been so, Jan surmised that her brother would still be alive and enjoying a significant presence in Jan's and Maureen's lives. So many times, Jan had considered saying to her father, "We want to love you, but you make it impossible for us to do so," but was too afraid of being rebuffed. She remembered asking Mike several years into their marriage, "Doesn't my father need love like everyone else?"

But Jan now understood that her father had belonged to a generation in which feelings were hardly ever discussed. Talking about one's fears or misgivings was a sign of weakness, and in those days a man had to appear strong and in charge at all times. Norman would have most likely dismissed all of her questions with the back of his hand, continuing to spew out a stream of profanities.

She considered visiting her father's gravesite in the New York cemetery, specifically to express the feelings she had kept bottled up for much of her life, but Mike suggested she should write her thoughts in a letter instead. "First, you'll stomp on it, and then we'll dispose of it once and for all. I'd prefer spending our money on a more upbeat vacation—somewhere romantic, just for the two of us."

Following Mike's advice, Jan wrote:

> *Dad, for my entire childhood I kept searching to be loved. Children naturally want to be loved. All children deserve to be loved. I deserved to be loved.*
>
> *I always hated you, but for good cause. You took advantage of me as if I was a mere object and not a human being. Why should a young child forever fear being decimated and tossed away like a piece of garbage—by a parent no less? What kind of parent constantly places a child in harm's way?*
>
> *I believed that there had to be some good in you and some good in Mom. I kept hoping that it would eventually show itself, but that never happened in your case. You tried so hard to be such a tough guy and you were, after all, the biggest weakling I ever met.*
>
> *You strove to manipulate your family and make us bend to your will. Looking back, it was as if*

*our spines had snapped in two. One by one, we
caved in to your control.*

   *Well, that jig is finally up. I am releasing
myself from your appalling curse. You're just not
worthy of being a part of my life any more. Mom
has passed on, and I have fulfilled the bitter,
senseless sentence that you condemned me to.*

After Jan read her letter out loud, Mike rewarded her
with a kiss and an enveloping bear hug. Together, they
walked hand in hand into their rear garden. He took the
letter from Jan's hand and placed it by her feet. "Go ahead,
do your stuff."

She growled as she shredded the letter to pieces.

Mike swept the fragments into a dustpan, tossed
them into an empty trashcan, added a lit match, and
encircled Jan's waist as they watched the letter disintegrate
into ashes.

Although peace was finally made between mother
and daughter, Alice and Jan never were able to fully resolve
their differences in a heart to heart talk—the kind of
discussion in which each woman would have spoken
honestly, without fears of recrimination or backlash. Alice
had been so brainwashed by Norman during their marriage
that Jan doubted if Alice was capable of ever discerning the
truth of any situation. How awful it must have been for her
mother to endure so much oppression and abuse for so long;
Alice's diseased body with its countless breakdowns was
surely evidence of that.

However, that opportunity was now lost forever and
Jan appreciated how important it was to talk to others while

the chance to do so still existed. She made a promise to maintain an open dialogue with Daniel after sharing with him how much of her obsession over his safety stemmed from the lack of good parenting that she, Maureen, and Henry had personally experienced.

"I realize that I overcompensated," Jan admitted, trying to keep her face centered in the screen as she conversed with Daniel over Skype—a new device that Daniel, conversant in all the latest technology, had insisted on Mike installing on their computer as Daniel walked him through the process. A jerky image of Daniel turned his head to utter something to what appeared to be a disjointed but very pregnant Emily. She appeared to be making cookies with a miniature sprite who kept dashing about and whom Jan guessed to be Asher. Jan waited until she had gained Daniel's attention once more. "I swung the pendulum too much in the opposite direction," she continued. "It was a mistake that I made while you were younger, Daniel."

Jan could hear Emily whisper to Daniel, "Go on, tell her. Don't keep a lid on your emotions; Now's your chance to say some things," and then Daniel announced reluctantly, "You were one of those annoying helicopter moms, for sure; that is when you weren't marching or picketing for practically every cause or handing out flyers on a street corner." Differing from his typical assertiveness, Daniel's voice now sounded tentative and unsure. "As a kid, I was embarrassed that every single person in my schools knew who you were. It was like you were in everybody's face."

Jan watched as two-year-old Asher suddenly appeared on the screen to show Daniel the spatula he was licking. Daniel removed the baseball cap with the ripped visor he had been wearing backwards and placed it on Asher's head.

"What are you doing, Asher? Making chocolate chip cookies with Mommy? Is that a blue checked apron you're wearing?" Jan hoped to gain a little of her grandson's attention, but Asher did not turn around to face the camera lens and propped himself up on his father's lap instead. The cookie dough got all over Daniel's hair, gym shorts, and orange and green jersey. Jan took in the vision of stubble running across Daniel's cheeks and contrasted that with her grandson's smooth skin. *Where have all the years gone? Wasn't Daniel just a freshman in college when he first bought that shirt?*

Emily came rushing to retrieve Asher. "Sorry, Mom. Hi, Mom. Bye, Mom," she said with Asher's legs clinging to her hips and Asher screaming, "I want sit Daddy's lap. I want sit Daddy's lap. Look at copooter."

"I tried to be the best of everything to so many people," Jan explained as Daniel cleaned his face with a baby wipe. For a moment, Jan wished he was a toddler once more, that she could be there washing his face for him. "I ended up giving less to the ones I cared most about," she lamented, feeling thankful that these sentiments could now be expressed so openly.

Daniel arose and suggested that he take the rest of the call from his office computer since there was too much noise and distraction going on in the kitchen with Emily and Asher's crying. Once they had been reconnected, Daniel shared with his mother, "It would have been nice to just have a regular, ordinary mother like most of my friends had."

"I don't think I knew what that was or how to behave that way," Jan uttered with regret. She wanted to add that she had done the best she could given the circumstances, but was afraid Daniel would think she was hoping to be excused for her past actions when what she really wanted was a path to a healthier mother/son relationship.

"Well, it put a lot of pressure on me. It was a hassle, you know? I was made fun of all the time. Every other day, you'd be at the principal's office making a whole load of noise about any little thing that the administration or teacher did to violate someone's rights."

"Is that such a bad thing?" Jan asked, seeing Daniel grimace. "Don't you believe that someone has to stand up to protect the people who can't stand up to protect themselves?"

"Sure, I can see that now, but…" Daniel hesitated mid-sentence.

"Please finish your thought," Jan prodded.

"Then, I thought you looked like the village idiot. That didn't do too much to help me with my own lack of self-confidence," Daniel stated awkwardly.

Jan leaned back in her upholstered swivel chair, pausing to take in a few deep breaths before answering. "Sometimes," she began slowly, "we inadvertently achieve the very thing we are hoping to avoid. I mistakenly thought I was teaching by example. I wanted you to be proud of me. I had hoped to earn your respect. By pretending to be stronger than what I actually was, I had hoped you would grow to be a strong, self-sufficient young man. I wanted you to know how much I cared about you because for any child not to feel loved or wanted is a very damaging, terrible thing."

Removing her elbows from the armrests, she clasped her hands and inched closer to the screen, saying, "I'm truly sorry, Daniel. I want you to know that I love you with all of my heart. If you allow me to do so, I'd like to make amends."

"What are we talking about here?" Daniel asked, a gigantic smirk plastered across his face. "New car? Vacation? Rolex? I have to consider if it'll be worth it." He pushed back on his chair and lifted his sneakers onto the desk.

"Ugh, not only does it look like you've got your father's hairy legs, but it sounds to me you've inherited your grandmother's sarcastic sense of humor. You're not going to say something really crass now, are you? Otherwise, I might have to think twice about my proposal."

"Like how I like both my soup and my women bubbling hot?" Daniel offered, beckoning Asher into the room after hearing his faint knock on the door.

Jan groaned and Daniel continued with his digs. "How about you should lose some weight, put on something a little nicer than the *schmatte* you're wearing, and go pick up my cleaning every week for an entire year?"

"But I live in Florida and you live on the west coast," Jan said, playing along.

Daniel lifted Asher to his lap and planted a kiss on his cheek. "That's shouldn't matter at all," he said to Jan. "If you *really* loved me, then you'd *do it*!"

"*Schmatte,*" Asher repeated, peering into the computer screen. "Hi, Nana," he said in a sweet, innocent voice that made Jan melt.

"How about if Papa and I come to Seattle to babysit for you while Mommy and Daddy take a vacation? Would you like that?"

"Uh huh, Nana," Asher replied, jumping up and down upon Daniel's knees.

"Now you're talking," Daniel said, slapping his desktop and then high-fiving with Asher. "Let me tell Emily to go fetch her calendar!"

***

It had been a few months short of two years since Alice's death, and Jan spontaneously decided to see if Charlotte was still employed at Glenbrook. Charlotte recognized Jan as soon as she stepped into the lobby, throwing her arms about her and landing a large kiss on each of Jan's cheeks. Jan laughed as Charlotte pulled Styrofoam peanuts out of her hair, placing them in a huge garbage bag filled with other peanuts to be used as stuffing for homemade ottomans and pillows. She appeared almost as Jan remembered her, with a few more gray strands at the hairline and extra padding at her waist and belly. Around her neck and shoulders were wrapped a series of colorful silk scarves, and on her feet, she wore orthopedic comfort shoes, which as Charlotte explained, "Provide the kind of support I need after having knee surgery. But you Jan, you look terrific! You haven't aged a day."

"Try telling that to my mirror," Jan kidded. "The over-sized tunic I have on works wonders at camouflaging unwanted, additional pounds."

When Jan drilled Charlotte on the names of the residents she used to know, Charlotte kept shaking her head.

"Denise? No, her heart finally gave out."

"Poor Gladys. Oh yes, we had to transfer her to the Alzheimer's wing."

"Helen? Oh, she's still around. Her hearing is worse, but she's doing okay. After Harold died, she moved in with James."

"Paul? He's recovering in the hospital from hip surgery."

"Had you heard that Mrs. Okeke was promoted, and she now has an office in the Delray location? She left here a year ago, right after our 'Buffet for 2006,' but we have lots of new faces who would love to partake in your Fireside Chats, Jan." Despite the passage of years, Charlotte still sparked with an abundance of zeal and joyfulness. "Would you consider giving it another go?"

Jan replied that she would give it serious consideration but would expect sufficient compensation for her services. She no longer felt obliged to constantly please others at her own expense, having learned from Rick to develop a better sense of her own value and self-worth. Unfortunately, Charlotte responded, "No can do; our budget is tighter than ever."

Jan leaned in closer to Charlotte and whispered, "I have something to tell you, but I'm not sure what you will do with this information."

"You've stirred my curiosity, so please hurry up and tell me. They're waiting on these peanuts upstairs, and I've got horse racing starting in ten minutes; that's what all these scarves are for. I hope it has nothing to do with Mr. Dean and that horrible drug situation."

"While my mother was a resident here, she went about stealing items that she gave to Sondra." A look of shock came across Charlotte's face as her lower lip fell and her muscles tensed. "I thought long and hard about reporting it before, but I decided not to step forward until this time," Jan continued, keeping the volume down. "Perhaps that was the wrong thing to do. My mother has now gone, and I know that Sondra is no longer associated with Glenbrook in any capacity."

"Whoa! What kind of place have I been working in all these years? Drugs? Stealing? How sure are you that this took place?" Charlotte inquired.

"Very sure, but it was for a very limited time—probably around the time that more of those complaints were being made to Mr. Dean." Jan added quickly, "Way before he was arrested, that is."

"A lot of those items claimed stolen actually did turn up, but not all of them," Charlotte conferred. "Mr. Dean loathed to pin the blame on just any employee without due cause, but he was never able to get to the crux of the problem, which ended as mysteriously as it began. Looking back in retrospect, I can understand why he was so reluctant to get the police involved." Charlotte began to sway from one foot to the other. She tapped Jan's hand and said, "I have to get the mat and cardboard horses out of the supply closet. You know how antsy everyone gets around here if the schedule goes off by a minute or two. Can we discuss this in detail another day?"

"Yes, of course," Jan replied, but then a haze of concern clouded her expression. "Do you suppose you'll be sharing this with Mrs. Okeke?"

"Most probably," Charlotte said. "It's really my duty to do so."

"I really don't want Sondra getting into trouble over this. If push came to shove, I wouldn't swear on the record to what I've just told you. Sondra is a more than decent person, and I was hoping for some guarantee from you that what I've told you will not adversely affect her job security."

Charlotte drew closer to Jan. "Well, now you've really got me in a bind. Again, I'm in a rush, but off the top of my head what I'm thinking is that I could make a note in her file, but not say anything at all to Mrs. Okeke. It's highly unlikely for anyone to now be nosing about Sondra's file, but if she ever came back here looking for a job, the entry would stand out like a red herring."

"I'd appreciate that, Charlotte," Jan said, kissing her on the cheek.

"Love you, babe," Charlotte shouted, on the run with the myriad of fabrics flying behind her. "It's just a slight way I can repay you for your past contribution, but I truly wish you would reconsider reinstating the Fireside Chats again. Like I said before, everyone enjoyed them."

Jan took a moment to reminisce about all the Glenbrook's sing-alongs, wine and cheese refreshers, and holiday buffets, pondering how much she had appreciated the opportunity to conduct the Fireside Chats. *Was it me, rather than the residents, who actually gained the most out of those experiences? I thought I was elevating their days, bringing a smile to their weathered faces, but all that time, their attention and approval was fulfilling a need in me.*

"How about if we try it out just once a month to start?" she called out to Charlotte, who spun around and thrust her two-thumbs-up signal elatedly into the air. "That's great news, but I want you starting sooner than later." Charlotte then tore up the stairs to the second-floor social room, yelling, "Mimi, I'm coming. I'm coming. Tell the crowd to settle down and save their voices for the races."

Jan retreated to the parking lot and called Mike once she was seated inside her car. She told him about seeing Charlotte and agreeing to conduct the Fireside Chats. "I think you'll enjoy that," he told her, free of any resentment as in the past.

"I'll be home in about an hour and half," she informed him. "You can count on it."

"Where are you off to between now and then?" Mike asked with mild curiosity. "The weather report said there was a thunderstorm on the way."

"I feel like paying a visit to my mother's grave," she said. "I'll be home before it starts to pour."

"From the tone of your voice, I can't tell if you're feeling happy or sad. This is the first time you'd be there since the funeral. Do you need me to go with you? I'm wrapping up my work and I can be home in fifteen minutes or so."

"I'm kind of feeling neutral: neither happy nor sad," Jan conveyed in earnest, "but thank you for being considerate enough to make the offer. Going to the cemetery wasn't anything I felt I had to do before."

"Maybe now you're looking for some closure." Mike offered. "Just remember to take your umbrella with you." Reluctant to end the call, he added, "How about I throw a little good news your way, just in case you need a little cheering up?"

"I'm not upset, but you can tell me anyway."

"Make believe you're hearing a drum roll because, ta-da! Maddy started walking today! Emily called here this afternoon and left the message. And, hold on to your hat— even though I know you never wear a hat—she said the four of them are coming to visit with us in the beginning of April."

"That's wonderful," Jan exclaimed, sharing in Mike's enthusiasm. "That means they'll be here for Passover. I can't wait!"

It took Jan thirty minutes traveling south on the Florida Turnpike to reach the funeral grounds in Fort Lauderdale where Alice had been buried. Looking out of her windshield, she saw a blanket of storm clouds traveling eastward bound. She parked her car in the closest lane to her mother's gravesite, grabbed her mini Tote's umbrella from the glovebox, and walked the short distance to the row of foxtail palm trees shading her mother's final resting place. Despite the lateness of the hour, the heat of the day had not dissipated. The high humidity made her feel like she was in a swimming pool with her clothes on. Jan took out a handkerchief to wipe the sweat from her forehead. Passing among the granite headstones and free-standing mausoleums, some of which were large enough to accommodate entire families, she took the time to read several of the inscriptions. Those dates indicating the loss of a young relative upset her the most. After finding her mother's grave, Jan stooped down to clean the simple footstone that was covered with twigs and other natural debris, placing a pebble on it that she had selected from a planting bed.

"This is going to be really tough for me, and I'm not so sure exactly what I want to say," Jan began. "All in all, you were a pretty pathetic mother, although I'm feeling awfully guilty even saying these words in such a hallowed place. Because I'm violating one of the Ten Commandments, I fear that God might send a supernatural entity to come down and punish me. However, on the other hand, the truth is that I have been unfairly treated and punished more than enough for one lifetime.

I believed I was so severely damaged that it was only by your good graces that I was allowed to keep on living. I bowed and served to your every need, but you never once lifted a finger or said a single word to try to halt me.

Mother, I have to wonder if you ever knew about the trap your husband first set for me. Were you, in some way, his co-conspirator? How much did it suit you to keep the charade going? His time with me meant less time with you? You and him—each with your own personal slave. How convenient!

I don't doubt that you had been living in your own personal hell and were subjected to immense brutality. I had witnessed your suffering, but at some point, I would have preferred you to attempt to stop the abuse. Any small gesture on your part would have made a significant impact on me and my siblings.

"Despite all your faults, the funny, outrageous truth, Mom, is that I still love you. I still can't say with certainty what you did was out of ignorance or as a result of your own pain, but in any case, I'm wiping the slate clean and wishing you happiness wherever you are."

Jan closed her eyes in silence. The sun, descending in the west, was still sending off enough heat that she could feel it on her cheeks. When she opened her eyes, she noticed two orange butterflies chasing each other within a stream of light. When the butterflies flew off to another row of markers, Jan then turned to walk toward her car. One or two drops fell from the sky. Reaching for her key, she stopped suddenly. She opened the zippered compartment of her pocketbook and lifted out from her cosmetic bag a lipstick in a lustrous black case and a small travel-size package of tissues. Reversing her direction, she headed back toward her mother's gravesite, placing the items next to the pebble on the footstone. "You probably have an infinite amount of lipsticks and tissues, hand-sized, facial-sized, and pocket-sized ones, in your present abode," she said, "but this lipstick is a Chanel in one of the latest colors, called *Passion Pink*. I even paid full price for it in Saks, so you should have nothing to complain about!"

The rain began to fall heavier, coming down in buckets, forming planes of curtains, but the Totes umbrella stayed closed in Jan's grasp. Jan hastened her pace. She didn't mind getting drenched, but she did not want to chance getting hit by lightning. She jumped behind her steering wheel and turned on the ignition. Entering Rock Island Boulevard, Jan kept her foot on the gas pedal, neither speeding nor crawling, but moving in line with the rest of the traffic.

###

Acknowledgements

I want to thank Fred Steinmark, who lent much support and advice during a challenging and lengthy writing process.

Dear Reader,

Thank you for reading my book.
If you enjoyed it, please take the time
to enter a review on Amazon.com,

Fran Steinmark

www.fransteinmark.com

www.ingramcontent.com/pod-product-compliance
Lightning Source LLC
Chambersburg PA
CBHW051523250626
47156CB00001B/200